UNDER THE WHISPERING DOOR

TJ Klune is a Lambda Literary Award-winning author (*Into This River I Drown*) and an ex-claims examiner for an insurance company. His novels include the Green Creek series, *The House in the Cerulean Sea*, *The Extraordinaries* and *Under the Whispering Door*. Being queer himself, TJ believes it's important – now more than ever – to have accurate, positive, queer representation in stories.

By TJ Klune

The House in the Cerulean Sea
Under the Whispering Door

UNDER THE WHISPERING DOOR

TJ KLUNE

TOR

First published 2021 by Tom Doherty Associates

This edition first published 2021 by Tor
an imprint of Pan Macmillan
The Smithson, 6 Briset Street, London EC1M 5NR
EU representative: Macmillan Publishers Ireland Ltd, 1st Floor,
The Liffey Trust Centre, 117–126 Sheriff Street Upper,
Dublin 1, D01 YC43
Associated companies throughout the world
www.panmacmillan.com

ISBN 978-1-5290-9227-1

9 8 7 6

A CIP catalogue record for this book is available from the British Library.

Printed in India by Gopsons Papers Pvt. Ltd., Noida

FSC
www.fsc.org
MIX
Paper from
responsible sources
FSC® C116313

For Eric.

I hope you woke up in a strange place.

Author's Note

This story explores life and love as well as loss and grief.

*There are discussions of death in different forms—
quiet, unexpected, and death by suicide.*

Please read with care.

CHAPTER 1

Patricia was crying.

Wallace Price hated it when people cried.

Little tears, big tears, full-on body-wracking sobs, it didn't matter. Tears were pointless, and she was only delaying the inevitable.

"How did you know?" she said, her cheeks wet as she reached for the Kleenex box on his desk. She didn't see him grimacing. It was probably for the best.

"How could I not?" he said. He folded his hands on his oak desk, his Arper Aston chair squeaking as he settled in for what he was sure was going to be a case of unfortunate histrionics, all while trying to keep from grimacing at the stench of bleach and Windex. One of the night staff must have spilled something in his office, the scent thick and cloying. He made a mental note to send out a memo to remind everyone that he had a sensitive nose, and that he shouldn't be expected to work in such conditions. It was positively barbaric.

The shades on the windows to his office were pulled shut against the afternoon sun, the air-conditioning blasting harshly, keeping him alert. Three years ago, someone had asked if they could move the dial up to seventy degrees. He'd laughed. Warmth led to laziness. When one was cold, one kept moving.

Outside his office, the firm moved like a well-oiled machine, busy and self-sufficient without the need for significant input, exactly as Wallace liked. He wouldn't have made it as far as he had if he'd had to micromanage every employee. Of course, he still kept a watchful eye, those in his employ knowing they needed to be working as if their lives depended on it. Their clients were the most important people on earth. When he said jump, he expected those within earshot to do just that without asking inconsequential questions like *how high?*

Which brought him back to Patricia. The machine had broken down, and though no one was infallible, Wallace needed to switch out the part for a new one. He'd worked too hard to let it fail now. Last year had been the most profitable in the firm's history. This year was shaping up to be even better. No matter what condition the world was in, someone always needed to be sued.

Patricia blew her nose. "I didn't think you cared."

He stared at her. "Why on earth would you think that?"

Patricia gave a watery smile. "You're not exactly the type."

He bristled. How dare she say such a thing, especially to her boss. He should've realized ten years ago when he'd interviewed her for the paralegal position that it'd come back to bite him in the ass. She'd been chipper, something Wallace had believed would lessen with time, seeing as how a law firm was no place for cheerfulness. How wrong he'd been. "Of course I—"

"It's just that things have been so *hard* lately," she said, as if he hadn't spoken at all. "I've tried to keep it bottled in, but I should have known you'd see right through it."

"Exactly," he said, trying to steer the conversation back on course. The quicker he got through this, the better off they'd both be. Patricia would realize that, eventually. "I saw right through it. Now, if you could—"

"And you *do* care," she said. "I know you do. I knew the moment you gave me a floral arrangement for my birthday last month. It was kind of you. Even though it didn't have a card or anything, I knew what you were trying to say. You appreciate me. And I so appreciate you, Mr. Price."

He didn't know what the hell she was talking about. He hadn't given her a single thing. It must have been his legal administrative assistant. He was going to have to have a word with her. There was no need for flowers. What was the point? They were pretty at first but then they died, leaves and petals curling and rotting, making a mess that could have been avoided had they not been sent in the first place. With this in mind, he picked up his ridiculously expensive Montblanc pen, jotting down a note (*IDEA FOR MEMO: PLANTS ARE TERRIBLE AND NO ONE SHOULD HAVE THEM*). Without looking up, he said, "I wasn't trying to—"

"Kyle was laid off two months ago," she said, and it took him longer than he cared to admit to place who she was talking about. Kyle was her husband. Wallace had met him at a firm function. Kyle had been intoxicated, obviously enjoying the champagne Moore, Price, Hernandez & Worthington had provided after yet another successful year. Face flushed, Kyle had regaled the party with a detailed story Wallace couldn't bring himself to care about, especially since Kyle apparently believed volume and embellishment were a necessity in storytelling.

"I'm sorry to hear that," he said stiffly, setting his phone on the desk. "But I think we should focus on the matter at—"

"He's having trouble finding work," Patricia said, crumpling up her tissue before reaching for another. She wiped her eyes, her makeup smearing. "And it couldn't come at a worse time. Our son is getting married this summer, and we're supposed to pay for half the wedding. I don't know how we'll manage, but we'll find a way. We always do. It's a bump in the road."

"Mazel tov," Wallace said. He didn't even know she had children. He wasn't one to delve into the personal lives of his employees. Children were a distraction, one he'd never warmed to. They caused their parents—his employees—to request time off for things like recitals and illness, leaving others to pick up the slack. And since Human Resources had advised him he couldn't ask his employees to avoid starting families ("You can't tell them to just get a *dog*, Mr. Price!") he'd had to deal with mothers and fathers needing the afternoon off to listen to their children vomit or screech songs about shapes and clouds or other nonsense.

Patricia honked again into her tissue, a long and terribly wet noise that made his skin crawl. "And then there's our daughter. I thought she was directionless and going to end up hoarding ferrets, but then the firm graciously provided her with a scholarship, and she finally found her way. Business school, of all things. Isn't that wonderful?"

He squinted at her. He would have to speak to the partners. He wasn't aware they offered scholarships. They donated to charities, yes, but the tax breaks more than made up for it. He didn't know what sort of return they'd see on giving money away for something as ridiculous as *business* school, even if it too could be written off. The daughter would probably want to do something as asinine as open a restaurant or start a nonprofit. "I think you and I have a different definition of wonderful."

She nodded, but he didn't think she was hearing him. "This job is so important to me, now more than ever. The people here are like family. We all support one another, and I don't know how I'd have made it this far without them. And to have you sense something was wrong and ask me to come in here so that I could vent means more to me than you will ever know. I don't care what anyone else says, Mr. Price. You're a good man."

What was *that* supposed to mean? "What is everyone saying about me?"

She blanched. "Oh, nothing bad. You know how it is. You started this firm. Your name is on the letterhead. It's . . . intimidating."

Wallace relaxed. He felt better. "Yes, well, I suppose that's—"

"I mean, *yes*, people talk about how you can be cold and calculating and if something doesn't get done the moment you want it to, you raise your voice to frightening levels, but they don't see you like I do. I know it's a front for the caring man underneath the expensive suits."

"A front," he repeated, though he was pleased she admired his sense of style. His suits *were* luxurious. Only the best, after all. It was why part of the package welcoming those new to the firm listed in detailed bullet points what was acceptable attire. While he didn't demand designer labels for all (especially since he could appreciate student debt), if anyone wore something obviously bought off a discount rack, they'd be given a stern talking to about having pride in their appearance.

"You're hard on the outside, but inside you're a marshmallow," she said.

He'd never been more offended in his life. "Mrs. Ryan—"

"Patricia, please. I've told you that before many times."

She had. "Mrs. Ryan," he said firmly. "While I appreciate your enthusiasm, I believe we have other matters to discuss."

"Right," she said hastily. "Of course. I know you don't like when people compliment you. I promise it won't happen again. We're not here to talk about you, after all."

He was relieved. "Exactly."

Her lip trembled. "We're here to talk about me and how difficult things have become lately. That's why you called me in after finding me crying in the supply closet."

He thought she'd been taking inventory and the dust had affected her allergies. "I think we need to refocus—"

"Kyle won't touch me," she whispered. "It's been years since I've felt his hands on me. I told myself that it's what happens when a couple has been together for so long, but I can't help but think there's more to it."

He flinched. "I don't know if this is appropriate, especially when you—"

"I *know*!" she cried. "How inappropriate can he be? I know I've been working seventy hours a week, but is it too much to ask for my husband to perform his matrimonial duties? It was in our *vows*."

What an awful wedding that must have been. They'd probably held the reception at a Holiday Inn. No. Worse. A Holiday Inn *Express*. He shuddered at the thought. He had no doubt karaoke had been involved. From what he remembered of Kyle (which was very little at all), he'd probably sung a medley of Journey and Whitesnake while chugging what he lovingly referred to as a brewski.

"But I don't mind the long hours," she continued. "It's part of the job. I knew that when you hired me."

Ah! An opening! "Speaking of hiring—"

"My daughter pierced her septum," Patricia said forlornly. "She looks like a bull. My little girl, wanting a matador to chase her down and stick things in her."

"Jesus Christ," Wallace muttered, scrubbing a hand over his face. He didn't have time for this. He had a meeting in half an hour that he needed to prepare for.

"I know!" Patricia exclaimed. "Kyle said it's part of growing up. That we need to let her spread her wings and make her own mistakes. I didn't know that meant having her put a gosh darn *ring* through her nose! And don't even get me started on my son."

"Okay," Wallace said. "I won't."

"He wants Applebee's to cater the wedding! *Applebee's*."

Wallace gaped in horror. He hadn't known awful wedding planning was genetic.

Patricia nodded furiously. "Like we could afford that. Money doesn't grow on trees! We've done our best to instill in our children a sense of financial understanding, but when you're young, you don't always have a firm grasp of it. And now that his bride-to-be is pregnant, he's looking to us for help." She sighed dramatically. "The only reason I can even get up in the morning is knowing I can come here and . . . escape from it all."

He felt a strange twist in his chest. He rubbed at his sternum. Most likely heartburn. He should have skipped the chili. "I'm glad we can be a refuge from your existence, but that's not why I asked you for this meeting."

She sniffled. "Oh?" She smiled again. It was stronger this time. "Then what is it, Mr. Price?"

He said, "You're fired."

She blinked.

He waited. Surely now she'd understand, and he could get back to work.

She looked around, a confused smile on her face. "Is this one of those reality shows?" She laughed, a ghost of her former exuberance he'd thought had long since been banished. "Are you filming me? Is someone going to jump out and shout *surprise*? What's that show called? *You're Fired, But Not Really*?"

"I highly doubt it," Wallace said. "I haven't given authorization to be filmed." He looked down at her purse in her lap. "*Or* recorded."

Her smile faded slightly. "Then I don't understand. What do you mean?"

"I don't know how to make it any clearer, Mrs. Ryan. As of today, you are no longer employed by Moore, Price, Hernandez & Worthington. When you leave here, security will allow you to gather up your belongings and then you'll be escorted from the building. Human Resources will be in touch shortly regarding any final paperwork in case you need to sign up for . . . oh, what was it called?" He flipped through the papers on the desk. "Ah, yes. Unemployment benefits. Because apparently, even if you're unemployed, you can still suckle from the teat of the government in the form of my tax dollars." He shook his head. "So, in a way, it's like I'm still paying you. Just not as much. Or while working here. Because you don't."

She wasn't smiling any longer. "I . . . *what*?"

"You're fired," he said slowly. He didn't know what was so difficult for her to understand.

"Why?" she demanded.

Now they were talking. The *why* of things was Wallace's specialty. Nothing but the facts. "Because of the amicus brief in the Cortaro matter. You filed it two hours past the deadline. The only reason it was pushed through was because Judge Smith owed me a favor, and even *that* almost didn't work. I had to remind him that I'd seen him and his babysitter-turned-mistress at the—it doesn't matter. You could've cost the firm thousands of dollars, and that doesn't even begin to cover the harm it would have caused our client. That sort of mistake won't be tolerated. I thank you for your years of dedication to Moore, Price, Hernandez & Worthington, but I'm afraid your services will no longer be required."

She stood abruptly, the chair scraping along the hardwood floors. "I didn't file it late."

"You did," Wallace said evenly. "I have the timestamp from the clerk's office here if you'd like to see it." He tapped his fingers against the folder sitting on his desk.

Her eyes narrowed. At least she wasn't crying any longer. Wallace could handle anger. On his first day in law school, he was told that lawyers, while a necessity in a functioning society, were always going to be the focal point of ire. "Even if I *did* file it late, I've never done anything like that before. It was one time."

"And you can rest easy knowing you won't do anything like it again," Wallace said. "Because you no longer work here."

"But . . . but my *husband*. And my *son*. And my *daughter*!"

"Right," Wallace said. "I'm glad you brought that up. Obviously, if your daughter was receiving any sort of scholarship from us, it's now rescinded." He pressed a button on his desk phone. "Shirley? Can you please make a note for HR that Mrs. Ryan's daughter no longer has a scholarship through us? I don't know what it entails, but I'm sure they have some form they have to fill out that I need to sign. See to it immediately."

His assistant's voice crackled through the speaker. "Yes, Mr. Price."

He looked up at his former paralegal. "There. See? All taken care of. Now, before you go, I'd ask that you remember we're professionals. There's no need for screaming or throwing things or making threats that will undoubtedly be considered a felony. And, if you could, please make sure when you clear out your desk that you don't take anything that belongs to the firm. Your replacement will be starting on Monday, and I'd hate to think what it would be like for her if she was missing a stapler or tape dispenser. Whatever knickknacks you have accumulated are yours, of course." He picked up the stress ball on his desk with the firm's logo on it. "These are wonderful, aren't they? I seem to remember you getting one to celebrate seven years at the firm. Take it, with my blessing. I have a feeling it will come in handy."

"You're serious," she whispered.

"As a heart attack," he said. "Now, if you'll excuse me, I have to—"

"You . . . you . . . you *monster*!" she shouted. "I demand an apology!"

Of course she would. "An apology would imply I've done something wrong. I haven't. If anything, you should be apologizing to me."

Her answering screech did not contain an apology.

Wallace kept his cool as he pressed the button on his phone again. "Shirley? Has security arrived?"

"Yes, Mr. Price."

"Good. Send them in before something gets thrown at my head."

The last Wallace Price saw of Patricia Ryan was when a large man named Geraldo dragged her away, kicking and screaming, apparently ignoring Wallace's warning about felonious threats. He was begrudgingly impressed with Mrs. Ryan's dedication to wanting to stick what she referred to as a *hot fire poker* down his throat until it—in her words—pierced his nether regions and caused extreme agony. "You'll land on your feet!" he called from the doorway to his office, knowing the entire floor was listening. He wanted to make sure they knew he cared. "A door closes, a window opens and all that."

The elevator doors slid shut, cutting off her outrage.

"Ah," Wallace said. "That's more like it. Back to work, everyone. Just because it's Friday doesn't mean you get to slack off."

Everyone began moving immediately.

Perfect. The machine ran smoothly once again.

He went back into his office, closing the door behind him.

He thought of Patricia only once more that afternoon, when he received an email from the head of Human Resources telling him that she would take care of the scholarship. That twinge in his chest returned, but it was all right. He'd stop for a bottle of Tums on his way home. He didn't give it—or Patricia Ryan—another thought. Ever forward, he told himself as he moved the email to a folder marked EMPLOYEE GRIEVANCES.

Ever forward.

He felt better. At least it was quiet now.

Next week, his new paralegal would start, and he'd make sure she knew he wouldn't tolerate mistakes. It was better to strike fear early rather than deal with incompetency down the road.

He never got the chance.

Instead, two days later, Wallace Price died.

CHAPTER 2

His funeral was sparsely attended. Wallace wasn't pleased. He couldn't even be quite sure how he'd gotten here. One moment, he'd been staring down at his body. And then he'd blinked and somehow found himself standing in front of a church, the doors open, bells ringing. It certainly hadn't helped when he saw the prominent sign sitting out front. A CELEBRATION OF THE LIFE OF WALLACE PRICE, it read. He didn't like that sign, if he was being honest with himself. No, he didn't like it one bit. Perhaps someone inside could tell him what the hell was going on.

He'd taken a seat on a pew toward the rear. The church itself was everything he hated: ostentatious, with grand stained-glass windows and several versions of Jesus in various poses of pain and suffering, hands nailed to a cross that appeared to be made of stone. Wallace was dismayed at how no one seemed to mind that the prominent figure displayed throughout the church was depicted in the throes of death. He would never understand religion.

He waited for more people to filter in. The sign out front said his funeral was supposed to start promptly at nine. It was now five till according to the decorative clock on the wall (another Jesus, his arms the hands of the clock, apparently a reminder that God's only son was a contortionist) and there were only six people in the church.

He knew five of them.

The first was his ex-wife. Their divorce had been a bitter thing, filled with baseless accusations on both sides, their lawyers barely able to keep them from screaming at each other across the table. She would've had to fly in, given that she'd moved to the opposite end of the country to get away from him. He didn't blame her.

Mostly.

She wasn't crying. He was annoyed for reasons he couldn't quite explain. Shouldn't she be sobbing?

The second, third, and fourth people he knew were the partners at the law firm Moore, Price, Hernandez & Worthington. He waited for others from the firm to join them, given MPH&W had been started in a garage twenty years before and had grown to be one of the most powerful firms in the state. At the very least, he expected his assistant, Shirley, to be there, her makeup streaked, a handkerchief clutched in her hands as she wailed that she didn't know how she'd go on without him.

She wasn't in attendance. He focused as hard as he could, willing her to pop into existence, wailing that it wasn't fair, that she *needed* a boss like Wallace to keep her on the straight and narrow. He frowned when nothing happened, a curl of unease fluttering in the back of his mind.

The partners gathered at the back of the church, near Wallace's pew, speaking in low tones. Wallace had given up trying to let them know he was still here, sitting right in front of them. They couldn't see him. They couldn't hear him.

"Sad day," Moore said.

"So sad," Hernandez agreed.

"Just the worst," Worthington said. "Poor Shirley, finding his body like that."

The partners paused, looking out toward the front of the church, bowing their heads respectfully when Naomi glanced back at them. She sneered at them before turning around toward the front.

Then:

"Makes you think," Moore said.

"It really does," Hernandez agreed.

"Absolutely," Worthington said. "Makes you think about a lot of things."

"You've never had an original thought in your life," Wallace told him.

They were quiet for a moment, and Wallace was sure they were lost in their favorite memories of him. In a moment, they'd start to fondly reminisce, each of them in turn giving a little story about the man they'd known for half their lives and the effect he'd had upon them.

Maybe they'd even shed a tear or two. He hoped so.

"He was an asshole," Moore said finally.

"Such an asshole," Hernandez agreed.

"The biggest," Worthington said.

They all laughed, though they tried to smother it to keep it from echoing. Wallace was shocked by two specific things. First, he wasn't aware one was allowed to laugh in church, especially when one was attending a funeral. He thought it had to be illegal, somehow. It was true that he hadn't been inside a church in decades, so it was possible the rules had changed. Second, where did they get off calling him an asshole? He was disappointed when they weren't immediately struck down by lightning. "Smite them!" he yelled, glaring up at the ceiling. "Smite them right . . . now . . ." He stopped. Why wasn't his voice echoing?

Moore, apparently having decided his grief had passed, said, "Did you guys catch the game last night? Man, Rodriguez was in rare form. Can't believe they called that play."

And then they were off, talking about sports as if their former partner wasn't lying in a seven-thousand-dollar solid red cherrywood casket at the front of the church, arms folded across his chest, skin pale, eyes closed.

Wallace turned resolutely forward, jaw clenched. They'd gone to law school together, had decided to start their own firm right after graduation, much to the horror of their parents. He and the partners had started out as friends, each young and idealistic. But as the years had gone by, they'd become something *more* than friends: they'd become colleagues, which, to Wallace, was far more important. He didn't have time for friends. He didn't need them. He'd had his job on the thirtieth floor of the biggest skyscraper in the city, his imported office furniture, and a too-big apartment that he rarely spent any time in. He'd had it all, and now . . .

Well.

At least his casket was expensive, though he'd been avoiding looking at it since he arrived.

The fifth person in the church was someone he didn't recognize. She was a young woman with messy black hair cut short. Her eyes were dark above a thin, upturned nose and the pale slash of her lips. She had her ears pierced, little studs that glittered in the sunlight filtering in through the windows. She was dressed in a smart pin-striped black suit, her tie bright red. A power tie if ever there was one. Wallace approved. All of his own ties were power ties. No, he wasn't exactly wearing a power tie at this moment. Apparently when you died, you continued to wear the last thing you had on before you croaked. It was unfortunate, really, given that he'd apparently died in his office on a Sunday. He'd come in to prepare for the upcoming week, and had thrown on sweats, an old Rolling Stones shirt, and flip-flops, knowing the office would be empty.

Which is what he found himself wearing now, much to his dismay.

The woman glanced in his direction, as if she'd heard him. He didn't know her, but he assumed he'd touched her life at some point if she was here. Perhaps she'd been a grateful client of his at one point. They all began to run together after a time, so that could be it too. He'd probably sued a large company on her behalf for hot coffee or harassment or *something*, and she'd gotten a massive settlement out of it. Of course she'd be grateful. Who wouldn't be?

Moore, Hernandez, and Worthington seemed to graciously decide their wild sporting-event conversation could be put on hold, walking past Wallace without so much as a glance in his direction and moving toward the front of the church, each of them with a solemn look on his face. They ignored the young woman in the suit, instead stopping near Naomi, leaning over one by one to offer their condolences. She nodded. Wallace waited for the tears, sure it was a dam ready to burst.

The partners each took a moment to stand in front of the casket, their heads bowed low. That sense of unease that had filled Wallace since he'd blinked in front of the church grew stronger, discordant and awful. Here he was, sitting in the back of the church, staring at himself in the *front* of the church, lying in a casket. Wallace was under no impression he was a handsome man. He was too tall, too gangly, his cheekbones wicked sharp, leaving his pale face in a state of perpetual gauntness. Once, at a company Halloween party, a group of children had been delighted by his costume, one bold tween saying that he made an excellent Grim Reaper.

He hadn't been wearing a costume.

He studied himself from his seat, catching glimpses of his body as the partners shuffled around him, the terrible feeling that something was off threatening to overtake him. The body had been dressed in one of his nicer suits, a Tom Ford sharkskin wool two-piece. It fit his thin frame well and made his green eyes pop. To be fair, it wasn't exactly flattering now, given that his eyes were closed and his cheeks were covered with enough rouge to make him look as if he'd been a courtesan instead of a high-profile attorney. His forehead was strangely pale, his short dark hair slicked back and glistening wetly in the overhead lights.

Eventually, the partners sat in the pew opposite Naomi, their faces dry.

A door opened, and Wallace turned to see a priest (someone else he didn't recognize, and he felt that discordance again like a weight on his chest, something off, something *wrong*) walk through the narthex, wearing robes as ridiculous as the church around them. The priest blinked a couple of times, as if he couldn't believe how empty the church was. He pulled back the sleeve of his robe to look at his watch and shook his head before fixing a quiet smile on his face. He walked right by Wallace without acknowledging him. "That's fine," Wallace called after him. "I'm sure you think you're important. It's no wonder organized religion is in the shape it's in."

The priest stopped next to Naomi, taking her hand in his, speaking in soft platitudes, telling her how sorry he was for her loss, that the Lord worked in mysterious ways, and while we may not always understand his plan, rest assured there was one, and this was part of it.

Naomi said, "Oh, I don't doubt that, Father. But let's skip all the mumbo-jumbo and get this show on the road. He's supposed to be buried in two hours, and I have a flight to catch this afternoon."

Wallace rolled his eyes. "Christ, Naomi. How about showing a little respect? You're in a *church*." *And I'm dead,* he wanted to add, but didn't, because that made it real, and none of this could be real. It couldn't.

The priest nodded. "Of course." He patted the back of her hand before moving to the opposite pews where the partners sat. "I'm sorry for your loss. The Lord works in mysterious—"

"Of course he does," Moore said.

"So mysterious," Hernandez agreed.

"Big man upstairs with his plans," Worthington said.

The woman—the stranger he didn't recognize—snorted, shaking her head.

Wallace glared at her.

The priest moved on, stopping in front of the casket, head bowed.

Before, there'd been pain in Wallace's arm, a burning sensation in his chest, a savage little twist of nausea in his stomach. For a moment, he'd almost convinced himself that it'd been the leftover chili he'd eaten the night before. But then he was on the floor of his office, lying on the imported Persian rug he'd spent an exorbitant amount on, listening to the fountain in the lobby gurgle as he tried to catch his breath. "Goddamn chili," he'd managed to gasp, his last words before he'd found himself standing *above* his own body, feeling like he was in two places at once, staring up at the ceiling while also staring *down* at himself. It took a moment before that division subsided, leaving him with mouth agape, the only sound crawling from his throat a thin squeak like a deflating balloon.

Which was *fine,* because he'd only passed out! That's all it was. Nothing more than heartburn and the need to take a nap on the floor. It happened to everyone at one point or another. He'd been working too hard as of late. Of course it'd finally caught up to him.

With that decided, he felt a bit better about wearing sweats and flip-flops and an old T-shirt in church at his funeral. He didn't even like the Rolling Stones. He had no idea where the shirt had come from.

The priest cleared his throat as he looked out at the few people gathered. He said, "It's written in the Good Book that—"

"Oh, for Pete's sake," Wallace muttered.

The stranger choked.

Wallace jerked his head up as the priest droned on.

The woman had her hand over her mouth like she was trying to stifle her laughter. Wallace was incensed. If she found his death so funny, why the hell was she even here?

Unless . . .

No, it couldn't be, right?

He stared at her, trying to place her.

What if she *had* been a client of his?

What if he'd gotten a less than desirable result for her?

A class-action lawsuit, maybe. One that hadn't netted as much as she'd hoped. He made promises whenever he got a new client, big promises of justice and extraordinary financial compensation. Where once he might have tempered expectations, he'd only grown more confident with every judgment in his favor. His name was whispered with great reverence in the hallowed halls of the courts. He was a ruthless shark, and anyone who stood in his way usually ended up flat on their back, wondering what the hell had happened.

But maybe it was more than that.

Had what started out as a professional attorney-client relationship turned to something darker? Perhaps she'd become fixated on him, enamored with his expensive suits and command of the courtroom. She told herself that she would have Wallace Price, or no one would. She'd stalked him, standing outside his window at night, watching him while he slept (his apartment being on the fifteenth floor didn't dissuade him of this notion; for all he knew, she'd climbed up the side of the building to his balcony). And when he was at work, she'd broken in and lain upon his pillow, breathing in his scent, dreaming of the day when she could become Mrs. Wallace Price. Then perhaps he'd spurned her unknowingly, and the love she'd felt for him had turned into a black rage.

That was it.

That explained everything. After all, it wasn't without precedent, was it? Because it was likely Patricia Ryan had *also* been obsessed with him, given her unfortunate reaction when he'd fired her. For all he knew, they were in cahoots with each other, and when Wallace had done what he did, they'd . . . what? Joined forces to . . . wait. Okay. The timeline was a little fuzzy for that to work, but *still*.

"—and now, I'd like to invite anyone who would like to say a few words about our dear Wallace to come forward and do so at this time." The priest smiled serenely. The smile faded slightly when no one moved. "Anyone at all."

The partners bowed their heads.

Naomi sighed.

Obviously, they were overcome, unable to find the right words to say in order to sum up a life well-lived. Wallace didn't blame them for that. How did one even begin to encapsulate all that he was? Successful, intelligent, hard-working to the point of obsession, and so much more. Of *course* they'd be reticent.

"Get up," he muttered, staring hard at those in the front of the church. "Get up and say nice things about me. Now. I *command you*."

He gasped when Naomi rose. "It worked!" he whispered fervently. "Yes. *Yes*."

The priest nodded at her as he stepped off to the side. Naomi stared down at Wallace's body for a long moment, and Wallace was surprised to see her face screw up like she was about to cry. Finally. *Finally* someone was going to show some kind of emotion. He wondered if she would throw herself at the casket, demanding to know why, why, *why* life had to be so unfair, and Wallace, I've always loved you, even when I was sleeping with the gardener. You know, the one who seemed averse to wearing shirts while he worked, the sun shining down on his broad shoulders, the sweat trickling down his carved abdominal muscles like he was a goddamn Greek statue that you pretended not to stare at too, but we both know that's crap, given that we had the same taste in men.

She didn't cry.

She sneezed instead.

"Excuse me," she said, wiping her nose. "That's been building for a while."

Wallace sunk lower in the pew. He didn't have a good feeling about this.

She moved in front of the church on the dais next to the priest. She said, "Wallace Price was . . . certainly alive. And now he's not. For the life of me, I can't quite say that's a terrible thing. He wasn't a good person."

"Oh my," the priest said.

Naomi ignored him. "He was obstinate, foolhardy, and cared only for himself. I could have married Bill Nicholson, but instead, I hooked up to the Wallace Price Express, bound for a destination of missed meals, forgotten birthdays and anniversaries, and the disgusting habit of leaving toenail clippings on the bathroom floor. I mean, come on. The trash bin was *right there.* How on earth do you miss it?"

"Terrible," Moore said.

"Exactly," Hernandez agreed.

"Put the clippings in the trash," Worthington said. "It's not that hard."

"Wait," Wallace said loudly. "That's not what you're supposed to be doing. You need to be *sad*, and as you wipe away tears, you talk about everything you'll miss about me. What kind of funeral *is* this?"

But Naomi wouldn't listen, which, really. When had she ever? "I've spent the last few days since I got the news trying to find a single memory of our time together that didn't fill me with regret or apathy or a burning fury that felt like I was standing on the sun. It took time, but I did find one. Once, Wallace brought me a cup of soup while I was sick. I thanked him. Then he went to work, and I didn't see him for six days."

"That's *it*?" Wallace exclaimed. "Are you *kidding* me?"

Naomi's expression hardened. "I know we're supposed to act and feel a certain way when someone dies, but I'm here to tell you that's bullshit. Sorry, Father."

The priest nodded. "It's okay, my child. Get it all out. The Lord doesn't—"

"And don't even get me started on the fact that he cared more about his work than making a family. I marked my ovulation cycle on his work calendar. Do you know what he did? He sent me a card that said CONGRATULATIONS, GRADUATE."

"Still holding onto that, are we?" Wallace asked loudly. "How's that therapy going for you, Naomi? Sounds like you should get a refund."

"Yikes," the woman in the pew said.

Wallace glared at her. "Something you'd like to add? I know I'm a catch, but just because I won't love you didn't give you the right to murder me!"

The sound he made when the woman looked directly at him is better left to the imagination, especially when she said quite loudly, "Nah. You're not exactly my type, and murder is bad, you know?"

Wallace practically fell out of the pew as Naomi continued to slander him in a house of God as if the strange woman hadn't spoken at all. He managed to grab the back of the pew, fingernails digging into the wood. He peered over the top, eyes bulging as he stared at the woman.

She smiled and arched an eyebrow.

Wallace struggled to find his voice. "You . . . you can see me?"

She nodded as she turned in her own pew, resting her elbow on the back. "I can."

He began to tremble, his hands gripping the pew so hard, he thought his fingers would snap. "How. What. I don't—*what*."

"I know you're confused, Wallace, and things can be—"

"I never told you my name!" he said shrilly, unable to stop his voice from cracking.

She snorted. "There's literally a sign with your picture on it below your name in the front of the church."

"That's not . . ." What? What wasn't it *exactly*? He pulled himself upright. His legs weren't quite working as he wanted them to. "Forget the damn sign. How is this happening? What the hell is going on?"

The woman smiled. "You're dead."

He burst out laughing. Yes, he could see his body in a casket, but that didn't mean anything. There had to be some mistake. He stopped laughing when he realized the woman wasn't joining in. "What," he said flatly.

"Dead, Wallace." Her face scrunched up. "Hold on. Trying to remember what the cause was. This is my first time, and I'm a little nervous." She brightened. "Oh, that's right! Heart attack."

And that was how he knew this wasn't real. A heart attack? Bullshit. He never smoked, he ate as best he could, and he exercised when he remembered. His last physical had ended with the doctor telling him that while his blood pressure was a little high, everything else seemed to be in working order. He couldn't be dead from a heart attack. It wasn't possible. He told her as much, sure that'd be the end of it.

"Riiiight," she repeated slowly, as if *he* were the idiot. "Hate to be a bummer, man, but that's what happened."

"No," he said, shaking his head. "I would know if I . . . I would have felt . . ." Felt what? Pain in his arm? The stuttering in his chest? The way he couldn't quite catch his breath no matter how hard he tried?

She shrugged. "I suppose it's one of those things." He flinched when she stood from the pew, making her way over to him. She was shorter than he expected, the top of her head probably coming up to his chin. He backed away from her as best he could, but he didn't get far.

Naomi was ranting about a trip to the Poconos they'd apparently taken ("He stayed in the hotel room the entire time on conference calls! It was our honeymoon!") as the woman sat on his pew, keeping a bit of distance between them. She appeared even younger than he first thought—perhaps early to mid-twenties—which somehow made things worse. Her complexion was slightly darker than his own, lips pulled back over small teeth in the hint of a smile. She tapped her fingers on the back of the pew before looking at him. "Wallace Price," she said. "My name is Meiying, but you can call me Mei, like the month, only spelled a little different. I'm here to bring you home."

He stared at her, unable to speak.

"Huh. Didn't know that'd shut you up. Should've tried that to begin with."

"I'm not going anywhere with you," he said through gritted teeth. "I don't know you."

"I should hope not," she said. "If you did, it'd be very weird." She paused, considering. "Weird*er*, at least." She nodded toward the front of the church. "Nice casket, by the way. Doesn't look cheap."

He bristled. "It isn't. Only the very best for—"

"Oh, I'm sure," Mei said. "Still. Pretty gnarly, right? Looking at your own body like that. Not a bad body, though. Little skinny for my tastes, but to each their own."

He bristled. "I'll have you know that I did just *fine* with my skinny—no. I won't be distracted! I demand you tell me what's going on *right this second*."

"Okay," she said quietly. "I can do that. I know this may be hard to understand, but your heart gave out, and you died. There was an autopsy, and it turned out you had blockages in your coronary arteries. I can show you the Y incision, if you want, though I'd advise against it. It's pretty gross. Did you know that once they perform the autopsy, they sometimes put the organs back inside in a bag along with sawdust before they close you up?" She brightened. "Oh, and I'm your Reaper, here to take you where you belong." And then, as if the moment wasn't strange enough, she made jazz hands. "Ta-da."

"Reaper," he said in a daze. "What is . . . that?"

"Me," she said, scooting closer. "I'm a Reaper. Once someone dies, there's confusion. You don't really know what's going on, and you're scared."

"I'm not scared!" This was a lie. He'd never been more frightened in his life.

"Okay," she said. "So you're not scared. That's good. Regardless, it's a trying time for anyone. You need help to make the transition. That's where I come in. I'm here to make sure said transition goes as smoothly as possible." She paused. Then, "That's it. I think I remembered to say everything. I had to memorize *a lot* to get this job, and I might have forgotten a detail here and there, but that's the gist of it."

He gaped at her. He barely heard Naomi yelling in the background, calling him a selfish bastard with absolutely no self-awareness. "Transition."

Mei nodded.

He didn't like the sound of that. "To *what*?"

She grinned. "Oh, man. Just you wait." She raised her hand toward him, turning her palm up. She pressed her thumb and middle fingers together and snapped.

The cool, spring sun was shining down on his face.

He took a stumbling step back, looking around wildly.

Cemetery. They were in a cemetery.

"Sorry about that," Mei said, appearing beside him. "Still getting the hang of it." She frowned. "I'm sort of new at this."

"What's happening!" he shrieked at her.

"You're getting buried," she said cheerily. "Come on. You'll want to see this. It'll help dispel any doubts you might have left." She grabbed him by the arm and pulled. He tripped over his own feet but managed to stay upright. His flip-flops slapped against his heels as he struggled to keep up. They weaved in and out of headstones, the sounds of busy traffic surrounding them as impatient cabbies honked their horns and shouted expletives out open windows. He tried to pull away from Mei, but her grip was tight. She was stronger than she looked.

"Here we are," she said, coming to a stop. "Right on time."

He peered over her shoulder. Naomi was there, as were the partners, all standing around a freshly dug rectangular hole. The expensive coffin was being lowered into the earth. No one was crying. Worthington kept looking at his watch and sighing dramatically. Naomi was tapping away on her phone.

Of all the things for Wallace to focus on, he was dumbstruck by the fact that there was no headstone. "Where's the marker? My name. Date of birth. An inspirational message saying I lived life to the fullest."

"Is that what you did?" Mei asked. She didn't sound like she was mocking him, merely curious.

He jerked his hand away and crossed his arms defensively. "Yes."

"Awesome. And the headstones usually come after the service. They still have to carve it and everything. It's this whole process. Don't worry about it. Look. There you go. Wave goodbye!"

He didn't wave.

Mei did, though, fingers wiggling.

"How did we get here?" he asked. "We were just in the church."

"So observant. That's really good, Wallace. We *were* just in the church. I'm proud of you. Let's say I skipped a couple of things. Gotta get a move on." She winced. "And that's my bad, man. Like, seriously, don't take this the wrong way because I totally didn't mean it, but I was a *little* late in getting to you. This is sort of my first time reaping on my own, and I screwed up. Went to the wrong place on accident." She smiled beatifically. "We cool?"

"*No*," he snarled at her. "We're *not cool*."

"Oh. That sucks. Sorry. I promise it won't happen again. Learning experience and all that. I hope you'll still rate my service a ten when you get the survey. It'd mean a lot to me."

He had no idea what she was talking about. He could almost convince himself that *she* was the crazy one, and nothing but a figment of his imagination. "It's been three days!"

She beamed at him. "Exactly! This makes my job so much easier. Hugo's gonna be so pleased with me. I can't wait to tell him."

"Who the hell is—"

"Hold on. This is one of my favorite parts."

He looked to where she was pointing. The partners stood in a line, with Naomi behind them. He watched as they all leaned down, one by one, scooping up a handful of dirt and dropping it into the grave. The sound of the dirt hitting the lid of the casket caused Wallace's hands to shake. Naomi stood with her handful of dirt over the open grave, and before she dropped it, a strange expression flickered across her face, there and gone. She shook her head, dropped the dirt, and then whirled around. The last he saw of his ex-wife was the sunlight on her hair as she hurried toward a waiting cab.

"Kinda brings it all home," Mei said. "Full circle. From the earth we came, and to the earth we return. Pretty, if you think about it."

"What's going on?" he whispered.

Mei touched the back of his hand. Her skin was cool, but not unpleasantly so. "Do you need a hug? I can give you a hug if you want."

He jerked his arm back. "I don't want a hug."

She nodded. "Boundaries. Cool. I respect that. I promise I won't hug you without your permission."

Once, when Wallace was seven, his parents had taken him to the beach. He'd stood in the surf, watching the sand rush between his toes. There was a strange sensation that rose through his legs to the pit of his stomach. He was sinking, though the combination of the whirling sand and white-capped water made it feel like so much more. It'd terrified him, and he'd refused to go back in the ocean, no matter how much his parents had pleaded with him.

It was this sensation Wallace Price felt now. Maybe it was the sound of the dirt on the casket. Maybe it was the fact that his picture was propped up next to the open grave, a floral wreath attached below it. In this picture, he was smiling tightly. His hair was styled perfectly, parted to the right. His eyes were bright. Naomi once said that he reminded her of the scarecrow from Oz. "If you only had a brain," she said. This had been during one of their divorce proceedings, so he'd discounted it as nothing but her trying to hurt him.

He sat down hard on the ground, his toes flexing into the grass over the tip of his flip-flops. Mei settled next to him, folding her legs underneath her, picking at a little dandelion. She plucked it from the ground, holding it close to his mouth. "Make a wish," she said.

He did not make a wish.

She sighed and blew on the dandelion seeds herself. They exploded into a white cloud, the bits catching on a breeze and swirling around the open grave. "It's a lot to take in, I know."

"Do you?" he muttered, face in his hands.

"Not literally," she admitted. "But I have a good idea."

He looked over at her, eyes narrowed. "You said this was your first time."

"It is. Solo, that is. But I went through the training, and did pretty good. Do you need empathy? I can give you that. Do you want to punch something because you're angry? I can help you with that too. Not me, though. Maybe a wall." She shrugged. "Or we can sit here and watch as they eventually come with a small bulldozer and shovel all the dirt on top of your former body thus cementing the fact that it's all over. Dealer's choice."

He stared at her.

She nodded. "Right. I could have phrased that better. Sorry. Still getting the hang of things."

"What is . . . ?" He tried to swallow past the lump in his throat. "What's happening?"

She said, "What's happening is that you lived your life. You did what you did, and now it's over. At least that part of it is. And when you're ready to leave here, I'll take you to Hugo. He'll explain the rest."

"Leave," he muttered. "With Hugo."

She shook her head before stopping herself. "Well, in a way. He's a ferryman."

"A what?"

"Ferryman," she repeated. "The one who will help you cross."

His mind was racing. He couldn't focus on any one single thing.

It all felt too grand to comprehend. "But I thought you were supposed to—"

"Aw. You do like me. That's sweet." She laughed. "But I'm just a Reaper, Wallace. My job is to make sure you get to the ferryman. He'll handle the rest. You'll see. Once we get to him, it'll be right as rain. Hugo tends to have that effect on people. He'll explain everything before you cross, any of those pesky, lingering questions."

"Cross," Wallace said dully. "To . . . where?"

Mei cocked her head. "Why, to what's next of course."

"Heaven?" He blanched, a terrible thought piercing through the storm. "Hell?"

She shrugged. "Sure."

"That doesn't explain anything at all."

She laughed. "I know, right? This is fun. I'm having fun. Aren't you?"

No, he really wasn't.

She didn't hurry him. They stayed even as the sky began to streak in pinks and oranges, the March sun setting low toward the horizon. They stayed even as the promised bulldozer came, the woman operating it deftly with a cigarette jammed between her teeth, smoke pouring from her nose. The grave filled quicker than Wallace expected. The first stars were starting to appear by the time she finished, though they were faint given the light pollution from the city.

And that was it.

All that was left of Wallace Price was a mound of dirt and a body that was going to be nothing but worm food. It was a profoundly devastating experience. He hadn't realized it would be. Strange, he thought to himself. How very strange.

He looked at Mei.

She smiled at him.

He said, "I . . ." He didn't know how to finish.

She touched the back of his hand. "Yes, Wallace. It's real."

And wonder of all wonders, he believed her.

She said, "Would you like to meet Hugo?"

No. He wouldn't. He wanted to run. He wanted to scream. He wanted to raise his fists toward the stars and rant and rave about the unfairness of it all. He had plans. He had goals. So much left to do, and now he'd never . . . he couldn't . . .

He startled when a tear slipped down his cheek. "Do I have a choice?"

"In life? Always."

"And in death?"

She shrugged. "It's a little more . . . regimented. But it's for your own good. I swear," she added quickly. "There are reasons these things happen the way they do. Hugo will explain it all. He's a great guy. You'll see."

That did not make him feel better.

But still, when she stood above him, holding her hand out, he only stared at it for a moment or two before taking it, allowing her to pull him up.

He turned his face toward the sky. He breathed in and out.

Mei said, "This is probably going to feel a little odd. But it's a longer distance, so it's to be expected. It'll be over before you know it."

But before he could react, she snapped again and everything exploded.

CHAPTER 3

Wallace was screaming when they landed on a paved road in the middle of a forest. The air was cold, but even as he continued to yell, no breath cloud formed in front of him. It didn't make sense. How could he be cold when he was dead? Was he actually breathing, or . . . No. No. Focus. Focus on the here. Focus on the now. One thing at a time.

"Are you done?" Mei asked him.

He realized he was still screaming. He snapped his mouth closed, pain bright as he bit into his tongue. Which, of course, set him off again, because how the hell could he feel *pain*?

"No," he muttered, backing away from Mei, thoughts jumbled in an infinite knot. "You can't just—"

And then he was hit by a car.

Wait.

He *should* have been hit by a car. The car approached, the headlights bright. He managed to bring up his hands in time to block his face, only to have the car go *through* him. Out of the corner of his eye, he saw the driver's face pass inches from his own. He didn't feel any of it.

The car continued down the road, the taillights flashing once before it rounded a corner and disappeared entirely.

He was frozen, hands extended in front of him, one leg raised, thigh pressed against his stomach.

Mei laughed loudly. "Oh, man. You should see the look on your face. Oh my god, it's *awesome*."

He gradually lowered his leg, half-convinced he'd fall right through the ground. He didn't. It was solid beneath his feet. He couldn't stop shaking. "How. What. Why. What. *What?*"

She wiped her eyes, still chuckling. "My bad. I should've warned you that could happen." She shook her head. "It's all good, though, right? I mean, how great is it that you can't be hit by cars anymore?"

"*That's* what you took away from this?" he asked incredulously.

"It's a pretty big thing if you think about it."

"I don't *want* to think about it," he snapped. "I don't want to think about any of this!"

Inexplicably, she said, "If wishes were fishes, we'd all swim in riches."

He stared after her as she started down the road. "That doesn't explain *anything*!"

"Only because you're being obstinate. Lighten up, man."

He chased after her, not wanting to be left alone in the middle of nowhere. In the distance, he could see the lights of what looked like a small village. He didn't recognize any of their surroundings, but she was talking a mile a minute, and he couldn't get a word in edgewise.

"He doesn't stand on ceremony or anything, so don't worry about that. Don't call him Mr. Freeman because he hates that. He's Hugo to everyone, okay? And maybe stop scowling so much. Or not, it's up to you. I won't tell you how to be. He knows that you . . ." She coughed awkwardly. "Well, he knows how tricky these things can be, so don't worry about it. Ask all the questions you need to. That's what we're here for." And then, "Do you see it yet?"

He started to ask what the hell she was talking about, but then she nodded toward his chest. He looked down, a scowl forming.

The pithy retort on the tip of his tongue was replaced by a cry of horror.

There, protruding from his chest, was a curved piece of metal, almost like a fishhook the size of his hand. Silver in color, it glinted in the low light. It didn't hurt, but it looked like it *should* have, given that the sharp tip appeared to be embedded into his sternum. Attached to the other end of the hook was a . . . cable? A thin band of what almost looked like plastic that flashed with a dull light. The cable stretched out on the road in front of them, leading away. He slapped against his chest, trying to knock the hook loose, but his hands passed right through it. The light from the cable intensified, and the hook vibrated warmly, filling him with an odd sense of relief that he hadn't expected given that he'd been skewered. This feeling was, of course, tempered by the fact that he *had* been skewered.

"What is it?" he yelled, still slapping at his chest. "Get it off, get it *off*!"

"Nah," Mei said, reaching over and grabbing his hands. "We really don't want to do that. Trust me when I say it's helping you. You need it. It's not gonna hurt you. I can't see it, but judging by your reaction, it's the same as all the others. Don't fuss with it. Hugo will explain, I promise."

"What is it?" he demanded again, skin prickling. He stared at the cable that stretched along the road in front of them.

"A connection." She bumped his shoulder. "Keeps you grounded. It leads to Hugo. He knows we're close. Come on. I can't wait for you to meet him."

The village was quiet. There seemed to be only a single main thoroughfare that went through the center. No traffic signals, no hustle and bustle of people on the sidewalks. A couple of cars passed by (Wallace jumping out of the way, not wanting to relive *that* experience again), but other than that, it was mostly silent. The shops on either side of the road had already closed for the day, their windows darkened, signs hanging from the doors promising to be back first thing in the morning. Their awnings stretched out over the sidewalk, all in bright colors of red and green and blue and orange.

Streetlamps lined either side of the road, their lights warm and soft. The road was cobblestone, and Wallace stepped out of the way as a group of kids on their bikes rode by him. They didn't acknowledge either him or Mei. They were laughing and shouting, cards attached to the spokes of their wheels with clothespins, their breath streaming behind them like little trains. Wallace ached a little at the thought. They were free, free in ways he hadn't been in a long time. He struggled with this, unable to shape it into anything recognizable. And then the feeling was gone, leaving him hollowed out and trembling.

"Is this place real?" he asked, feeling the hook in his chest grow warmer. The cable didn't go slack as he expected it to as they continued on. He'd thought he would be tripping over it by now. Instead, it remained as taut as it'd been since he'd first noticed it.

Mei glanced at him. "What do you mean?"

He didn't quite know. "Are they . . . is everyone here dead?"

"*Oh*. Yeah, no. I get it. Yes, this place is real. No, everyone isn't dead. This is just like everywhere else, I suppose. We did have to travel pretty far, but it's nowhere you couldn't have gone on your own had you ever decided to leave the city. Doesn't sound like you got out very much."

"I was too busy," he muttered.

"You have all the time in the world now," Mei said, and it *startled* him how pointed that was. His chest hitched, and he blinked against the sudden burn in his eyes. Mei walked lazily down the sidewalk, glancing over her shoulder to make sure he followed.

He did, but only because he didn't want to be left behind in an unfamiliar place. The buildings that had seemed almost quaint now loomed around him ominously, the dark windows like dead eyes. He looked down at his feet, focusing on putting one foot in front of the other. His vision began to tunnel, his skin thrumming. That hook in his chest was growing more insistent.

He'd never been more scared in his life.

"Hey, hey," he heard Mei say, and when he opened his eyes, he found himself crouched low to the ground, his arms wrapped around his stomach, fingers digging into his skin hard enough to leave bruises. If he could even *get* bruises. "It's okay, Wallace. I'm here."

"Because *that's* supposed to make me feel better," he choked out.

"It's a lot for anyone. We can sit here for a moment, if that's what you need. I'm not going to rush you, Wallace."

He didn't know what he needed. He couldn't think clearly. He tried to get a handle on it, tried to find something to grasp onto. And when he found it, it came from within him, a forgotten memory rising like a ghost.

He was nine, and his father asked him to come into the living room. He'd just gotten home from school and was in the kitchen making a peanut-butter-and-banana sandwich. He froze at his father's request, trying to think of what he could have done to get in trouble. He'd smoked a cigarette behind the bleachers, but that had been weeks ago, and there was no way his parents could have known unless someone had told them.

He left the sandwich on the counter, already making excuses in his head, forming promises of *I'll never do it again, I swear, it was just one time.*

They were sitting on the couch, and he stopped cold when he saw his mother was crying, though she looked like she was trying to stifle it. Her cheeks were streaked, the Kleenex tightened into a little ball in her hand. Her nose was running, and though she tried to smile when she saw him, it trembled and twisted down as her shoulders shook. The only time he'd seen her cry before had been over a random movie where a dog had overcome adversity (porcupine quills) in order to be reunited with its owner.

"What's wrong?" he asked, unsure of what he should do. He understood the idea of consoling someone but had never actually put it into practice. They weren't a family free with affection. At best, his father shook his hand, and his mother squeezed his shoulder whenever they were pleased with him. He didn't mind. It was how things were.

His father said, "Your grandfather passed away."

"Oh," Wallace breathed, suddenly itchy all over.

"Do you understand death?"

No, no, he didn't. He knew what it was, knew what the word meant, but it was a nebulous thing, an event that occurred for other people far, far away. It'd never crossed Wallace's mind that someone *he* knew could die. Grandpa lived four hours away, and his house always smelled like sour milk. He'd been fond of making crafts out of his discarded beer cans: planes with propellers that actually moved, little cats that hung on strings from the ceiling of his porch.

And since he was a child grappling with a concept far bigger than he, the next words out of his mouth were: "Did someone murder him?" Grandpa was fond of saying how he'd fought in the war (which war, exactly, Wallace didn't know; he'd never been able to ask a follow-up question), which was usually followed by words that caused Wallace's mother to yell at her father while she covered Wallace's ears, and later, she'd tell her only son to *never* repeat what he'd heard because it was grossly racist. He could understand if someone had murdered his grandpa. It actually made a lot of sense.

"No, Wallace," his mother choked out. "It wasn't like that. It was cancer. He got sick, and he couldn't go on any longer. It's . . . it's over."

This was the moment Wallace Price decided—in the way children often do, absolute and fearless—never to let that happen to him. Grandfather was alive, and then he wasn't. His parents were upset at the loss. Wallace didn't like to be upset. So he tamped it down, shoving it into a box and locking it tight.

He blinked slowly, becoming aware of his surroundings. Still in the village. Still with the woman.

Mei hunkered down before him, her tie dangling between her legs. "All right?"

He didn't trust himself to speak, so he nodded, though he was the furthest thing from *all right*.

"This is normal," she said, tapping her fingers against her knee. "It happens to everyone after they pass. And don't be surprised if it happens a few more times. It's a lot to take in."

"How would you know?" he mumbled. "You said I was your first one."

"First one *solo*," she corrected. "I put in over a hundred hours of training before I could go out on my own, so I've seen it before. Think you can stand?"

No, he didn't. He did anyway. He was a little unsteady on his feet, but he managed to stay upright through sheer force of will. That hook was still there in his chest, the cable still flashing dimly. For a moment, he thought he felt a gentle tug, but he couldn't be sure.

"There we go," Mei said. She patted his chest. "You're doing well, Wallace."

He glared at her. "I'm not a child."

"Oh, I know. It's easier with kids, if you can believe that. The adults are the ones that're usually the problem."

He didn't know what to say to that, so he said nothing at all.

"Come on," she said. "Hugo's waiting for us."

They reached the end of the village a short time later. The buildings stopped, and the road that stretched before them wound its way through the coniferous forest, the scent of pine reminding Wallace of Christmas, a time when all the world seemed to take a breath and forget—even just for a little while—how harsh life could be.

He was about to ask how far they had to walk when they reached a dirt road outside of the village. A wooden sign sat next to the road. He couldn't make out the words in the dark, not until he'd gotten closer.

The letters had been carved into the wood with the utmost care.

CHARON'S CROSSING
TEA AND TREATS

"Char-ron?" he said. He'd never heard such a word before.

"Kay-ron," Mei said, enunciating slowly. "It's a bit of a joke. Hugo's funny like that."

"I don't get it."

Mei sighed. "Of course you don't. Don't worry about it. As soon as we get to the tea shop, it'll—"

"Tea shop," Wallace repeated, eyeing the sign with disdain.

Mei paused. "Wow. You've got something against tea, man? That's not gonna go over well."

"I don't have anything against—I thought we were going to meet God. Why would he—"

Mei burst out laughing. "*What?*"

"Hugo," he said, flustered. "Or whoever."

"Oh man, I cannot *wait* to tell him you said that. Holy crap. That's gonna go right to his head." She frowned. "Maybe I won't tell him."

"I don't see what's so funny."

"I know," she said. "That's what's so funny about it. Hugo's not God, Wallace. He's a ferryman. I told you that. God is . . . the idea of God is a human one. It's a little more complicated than that."

"What?" Wallace said faintly. He wondered if it was possible to have a second heart attack, even though he was already dead. And then he remembered he couldn't actually *feel* his heart beating anymore, and the desire to curl up into a little ball once again started to take over. Agnostic or not, he hadn't expected to hear something so enormous said so easily.

"Oh, no," Mei said, grabbing onto his hand to make sure he stayed on his feet. "We're not going to lie down here. It's only a little bit farther. It'll be more comfortable inside."

He let himself be pulled down the road. The trees were thicker, old pines that reached toward the starry sky like fingers from the earth. He couldn't remember the last time he'd been in a forest, much less at night. He preferred steel and honking horns, the sounds of a city that never went to sleep. Noise meant he wasn't alone, no matter where he was. Here, the silence was all-consuming, suffocating.

They rounded a corner, and he could see warm lights through the trees like a beacon calling, calling, calling him. He barely felt his feet on the ground. He thought he might be floating but couldn't bring himself to look down to see.

The closer they got, the more the hook tugged at his chest. It wasn't quite irritating, but he couldn't ignore it. The cable continued on down the road.

He was about to ask Mei about it when something moved on the road ahead of them. He flinched, mind constructing a terrible creature crawling from the shadowy woods with sharp fangs and glowing eyes. Instead, a woman appeared, hurrying down the road. The closer she got, the more details filled in. She looked middle-aged, her mouth set in a thin line as she pulled her coat tighter around her. She had bags under her eyes, dark circles that looked as if they'd been tattooed on her face. Wallace didn't know why he was expecting some kind of acknowledgment, but she passed by them without so much as a glance in their direction, blond hair trailing behind her as she moved quickly down the road.

Mei had a pinched look on her face, but she shook her head and it was gone. "Come on. Don't want to keep him waiting any more than we already have."

He didn't know what he was expecting after reading the sign. He'd never really been inside something that could be called a *tea shop* before. He'd gotten his morning coffee from the cart in front of the office building. He wasn't a hipster. He didn't have a man bun or an ironic sense of fashion, his current outfit be damned. The glasses he usually wore while reading were, while expensive, utilitarian. He didn't belong in something that could be described as a *tea shop*. What a preposterous idea.

Which was why he was surprised when they came to the shop itself to see that it looked like a house. Granted, it was unlike any house he'd ever seen before, but a house all the same. A wooden porch wrapped around the front, large windows on either side of a bright green door, light flickering from within like candles had been lit. A brick chimney sat on the roof with a little curl of smoke coming out the top.

But that was where the similarity to any house Wallace had ever seen ended. Part of it had to do with the cable extending from the hook in his chest and up the stairs, disappearing into the closed door. *Through* the closed door.

The house itself looked as if it had started out one way, and then halfway through the builders had decided to go in another direction entirely. The best way Wallace could think of to describe it was that it looked like a child stacking block after block on top of one another, making a precarious tower. The house looked as if even the smallest breeze could send it tumbling down. The chimney wasn't crooked, per se, but more *twisted*, the brickwork jutting out at impossible angles. The bottom floor of the house appeared sturdy, but the second floor hung off to one side, the third floor to the opposite side, the *fourth* floor right in the middle, forming a turret with drapes drawn across multiple windows. Wallace thought he saw one of the drapes move as if someone were peering out, but it could have been a trick of the light.

The outside of the house was constructed with panel siding.

But also brick.

And . . . adobe?

One side appeared to be built out of logs, as if it'd been a cabin at one point. It looked like something out of a fairy tale, an unusual house hidden away in the woods. Perhaps there'd be a kindly woodsman inside, or a witch who wanted to cook Wallace in her oven, his skin cracking as it blackened. Wallace didn't know which was worse. He'd heard too many stories about terrible things happening in such houses, all in the name of teaching a Very Valuable Lesson. This did nothing to make him feel better.

"What is this place?" Wallace asked as they stopped near the porch. A small green scooter sat next to a flower bed, the blooms wild in yellows and greens and reds and whites, but muted in the dark.

"Awesome, right?" Mei said. "It's even crazier on the inside. People come from all over to see it. It's pretty famous, for obvious reasons."

He pulled his arm from her as she tried to walk toward the porch. "I'm not going inside."

She glanced over her shoulder. "Why not?"

He waved at the house. "It doesn't look safe. It's obviously not up to code. It's going to fall down at any moment."

"How do you know that?"

He stared at her. "We're seeing the same thing, right? I'm not going to be trapped inside when it collapses. It's a lawsuit waiting to happen. And I *know* about lawsuits."

"Huh," Mei said, looking back up at the house. She tilted her head back as far as she could. "But . . ."

"But?"

"You're dead," she said. "Even if it did fall down, it wouldn't matter."

"That's . . ." He didn't know what that was.

"And besides, it's been like this for as long as I've lived here. It hasn't fallen down yet. I don't think today will be that day either."

He gaped at her. "You *live* here?"

"I do," she said. "It's our home, so maybe show some respect? And don't worry about the house. If we worry about the little things all the time, we run the risk of missing the bigger things."

"Has anyone ever told you that you sound like a fortune cookie?" Wallace muttered.

"No," Mei said. "Because that's kind of racist, seeing as how I'm Asian and all."

Wallace blanched. "I . . . that's not—I didn't mean—"

She stared at him a long moment, letting him sputter before saying, "Okay. So you didn't mean it that way. Glad to hear it. I know this is all new for you, but maybe think before you talk, yeah? Especially since I'm one of the few people who can even see you."

She took the steps on the porch two at a time, stopping in front of the door. Potted plants hung from the ceiling, long vines draping down. A sign sat in the window that read CLOSED FOR PRIVATE EVENT. The door itself had an old metal knocker in the shape of a leaf. Mei lifted the knocker, tapping it against the green door three times.

"Why are you knocking on the door?" he asked. "Don't you live here?"

Mei looked back at him. "Oh, I do, but tonight's different. This is how things go. Ready?"

"Maybe we should come back later."

She smiled like she was amused, and for the life of him, Wallace couldn't see what was so funny. "Now's as good as time as any. It's all about the first step, Wallace. You can do it. I know faith is hard, especially in the face of the unknown. But I have faith in you. Maybe have a little in me?"

"I don't even know you."

She hummed a little under her breath. "Sure you don't. But there's only one way to fix that, right?"

He glared at her. "Really working for that ten, aren't you?"

She laughed. "Always." She put her hand on the doorknob. "Coming?"

Wallace looked back down the road. It was full-on dark. The sky was a field of stars, more than he'd ever seen in his life. He felt small, insignificant. And lost. Oh, was he lost.

"First step," he whispered to himself.

He turned back toward the house. He took a deep breath and puffed out his chest. He ignored the ridiculous slap his flip-flops made as he climbed the porch steps. He could do this. He was Wallace Phineas Price. People cowered at the sound of his name. They stood before him in *awe*. He was cool and calculating. He was a shark in the water, always circling. He was—

—tripping when the top step sagged, causing him to stumble forward.

"Yeah," Mei said. "Watch the last one. Sorry about that. Been meaning to tell Hugo to get that fixed. Didn't want to interrupt your moment or whatever was happening. It seemed important."

"I hate everything," Wallace said through gritted teeth.

Mei pushed open the door to Charon's Crossing Tea and Treats. It creaked on its hinges, and warm light spilled out, followed by the thick scent of spices and herbs: ginger and cinnamon, mint and cardamom. He didn't know how he was able to distinguish them, but there it was all the same. It wasn't like the office, a place more familiar than even his own home, stinking of cleaning fluids and artificial air, all steel and without whimsy, and though he hated that stench, he was used to it. It was safety. It was reality. It was what he knew. It was *all* he knew, he realized with dismay. What did that say about him?

The cable attached to the hook vibrated once more, seeming to beckon him forward.

He wanted to run as far as his feet could carry him.

Instead, with nothing left to lose, Wallace followed Mei through the door.

CHAPTER 4

He expected the inside of the house to look like the outside, a mish-mash of architectural atrocities better suited for demolition than habitation.

He wasn't disappointed.

The light was low, coming from mismatched sconces bolted to the walls and an obscenely large candle sitting on a small table near the door. Plants hung from the vaulted ceiling in wicker baskets, and though none of them were flowering, the scent of them was almost overwhelming, mixing with the powerful smell of spices that seemed embedded into the walls. The vines trailed toward the floor, swaying gently in the breeze through the open window on the far wall. He started to reach for one, suddenly desperate to feel the leaves against his skin, but he curled his hand at the last moment. He could smell them, so he knew they were there even if his eyes were playing tricks on him. And Mei could touch him—in fact, he could still feel the ghost of her fingers on his skin—but what if that was it? Wallace had never been a man of leisure, stopping to smell the roses, or so the saying went. Doubt, then, doubt creeping up on him, sliding over his shoulders and weighing him down, fingers like claws digging in.

A dozen tables sat in the middle of the large room, their surfaces gleaming as if freshly wiped down. The chairs tucked underneath were old and worn, though not shabby. They too were mismatched, some with wooden seats and backs, others with thick and faded cushions. He even saw a moon chair in one corner. He hadn't seen one of those since he was a kid.

He barely heard Mei close the door behind them. He was distracted by the walls of the room, his feet moving him toward them of their own volition. They were covered in pictures and posters, some framed, some held up by pushpins. They told a story, he thought, but one he couldn't follow. Here was a picture of a waterfall, the spray catching the sunlight in rainbow fractals. Here was a shot of an island in a cerulean sea, the trees so thick, he couldn't see the ground. Here was a gigantic mural of the pyramids, drawn with a deft but unpracticed hand. Here was a photograph of a castle on a cliff, the stone crumbling and being overtaken by moss. Here was a framed poster of a volcano rising above the clouds, lava bursting in hot arcs. Here was a painting of a town in the throes of winter, the lights bright and almost twinkling, reflecting off an unmarked layer of snow. Strangely, they all caused a lump in Wallace's throat. He had never had time for such places, and now, he never would.

Shaking his head, he moved on, glancing at a fireplace that made up half of the wall to his right, the wood shifting as the embers sparked. It was made of white stone, the mantle, oak. Atop the mantle were little knickknacks: a wolf carved from stone, a pinecone, a dried rose, a basket of white rocks. Above the fireplace, a clock, but it appeared to be broken. The second hand was twitching, but it never advanced. A high-backed chair sat in front of the fireplace, a heavy blanket hanging off the armrest. It looked . . . welcoming.

Wallace glanced to the left to see a counter with a cash register and an empty, darkened display case with little handwritten signs taped against the glass advertising a dozen different types of pastries. Jars lined the walls behind the counter. Some were filled with thin leaves, others with powder in various shades. Little handwritten labels sat in front of each one, describing even more varieties of tea.

A large chalkboard hung on the wall above the jars, next to a pair of swinging doors with porthole windows. Someone had drawn little deer and squirrels and birds on the chalkboard in green and blue chalk, surrounding a menu that seemed to go on forever. Green tea and herbal tea, black tea and oolong. White tea, yellow tea, fermented tea. Sencha, rose, yerba, senna, rooibos, chaga tea, chamomile. Hibiscus, essiac, matcha, moringa, pu-erh, nettle, dandelion tea . . . and he remembered the graveyard where Mei had plucked the dandelion puffball from the ground and blown on it, the little white wisps floating away.

They were all printed around a message in the center of the board. The words, written in spiky and slanted letters, read:

The first time you share tea, you are a stranger.
The second time you share tea, you are an honored guest.
The third time you share tea, you become family.

The entire place felt like a fever dream. It couldn't be real. It was too . . . something, something that Wallace couldn't quite put his finger on. He stopped in front of the display case, staring at the message on the chalkboard, unable to look away.

Unable, that was, until a dog ran out of a wall.

He shrieked as he stumbled backward, not believing his eyes. The dog, a large black mutt with a white pattern on its chest that almost looked like a star, rushed toward him, barking its fool head off. Its tail swishing furiously, it circled Mei, back end wiggling as it rubbed up against her.

"Who's a good boy?" Mei cooed in a tone of voice that Wallace despised. "Who's the best boy in the entire world? Is it *you*? I think it's *you*."

The dog, apparently in agreement that it was the best boy in the entire world, barked cheerfully. Its ears were large and pointed, though the left one flopped over. It collapsed in front of Mei, rolling over onto its back, legs kicking as Mei sank to her knees—seeming to disregard the fact that she was wearing a suit, much to Wallace's consternation—rubbing her hands along its stomach. Its tongue lolled out of its mouth as it looked at Wallace. It rolled back over and climbed to its feet, shaking itself from side to side.

And then it jumped on Wallace.

He barely got his hands up in time before it crashed into him, knocking him off his feet. He landed on his back, trying to shield his face from the frantic, wet tongue licking all the exposed skin it could find.

"Help me!" he shouted. "It's trying to kill me!"

"Yeah," Mei said. "That's not quite what he's doing. Apollo doesn't kill. He loves." She frowned. "Quite a bit, apparently. Apollo, no! We don't hump people."

And then Wallace heard a dry, rusty chuckle followed by a deep, crackly voice. "Don't usually see him so excited. Wonder why that is?"

Before Wallace could focus on *that*, the dog jumped off him and took off toward the closed double doors behind the counter. But rather than pushing the doors open, it went *through* them, the doors unmoving. Wallace sat up in time to see the tip of its tail disappear. The cable from his chest wrapped around the counter, and he couldn't see where it led to.

"What the hell was that?" he demanded, hearing the dog bark somewhere in the house.

"That's Apollo," Mei said.

"But—it—he walked through *walls*."

Mei shrugged. "Well, sure. He's dead like you."

"*What?*"

"Quick one you've got there," that crackly voice said, and Wallace turned his head toward the fireplace. He yelped at the sight of an old man peering around the side of the high-backed chair. He looked ancient, his dark brown skin heavily wrinkled. He grinned, his strong teeth catching the firelight. His eyebrows were large and bushy, his white Afro sitting on his head like a wispy cloud. He smacked his lips as he chuckled again. "Good on you, Mei. Knew you could do it."

Mei blushed, shuffling her feet. "Thanks. Had a little trouble there at the beginning, but I got it all sorted out." Wallace barely heard her as he continued to mention sexually aggressive ghost dogs and old men appearing out of nowhere. "I think."

The man pushed himself up from the chair. He was short and slightly hunched. If he cleared five feet, Wallace would be surprised. He wore flannel pajamas and an old pair of slippers. A cane leaned against the side of the chair. The old man grabbed it and shuffled forward. He stopped next to Mei, squinting down at Wallace on the floor. He tapped the end of the cane against Wallace's ankle. "Ah," he said. "I see."

Wallace didn't want to know what he saw. He should have never followed Mei into the tea shop.

The man said, "Kinda squirrely, ain't ya?" He tapped his cane against Wallace again.

Wallace batted it away. "Would you stop that?!"

The man didn't stop that. In fact, he did it once more. "Trying to make a point."

"What are you—" And then Wallace knew. This had to be Hugo, the man Mei brought him to see. The man who wasn't God, but something she'd called a ferryman. Wallace didn't know what he was expecting; perhaps a man in white robes and a long flowing beard, surrounded by blazing light, a wooden staff instead of a cane. This man looked at least a thousand years old. He had a presence about him, something Wallace couldn't quite place. It was . . . calming? Or so close to it that it didn't matter. Maybe this was part of the process, what Mei had called the *transition*. Wallace wasn't sure *why* he needed to be beaten with a cane, but if Hugo deemed it necessary, then who was Wallace to say otherwise?.

The man pulled the cane back. "Do you understand now?"

No, he really didn't. "I think so."

Hugo nodded. "Good. Up, up. Shouldn't stay on the floor. Gets drafty. Don't want to catch your death." He cackled as if it were the funniest thing in the world.

Wallace laughed too, though it was incredibly forced. "Ha-ha, yeah. That's . . . hysterical. I get it. Jokes. You tell jokes."

Hugo's eyes twinkled with undisguised mirth. "It helps to laugh, even when you don't feel like laughing. You can't be sad when you're laughing. Mostly."

Wallace slowly rose to his feet, eyeing the two in front of him warily. He brushed himself off, aware of how ridiculous he looked. He pulled himself to his full height, squaring his shoulders. In life, he'd been an intimidating man. Just because he was dead didn't mean he was going to get jerked around.

He said, "My name is Wallace—"

The man said, "Tall fella, ain't ya?"

Wallace blinked. "Uh, I . . . guess?"

The man nodded. "In case you didn't know. How's the weather up there?"

Wallace stared down at him. "What?"

Mei covered her mouth with her hand, but not before Wallace could see the smile growing.

The man (Hugo? God?) shuffled forward, knocking his cane against Wallace's leg again as he circled around him. "Uh-huh. Okay. I see. So. Right. We can work with this, I think." He reached up and pinched Wallace's side. Wallace yelped, knocking his hand away. Hugo shook his head as he completed his circle, once again standing next to Mei, resting on his cane. "Hell of a first case to get assigned, Mei."

"Right? But I think I'm getting through to him." She glanced at Wallace with a frown. "Maybe."

"You didn't do *anything*," Wallace snapped.

Hugo nodded. "This one's gonna give us trouble. Wait and see." He grinned, the lines around his eyes cavernous. "I like the ones who cause trouble."

Wallace bristled. "My name is Wallace Price. I'm an attorney from—"

Hugo ignored him, looking at Mei and smiling. "How was your trip, dear? Got a little lost, did you?"

"Yeah," Mei said. "The world is bigger than I remember, especially going on my own."

"It usually is," Hugo said. "That's the beauty of it. But you're home now, so don't you worry. Hopefully, you won't get sent out again right away."

Mei nodded as she stretched her arms above her head, back popping loudly. "No place like home."

Wallace tried again. "I'm told I died from a heart attack. I'd like to lodge a formal complaint, seeing as how—"

"He's taking to being dead pretty well," Hugo said, eyeing Wallace up and down. "Usually there's screaming and yelling and threats. I like it when they threaten."

"Oh, he had his moments," Mei said. "But on the whole, not too bad. Guess where I found him?"

Hugo eyed Wallace up and down. Then, "Where he died. No, wait. At his home, trying to figure out why he couldn't make anything work."

"His funeral," Mei said, and Wallace was offended by how gleeful she sounded.

"No," Hugo breathed. "Really?"

"Sitting in a pew and everything."

"Wow," Hugo said. "That's embarrassing."

"I'm standing right here," Wallace snapped.

"Of course you are," Hugo said, not unkindly. "But thank you for making that known."

"Look, Hugo, Mei said you could help me. She said she had to bring me to you because you're the ferryman, and you're supposed to do . . . something. I admit I wasn't really paying attention to that part, but that is *beside the point.* I don't know what kind of racket you're running here, and I don't know who put you up to this, but I would really rather not be dead if at all possible. I have far too much work to do, and this has been an awful inconvenience. I have *clients.* I have a brief due by the end of the week that can't be delayed!" He groaned, mind racing. "And I'm supposed to be in court on Friday for a hearing that I can't miss. Do you know who I am? Because if you *do,* then you know I don't have time for this. I have responsibilities, yes, *extremely* important responsibilities that can't be ignored."

"Of course I know who you are," Hugo said dryly. "You're Wallace."

Relief like he'd never before experienced washed over him. He'd come to the right person. Mei, whoever—or *whatever*—she was, seemed to be an underling. A drone. Hugo was in the position of power. Always, always speak to the manager to get results. "Good. Then you understand that this won't do at all. So if you could do whatever you need to in order to fix this, I would be greatly appreciative." And then, just because he couldn't be absolutely sure this man wasn't God, he added, "Please. Thank you. Sir."

"Huh," Hugo said. "That was a bit of a word salad."

"He tends to do that," Mei whispered loudly. "Probably because he was a lawyer."

The old man eyed Wallace up and down. "Called me Hugo. You hear that?"

"I did," Mei said. "Maybe we should—"

"Hugo Freeman, at your service." He bowed as low as he could.

Mei sighed. "Or we could do it this way."

Hugo snorted. "Learn to have a little fun. It doesn't always have to be doom and gloom. Now, where were we? Ah, yes. I'm Hugo, and you're upset you're dead, but not because of friends or family or some other such drivel, but because you have work to do, and this is an inconvenience." He paused, considering. "An *awful* inconvenience."

Wallace was relieved. He expected more of a fight. He was pleased he didn't need to resort to threats of legal action. "Exactly. That's exactly it."

Hugo shrugged. "All right."

"Really?" He could be back into the office by tomorrow afternoon at the latest, maybe the day after depending on how long it took him to get home. He'd have to demand that Mei bring him back as he didn't have his wallet. If push came to shove, he'd phone the firm and have his assistant buy him a plane ticket. Sure, he didn't have his driver's license, but something so trivial wouldn't stop Wallace Price. As a last resort, he could take the bus, but he wanted to avoid it if he could. He had almost a week's worth of work to catch up on, but it was a small price to pay. He'd have to find a way to explain the whole funeral/open casket thing, but he'd figure it out. Naomi would be disappointed she wasn't getting anything from his estate, but screw her. She'd been mean at the funeral.

"Okay," he said. "I'm ready. How do we do this? Do you . . . chant or something? Sacrifice a goat?" He grimaced. "I really hope you don't have to sacrifice a goat. I get squeamish around blood."

"You're in luck," Hugo said. "We're fresh out of goats."

Wallace sagged. "Great. I'm ready to be alive again. I learned my lesson. I promise to be nicer to people and blah, blah, blah."

"The joy I feel knows no bounds," Hugo said. "Raise your arms above your head."

Wallace did just that.

"Now jump up and down."

Wallace did, the cable rising and falling from the floor.

"Repeat after me: 'I want to be alive.'"

"I want to be alive."

Hugo sighed. "You gotta mean it. Really let me hear it. Make me *believe*."

"I want to be alive!" Wallace shouted as he jumped up and down, arms above his head. "I want to be alive! I want to be alive!"

"There it is!" Hugo cried. "I can feel something happening. It's really coming. Keep going! Jump in circles!"

"I want to be alive!" Wallace bellowed as he jumped in a circle. "I want to be alive! I want to be alive!"

"And *stop*. Whatever you do, *don't move*."

Wallace froze, arms above his head, one leg raised, his flip-flop dangling off his foot. He could feel it working. He didn't know how, but he did. Soon, this would all be over and he'd go back to living.

Hugo's eyes widened. "Stay like that until I say so. Don't even *blink*."

Wallace didn't. He stayed exactly as he was. He'd do anything to make this right again.

Hugo nodded. "Good. Now, I want you to repeat after me again: 'I am an idiot.'"

"I am an idiot."

"'And I'm dead.'"

"And I'm dead."

"'And there's no way for me to come back to life because that's not how it works.'"

"And there's . . . what?"

Hugo doubled over, wheezing out grating laughter. "Oh. Oh my. You should see the look on your face. It's priceless!"

The skin under Wallace's right eye twitched as he lowered his arms slowly, putting his foot back onto the floor. "*What?*"

"You're *dead*," Hugo exclaimed. "You can't be brought back to life. That's not how anything works. Honestly." He elbowed Mei in the side. "You see this? What a goof. I like him. It'll be a shame to see him go. He's fun."

Mei glanced toward the double doors. "You're going to get us in trouble, Nelson."

"Bah. Death doesn't need to always be sad. We need to learn to laugh at ourselves before we—"

"Nelson," Wallace said slowly.

The man looked at him. "Yes?"

"She called you Nelson."

"That's because it's my name."

"Not Hugo."

Nelson waved his hand. "Hugo is my grandson." He narrowed his eyes. "And you won't tell him what we did if you know what's good for you."

Wallace gaped at him. "Are you . . . are you *serious*?"

"As a heart attack," Nelson said as Mei choked. "Oops. Too soon?"

Wallace took a stuttering step toward the man—to do what, he didn't know. He couldn't think, couldn't form a single word. He tripped over his own feet, falling forward toward Nelson, eyes wide, a sound like a door creaking escaping his throat.

But he didn't crash into Nelson, because Nelson disappeared, causing Wallace to land roughly on the floor, facedown.

He raised his head in time to see Nelson blink back into existence a few feet away, near the fireplace. He wiggled his fingers at Wallace.

Wallace rolled over onto his back, staring up at the ceiling. His chest heaved (pesky thing, that, seeing as how his lungs weren't exactly necessary at this point), and his skin thrummed. "You're dead."

"As a doornail," Nelson said. "It was a relief, really. This old body had worn down, and try as I might, I couldn't make it work like I wanted it to anymore. Sometimes, death is a blessing, even if we don't realize it right away."

Another voice came then, deep and warm, the words sounding as if they had weight, and there was a mighty tug at that hook in Wallace's chest. It should have hurt. It didn't.

It almost felt like relief.

"Grandad, are you making trouble again?"

Wallace turned his head toward the voice.

A man appeared through the double doors.

Wallace blinked slowly.

The man smiled quietly, his teeth shockingly bright. The front two were a bit crooked and strangely charming. He was, perhaps, an inch or two shorter than Wallace, with thin arms and legs. He wore jeans and an open-collared shirt under an apron with the words CHARON'S CROSSING stitched across the front. The front of the apron bulged slightly against the gentle swell of his stomach. His skin was deep brown, his eyes almost hazel with shots of green through them. His hair was similar to the old man's, tight coils in a short Afro, though his was black. He seemed young; not quite as young as Mei, but surely younger than Wallace. The floorboards creaked with every step he took.

He set down the tray he was carrying onto the counter, a teapot clanking against the oversized teacups. It smelled like peppermint. He walked around the counter. Wallace saw the dog—Apollo—weaving around and then *through* the man's legs. The man laughed at the dog. "I can see that. Curious, right?"

The dog barked in agreement.

Wallace stared as the man approached. He didn't know why he focused on the man's hands, fingers oddly delicate, palms paler than the backs, nails like crescent moons. He rubbed his hands together before he crouched down near Wallace, keeping some distance from him as if he thought Wallace was skittish. It was only then Wallace noticed the cable attached to his chest extended to the man, though there didn't appear to be a hook. The cable disappeared into his ribcage, right where his heart should be.

"Hello," the man said. "Wallace, right? Wallace Price?"

Wallace nodded, unable to find his voice.

The man's smile widened, and the hook in Wallace's chest felt like it was burning. "My name is Hugo Freeman. I am a ferryman. I'm sure you have questions. I'll do my best to answer them all. But first things first. Would you like a cup of tea?"

CHAPTER 5

Wallace had never been a fan of tea. If pressed, he would say he never really saw what the fuss was about. It was dry leaves in hot water.

And it probably didn't help that he was still staring at the man known as Hugo Freeman. He moved with grace, every action deliberate, almost as if he were dancing. He didn't reach out to help Wallace to his feet, but instead motioned for him to pick himself up off the floor. Wallace did, though he kept his distance. If there ever were a god, it would be this man, no matter what Mei had told him. For all he knew, it was another trick, a test to see how he would act. He needed to be careful here, especially if he was going to insist this man give him back his life. It didn't help that the cable seemed to connect the two of them, stretching and shrinking depending upon how close they were to each other.

Apollo sat at Hugo's feet near the counter, staring up adoringly at him, tail thumping silently against the floor. Mei helped Nelson toward the counter, though he was grumbling that he could do it himself.

Wallace watched as Hugo picked up the steaming pewter teapot from the tray. He raised the pot toward his face, inhaling deeply. He nodded and said, "It's had time to steep. Should be ready now." He looked up at Wallace almost apologetically. "It's organic loose leaf, which didn't seem to fit what I know of you, but I have a pretty good track record for such things. For all I know, everything you like is organic. And peppermint."

"I don't like organic anything," Wallace muttered.

"That's okay," Hugo said as he began to pour the tea. "I think you'll like this." There were four cups, each with a different floral design. He motioned for Wallace to take the cup with the flowers that rose along the sides and into the interior of the cup.

"I'm dead," Wallace said.

Hugo beamed at him. "Yes. Yes, you are."

Wallace ground his teeth together. "That's not what—forget it. How the hell can I pick up the cup?"

Hugo laughed. It was a low and rumbly thing that started in his chest and poured out from his mouth. "Ah. I see. And anywhere else, you might have a point. But not here. Not with these. Try it. I promise you won't be disappointed."

No one could promise that with any certainty. The only thing he'd been able to touch was Mei and the ground beneath his feet. And Apollo, but the less said about that the better. This felt like a test, and he didn't trust this man as far as he could throw him. Wallace had never thrown a man before, and he didn't want to start now.

He sighed and reached for the cup, expecting his hand to pass through it, ready to glare at Hugo as if to say *See?*

But then he felt the warmth of the tea, and he gasped when his fingers touched the surface of the cup. It was solid.

It was solid.

He hissed when he jerked his hand up, sloshing tea over the side of the cup and onto his fingers. There was a brief flare of heat, but then it was gone. He looked at his fingers. They were pale as always, the skin unblemished.

"These teacups are special," Hugo said. "For people like you."

"People like me," Wallace echoed dully, still staring at his fingers.

"Yes," Hugo said. He finished pouring the tea into the remaining cups and set the teapot back onto the tray. "Those who have left one life in preparation for another. They were a gift when I became what I am now."

"A ferryman," Wallace said.

Hugo nodded. "Yes." He tapped the stitched lettering on his

chest. He didn't seem to notice the cable, his fingers disappearing through it. "Do you know Charon?"

"No."

"He was the Greek ferryman who carried souls to Hades over the rivers Styx and Acheron that divided the world between the living and the dead." Hugo chuckled. "It lacks subtlety, I know, but I was younger when I named this place."

"Younger," Wallace repeated. "You're already young." Then, unsure if he was insulting a sort of deity who was apparently in charge of . . . something, he quickly added, "At least you look like you are. I mean, I don't know how this works, and—"

"Thank you," Hugo said, lips quirking as if he found Wallace's discomfort amusing.

"Oh boy," Nelson grumbled, picking up his teacup and slurping along the edges. "He's an old man now. Maybe not as old as me, but he's getting there."

"I'm thirty," Hugo said dryly. He gestured toward the cup on the table in front of Wallace. "Drink up. It's best when it's hot."

Wallace eyed the tea. There were bits of *something* floating at the top. He wasn't sure he wanted to drink it, but Hugo was watching him closely. It didn't seem to be hurting Mei or Nelson, so Wallace gingerly picked up the cup, bringing it close to his face. The scent of peppermint was strong, and Wallace's eyes fluttered shut of their own accord. He could hear Apollo yawning in the way dogs do, and the bones of the house as it settled, but the floor and walls fell away, the roof rocketing up toward the sky, and he was, he was, *he was*—

He opened his eyes.

He was home.

Not his *current* home, the high-rise apartment with the imported furniture and the red accent wall he thought about painting over and the picture windows that opened up to a city of metal and glass.

No, it was his *childhood* home, the one with the stairs that creaked and the water heater that never had enough hot water. He stood in the doorway to the kitchen, Bing Crosby singing on the old radio, telling everyone who could hear to have yourself a merry little Christmas.

"Until then," his mother sang as she spun through the kitchen, "we'll have to muddle through somehow."

It was snowing outside, and garlands stretched along the top of the cabinets and on the windowsills. His mother laughed to herself as the oven dinged. She grabbed an oven mitt with a snowman printed on it from the counter. She opened the oven door, the hinges squealing, and pulled out a sheet of homemade candy canes. Her holiday specialty, a recipe she'd learned from her mother, a heavy-set Polish woman who called Wallace *pociecha*. The scent of peppermint filled the room.

His mother looked up at him standing in the doorway, and he was *ten* and *forty* all at the same time, in his sweats and flip-flops, but also in flannel pajamas, his hair a mess, his toes bare on the cold floor. "Look," she said, showing him the candy canes. "I think it's the best batch yet. *Mamusia* would be proud, I think."

Wallace doubted that. His grandmother had been a frightening woman with a sharp tongue and blunt insults. She died in a home for the elderly. Wallace had been sad and relieved all at once, though he'd kept that thought to himself.

He took a step toward his mother, and at the same time felt the warm bloom of the tea as it slid down his throat and settled in his belly. It tasted like the candy canes smelled, and it was too much, too jarring, because it couldn't be real. Yet he could taste her candy canes as if she were really there, and he said, "Mom?" but she didn't respond, instead humming along as Bing Crosby gave way to Ol' Blue Eyes.

He blinked slowly.

He was in a tea shop.

He blinked again.

He was in the kitchen of his childhood home.

He said, "Mom, I—" and there was a sting in his heart, a sharp jab that caused him to grunt. His mother had died. One minute she was there, and the next she was gone, his father speaking gruffly into the phone, telling him it'd been quick, that by the time they'd caught it, it'd already been too late. Metastasized, one of his cousins had told him later, in her lungs. She hadn't wanted Wallace to know, especially since they hadn't spoken in close to a year. He'd been so angry at her for this. For everything.

This is what the tea tasted like. Memory. Home. Youth. Betrayal. Bittersweet and warm.

Wallace blinked and found himself still in the tea shop, the cup shaking in his hands. He set it back down on the counter before it spilled more.

Hugo said, "You have questions."

In a shaky voice, Wallace replied, "That is quite possibly the biggest understatement ever spoken by the human tongue."

"He tends to be hyperbolic," Mei said to Hugo, as if that explained everything.

Hugo lifted his own teacup, taking a sip. His brow furrowed for a moment before smoothing out. "I'll answer them as best I can, but I don't know everything."

"You don't?"

Hugo shook his head. "Of course not. How could I?"

Frustrated, Wallace snapped, "Then I'll make this as simple as possible. Why am I here? What's the point of all of this?"

Mei laughed. "*That's* what you call simple? Rock on, man. I'm impressed."

"You're here because you died," Hugo said. "As for your other question, I don't know if I can answer it for you, at least not on the scale you mean. I don't think anyone can, not fully."

"Then what's the point of *you*?" he demanded.

Hugo nodded. "That I can answer. I'm a ferryman."

"I told him that," Mei whispered to Nelson.

"It's hard to retain information right after," Nelson whispered back. "We'll give him a little longer."

"And what does a ferryman do?" Wallace asked. "Are you the only one?"

Hugo shook his head. "There are many of us. People who . . .

well. People who have been given a job. To help others like yourself. To make sense of what you're feeling at the moment."

"I already have a therapist," Wallace snapped. "He does what I pay him for, and I have no complaints."

"Really?" Mei said. "No complaints. None whatsoever."

"Mei," Hugo warned again.

"Yeah, yeah," she muttered. She drank from her own tea. Her eyes widened slightly before she drank the rest in three huge gulps. "Holy crap, this is good." She looked up at Wallace. "Huh. I didn't expect that from you. Congrats."

Wallace didn't know what she was on about and didn't care to ask. That hook in his chest felt heavier, and though it tugged pleasantly, he was growing annoyed at the sensation. "I'm in the mountains."

"You are," Hugo agreed.

"There are no mountains near the city."

"There aren't."

"Which means we've come a long way."

"You have."

"Even if you're not the ferryman for everyone," Wallace said, "how does that work? People die all the time. Hundreds. Thousands. There should be more here. Why isn't there a line out the door?"

"Most of the people in the city go to the ferrywoman *in* the city," Hugo said, and Wallace was unnerved by how carefully he seemed to be choosing his words. "Sometimes, they get sent on to me."

"Overflow."

"Something like that," Hugo said. "To be honest, I don't always know why people such as yourself are brought to me. But it's not my job to question the *why*. You're here, and that's all that matters."

Wallace gaped at him. "You don't question the *why*? Why the hell not?" The *why* of things was Wallace's specialty. It led to truths that some tried to keep hidden. He looked at Mei, who grinned at him. No help there. Nelson, though. Nelson was in the same boat as he was. Maybe he could be of some use. "Nelson, you're—"

"Oh no," Nelson said, glancing at his bare wrist. "Would you look at the time. I do believe I'm supposed to be sitting in my chair in front of the fire." He shuffled away toward the fireplace, leaning on his cane. Apollo trailed after him, though he glanced back at Hugo as if to make sure he was staying right where he was.

That certainly didn't make Wallace feel better. "Somebody had better give me some answers before I . . ." He didn't know how to finish that.

Hugo reached up and scratched the back of his neck. "Look, Wallace—may I call you Wallace?" Then, without waiting for an answer, "Wallace, death is . . . complicated. I can't even begin to imagine what's going through your head right now. It's different for everyone. No two people are the same, in life or in death. You want to rant and rave and threaten. I get that. You want to bargain, make a deal. I get that too. And if it makes you feel better, you can say whatever you want here. No one will judge you."

"At least not out loud," Nelson said from his chair.

"You had a heart attack," Hugo said quietly. "It was sudden. There was nothing you could have done to stop it. It wasn't your fault."

"I know that," Wallace snapped. "I didn't *do* anything." He paused. "Wait, how did you know how I . . ." He couldn't finish.

"I know things," Hugo said. "Or, rather, I'm shown things. Sometimes it's . . . vague. An outline. Other times, it's crystal clear, though those are rare. You were clear to me."

"I expect I would be," Wallace said stiffly. "Which makes this easier, because I don't know how much clearer I can be. Send me back."

"I can't do that."

"Then find me someone who can."

"I can't do that either. That's not how it works, Wallace. A river only moves in one direction."

Wallace nodded, mind racing. He obviously wasn't being heard. He wouldn't find any help here. "Then I bid you good day, and request I be returned to the city. If you can't help me, I'll figure it out on my own." He didn't know *how*, exactly, but anything would be better than being here and hearing nothing but these three idiots talking in circles.

Hugo shook his head. "You can't leave."

Wallace narrowed his eyes. "Are you saying I'm trapped here? Keeping me against my will? That's kidnapping. I'll see you all brought up on charges for this, don't think I won't."

Hugo said, "You're standing."

"What?"

Hugo nodded toward the floor. "Can you feel the floor beneath your feet?"

Wallace flexed his toes. Through the thin, cheap flip-flops, he could feel the pressure of the wood floor against the bottoms of his feet. "Yes."

Hugo lifted a spoon off the tray and set it on the counter. "Pick that spoon up."

"Why?"

"Because I asked you to. Please."

Wallace didn't want to. He couldn't see the point. But instead of arguing, he stepped back up to the counter. He stared down at the spoon. It was such a little thing. Flowers had been carved into the handle. He reached down to pick it up. His hands shook as his finger curled around the handle, and he lifted it.

"Good," Hugo said. "Now put it back down."

Grumbling under his breath, he did as he was told. "Now what?"

Hugo looked at him. "You're a ghost, Wallace. You're dead. Pick it up again."

Rolling his eyes, he made to do just that. Only this time, his hand passed right through it. Not only that, his hand went *into* the countertop. There was a strange buzzing sensation prickling along his skin, and he gasped as he pulled his hand back as if it were burned. All his fingers were still attached, and the buzzing was already fading. He tried it again. And again. And again. Each time, his hand passed through the spoon and into the counter.

Hugo reached out for Wallace's hand, but stopped above it, hovering and coming no closer. "You were able to do it the first time because you've always been able to. You expected it because that's the way it's always worked for you. But then I reminded you that you've passed, and you could no longer touch it. Your expectations changed. You should have *un*expected it." He tapped the side of his head. "It's all about your mind and how you focus it."

Wallace started to panic, throat closing, hands shaking. "That doesn't make any sense!"

"That's because you've been conditioned your entire life to think one way. Things are different now."

"Says *you*." He reached for the spoon again but jerked his arm up when it passed through it once more. His hand caught the teacup, knocking it over. Tea spilled onto the counter. He stumbled back, eyes wide, teeth grinding together. "I . . . I can't be here. I want to go home. Take me home."

Hugo frowned as he came around the counter. "Wallace, you need to calm down, okay? Take a breath."

"Don't tell me to calm down!" Wallace cried. "And if I'm dead, why are you telling me to breathe? That is *impossible*."

"He's got a point," Mei said as she finished her second cup of tea.

For every step Hugo took toward him, Wallace took an answering step back. Nelson peered around the edge of the chair, a hand resting on the top of Apollo's head. The dog's tail thumped, keeping time like a silent metronome.

"Stay back," he snarled at Hugo.

Hugo raised his hands placatingly. "I'm not going to hurt you."

"I don't believe you. Don't come near me. I'm leaving, and there's nothing you can do to stop me."

"Oh no," Mei breathed. She set down her teacup and stared at Wallace. "That's definitely not a good idea. Wallace, you can't—"

"Don't tell me what I can't do!" he shouted at her, and the light bulb in one of the sconces sizzled and snapped before the glass shattered. Wallace jerked his head toward it.

"Uh-oh," Nelson whispered.

Wallace turned and ran.

CHAPTER 6

The first obstacle was the door.

He grabbed for the handle.

His hand passed right through it.

With a strangled yell, he jumped at the door. *Through* the door. He opened his eyes, finding himself on the porch of the tea shop. He looked down. All his bits and bobs still seemed to be attached, though the hook and cable were still there, the latter extending back into the tea shop. Something heavy moved thunderously toward the door, and he leapt from the porch, landing on the gravel. The stars stuttered in the sky above him, the trees more ominous than they'd been when he'd first arrived. They seemed to bend and sway as if beckoning him. He stumbled when he thought he saw movement off in the trees to his left, a great beast watching him, a crown of antlers atop its head, but it had to be a trick of the shadows because when he blinked, all he saw were branches.

He took off down the road, heading back the way he'd come earlier with Mei. If he got to the village, he could find someone to help him. He'd tell them about the crazy people in the tea shop in the middle of the woods.

The hook in his chest pulled sharply, the cable growing taut as it wrapped around his side. He almost fell to his knees. He managed to stay upright, flip-flops snapping against the bottoms of his feet. How on earth had he ever thought flip-flops were a good idea?

He glanced back over his shoulder toward the tea shop in time to see Mei and Hugo burst out onto the porch, shouting after him. Mei said, "Of all the stupid things" just as Hugo said, "Wallace, *Wallace*, you can't, you don't know what's out there—" but Wallace doubled down, running as fast as he could.

He'd never been much of a runner, much less a jogger of any

kind. He had a treadmill in his office, often walking long distances on it while on conference calls. He had time for little else, but at least it was something.

He was surprised, then, to find that his breath didn't catch in his chest, that no stitch formed in his side. Even wearing flip-flops didn't seem to slow him down much. The air was strangely stagnant, thick and oppressive, but he was *running*, running faster than he ever had in his life. He glanced down in shock at his own legs. They were almost a blur as his feet met the pavement of the road that led to the village. He laughed despite himself, a wild cackle that he'd never heard himself make before, sounding as if he were half out of his mind.

He looked back over his shoulder again.

Nothing there, no one chasing after him, no one shouting his name, only the empty, dark road that led to destinations unknown.

It should have made him feel better.

It didn't.

He ran as fast as he could toward a gas station ahead, the sodium arc lights lit up like a beacon, moths fluttering around them. An old van sat parked next to one of the pumps, and he could see people moving around inside. He ran toward it, only stopping when he reached the automatic doors.

They didn't open.

He jumped up and down in front of them, waving his arms.

Nothing.

He shouted, "Open the doors!"

The man behind the counter continued to look bored, tapping on his phone.

A woman toward the back of the store stood in front of a drink cooler, scratching her chin as she yawned.

He growled under his breath before reaching out to pry the doors open. His hands went right through them.

"Oh, right," he said. "Dead. Goddammit."

He walked through the doors.

The moment he entered, the fluorescent lights in the store above him flared and buzzed. The man behind the counter—a kid with enormous eyebrows and a face dotted with dozens of freckles—frowned as he looked up. He shrugged before going back to his phone.

Wallace smacked it out of his hands.

At least he tried to.

It didn't work.

He also tried to grab the man by the face with the same amount of success. Wallace recoiled when his thumb went into the man's *eye*. "This is so stupid," he muttered. He turned toward the woman in the back, still staring at the coolers. He went to her without much hope. She didn't hear him. She didn't see him. Instead, she picked out a two-liter of Mountain Dew.

"That's disgusting," he told her. "You should feel ashamed. Do you even know what's in that?"

But his opinion went unnoticed.

The automatic doors slid open, and Wallace ducked down when the clerk said, "Hey, Hugo. You're out late."

"Couldn't sleep," Hugo said. "Thought I'd pick a few things up."

Wallace tried to lean against a shelf of potato chips. He cursed when he fell back through them, blinking rapidly as he was *inside* the shelf. He jerked forward, ready to flee when the doors slid open again. He froze when the man behind the counter said, "Hey, Mei. Can't sleep either?"

"You know how it is," Mei said. "Boss man's up, so that means I'm up too."

The man could see her.

He could *see her.*

Which meant—

Wallace had no idea what that meant.

Before he could even begin to process this new information, a curious thing happened: bits of dust floated up around him.

He frowned at them, watching as they rose before his face, heading toward the ceiling. The motes of dust were oddly colored, almost flesh-like. He reached out to touch a rather large flake, but his hand froze when he saw where the dust was coming from.

His own arms.

His skin was flaking off, bit by bit, the top layer of derma floating up and away.

He yelped as he furiously brushed his arms.

"Got you," Mei said, appearing beside him. And then, "Oh crap. Wallace, we have to get you—"

He leapt forward toward the coolers.

Through the coolers.

He yelled incoherently as he went through a row of soda, and then a wall of cement. He was outside again, on the side of the store. He ran his hands over his arms as his skin continued to flake. The hook in his chest twisted angrily, the cable running back into the wall he'd just rushed through. He ran around the back of the store. An empty field stretched behind it under a night sky that seemed infinite. On the other side was another neighborhood, the houses close together, some with lights on, others dark and foreboding. He took off toward them, still rubbing his arms frantically.

He crossed the field and went between two houses. Music blared from the house on his right; the house to his left was silent and dark. He burst through the wall of the right house directly into a bedroom where a woman in a full-body suit of red leather slapped a riding crop against her palm, her attention on a man in footie pajamas who said, "This is going to be so *awesome*."

"Oh dear god," Wallace croaked before backing out of the house slowly. He turned toward the street in front of the houses.

He paused when his feet met pavement. He wasn't sure where to go, and now the skin on his legs was flaking off through his sweats and off the top of his feet. His ears were ringing, and the world had taken on a hazy glow, the colors running together. The cable flashed violently, the hook shaking.

He hurried down the sidewalk, wanting to get as far as he could. But it was as if the bottoms of his flip-flops had melted, sticking to the concrete. Each and every step was harder than the one before it, like he was moving under water. He grunted at the exertion. The ringing in his ears grew louder, and he couldn't focus. He gritted his teeth as he tried to push through it. The fingernail from the pinkie of his right hand slid off and disintegrated.

He curled his hand into a fist as he looked up. There, standing in the middle of the street, was a man.

But he was wrong, somehow, off in ways that turned Wallace's skin to ice. The man was hunched over, his back to Wallace, his shirtless torso covered in gray, sickly skin, his spine jutting out sharply. His shoulders shook as if he were heaving. His pants hung low on his hips. His sneakers were scuffed and dirty. His arms hung boneless at his sides.

A chill ran down Wallace's spine even as he took another step, everything in him screaming to back away, to run before the man turned around. He didn't want to see what the man's face looked like, sure it would be just as terrible as the rest of him. All sound seemed muffled, as if his ears were stuffed with cotton. When he spoke, it sounded like it came from someone else, his voice cracking. "Hello? Are you . . . can you hear me?"

The man's head snapped up as his arms twitched. On either wrist, angry welts rose the length of his forearms, making a T shape.

He turned around slowly.

Wallace Price was clinical to an almost inhuman degree. Details were his job, the little things others might have missed, something said in passing in a deposition or during intake interviews. And it was this attribute that caused him to catalogue each and every bit of the man before him: the dull, dead hair, the open mouth with blackened teeth, the horrifying, flat look in his eyes. The thing was *shaped* like a human, but he looked feral, dangerous, and if Wallace had felt fear before, it was nothing compared to what roared through him now. A mistake. He'd made a mistake. He should've never tried to speak to this . . . this thing, whatever it was. Even as his skin continued to rise around him, Wallace tried to take a step back.

His legs didn't work.

The stars blotted out until all Wallace knew was the dark of night, shadows stretching around him, reaching, reaching.

The man moved toward him, but it was awkward, as if the joints in his knees were frozen. He rocked from side to side with each step. He raised an arm, all fingers pointed toward the ground except one that was trained on Wallace. He opened his mouth again but no words came out, only a low animalistic grunt. Wallace's mind whited out in terror, and he knew, he *knew* that when the man touched him, his skin would be thin like paper, dry and catastrophic. And though he'd been told God didn't exist, Wallace prayed then, for the first time in years, a dying gasp of a thought that arced through his head like a shooting star: *!!HELP ME OH PLEASE MAKE IT STOP!!*

Movement then, sudden and quick as Hugo appeared between them, his back to Wallace. Relief like Wallace had never felt before bowled through him, knocking violently through his ribcage. The cable had shrunk to only a couple of feet, extending from Wallace around to Hugo's chest.

He said, "Cameron, no. You can't. He's not yours."

A dull clacking sound followed, and though Wallace couldn't see the man, he knew the noise came from him snapping his teeth together.

"I know," Hugo said quietly. "But he's not for you. He never was."

Wallace jerked his head when Mei appeared beside him. She frowned as she stood on her tiptoes, looking over Hugo's shoulder. "Crap." She dropped back down on her heels before raising her hands close to her chest, left palm toward the sky. She tapped the fingers of her right hand against her left palm in a staccato beat. A little burst of light came from her hand, and she reached over, grabbing Wallace by the arm.

"Get him home," Hugo said.

"What about you?" she asked, already pulling Wallace away. She grimaced when the skin of his wrist filtered through her grip.

"I'll follow," Hugo said, staring straight ahead at the man before him. "I need to make sure Cameron stays where he is."

Mei sighed. "Don't do anything stupid. We've already had enough of that for one day."

Right before Mei pulled him around the corner, Wallace glanced back once. Cameron had tilted his head toward the sky, mouth open, white tongue stuck out as if he were trying to catch snow. Later, Wallace would realize that it wasn't flakes of snow that fell onto Cameron's tongue.

He didn't speak the entire way back.

Mei did, however, muttering under her breath that of *course* her first assignment would be such a pain in the ass, she was being tested, but by god, she was going to see this through if it was the last thing she ever did.

Wallace's mind whirled. He noticed with no small amount of dread-tinged awe that the closer they got back to the tea shop, the less his skin disintegrated. It became less and less until they hit the dirt road that led to Charon's Crossing, where it ceased entirely. He looked down at his arms to see they looked as they always had, although the hairs were standing on end. The hook and cable were still attached to him, though the cable itself now led to where they'd just come from.

Mei dragged him up the porch stairs and shoved him through the door. "Stay here," she said before slamming the door in his face. He went to the window and looked out. She stood on the porch, wringing her hands as she stared out into the dark.

"What the hell?" Wallace whispered.

"Saw one, did you?"

He whirled around. Nelson, sitting in his chair in front of the fireplace. The fire was mostly embers now, the remaining charred log glowing red and orange. Apollo lay in front of the chair on his back, his legs kicking in the air. He snorted as he fell to his side, jaws opening in a yawn before he closed his eyes.

Wallace shook his head. "I . . . don't know what I saw."

Nelson grunted as he rose from the chair, using the cane to prop himself up. Wallace didn't know why he hadn't noticed before, but Nelson's slippers were little felt rabbits, the ears floppy and frayed. He glanced back out the window. Mei paced, the road in front of the tea shop dark and empty.

Nelson smacked his lips as he shuffled over to him. He looked Wallace up and down before peering out the window. "Still intact, I see. You should thank your lucky stars."

Wallace wasn't sure how intact he was. It was as if his mind had blown away on the wind with the other pieces of him. He couldn't focus, and he felt cold. "What happened to me? The . . . man. Cameron."

Nelson sighed. "Poor soul. Figured he was still lurking out there."

"What's wrong with him?"

"He's dead," Nelson said. "A couple of years, or thereabouts. Time . . . slips a little in here. Sometimes it crawls to a halt, and then it skips and jumps. It's part of living with a ferryman. Look, Mr. Price, you need to—"

"Wallace."

Nelson blinked owlishly. Then, "Wallace, you need to keep your focus on yourself. Cameron doesn't concern you. There's nothing you can do for him. How far did you get before it happened to you?"

Wallace considered pretending he had no idea what Nelson was talking about. Instead, he said, "The gas station."

Nelson whistled lowly. "Farther than I expected, I'll give you that." He hesitated. "That world is for the living. It no longer belongs to those of us who've passed. And those who try to make it, lose themselves. Call it insanity, call it another form of death. Regardless, the moment you walk out these doors, it begins to pull at you. And the longer you stay out there, the worse it gets."

Horrified, Wallace said, "I was out there. For *days*. Mei didn't show up until my funeral."

"The process sped up the moment you stepped foot into Charon's

Crossing. And if you try to leave, the same thing will happen to you that happened to Cameron."

Wallace reared back. "I'm trapped here."

Nelson sighed. "That's not—"

"It *is*. You're telling me that I can't leave. Mei kidnapped me and brought me here, and I'm a damn prisoner!"

"Bull," Nelson said. "There's a staircase at the back of the house. It'll take you to the fourth floor. On the fourth floor is a door. You can go through that door, and all of this, *everything* will fade away. You'll leave this place behind, and you'll know only peace."

It struck Wallace then, something he hadn't even considered. He didn't know why he hadn't seen it before. It was as clear as day. "You're still here."

Nelson eyed him warily. "I am."

"And you're dead."

"Nothing gets by you, does it?"

"You haven't crossed." Wallace's voice began to rise. "Which means everything you're saying is bullshit."

Nelson placed his hand on Wallace's arm, squeezing tighter than Wallace expected. "It's not. I wouldn't lie to you, not about this. If you leave this place, you'll end up like Cameron."

"But you're not."

"No," Nelson said slowly. "Because I've never left."

"How long have you been—"

Nelson sniffed. "It's rude to ask about another person's death."

Wallace blanched, uncharacteristically flustered. "I didn't mean to—"

Nelson laughed. "I'm giving you crap, boy. Need to have my fun where I can get it. Been dead for a few years."

Wallace reeled. *Years*. "But you're still here," he said faintly.

"I am. And I have my reasons, but never you mind what those are. I stay here because I choose to. I know the risks. I know what it means. They tried to make me move on, but I gave 'em the ol' what for." He shook his head. "But you can't let that affect what Hugo needs to do for you. Take the time you need, Wallace. There's no rush, so long as you realize this is the last place you'll ever be before you cross, if you know what's good for you. If you can accept that, then we'll be right as rain. Look. Here he comes."

Wallace turned back toward the window. Hugo was walking down the road, hands in the pockets of his apron, head bowed.

"Such a good boy," Nelson said fondly. "Empathetic almost to a fault, ever since he was a tyke. Causes him to take the weight of the world on his shoulders. You would do well to listen to him and learn from him. I don't know if you could find yourself in better hands. Remember that before you start hurling accusations."

Mei waited for Hugo on the porch. Hugo looked up at her, smiling tiredly. When they spoke, their voices were muffled but clear. "It's all right," he said. "Cameron's . . . well. He's Cameron. Wallace?"

"Inside," Mei said. Then, "Do you think it'll bring the Manager?"

Hugo shook his head. "Probably not. But weirder things have happened. We'll explain if he does come."

"The Manager?" Wallace whispered.

"Ooh, you don't want to know," Nelson muttered, picking up his cane as he shuffled back toward his chair. "Trust me on that. Mei and Hugo's boss. Nasty fellow. Pray you don't ever have to meet him. If you do, then I suggest you do whatever he says." He brushed a hand over Apollo's back as the dog rose. Apollo barked happily as he paced back and forth in front of the door. He backed up as it opened, Mei talking a mile a minute as Hugo trailed in after her. Apollo circled around the both of them. Hugo held out his hand. Apollo sniffed his fingers and tried to lick them, but his tongue went right through Hugo's hand.

"All right?" Hugo asked even as Mei glared at Wallace.

No, Wallace wasn't all right. Nothing about this was all right. "Why didn't you tell me I'm a prisoner?"

Hugo sighed. "Grandad."

"What?" Nelson said. "Had to scare him straight." He paused, considering. "Something you probably don't know a thing about, isn't that right? Because of the whole gay—"

"Grandad."

"I'm old. I'm allowed to say whatever I want. You know this."

"Pain in my ass," Hugo mumbled, but Wallace could see the quiet smile on his face. The hook tugged gently in his chest, warm and soft. Hugo's smile faded as he glanced at Wallace. "Come with me."

"I don't want to go through the door," Wallace blurted. "I'm not ready."

"The door," Hugo repeated.

"At the top of the stairs."

"*Grandad.*"

"Eh?" Nelson said, cupping his ear. "Can't hear you. Must be going deaf. Woe is me. As if my life wasn't hard enough already. No one should talk to me for the rest of the night so I can collect myself again."

Hugo shook his head. "You'll get yours, old man."

Nelson snorted. "Shows what you know."

Hugo glanced at Wallace. "I'm not going to take you to the door. Not until you're ready. I promise."

Wallace didn't know why, but he believed him. "Where are we going?"

"I want to show you something. It won't take long."

Mei was glaring at him. "You try to run again, I'll drag you back by your hair."

Wallace had been threatened before—many times, in fact; such was the life of a lawyer—but this was one of the first times he actually believed it. For someone so small, she was positively terrifying.

Before he could speak, Hugo said, "Mei, could you finish up the prep work for tomorrow? Shouldn't be much left. I got through most of it before you got back."

She muttered more threats as she pushed by Hugo and headed

through the double doors behind the counter. As the doors swung back and forth, Wallace could see what looked to be a large kitchen, the appliances steel, the floor covered in square tiles.

Hugo nodded toward a hallway at the back of the room. "Come on. You'll like this, I think."

Wallace doubted that immensely.

CHAPTER 7

Apollo seemed to know where they were going, prancing down the hallway, tail wagging. He looked back every now and then to make sure Hugo followed.

Hugo went through another entryway without looking back to see if Wallace would follow. The walls were covered in wallpaper, old but clean: little flowers were etched in that seemed to bloom as they walked by, though Wallace thought it might have been a trick of the light. A door on the right led to a small office, a desk inside covered with papers next to an ancient computer.

A door on the left was closed, but it seemed to be another way into the kitchen. He could hear Mei moving around inside along with the clatter of dishes as she sang at the top her lungs, a rock song that had to be older than she was. But since Wallace couldn't be sure how old she was (or, if he was being honest with himself, *what* she was), he decided to let it pass without comment.

Another door on the right led to a half bathroom with a sign hanging on it that read: GUYS, GALS, & OUR NONBINARY PALS. Beyond it was a set of stairs, and if Wallace still had a heartbeat, he was sure it'd be racing.

But Hugo paid it no mind, passing the stairs, heading for a door at the end of the hall. Apollo didn't wait for him to open it, instead walking through it. Wallace learned then that he still wasn't used to such things, and though he was sure he could do the same, he waited for Hugo to open the door.

It led outside and into darkness.

Wallace hesitated until Hugo motioned for him to walk through. "It's okay. It's just the backyard. Nothing will happen to you out there."

The air was cooler still. Wallace shivered and wondered again *why* he was shivering. He could make out Apollo's tail down in the yard, but it took time for his eyes to adjust. He gasped quietly as Hugo flipped a switch near the door.

Strings of light that hung above them burst to life. They stood on a back deck of sorts. There were more tables on it, the chairs turned over and set atop them. The lights had been strung around the deck railing and the eaves overhead. More plants were hanging down, bright flowers that had turned in on themselves against the night.

"Here," Hugo said. "Watch." He went to the edge of the deck near a set of stairs. He flipped another switch set against a wooden strut, and more lights turned on below the deck, revealing dry, sandy soil and row after row of . . .

"Tea plants," Hugo said before Wallace could ask. "I try to grow as much of my own as I can, only importing leaves that wouldn't survive the climate. There's nothing like a cup of tea from leaves that you've grown yourself."

Wallace watched as Apollo trotted up and down the rows of plants, stopping only briefly to sniff at the leaves. Wallace wondered if he could actually smell anything. Wallace could, a deep and earthy scent, one which grounded him more than he expected.

"I didn't know they grew from the ground," Wallace admitted.

"Where did you think they came from?" Hugo asked, sounding amused.

"I . . . never really thought about it, I guess. I don't have time for such things." As soon as the words left his mouth, he realized how it sounded. Normally, he wouldn't have given it a second thought, but these were strange days. "Not that it's a *bad* thing, but . . ."

"Life gets away from you," Hugo said simply.

"Yeah," Wallace muttered. "Something like that." Then, "Why tea?"

He followed Hugo down the stairs. The plants were tall, the biggest and most mature rising to Wallace's waist. In passing, almost at the back of his mind, he noticed the cable stretched tight between himself and Hugo.

He stopped when Hugo crouched down, reaching out to touch the leaves of one of the tallest plants. The leaves themselves were small and flat and green. He touched one briefly, his fingers trailing along the tip. "Guess how old this plant is."

"I don't know." He looked around at the other plants. "Six months? A year?"

Hugo chuckled. "A little older than that. This one was one of my first. It's ten years old next week."

Wallace blinked. "Come again?"

"Growing tea isn't for everyone," Hugo said. "Most tea plants don't mature until around three or four years. You can harvest the leaves before then, but something's missing from the flavor and scent. You have to put in the time and have patience. Too early, and you risk killing the plant and having to start all over again."

"Is this one of those times where we're talking about one thing, but you mean something else entirely?"

Hugo shrugged. "I'm talking about tea plants, Wallace. Something on your mind?"

Wallace wasn't sure he believed him. "I have many things on my mind."

Hugo said, "In the fall, some of the plants flower, these little things with a yellow center and white petals. The smell is indescribable. It mingles with the scent of forest, and there's nothing like it in all the world. It's my favorite time of year. What's yours?"

"Why do you care?"

"It's just a question, Wallace."

Wallace stared at him.

Hugo let it go. "Sometimes, I talk to the plants. It sounds weird, I know, but studies have been done showing plants respond to encouragement. It's not conclusive, and it's not necessarily the wording as much as it is the vibrations of the voice. I'm thinking of setting up speakers sometime soon, to play music for the plants to hear. Have you ever talked to a plant?"

"No," he said, distracted by the rows of green, the dark soil holding them in place. They were planted with about four or five feet between them, the leaves glossy in the starlight, and pungent, so much so that it caused Wallace to wrinkle his nose. It wasn't a bad smell (quite the contrary, in fact), just overwhelming. "That's stupid."

Hugo smiled. "A little bit. But I do it anyway. What could it hurt, right?" He looked back down at the plant before him. "You have to be careful when you harvest the leaves. If you're too rough, you can end up killing the plant. It took me a long time to get it right. I can't even begin to tell you how many I've had to pull out and throw away because of my own haste."

"Plants are living things," Wallace said.

"They are. Not like you and me, but in their own way."

"Are there ghost plants?"

Hugo stared at him, mouth agape.

Wallace scowled at him. "Don't give me that look. You told me to ask questions."

Hugo closed his mouth as he shook his head. "No, it's not—I've never thought about it that way. Curious." He squinted up at Wallace. "I like where your mind goes."

Wallace looked away.

"No," Hugo said. "I don't think there are ghost plants, though it would be wonderful if there were. They're alive, yes. And maybe they respond to encouragement. Or maybe they don't and it's a little story we like to tell ourselves to make the world seem more mysterious than it actually is. But they don't have a soul, at least none that I'm aware of. That's the difference between us and them. They die, and that's it. We die and—"

"End up at a tea shop in the middle of nowhere against our will," Wallace said bitterly.

Hugo sighed. "Let's try something else. Did you like being alive?"

Taken aback, Wallace said, "Of course I do." His expression hardened. "Did. Of course I did." It rang false even to his own ears.

Hugo brushed his hands against his apron as he stood slowly. "What did you like about it?" He continued on down the row of plants.

Against his better judgment, Wallace followed him. "Doesn't everyone like being alive?"

"Most people, I think," Hugo said. "I can't speak for everyone. But you're not most people, and no one else is here, which is why I'm asking you."

"What do *you* like about it?" Wallace asked, flinging the question back at him. He felt skittish, irritation growing.

"Many things," Hugo said easily. "The plants, for one. The earth beneath my feet. This place. It's different here, and not just because of what I am or what I do. For a long time, I couldn't breathe. I felt . . . stifled. Crushed. Like there was this weight on my shoulders and I didn't know how to get it off." He glanced back at Wallace. "Do you know what that feels like?"

He did, but he wasn't going to admit it here. Not now. Not ever. "You're not my therapist."

Hugo shook his head. "No, I'm not. Not exactly qualified for something like that, though I do play the role now and then. It's all part of the gig."

"The gig," Wallace repeated.

"Selling tea," Hugo said. "People come in, and some of them don't have any idea what they're looking for. I try to get to know them, to find out what they're all about before deciding on what kind of tea would be the best fit. It's a process of discovery. I usually get it right, though not always."

"Peppermint," Wallace said.

"Peppermint," Hugo agreed. "Did I get that right?"

"You hadn't even met me."

He shrugged. "I get a feeling, sometimes."

"A feeling." Wallace did nothing to stop the scorn dripping from his words. "You have to know how that sounds."

"I do. But it's just tea. Nothing to get so worked up about."

Wallace felt like screaming. "You got a *feeling* that told you peppermint."

"It did." He stopped in front of another plant, crouching down and picking up dead leaves off the ground. He put them in a pocket on his apron with the utmost care, as if he was worried about crushing them. "Was it wrong?"

"No," Wallace said begrudgingly. "It wasn't wrong." He thought Hugo would ask him to explain, what the peppermint meant.

He didn't. "Good. I like to think I'm pretty spot-on, but as I said, it doesn't always work. I try to be careful about it. You don't want to end up missing the forest for the trees."

Wallace had no idea what that meant. Everything was topsy-turvy, and the hook in his chest was tugging again. He wanted to tear it out, consequences be damned. "I liked being alive. I want to be alive again."

"Kübler-Ross."

"What?"

"There was a woman named Elisabeth Kübler-Ross. Have you ever heard of her?"

"No."

"She was a psychiatrist—"

"Oh dear god."

"A psychiatrist who studied death and near-death experiences. You know, you're rising above your body toward a bright white light, though I expect it's a little more complicated than that. A lot of it can be difficult to understand." He rubbed his jaw. "Kübler-Ross talked about stuff like transcendence of ego and spatiotemporal boundaries. It's complex. And I'm really not."

"You're not?" Wallace asked incredulously.

"Careful, Wallace," Hugo said, lips quirking. "That almost sounded like a compliment."

"It *wasn't*."

Hugo ignored him. "She was known for many things, but I think her biggest accomplishment was the Kübler-Ross model. Do you know what that is?"

Wallace shook his head.

"You probably do, though not by that name. And sure, some of the research since then doesn't agree with her findings, but I think it's a good place to start. It's the five stages of grief."

Wallace wanted to go back inside. Hugo once again rose to his feet, turning to face him. He didn't come any closer, but Wallace couldn't move, mouth almost painfully dry. He was a tea plant, rooted in place, not yet mature enough to be harvested. The cable thrummed between them.

Hugo said, "I've done this long enough to see how right she was. Denial. Anger. Bargaining. Depression. Acceptance. It's not always in that order, and it's not always every single step. Take you, for example. You seemed to skip right over denial. You've got the anger part down pat with a little bit of bargaining mixed in. Maybe more than a little bit."

Wallace stiffened. "That doesn't sound like it's for the dead. It's for the people who are left behind. I can't grieve for myself."

Hugo shook his head slowly. "Of course you can. We do it all the time, regardless of if we're alive or not, over the small things and the big things. Everyone is a little bit sad all the time. Yes, Kübler-Ross was talking about the living, but it fits just as well for people like you. Maybe even better. I've often wondered what it was like for her, after she passed. If she went through it all herself, or if there were still surprises left to find. What do you think?"

"I have no idea what you're talking about."

"Okay," Hugo said.

"Okay?"

"Sure. Do you like the plants?"

Wallace glared at him. "They're plants."

"Hush," Hugo said. "Don't let them hear you say that. They're very sensitive."

"You're out of your mind."

"I prefer to think of myself as eccentric." His smile returned. "At least that's what the people in town think of me. Some even believe this place is haunted." He laughed to himself. Wallace was never one for noticing how people sounded when they laughed, but there was a first time for everything. It was a full-body thing for Hugo, low and deep.

"That doesn't bother you?"

Hugo cocked his head. "No. Why would it? It's true. You're a ghost. Grandad and Apollo too. And you're not the first, nor will you be the last. Charon's Crossing is always haunted, though not like most people think. We don't have anyone rattling chains or causing a ruckus." He frowned. "Well, most of the time we don't. Grandad can get a little ornery when the health inspector comes around, but usually we tend to avoid the trappings of a haunted house. It'd be bad for business."

"They're still here," Wallace said. "Nelson. Apollo."

Hugo stepped around him, heading back toward the house. He trailed his fingers along the tops of the tallest plants. They bent with his touch before snapping back upright. "They are."

Wallace followed him. "Why?"

"I can't speak for Grandad," Hugo said. "You'll have to ask him."

"I did."

Hugo glanced back, a look of surprise on his face. "What did he say?"

"That it was none of my business."

"Sounds about right. He's stubborn that way."

"And Apollo?"

The dog barked at the sound of his name, guttural and sharp. He came bounding up one of the rows to their left. No dust or dirt rose when his paws hit the ground. He stopped near the porch, back arched, nose and whiskers twitching as he stared off into the dark forest. Wallace couldn't see far, and it struck him how different the night was here compared to the city, the shadows almost alive, sentient.

"I don't know that I can answer that either," Hugo said. Before Wallace could respond, he added, "Not because I don't want to, but because I don't know, exactly. Dogs don't—they're not like us. They're . . . pure in a way we aren't. I've never had another dog come here before, needing help to cross. I've heard stories of ferrymen and women whose job it is to handle certain animals, but that's not what I do. I'd love it, though. Animals aren't as complicated as people."

"Then why would he—" Wallace stopped. Then, "He was yours."

Hugo paused at the bottom of the steps. Apollo stared up at him adoringly, a goofy smile on his face, whatever had captured his attention in the trees forgotten. Hugo held his hand toward Apollo's snout. The dog sniffed his fingers. "He was," Hugo said quietly. "He is. He was a service dog. Or at least he tried to be. Failed most of his training, but that's okay. I still love him all the same."

"Service dog?" Wallace asked. "Like for . . ." He didn't know how to finish.

"Oh, probably not like you're thinking," Hugo said. "I'm not a veteran. I don't have PTSD." He shrugged. "When I was younger, things were difficult. Days I could barely get myself out of bed. Depression, anxiety, a whole matter of diagnoses I didn't know how to handle. There were doctors and medications and 'Do this, Hugo, do that, Hugo, you'll feel better if you just *let* yourself feel better, Hugo.'" He chuckled. "I was a different person then. I didn't know what I know now, though it'll always be part of me." He nodded toward Apollo. "One day, I heard this little yipping outside my window. It was raining and had been for what felt like weeks. I almost ignored the sound I heard, wanting to pull the covers over my head and shut everything out. But something made me get up and go outside. I found this dog shivering under a bush on the side of my house, so emaciated, I could count his ribs through his skin. I picked him up and took him inside. I dried him off and fed him. He never left. Funny, right?"

"I don't know."

"It's okay not to know," Hugo said. "We don't know most things, and we never will. I don't know how he came to be here, or where he came from. Thought he might make a good service dog. Seemed smart enough. And he was—is. Didn't really take, though. He was too distracted by most everything, but who could blame him? Certainly not me, because he tried his best, and that's all that matters. Turned out he was this . . . this part I didn't know I was missing. He wasn't the answer to everything, but it was a start. He lived a good life. Not as long as I would've liked, but still good."

"But he's here."

"He is," Hugo agreed.

"Trapped here," Wallace said, his hands curling into fists.

Hugo shook his head. "No. He has a choice. I tried to lead him to the door at the top of the stairs time and time again. I told him it was okay to go to whatever's next. That I would never forget him and would always be thankful for the time we had together. But he made his choice. Grandad made his choice." He glanced back at Wallace. "You have a choice too, Wallace."

"Choice?" Wallace spat. "If I leave, I turn into one of those . . . those *things*. If I step foot outside this place, I turn into dust. And don't even get me started on this ridiculous thing in my chest." He looked down at the cable stretching between them. It flashed once. "What is this?"

"Mei calls it the red thread of fate."

Wallace blinked. "It's not red. Or a thread."

"I know," Hugo said. "But it's apt, I think. Mei said . . . how did she put it? Ah, right. In Chinese myth, the old gods tie a red thread around the ankles of those who are destined to meet, who are meant to help one another. It's a pretty thought, isn't it?"

"No," Wallace said bluntly. "It's a shackle. A chain."

"Or it's a tether," Hugo said, not unkindly. "Though I know it doesn't seem like that to you now. It keeps you grounded while you're here. It helps me to find you if you're ever lost."

That certainly didn't make him feel any better. "What happens if I remove it?"

Hugo looked grim. "You'll float away."

Wallace was gobsmacked. "*What?*"

"If you try to remove it while you're on the grounds of the tea shop, you'll . . . rise. And I don't know if you'll ever stop. But if you remove it *off* grounds, you begin to lose your humanity, flaking away until all that's left is a shell."

Wallace spluttered. "That . . . that doesn't make any sense! Who the hell makes up these rules?"

Hugo shrugged. "The universe, I expect. It's not a bad thing,

Wallace. It helps me help you. And while you're here, all I can do is show you your options, the choices laid out in front of you. To make sure you understand there's nothing left for you to fear."

Wallace's eyes stung. He blinked rapidly, unable to meet Hugo's gaze. "You can't say that. You don't know what it's like. It's not fair."

"What isn't?"

"This!" Wallace cried, waving his arms around wildly. "All of it. Everything. I didn't ask for this. I don't *want* this. I have things to do. I have responsibilities. I have a *life*. How can you say I have a choice when it comes down to becoming like Cameron or going through your damn door?"

"I guess the denial was there all along."

Wallace glared at him. "I don't like you." It was petulant and mean, but Wallace couldn't bring himself to care.

Hugo didn't rise to the bait. "That's okay. We'll get there. I won't force you into anything you don't want to do. I'm here to guide you. All I ask is that you let me try."

Wallace swallowed past the lump in his throat. "Why do you care so much? Why do you do what you do? *How* do you do what you do? What's the point of all of this?"

Hugo grinned. "That's a start. There might be hope for you yet."

And with that, he walked up the porch stairs, Apollo bounding up beside him. He stopped at the door, looking back at Wallace still standing amongst the tea leaves. "You coming?"

Wallace hung his head and trudged up the stairs.

Hugo yawned as he closed the door behind them. He blinked sleepily, rubbing his jaw. Wallace could hear the clock in the front tick, tick, ticking. Before he'd fled the tea shop, the seconds had seemed lost, stuttering and stopping, stuttering and stopping. It sounded as if it'd smoothed out. It was normal again. Wallace didn't know what that meant.

"It's late," Hugo told him. "Our days start early here. Pastries needs to be baked, and tea needs time to steep."

Wallace felt awkward, unsure. He didn't know what was supposed to happen next. "Fine. If you could show me to my room, I'll let you be."

"Your room?"

Wallace ground his teeth together. "Or give me a blanket and I can sleep on the ground."

"You don't need to sleep."

Wallace flinched. "What?"

Hugo stared at him curiously. "Have you slept since you died?"

Well . . . no. He hadn't. But there hadn't been time. He'd been far too busy trying to make sense of all this drivel. The very idea of sleep hadn't even crossed his mind, even when things had gotten a bit hazy and he'd found himself at his own funeral. And then Mei had shown up and dragged him to this place. So, no. He hadn't slept. "I had things to do."

"Of course you did. Are you tired?"

He wasn't, which was strange. He should've been exhausted. With everything that had happened, he expected to be drained and moving sluggishly. But he wasn't. He'd never felt more awake. "No," he muttered. "That doesn't make sense."

"You're dead," Hugo reminded him. "I think you'll find sleep is the least of your worries from here on out. In all my years as a ferryman, I've never come across a sleeping ghost. That would be something new. You could try, I suppose. Let me know how that works out."

"So what am I supposed to do?" Wallace demanded. "Stand here and wait for you to wake up?"

"You could," Hugo said. "But there are more comfortable places for you to wait."

Wallace scowled at him. "You're not funny."

"A little," Hugo said. "You can do whatever you want, so long as you don't leave the grounds of the tea shop. I'd rather not have to chase after you again."

"Whatever I want?"

"Sure."

For the first time since he'd arrived in the tea shop, Wallace smiled.

"Mei."

"G'way."

"Mei."

"Time 'zit."

"Mei. Mei. *Mei*."

She sat up in her bed, the blankets falling around her waist. She wore an oversized shirt with the face of Friedrich Nietzsche printed on it. She jerked her head back and forth before settling on Wallace, standing in the corner of her room. "What? What is it? What's wrong? Are we under attack?"

"No," Wallace said. "What are you doing?"

She stared at him. "I'm *trying* to sleep."

"Oh, really? How's that working out for you?"

She started to frown. "Not well."

"Did you know I can't sleep ever again?"

"Yes," she said slowly.

He nodded. "Good." He turned around and walked through the wall out of her room.

"Oooooh!" he moaned as loudly as he could. "Oooooooh!" He paced up and down the hall of the bottom floor, a little perturbed that he couldn't seem to stomp his feet no matter how hard he tried. He banged his hands on the walls, but he kept almost falling through. Which is why he found himself bellowing out every ghost noise he'd ever heard in horror movies. He was disappointed he had no chains to clank. "I'm deaaaad. *Deaaaaaaaad!* Woe is meeee."

"Would you shut *up*!" Mei shouted from her room.

"Make me!" he bellowed back, and then redoubled his efforts.

Wallace continued on for sixteen more minutes before he took a cane upside the head.

"*Ow!*" he cried, rubbing the back of his skull. He whirled around to see Nelson standing before him, brow furrowed. "What was that for?"

"Are you going to behave? If not, I can do it again."

He reached for Nelson's cane, meaning to take it from him and toss it away, only to come up with nothing, taking a stumbling step forward where Nelson had stood before he'd disappeared into thin air.

Wallace's eyes bulged as he looked around the empty tea shop wildly. "Um," he said. "Hello? Where . . . where did you go?"

"Boo," a voice whispered in his ear.

Wallace didn't so much scream as squeak. He almost fell over as he turned around. Nelson stood behind him, arching a bushy white eyebrow. "How did you do that?"

"I'm a ghost," Nelson said dryly. "I can do almost anything." He raised the cane as if to strike Wallace again. Wallace reared back. "That's better. Enough with this nonsense. You may not like being here, but that doesn't mean you can make the rest of us suffer because of it. Either keep your mouth closed or come with me."

"Why would I go *anywhere* with you?"

"Oh, I don't know," Nelson said. "Maybe because I'm the only other human ghost here besides you? Maybe because I've been dead far longer than you have, and therefore know much more than you? Or maybe, just maybe, because I don't sleep either and it would be nice to have someone to stay up with? Pick one, boy, or don't pick anything at all, so long as you stop this infernal racket before I show you the end of my cane again."

"Why would you want to help me?"

Nelson's eyebrows rose on his forehead. "You think this is about you?" He scoffed. "It's not. I'm helping my grandson. And don't you forget it." He pushed by Wallace and shuffled down the hall toward the front of the house, the little ears on his rabbit slippers flopping around. "About you," he muttered. "Bah."

Wallace stared after him. He thought about picking right up where he'd left off, but the threat of the cane wasn't pleasant. He hurried after the old man.

Nelson went back to his chair in front of the fire, grunting as he sat down. Apollo was lying on his side in front of the fire, chest rising and falling slowly. Someone had cleaned up the glass from the bulb that had shattered earlier, and the lights from the sconces were dimmed.

"Pull up a chair," Nelson said without looking at him.

Wallace sighed, but did as he was asked.

At least he tried to.

He went to the table closest to him and reached for one of the overturned chairs. He frowned when his hand went through the chair leg. He breathed heavily through his nose as he tried again with the same results. And again. And again. And *again*.

Wallace heard Nelson laughing, but ignored him. If Nelson could sit in a chair, then it was something Wallace could do too. He just needed to figure out how.

He grew even more frustrated a few moments later when he still couldn't touch the chair.

"Acceptance."

"What?"

"You've accepted you're dead," Nelson said. "At least a little bit. You think you can't interact with the corporeal world because of it. Your mind is playing tricks on you."

Wallace scoffed. "Isn't that what you all wanted me to do? Accept that I'm dead?"

He didn't like the smile that grew on Nelson's face. "Come here."

Wallace did.

Nelson motioned for him to sit on the floor before him. Wallace sighed, but he had no other choice. He sank to the floor, crossing his legs, hands twitching on his knees. Apollo raised his head and looked at him. His tail thumped. He turned himself toward Wallace, rolling onto his back, legs kicking in the air. When Wallace didn't accept the obvious invitation to scratch his stomach, he whined pitifully.

"No," Wallace said. "Bad dog."

Apollo farted in reply, a long sonorous sound.

"Oh my god," Wallace mumbled, unsure how he would find the strength to make it through the night.

"Who's a good boy?" Nelson cooed. Apollo almost knocked Wallace over as he wiggled at the praise.

"Are you going to help me or not?"

"Ask me nicely," Nelson said, sitting back in his chair. "Just because we're dead doesn't mean we don't have to use our manners."

"Please," Wallace said, grinding his teeth together.

"Please what?"

Wallace wished they were both alive so he could murder Nelson. "Please help me."

"That's better," Nelson said. "How's the floor? Is it comfortable?"

"No."

"But you're sitting on it. You expect it. The floor is always there. You don't think about it. Except now you are, aren't you?"

He was. He was thinking about it quite a bit.

Which is why he suddenly found himself sinking *through* the floor.

He scrabbled for purchase, trying to reach for something to keep him from falling farther. He was up to his chest by the time Nelson held out his cane, cackling as he did so. Wallace grabbed ahold of it as if it were a lifeline and pulled himself back up, only to start sinking again almost immediately.

"Stop thinking about it," Nelson told him.

"I *can't*!" In fact, it was all he could think about. And even worse, he wondered what would happen if he fell through the floor completely, only to hit the earth beneath and then go through *that*.

But before he sank to the center of the earth only to perish (possibly) in the molten core, Nelson said, "Did it hurt when you died?"

He blinked, his grip on the cane tight. "What?"

"When you died," Nelson said. "Did it hurt?"

"I . . . a little. It was quick. One moment I was there, and then I wasn't. I didn't know what was happening. I don't see what that has to do with—"

"And when you were there and then you weren't, what was the first thing that went through your head?"

"That it couldn't be real. That there had to be some mistake. Maybe even just an awful dream."

Nelson nodded as if that were the answer he expected. "What made you realize you weren't dreaming?"

He hesitated, his grip tightening on the cane. "Something I remembered. I'd heard or read it. That it wasn't possible for you to see your own face in a dream with any real clarity."

"Ah," Nelson said. "And it was clear for you."

"Crystal," Wallace said. "I could see the indents on my nose from my reading glasses, the stubble on my chin and cheeks. That's when I first started thinking it might not be a dream." A fleeting thought, one he'd shoved away as hard as possible. "And then . . ." He swallowed thickly. "At the funeral. Mei was . . . I'd never seen her before."

"Exactly," Nelson said. "The mind is a funny thing. When we dream, our subconscious isn't capable of constructing new faces out of nothing. Anyone we see in our dreams is someone we've seen before, even if only in passing. And when we're awake, everything is clear because we see it with our eyes. Or hear it with our ears, smell it with our noses. It's not like that when you're dead. You have to start from scratch. You need to learn to trick yourself into believing the unexpected. And would you look at that. You did. It's a start."

Wallace looked down. He was once again sitting on the floor. It felt solid beneath him. Before he could think about falling once again, he said, "You distracted me."

"It worked, didn't it?" He pulled his cane back and set it against the chair. "You're very lucky to have me."

"I am?" He was dubious at best.

"Absolutely," Nelson said. "When I died, I had to learn all of this on my own. Hugo wasn't pleased with me but kept his protestations to a minimum. One shouldn't speak ill of the dead, after all. It took time. It was like learning to walk all over again." He chuckled. "I had quite a few stumbles here and there. Broke a few teacups, much to Hugo's dismay. He loves his teacups."

"He seems to have an unhealthy fascination with tea," Wallace mumbled.

"He got that from me," Nelson said, and Wallace almost felt bad. Almost. "Taught him everything he knows. He needed focus, and the growing of tea plants provided that for him."

"Why are you helping me?"

Nelson cocked his head. "Why wouldn't I? It's the right thing to do."

Wallace was confused. "But I'm not giving you anything in return. I can't. Not like this."

Nelson sighed. "That's a strange way to look at things. I'm not helping you because I expect you to give me anything. Honestly, Wallace. When was the last time you ever did anything without expecting something in return?"

2006. Wallace had loose change in his pocket that annoyed him. A homeless man had been panhandling on the street corner near his office. He'd dropped the change into the man's cup. It totaled seventy-four cents. The man thanked him. Ten minutes later, Wallace had forgotten he existed. Until now.

He said, "I don't know."

"Huh," Nelson said. "That sure is . . . what it is. You've already got a leg up on me in one regard."

"I do?"

Nelson nodded toward the sconces on the wall. "Shorted out that light bulb. Broke the glass. Took me a long time to work up that amount of energy."

"I didn't mean to," Wallace admitted. "I wasn't—I was angry."

"So I noticed." His brow furrowed again. "Best you avoid anger if at all possible. It can cause all manner of situations better left avoided."

Wallace closed his eyes. "I have a feeling that's easier said than done."

"It is," Nelson said. "But you'll get there. At least you will if you don't decide to go through that door."

Wallace's eyes snapped open. "I don't want to—"

Nelson held up his hands. "You'll know when the time is right. I will say it's nice to have someone to talk to so late at night. Helps pass the time."

"Years," Wallace said. "You said you'd been dead a few years."

"That's right."

Wallace's stomach twisted strangely. It wasn't unlike the hook in his chest, though it burned more. "You've been here every night by yourself?"

"Most nights," Nelson corrected gently. "Every now and then, someone like you comes along, though they don't tend to stay very long. It's transitionary. One foot in one world, and the other in the next."

Wallace turned toward the fire. It was almost out. "I don't want to talk about it anymore."

"Ah," Nelson said. "Of course not. What would you like to talk about?"

But Wallace didn't reply. He lay down on the floor and curled in on himself, arms wrapped around his chest, knees against his stomach. The hook in his chest vibrated, and he hated it. He closed his eyes and wished he could go back in time when everything made sense. It hurt more than he expected.

"Okay," Nelson said quietly. "We can do this too. Take all the time you need, Wallace. We'll be here when you're ready. Isn't that right, Apollo?"

Apollo woofed, tail thumping silently on the floor.

CHAPTER 8

He opened his eyes again when he heard an alarm clock ringing from somewhere upstairs. It was still dark outside, and the clock above the fireplace said it was half past four in the morning.

He hadn't slept. No matter how hard he tried, he couldn't get himself to relax. It didn't help that he wasn't even remotely tired. He'd drifted, not quite dozing. He replayed the moment right before his death over and over again in his mind, wondering if he could have done anything different. He could think of nothing, and it only made him feel worse.

Pipes in the walls groaned and creaked as someone turned on a shower overhead. The sound of the water brought a fresh wave of misery. He'd never take another shower again.

Mei was the first to come down the stairs. Apollo greeted her, tail wagging. She yawned, jaw cracking as she rubbed between his ears. She wasn't wearing a suit like she'd been the day before. Instead, she wore a pair of black slacks and a crisp white collared shirt under an apron like the one Hugo had worn the night before.

Nelson was gone from his chair. Wallace hadn't even heard him leave.

"Why are you lying on the floor?" Mei asked.

"Why do we do anything that we do?" Wallace said dully. "There's no point."

"Oh man," Mei said. "It's far too early for your existential angst. At least let me wake up more before having to deal with such a bummer."

He closed his eyes again.

And opened them when he felt someone above him.

Hugo stood there, staring down at him, dressed as he'd been the day before. The only difference was the bright pink bandana around his head. Wallace hadn't even heard him approach. He glared at the cable that connected them.

Hugo smiled. "What's this?"

"How are you so quiet?" Wallace asked.

"Practice," Hugo said with a chuckle as he patted the slope of his stomach. "Or maybe you weren't paying attention. Come on. Get up."

"Why?" He hugged his legs tighter.

"Because I want to show you the kitchen."

"It's a kitchen," Wallace said. "Once you've seen one, you've seen them all."

"Humor me."

"I highly doubt I want to do that at all."

Hugo nodded. "Suit yourself. Apollo."

Wallace yelped as the dog ran through the closest wall. He circled around Hugo, sniffing his feet and legs. Once he'd finished his inspection, he sat down next to Hugo, his one ear flopping over.

"Good boy," Hugo said. He nodded toward Wallace. "Lick."

Wallace said, "*What?* Wait, no! No lick! No—"

Apollo licked quite furiously. His tongue slobbered on Wallace's face and then his arms when he tried to shield himself from what most certainly amounted to assault by canine. He attempted to shove the dog off him, but Apollo was heavy. His breath was terrible, and for a brief moment, Wallace wondered about his *own* breath, because he hadn't brushed his teeth in days. But then that train of thought derailed quite spectacularly when he opened his mouth to shout, only to have dog tongue brush against his own.

"Ack! No! Why! *Why.*"

"Apollo," Hugo said mildly.

Apollo immediately stepped back, sitting once again beside Hugo, looking down at Wallace as if *he* were the asshole in this situation.

"Kitchen?" Hugo asked.

"I will destroy everything you love," Wallace threatened.

"Does that ever work on anyone?" Hugo sounded honestly curious.

"*Yes*. All the time." Granted, he hadn't used those *exact* words before, but people had learned to fear him. Those in his employ, those *not* in his employ. Colleagues. Judges. A few children, but the less said about that the better.

"Oh," Hugo said. "Well. Until you do that, you should come and see my scones. I'm proud of them."

"*Your* scones?" Mei shouted from the kitchen. "How very dare you!"

Hugo laughed. "You see what I have to deal with? Get up, Wallace. You don't want to be there when we open. People will walk all over you, and no one wants that. You least of all."

He turned on his heel and walked around the counter before pushing through the double doors, Apollo trailing after him.

Wallace gave very serious thought to staying right where he was.

In the end, he got up.

But only because he chose to.

The kitchen was far bigger than he thought it'd be. It was a galley kitchen: on one side were two industrial-size ovens and a stove with eight different metal burners, almost all in use. On the other was a sink and the largest refrigerator Wallace had ever seen. At the back of the kitchen was a small breakfast nook with a table near bay windows that looked out onto the tea garden.

Mei had flour on her forehead as she moved from one side of the kitchen to the other, frowning at the bubbling pots on the stove before muttering, "Is it supposed to do that?" She shrugged and bent over to stare into each oven.

A radio sat on top of a cabinet, and Wallace was shocked at the heavy metal music pouring from the speakers, thunderous and awful and in . . . German? Mei made it worse by singing along in an off-putting guttural voice. It sounded like she was trying to summon Satan. Wallace wouldn't put it past her to be doing just that. And oh, did *that* start a line of thought he didn't want to even consider.

He startled when he saw Nelson sitting in one of the chairs at the table, hands resting on his cane. He'd . . . changed his clothes? Gone were the pajamas and bunny slippers. He now wore a thick blue sweater over tan slacks and shoes with Velcro straps. And he too was grunting along with the music as if he knew each and every word.

"How did you do that?" Wallace demanded.

Everyone stopped to stare at him, Hugo in the process of tying his apron.

"Do what?" Mei asked as she reached up to turn the radio volume down.

"I'm not talking to—Nelson, how did you do that?"

Nelson looked around as if there were some other Nelson in the kitchen. When he saw there wasn't, he said, "Me?"

Maybe sinking through the floor wasn't such a bad idea. "Yes, *you*. You changed your clothes!"

Nelson looked down at himself. "Why shouldn't I have? Pajamas are for nighttime. Do you not know that?"

"But—that's—we're *dead*."

"Acceptance," Mei said. "Cool." She started furiously stirring the pots again, one after the other.

"And?" Nelson said. "Just because I'm dead doesn't mean I don't like to look my best." He held up his shoes, wiggling his feet. "Do you like them? They're Velcro, because laces are for suckers."

No, Wallace didn't like them. "How did you do that?"

"Oh!" Nelson said brightly. "Well, it's the unexpected thing we were talking about last night after you sank through the floor."

"After what?" Hugo asked, eyebrows rising on his forehead.

Wallace ignored him. "Can I do that?"

Nelson shrugged. "I don't know. Can you?" He raised his cane and thumped it on the floor. And just like that, he was wearing a pinstriped suit, not unlike one Wallace had hanging in his own closet. He thumped the cane again, and he was wearing jeans and a heavy winter coat. He thumped the cane *again*, and was in a tuxedo, his top hat tilted jauntily on his head. The cane hit the floor one more time and he was in his original outfit, Velcro shoes and all.

Wallace gaped at him.

Nelson preened. "I'm very good at most things."

"Grandad," Hugo warned.

Nelson rolled his eyes. "Hush, you. Let me have my fun. Wallace, come here."

Wallace went. He stopped in front of Nelson, who looked him up and down critically. "Uh-huh. Yes. Quite. I see. That's . . . unfortunate." He squinted at Wallace's feet. "Flip-flops. Never had use for them myself. My toenails are too long."

Wallace grimaced. "That doesn't sound like something to be shared."

Nelson shrugged. "We have no secrets here."

"We should," Hugo muttered, pulling a tray of scones out of one of the ovens. They were thick and fluffy, bits of chocolate oozing. Wallace might have noticed them more if he hadn't been thoroughly distracted by the fact that he could *change clothes at a whim*.

"How does it work?" he asked.

Nelson scrunched up his face. "You have to want it hard enough."

Wallace wanted it more than anything. *Almost* anything. "Done. What else?"

"That's it."

"Are you messing with me?"

"I wouldn't dream of it," Nelson assured him. "Think about what you'd like to wear, how it feels against your skin, how it looks upon your frame. Close your eyes."

Wallace did, feeling a little awkward. The last time Nelson told him to do something, he'd been jumping in circles. The song ended and another started, this one apparently with even more screams.

"Now, picture an outfit in your head. Start with something simple. A pair of slacks and a shirt. You don't want to try layers, at least not yet. You'll get there."

"Okay," Wallace whispered. "Slacks and a shirt. Slacks and a shirt. Got it."

"Can you see yourself?"

He could. He stood in his apartment bedroom in front of the mirror hanging on the back of the door. His closet was open. In the streets below, horns honked, men and women in construction hats shouting and laughing. A busker played a cello on the street corner. "Yes. I can see it."

"Now, make it happen."

Wallace opened one eye balefully. "I think I'm going to need a little more than that."

He yelped when he got a cane upside his shins. "You're not focusing."

He closed his eyes again and took a breath, letting it out slow. "Right. Focusing. Slacks and a button-up shirt. Slacks and a button-up shirt."

The strangest thing happened.

He felt his skin tingling as if a low electric current began to run through him. It started at his toes and worked its way up his legs and into his chest. The hook—always there, and he was already getting used to it, much to his chagrin—twisted slightly.

"Oh my," Nelson said as Mei started choking.

Wallace opened his eyes. "What? Did it work?"

"Um," Nelson said. He cleared his throat. "I . . . think so? Do you often find yourself wearing that? No judgment, of course. What you do in your free time is your own business. I just don't know if it's appropriate for the tea shop."

"What—" Wallace looked down.

He'd changed his clothes. The sweats and shirt and flip-flops were gone.

He made a strangled noise when he saw he now wore a striped bikini that left little to the imagination. And it wasn't only bikini *bottoms*, no. He also had the top across his chest, the straps tied around his neck, the ends dangling down his back. His feet were bare, but that was the least of his problems. "What is this?!" he shrieked. "What have you done to me?!"

Nelson huffed. "That had nothing to do with me. It's all you." He squinted at Wallace. "Is this what you wore in your free time? Seems a little . . . tight. Again, no judgment." He was lying, obviously. His voice carried quite a bit of judgment.

It was about this time Wallace lamented that humans had evolved with only two hands. He tried to cover his crotch with one hand while pressing the other futilely against his chest as if it would actually do anything.

Mei whistled lowly. "You pull that off better than I'd have thought. I'm actually a little jealous. You've got a cute butt."

He whirled around, both hands now covering his rear. He glared at Mei. She smiled sweetly at him.

"Grandad," Hugo said.

Nelson scowled. "It wasn't me. I honestly wasn't expecting it to work. It took me months to figure out how to change my clothes. How was I to know he'd be able to do it on his first try? He's pretty good at this whole ghost thing." He grimaced as he stared at Wallace. "Maybe a little too good."

Wallace wondered what it said about his life (and death) that he'd ended up in a kitchen in a lopsided house in the middle of nowhere wearing nothing but a bikini.

"It's all right," Hugo said gently as Wallace looked around for something to cover himself up, only to remember he couldn't actually *touch* anything. "It doesn't always work the first time. You've just glitched a little."

"Glitched," Wallace said with a snarl. "It's riding up my—how do I fix this?"

"I don't know if you can," Nelson said gravely. "You might be stuck like this for the rest of your time here. And beyond."

Hugo sighed. "You won't. Grandad is having you on. You should've seen the first time he managed to change his clothes. Ended up wearing a full Easter rabbit costume."

"Even had a basket with little plastic eggs," Nelson agreed.

"Strange thing, that. The eggs were filled with cauliflower, which is, of course, disgusting."

"You *knew* this was going to happen," Wallace snapped.

"Of course I didn't," Nelson replied. "I thought you'd stand there scrunching up your face for a good thirty minutes before giving up." He chuckled. "This is far more entertaining. I'm so glad you came here. You certainly know how to liven this place up." He grinned. "Get it? Liven? It's funny because you're not alive. Oh, wordplay. How I adore you."

Wallace had to remind himself that from a legal perspective, striking the elderly was frowned upon (and against the law), even if said elderly deserved it. "Change me back!"

But before Nelson could open his mouth—and undoubtedly make things worse, Wallace thought—Hugo said, "Wallace, look at me."

He did. He felt almost helpless not to. The cable thrummed between them.

Hugo nodded. "It's okay. A little hiccup. It happens. Nothing to get upset about."

"You're not the one wearing a bikini," Wallace reminded him.

Hugo smiled. "No, I don't suppose I am. It's not so bad, though. You've got the legs for it."

Wallace groaned as Mei started choking again.

Hugo held up his hand toward Wallace's chest, his fingers and palm a few inches from Wallace's skin. The hook vibrated softly. Wallace sucked in a breath. His anger was fading along with his mortification. He didn't feel *good*, not exactly, but he was growing calmer. "What are you doing?"

"Helping," Hugo said, lines appearing on his forehead. "Close your eyes."

He did.

And strangely, he thought he could feel the heat from Hugo's hand, though that should have been impossible. Wallace could touch the dog, he could touch Nelson and Mei (and she all of them), but he couldn't touch Hugo. There seemed to be rules in place, rules that he was beginning to learn even if they were nonsensical. That tingling sensation returned, running along his skin. "It comes from the earth," Hugo said quietly. "Energy. Life. Death. All of it. We rise and we fall and then we rise once more. We're all on different paths, but death doesn't discriminate. It comes for everyone. It's what you do with it that sets you apart. Focus, Wallace. I'll show you where to look. You'll get it. All it takes is a little—there. See?"

Wallace opened his eyes and looked down.

Flip-flops. Sweats. Old shirt. Just like it'd been before.

"How did you do that?" he asked, pulling at his shirt.

"I didn't do anything," Hugo said. "You did. I merely helped you find direction. Better?"

Much. He never thought he'd be so relieved to see his flip-flops again. "I guess."

Hugo nodded. "You'll figure it out. I have faith in you." He took a step back. "If you stay for long, that is." A funny look crossed his face, but it was gone before Wallace could make sense of it. "I'm sure that whatever comes next, you won't have to worry about such things."

That sounded ominous. "Do—do people not wear clothes in the . . . Heaven? Afterlife? What do I even call it?"

Nelson laughed. "Oh, I'm sure you'll find out one way or another. For all we know, it's a gigantic nudist colony."

"So, Hell, then," Wallace muttered.

"What do you think of the scones?" Hugo asked, nodding toward the tray sitting on the stove.

Wallace sighed. "I can't eat them, can I?"

"No."

"Then why on earth would I care what they look like?" He didn't say that he could smell them, the scent thick and warm, because it made him feel alone. Strange that scones could do such a thing, almost making him reach out and fail at touching something he could never have.

Hugo looked down at them then back at Wallace. "Because they look nice. It's not always about what we can or can't have, but the work we put into it."

Wallace threw up his hands. "That doesn't—you know what? Fine. They look like scones."

"Thank you," Hugo said seriously. "That's nice of you to say."

Wallace groaned.

At promptly half past seven, Charon's Crossing opened for business.

Wallace watched as Hugo unlocked the front door, flipping the sign in the window from CLOSED to WE'RE OPEN! COME ON IN! He didn't know what to expect. The tea shop was removed from the town, and he thought if there were any customers at all, they'd trickle in slowly throughout the day.

So, imagine his surprise when he saw people already waiting outside. As soon as the lock clicked on the door, it opened, a stream of people pouring in.

Some formed a line at the counter, greeting Hugo as if they'd known him for a long time. Others sat at the tables, rubbing sleep from their eyes as they yawned. They wore business attire or uniforms for their places of employment. There were young people in beanies, their bags slung over their shoulders. He was shocked when no one immediately pulled out a laptop or stared down at their phones.

"No Wi-Fi," Mei said when he asked. She was bustling around the kitchen with practiced ease. "When people come here, Hugo wants them to talk to one another instead of being fixated on a screen."

"Of course he does," Wallace said. "It's a hipster thing, isn't it?"

Mei turned slowly to stare at him. "Please let me be there when you say that to Hugo. I want to see the look on his face when you call him a hipster. I need it like air."

Hugo rang up the orders on his old cash register, his smile never faltering as he put pastries in little bags or delivered teapots to waiting tables. Wallace stayed in the kitchen, watching him through the porthole windows. He thought about going out to the front, but he stayed right where he was. He told himself it was because he didn't want to get in the way.

Not that he could.

Nelson went back to his chair in front of the fireplace. Wallace noticed no one ever tried to sit in the chair, though they couldn't see it was taken. Apollo moved around from table to table, tail wagging even though he was ignored.

It was close to nine when the door opened once more. A woman entered. She wore a heavy coat, the front buttoned up to her throat. She was pale and wan with dark circles under her eyes. She didn't go to the counter; instead, she went and sat at an empty table near the fireplace.

Wallace frowned through the window. It took him a moment to place her. He'd seen her the night before when Mei had brought him to Charon's Crossing. She'd been walking swiftly away from the tea shop.

"Who is that?" Wallace asked.

"Who?" Mei came to the door, standing on her tiptoes to look through the porthole next to him.

"The woman near Nelson. She was here last night when we arrived. She walked right by us."

Mei sighed as she dropped back down to her heels. "That's Nancy. Shit, she's early. She usually comes in the afternoon. Must have been a bad night." She wiped her hands on her apron. "I'll have to go out and run the register. You gonna stay here?"

"Why do you have to—" He stepped back when Mei pushed her way through the door. He watched as she went to Hugo, whispering in his ear. He looked at the woman sitting at the table before nodding. Hugo moved around the counter, picking up another pot of tea and a single cup, setting it on a tray. He carried it over to the woman. She didn't acknowledge him as he placed the tray on the table. She continued to look out the window as she clutched at the purse in her lap.

Hugo sat in the empty chair on the other side of the table. He didn't speak. He poured the tea into the cup, the steam rising up in wisps. He set the pot back down on the tray before lifting the cup and setting it on the table in front of the woman.

She ignored it, and him.

Hugo didn't seem put out. He folded his hands on the table and waited.

Wallace wondered if this woman was another ghost, a spirit like himself. But then a man came to the table, putting his hand on Hugo's shoulder and speaking quietly. The man nodded at the woman before leaving out the front door.

Hugo and the woman stayed that way for almost an hour. The woman never drank from the proffered tea, and she never spoke. Neither did Hugo. It was as if they were simply existing in the same space.

When the line at the counter had thinned, Mei came back into the kitchen. "What are they doing?"

Mei shook her head. "It's not—I don't think it's my place to say."

Wallace scoffed. "Does no one here actually say anything of any substance?"

"We do," Mei said, opening a pantry door and pulling down a plastic tub filled with individual packets of sugar and creamer. "You're just not hearing what you want to hear. I know it might be hard to understand, but not everything is about you, Wallace. You have your own story. She has hers. If you're meant to know what it is, you will."

He felt properly rebuked. And worse, he thought she had a point.

Mei sighed. "You're allowed to ask questions. In fact, it's good that you do. But her business is between her and Hugo." She carried the tub toward the doors. Wallace stepped out of her way. Before she went through, she stopped, looking up at him. She hesitated. Then, "Hugo will probably give you the specifics if you ask, but know she has her reasons for being here. You know how you're my first solo case?"

Wallace nodded.

Mei gnawed on her bottom lip. "Hugo had another Reaper before me. He'd been with Hugo since he started as a ferryman. There were . . . complications, and not just pertaining to Cameron. The Reaper pushed when he shouldn't have, and mistakes were made. I didn't know him, but I heard the stories." She brushed her bangs back off her forehead. "We're here to guide, to help Hugo and the people we bring here. But his first Reaper forgot that. He thought he knew better than Hugo. And it didn't end well. The Manager had to get involved."

Wallace had heard that name before. Nelson had called him a nasty fellow. "The Manager?"

"It's best you don't know him," Mei said quickly. "He's our boss. He's the one who assigned me to Hugo and trained me on how to reap. It's . . . better when he's not here. We don't want to draw his attention."

The hairs on the back of his neck stood on end. "What does he do?"

"Manages," Mei said as if that explained everything. "Don't worry about it. It has nothing to do with you, and I don't think you'll ever have to meet him." And then, under her breath, "At least I hope you won't." She pushed her way through the doors.

Wallace looked out the porthole again in time to see the woman—Nancy—looking as if she were about to speak. She opened her mouth, and then closed it. Her lips stretched into a thin, bloodless line. She stood abruptly, the chair scraping along the floor. The din of the tea shop quieted as everyone turned to look at her, but she only had eyes for Hugo. Wallace flinched at her expression of rage. Her eyes were almost black. He thought she was going to reach out and strike Hugo. She didn't, instead stepping around the table and heading toward the door.

She stopped only when Hugo said, "I'll be here. Always. Whenever you're ready, I'll be here."

Her shoulders slumped as she left Charon's Crossing.

Hugo watched her through the window as she walked away. Mei went to the table, putting her hand on his shoulder. She spoke quietly, words Wallace couldn't make out. Hugo sighed and shook his head before gathering up the teacup and putting it back on the tray. Mei stepped back as he rose, lifting the tray with one hand and walking back toward the kitchen.

Wallace backed away quickly, not wanting to get caught spying. He pretended to be studying the appliances as the doors swung open and Hugo entered the kitchen. The noise of Charon's Crossing picked up again.

"You don't have to stay back here," Hugo said.

Wallace shrugged awkwardly. "I didn't want to get in the way." He knew how ridiculous that sounded. He didn't know how to quite put into words what he really meant, that he didn't want people to be walking around (or, heaven forbid, through) him as if he weren't there at all.

Hugo set the tray near the sink. "This place is yours as much as it is ours while you're here. I don't want you to feel trapped."

"I am, though," Wallace reminded him, nodding toward the cable. "Remember? It was a whole ordeal last night."

"I remember," Hugo said. He looked down at the tea in the cup, shaking his head. "But while you're here, you can go anywhere on the grounds you wish. I don't want you to feel like you can't."

"Why do you care if I feel trapped?"

Hugo glanced at him. "Why wouldn't I?"

He was so goddamn frustrating. "I don't get you."

"You don't know me." It wasn't mean, just a statement of fact. Hugo held up his hand before Wallace could retort. "I know how that sounds. I'm not trying to be flippant, I promise." He lowered his hand, looking down at the tray. The tea had cooled, the liquid dark. "It's easy to let yourself spiral and fall. And I was falling for a long time. I tried not to, but I did. Things weren't always like this. There wasn't always a Charon's Crossing. I wasn't always a ferryman. I made mistakes."

"You did?" Wallace didn't know why he sounded so incredulous.

Hugo blinked slowly. "Of course I did. Regardless of what else I am or what I do, I'm still human. I make mistakes all the time. The woman I was sitting with, Nancy, she's . . ." He shook his head. "I try to be the best ferryman I can be because I know people are counting on me. I think that's all anyone can ask for. I've learned from my mistakes, even as I continue to make new ones."

"I don't know if that makes me feel any better," Wallace said.

Hugo laughed. "I can't promise I won't screw up somehow, but I want to make sure your time here is restful and calm. You deserve it, after everything."

Wallace looked away. "You don't know me."

"I don't," Hugo said. "But that's why we're doing what we're doing now. I'm learning about you so I know how best to help you."

"I don't want your help."

"I know you think that," Hugo said. "But I hope you realize that you don't have to go this alone. Can I ask you a question?"

"If I say no?"

"Then you say no. I'm not going to pressure you into something you're not ready for."

He didn't know what else he had to lose. "Fine. Ask your question."

"Did you have a good life?"

Wallace jerked his head up. "What?"

"Your life," Hugo said. "Was it good?"

"Define good."

"You're hedging."

He was, and he hated how easily Hugo saw that. It made his skin itch. He felt on display, showing things he didn't think he'd ever be ready to show. He wasn't obfuscating; he genuinely had never thought about it that way. He woke up. He went to work. He stayed at work. He did his job, and he did his job well. Sometimes he lost. Most times he didn't. There was a reason the firm had been as successful as it was. What else was there to life aside from success? Nothing, really.

Sure, he'd had no friends. No family. He had no partner, no one to grieve over him as he'd lain in an expensive coffin in the front of a ridiculous church, but that shouldn't be the only measure of a life well-lived. It was all about perspective. He'd done important things, and in the end, no one could have asked any more of him.

He said, "I lived."

"You did," Hugo said, still holding onto the teacup. "That doesn't answer my question."

Wallace scowled. "You're not my therapist."

"So you've said." He lifted the cup and poured the tea out into the sink. It looked as if it pained him to do so. The dark liquid splattered against the sink before Hugo turned on the faucet and washed away the dregs.

"Is this . . . is this how you are with the others?"

Hugo switched off the faucet and set the teacup gently in the sink. "Everyone's different, Wallace. There's no one way to go about this, no uniform rules in place that can be applied to every single person like you who comes through my doors. That wouldn't make sense because you're not like everyone else, just as they're not you." He looked out the window above the sink. "I don't know who or what you are yet. But I'm learning. I know you're scared, and you have every right to be."

"Damn right I am," Wallace said. "How could I not be?"

Hugo smiled quietly as he turned toward Wallace. "That might be the most honest thing you've said since you got here. Would you look at that? You're making progress. That's great."

The praise shouldn't have warmed him as much as it did. It felt unearned, especially when he didn't want it. "Mei said you had another Reaper before her."

Hugo's smile faded as his expression hardened. "I did. But that discussion is off-limits. It has nothing to do with you."

Wallace took a step back, and for the first time since he could remember, he wanted to apologize. It was strange, this, made worse by how *hard* it seemed to get the words out. He frowned and pushed through it. "I'm . . . sorry?"

Hugo sagged, hands on the counter in front of the sink. "If I'm going to ask you questions, you should be able to do the same. There are some things I don't like to talk about, at least not yet."

"Then you can understand if I'm the same way."

Hugo looked up in surprise. The smile returned. "I . . . yeah. Okay. I can see that. That's only fair."

And with that, he turned and walked out of the kitchen, leaving Wallace to stare after him.

CHAPTER 9

Charon's Crossing stayed relatively busy for most of the day. There was a lull mid-afternoon before more people came as the blue sky started to shift toward the encroaching dark. Wallace stayed in the kitchen, feeling voyeuristic as he watched the customers filter in and out.

He was surprised (Mei be damned) to see that not a single person tried to boot up a laptop or spend any time on their phones. Even those who came alone seemed happy enough to just sit in their chairs, taking in the noise of the tea shop. He was slightly amused (and more than a little horrified) when he tried to figure out what day it was, only to realize he had no idea. It took him a moment to count back the days. He'd died on a Sunday. His funeral had been Wednesday.

Which meant today was Thursday, though it felt like weeks had passed. If he were still alive, he'd be in the office, his day hours from being over. He always kept himself busy to the point of exhaustion, so much so that he'd usually collapse by the time he got home, falling face-first onto his bed until his alarm blared bright and early the next morning to begin all over again.

It was illuminating.

All that work, all that he'd done, the life he'd built. Had it mattered? What had been the point of anything?

He didn't know. It hurt to think about.

With these thoughts thundering around his head, he played the part of the voyeur as he had nothing else to do.

Mei was in and out of the kitchen, telling Wallace she preferred to stay in the back if at all possible. "Hugo's the people person," she told him. "He likes to talk to everyone. I don't."

"You're in the wrong line of work if that's the case."

She shrugged. "I like the dead more than the living. Dead people usually don't care about the little annoyances of life."

He hadn't thought about it that way. He'd give anything for those annoyances again. Hindsight was a bitch of a thing.

Nelson stayed, for the most part, in his chair in front of the fireplace. Other times, he wandered between the tables, nodding along with conversations he could take no part in.

Apollo was in and out of the house. Wallace heard him barking ferociously at a squirrel, incensed that the squirrel ignored him completely.

But it was Hugo who Wallace watched the most.

Hugo, who seemed to have all the time in the world for anyone who asked for his attention. A gaggle of older women came in the early afternoon, fawning and cooing over him, pinching his cheeks and giggling when he blushed. He knew them all by name, and they clearly adored him. They all left with smiles on their faces, paper cups of tea steaming in their hands.

It wasn't just the older women. It was everyone. Kids demanded he lift them up and he did, but not with his hands. They held onto his thinly muscled biceps as he raised his arms, their feet kicking into nothing, their laughter bright and loud. Younger women flirted, batting their eyes at him. Men shook his hand furiously, their grips looking strong as their arms pumped up and down. They called him by his first name. They all seemed delighted to see him.

By the time Hugo turned the sign on the window to CLOSED and locked the door, Wallace was wrung out. He didn't know how Hugo and Mei could do this day in and day out. He wondered if it ever felt too big for them, facing the clear evidence of life, knowing what waited for everyone after.

Speaking of.

"Why aren't there other people here?" he asked as Mei lugged in a wash bin full of dirty dishes. Through the swinging door, he could see Hugo had picked up a broom and was sweeping the floor as he overturned the chairs.

She grunted as she set the bin on the counter next to the sink. "What?"

"Other people," Wallace repeated. Then, "Ghosts. Or whatever."

"Why would there be?" Mei asked, beginning to load the dishwasher for the sixth time that day.

"People die all the time."

Mei gasped. "They *do*? Oh my god, this changes everything. I can't believe I never—oh, now *that's* a look on your face for sure."

Wallace grimaced. "Whoever told you that you were funny obviously lied and you should feel bad about it."

"I don't," Mei assured him. "Like, at all."

"Like, totally."

"Sounds like we spoke to the same person."

"Hey!"

"There aren't other ghosts here because we haven't received a new assignment yet. Some days, it's back-to-back and things overlap. And then there are other days when we don't get anyone at all." She glanced at him before going back to the dishwasher. "We don't usually have long-term tenants. And no, Nelson and Apollo don't count. I think the most we ever had at one time was . . . three, not including them. It got a little crowded."

"Of course they don't count," Wallace muttered. "What's the longest someone has been here?"

"Why? Thinking about setting down roots?"

He crossed his arms defensively. "No. I'm just asking."

"Ah. Right. Well, I know Hugo had someone who stayed for two weeks. That was . . . a hard case. Deaths by suicide usually are."

Wallace swallowed thickly. "I can't imagine having to deal with that."

"I don't *deal* with it," Mei said sharply. "And neither does Hugo. We do what we do because we want to help people. We aren't here because we have to be. We're here because we choose to be. Remember that distinction, yeah?"

"Okay, okay. I didn't mean anything by it." He'd struck a nerve he didn't even know to aim for. He needed to be careful.

She relaxed. "I won't pretend to say I understand what you're going through. How can I? And even if I *thought* I knew what it's like, I'd probably still be wrong. It's different for everyone, man. What the people went through before you and those who will come after you, it's never going to be the same thing twice. But that doesn't mean I don't know what I'm doing."

"You're new," Wallace reminded her.

"I am. I was training for only two years before I was given your case. That's quicker than any other Reaper in history."

That certainly didn't make him feel any better. He changed tack, an old trick he'd learned to try to catch people off guard. It was mostly force of habit because he wasn't quite sure what he was looking for. "At the convenience store."

"What about it?" She closed the dishwasher before leaning against it, waiting for him to continue.

"The clerk," Wallace said. "He could see you. And the people here can too."

"They can," she said slowly.

"But the people at my funeral couldn't."

"Is there a question in there somewhere?"

He scowled at her. "Are you always this aggravating?"

She shrugged. "Depends on who you ask."

"Are you . . . human?" He knew how ridiculous that sounded, but then he remembered he was a ghost talking to a woman who could snap her fingers and drag him hundreds of miles in an instant.

"Sort of," she said. She hoisted herself up onto the counter, legs and feet dangling against a row of wooden cabinets. "Or, rather, I used to be. I've still got all my human parts, if that's what you meant."

"I don't think that's what I meant at all. I'm not thinking about your parts."

She snorted. "I know. I'm just giving you shit, man. Lighten up a little. There's not a whole lot for you to worry about anymore."

That stung more than he cared to admit. "That's not true," he said stiffly.

She sobered. "Hey, no. I didn't mean it like—you're allowed to ask questions, Wallace. In fact, if you didn't, I'd be concerned. It's natural. This is something you've never experienced before. Of course you'll want to try to figure out everything right away. It can't be easy not getting the answers you're used to hearing. I wish I could *give* you all the answers, but I don't have them. I don't know if anyone does, not really." She squinted at him. "Did that help?"

"I have no idea how to answer that."

"Good," she said.

He blinked, confused. "It is?"

She nodded. "Maybe it's just me, but I think I'd feel relieved finding out there are things I don't know about. It can't be healthy the other way, you know?"

"Obviously," he said faintly. "I died."

She laughed and looked shocked because of it. "Obviously. Don't try to force it, Wallace. It'll come when it comes. I've seen it before. You'll know when the time is right."

He thought she was speaking about more than the contents of their conversation, and his mind drifted to the door upstairs. He hadn't worked up the courage to find it, much less ask more about it.

"Time moves a little different here," she said. "I don't know if you noticed that, but there's—"

"The clock."

She arched an eyebrow. "The clock?"

"Last night, when we got here. The second hand was stuttering. It moved back and forth or sometimes not at all."

She seemed impressed. "Noticed that, huh?"

"Hard not to. Is it always like that?"

She shook her head. "Only when we have visitors like yourself, and only on the first day. It's meant to give you time to acclimate. To get an understanding of the position you find yourself in. Most of the time, it means sitting there, waiting for someone like you to speak."

"I ran instead," Wallace said.

"You did. And the clock began to move like it normally does the moment you left. It happens at all places like this."

"Nelson called it a way station."

"That's a good way to put it," Mei said. "Though, I think of it more as a *waiting* station."

"What am I waiting for?" Wallace asked, aware of how monumental the question felt.

"That's for you to decide, Wallace. You can't force this, and no one here is going to try to push you into something you're not ready for. Hope for the best; you know?"

"That's not very reassuring."

"It's worked so far. Mostly."

Cameron. That wasn't a topic he was prepared for. He still could hear the wordless sound the man had made at the sight of him. If he could still dream, he thought he'd have nightmares because of it. "Why do you do this?"

"That's a little personal."

He blinked. "Oh. I . . . suppose it is. You don't have to say anything if you don't want to."

"Why do you want to know?" Her tone gave nothing away.

Wallace struggled with what to say. He landed on, "I'm trying."

She didn't let him off the hook. He was a little in awe of her. "Trying to what, Wallace?"

He looked down at his hands. "Trying to be . . . better. Isn't that what you're supposed to be helping me with?"

The backs of her shoes hit the lower cabinets, causing the doors to rattle. "I don't think it's our job to make you better. Our job is to get you through the door. We give you the time to make peace with it, but anything else beyond that is up to you."

"Okay," he said helplessly. "I . . . I'll remember that."

She stared at him for a long moment. Then, "Before I came here, I didn't know how to bake."

He frowned. What did *that* have to do with anything?

"I had to learn," she continued. "Growing up, we didn't bake.

We didn't use an oven. We had a dishwasher, but we never used it because dishes needed to be handwashed, and then put into the dishwasher to be used as a drying rack." She grimaced. "Have you ever tried to whisk eggs? Man, that shit is *hard*. And then there was the time I made the dishwasher overflow with soap until it flooded the kitchen. Felt a little bad about that."

"I don't understand," Wallace admitted.

"Yeah," Mei muttered, rubbing a hand over her face. "It's a cultural thing. My parents emigrated to this country when I was five. My mother, she . . . well. She was fascinated by the idea of being American. Not Chinese. Not Chinese American. American. She didn't like her history. China in the twentieth century was filled with war and famine, oppression and violence. During the Cultural Revolution, religion was outlawed, and anyone who disobeyed was beaten or killed or just . . . disappeared into thin air."

"I can't imagine what that's like," Wallace admitted.

"No, you can't," she said bluntly. "My mom wanted to escape it all. She wanted fireworks on the Fourth of July and picket fences, to become someone different. She wanted the same for me. But even coming here, there were certain things she still believed. You don't go to bed with wet hair because you'll get a cold in your head. Don't write names in red ink, because that's taboo." She looked away. "When I started . . . manifesting, I thought something was wrong with me, that I was sick. Seeing things that weren't there. She wouldn't hear of it." She laughed hollowly. "I know you probably don't get this, but we don't talk about stuff like that in my family. It's . . . ingrained. She wouldn't let me get help, to see a doctor, because for all that she wanted to be American, there were still some things that just wouldn't do. After all, what would the neighbors think if they found out?"

"What happened?" Wallace asked, unsure if it was his place.

"She tried to keep me hidden away," Mei said. "Kept me at home, telling me that I was acting out, that nothing was wrong with me. Why would I do this to her after all she'd done to give me a good life?" She smiled weakly. "When that still didn't work, I was given a choice. Either her way or the highway. She said it just like that, and she was so *proud* of it, because it was such an American thing to say."

"Christ," Wallace breathed. "How old were you?"

"Seventeen. Almost ten years ago now." She gripped the countertop on either side of her legs. "I went out on my own. Made good decisions. Sometimes not-so-good decisions, but I learned from them. And she's . . . well. She's not gotten *better*, exactly, but I think she's trying. It'll take time to rebuild what we had before, if that's even possible, but we talk on the phone a few times a month. In fact, she was the first one to reach out. I talked it over with Hugo, and he thought it might be an olive branch, but ultimately, it was up to me to decide." She shrugged. "I missed her. Even with all that happened. It was . . . nice to hear her voice. Toward the end of last year, she even asked me to come back and visit her. I told her I wasn't ready for that, at least not yet. I haven't forgotten what she said to me before. She was disappointed, but said she understood and didn't push it. Still doesn't change what I see."

"And what's that?"

"People like you. Ghosts. Wandering souls who haven't yet found their way." She sighed. "You know bug zappers? Those electric blue lights that hang on porches and torch the bugs that fly into them?"

He nodded.

"I'm sort of like that," she said. "Except for ghosts, not bugs, and I don't fry them when they get close. They're attracted to something in me. When I first started seeing them, I didn't know how to make it stop. It wasn't until . . ."

"Until?"

Her eyes slid unfocused as she looked off into nothing. "Until someone came for me and offered me a job. He told me who—*what* I was. And with the proper training, what I could do. He brought me here to Hugo, to see if we'd make a good match."

"The Manager," Wallace said.

"Yeah. But don't worry about him. He's nothing we can't handle."

"Then why do you seem so scared of him?"

She startled. "I'm not scared of anything."

He didn't think that was true. If she was telling the truth and was human, she'd always have to be scared of something. That was how humanity worked. Survival instinct was based on a healthy dose of fear.

"I'm wary of him," she said. "He's . . . intense. And that's putting it mildly. I'm grateful he brought me here and taught me what he knows, but it's better when he's gone."

From everything he'd heard about the Manager, Wallace hoped he'd stay gone. "And he . . . what? Made you this way?"

She shook her head. "He fine-tuned what was already there. I'm a sort of medium, and *yes*, I know how that sounds, so you can shut your mouth."

He did.

"I have . . ." She paused. Then, "It's like when you're standing in a doorway. You have one foot on one side, and the other foot on the other side. You're in two places at once. That's me. He just showed me how to lean into one side of the doorway, and how to pull myself back."

"How can you do this?" Wallace asked, suddenly feeling very small. "How can you be surrounded by death all the time and not let it get to you?"

"I wish I could tell you it's because I always wanted to help people," Mei said. "But that would be a lie. I didn't . . . I didn't know how to *be*. I had to unlearn so many things I'd been taught. Hell, the first time Hugo hugged me, I didn't hug him back because that's not something I'd ever really had before. Contact, much less physical affection, wasn't something I was used to. It took me a while to appreciate it for what it was." She grinned at him. "Now, I'm pretty much the best hugger."

Wallace remembered how her hand had felt in his the first time, the relief that'd washed over him. He couldn't imagine going an entire life without knowing something like that.

"It's like you, in a way," she said. "You need to unlearn all that you know. I wish I could just flip a switch for you, but that's not how it works. It's a process, Wallace, and it takes time. For me, it started when I was shown the truth. It changed me, though definitely not right away." She hopped down from the counter, though she kept the distance between them. "I do what I do because I know there's never been a time in your life when you've been more confused or more vulnerable. And if I can do something to at least alleviate that a little bit, then so be it. Death isn't a final ending, Wallace. It *is* an ending, sure, but only to prepare you for a new beginning."

He was stunned when he felt a tear trickle down onto his cheek. He brushed it away, not able to look at Mei as he did so. "You're awfully strange."

He heard the smile in her voice. "Thank you. That might be the nicest thing you've ever said to me. You're awfully strange too, Wallace Price."

Hugo was in front of the fireplace when Wallace left the kitchen, putting logs in under the direct supervision of Nelson. Apollo sat on his haunches, looking between the two of them, tongue hanging out of his mouth as he panted. "Higher," Nelson said. "Make it a big one. I've got a chill in my bones. Gonna be a cold night. Spring often lies with hints of green and sun."

"Of course it does," Hugo said. "Don't want you to be cold."

"Absolutely," Nelson agreed. "I could catch my death, and then where would you be?"

Hugo shook his head. "I don't even want to imagine."

"Good man. Ah, there it is." The fire grew, the flames bright. "Always said that having a good fire and good company is all a person needs."

"Funny," Hugo said. "I don't think I've ever heard you say that before."

Nelson sniffed. "Then you weren't listening. I say it all the time. I'm your elder, Hugo, which means you should be hanging on to my every word and believing everything I say."

"I do," Hugo assured him as he stood. "I couldn't ignore you if I tried."

"Damn right," Nelson said. He tapped his cane on the floor, and he was back in his pajamas, bunny slippers and all. "That's better. Wallace, don't stand there gawking. It's unbecoming. Get your butt over here and let me look at you."

Wallace went.

"All right?" Hugo asked as Wallace stopped awkwardly next to Nelson's chair.

"I have no idea," Wallace said.

Hugo beamed at him as if Wallace had said something profound. "That's wonderful."

Wallace blinked. "It is?"

"Very. Not knowing is better than pretending to know."

"If you say so," Wallace muttered.

Hugo grinned. "I do. Hang out here with Grandad for me, okay? I'll be back in a little bit."

He headed for the kitchen before Wallace could ask where he was going.

Nelson craned his neck around the chair, waiting for the kitchen doors to swing shut before he looked at Wallace. "They're eating," he whispered as if revealing a great secret.

Wallace looked down at him. "What?" But now that Nelson had mentioned it, he could smell it, the scents filling his nose. Meatloaf? Yes, meatloaf. Roasted broccoli on the side.

"Supper," Nelson said. "They don't eat in front of us. It's rude."

"It is?" He grimaced. "Do they talk with their mouths full of food?"

Nelson rolled his eyes. "They don't eat in front of us because we can't eat. Hugo thinks it's like dangling a bone in front of a dog but then taking it away."

Apollo's ears quirked at the word *bone.* He stood and began to nose Nelson's knees as if he thought Nelson had a treat to offer him. Nelson scratched between his ears instead.

"We can't . . . eat?" Wallace said.

Nelson glanced at him. "Are you hungry?"

No, he wasn't. He hadn't even *thought* about eating, even when the scones had come out of the oven that morning. They'd smelled delicious, and he knew they'd be light and fluffy, melting on his tongue, but it was almost an afterthought. "We can't eat," he said.

"Nope."

"We can't sleep."

"Nope."

Wallace groaned. "Then what the hell *can* we do?"

"Rock a bikini, I guess. You've got that down pat."

"You're never going to let me forget that, are you?"

"Never," Nelson said. "It was enlightening to see that you were a proponent of manscaping when you were alive. I'd hate to think you'd neglect it only to spend your time here with a topiary garden in your pants."

Wallace gaped at him.

Nelson tapped his cane on the floor. "Sit down. I don't like it when people hover."

"I'm not sitting on the floor."

"Okay," Nelson said. "Then pull up a chair."

Wallace turned to do just that, stopping halfway to the nearest table before he remembered he *couldn't*. He frowned as he turned back to Nelson. "That's not funny."

Nelson squinted at him. "It wasn't supposed to be. I wasn't telling a joke. Would you like me to tell you a joke?"

No, he really wouldn't. "That's fine, you don't need to—"

"What is a ghost's favorite fruit?"

This was definitely Hell. He didn't care what Mei or Hugo said. "I really don't—"

"Booberries."

Wallace felt his eye twitch. "I can just sit on the floor."

"What kind of a street does a ghost live on?"

"I don't care."

"A dead end."

Silence.

"Huh," Nelson said. "Nothing? Really? That was one of my better ones." He frowned. "I suppose I can pull out the big guns, if you think it'd help. What does a ghost do to stay safe in a car? He puts on his sheet belt."

Wallace sank down to the floor. Apollo was delighted by this, lying down next to Wallace and rolling onto his back, staring at Wallace pointedly. "No more. Please. I'll do anything." He reached over absentmindedly and scratched Apollo's belly.

"*Any*thing?" Nelson said, sounding rather gleeful. "I'll have to keep that in mind."

"That wasn't an offer."

"Sounded like one. Don't write checks your butt can't cash is what I always say."

Wallace doubted that. He looked at the fire. He could feel the heat from it, though he didn't understand how that was possible. "How can you stand it?"

"What?" Nelson asked, settling back in his chair.

"Staying here."

"It's not a bad place," Nelson said sharply. "It's quite nice, if you ask me. There are worse places I could be."

"No, I'm—that's not what I meant."

"Then say what you mean. Seems easy enough, right?"

"And that's another thing," Wallace said without thinking. "You can change your clothes."

"It's not *that* hard. You just need to have focus."

Wallace shook his head. "Why are you the way you are?"

"Like . . . physically? Or philosophically? If it's the latter, I hope you're ready for a long story. It all started when I was—"

"Physically," Wallace said. "Why are you still old?"

Nelson cocked his head. "Because I *am* old. Eighty-seven, to be exact. Or, rather, that's how old I was when I bit the big one."

"Why don't you make yourself younger?" Wallace asked. "Are you—" *we*, though that went unsaid—"stuck like this forever?"

He startled when Nelson laughed loudly. He looked up in time to see Nelson wiping his eyes. "Oh, you are a delight. Getting right to the meat of it. I thought that would take at least another week or two. Possibly seven."

"Glad I can buck your expectations," Wallace mumbled.

"It's simple, really," Nelson said, and Wallace tried to hide how eager he was to hear the answer. "I like being old."

That . . . wasn't the answer he'd expected. "You do? Why?"

"Spoken like a young person."

"I'm not *that* young."

"I can see that," Nelson said. "Worry lines around your eyes, but none around your mouth. Didn't laugh much, did you."

It wasn't a question. And even if it was, Wallace didn't know how to answer without sounding defensive. Instead, he lifted his hand to his face, touching the skin near his eyes. He'd never been one to worry about such things. He had expensive clothes, and his haircuts cost enough to feed a family of four for a week. But even though he put on an imposing display, he never thought much about the person underneath it all. He was far too busy to care about such things. If there were times he'd caught his reflection in the mirror in his bedroom, it was only given a passing thought. He hadn't been getting any younger. Maybe if he'd cared more, he wouldn't be here. That line of thinking felt dangerous, and he pushed it away.

"I could change how I look," Nelson said. "I think. I've never tried, so I don't know if it would work or not. But I don't imagine we have to stay as we were when we died if we don't want to."

Wallace looked down at the floor warily. He wasn't sinking, so he supposed that was a start.

"Tell me something no one else knows."

"Why?"

"Because I asked you to. You don't have to if you don't want to, but I find it helps to speak some things out loud rather than keep them bottled up. Quick. Don't think about it. The first thing that comes to your mind."

And Wallace said, "I think I was lonely," surprising even himself. He frowned and shook his head. "That's . . . not what I meant to say. I don't know why that came out. Forget it."

"We can if you want," Nelson said, not unkindly.

He didn't push. Wallace felt a strange surge of affection for him, foreign and warm. It was . . . odd, this feeling. He couldn't remember the last time he'd cared for anyone but himself. He didn't know what that made him. "I didn't have . . . this."

"This?"

Wallace waved his hand around. "This place. These people, like you have."

"Ah," Nelson said, as if that made perfect sense.

He wondered how this man could say so much by saying so little. While words had always been easy for Wallace, it was his power of observation that set him apart from his peers. Noticing the little tics people had when they were sad or happy or troubled. When they were lying, eyes turned down, shifting side to side, mouth twisted, something Wallace prided himself in knowing. How strange, then, that he hadn't been able to turn that on himself. Denial, maybe? That didn't make him feel better. Introspection wasn't exactly his forte, but how could he have not seen any of this before?

Nelson didn't seem to have that problem, which humbled Wallace more than he expected. "I didn't see it, then," he admitted. He scrubbed a hand over his face. "I had privilege. I lived a *life* of privilege. I had everything I thought I wanted and now . . ." He didn't know how to finish.

"And now that's all been stripped away, leaving you only with yourself," Nelson said quietly. "Hindsight is a powerful thing, Wallace. We don't always see what's right in front of us, much less appreciate it. It's not until we look back that we find what we should have known all along. I won't have you thinking I'm a perfect man. It would be a lie. But I've learned that maybe I was a better person than I expected. I think that's all anyone can ask for." Then, "Did you have anyone to help chase the loneliness away?"

He hadn't. He tried to remember how things had been before

it'd all fallen apart, how Naomi had looked to him with light in her eyes, the corners of her mouth quirking up softly. She hadn't always despised him. There had been love between them, at one point. He'd taken it for granted, thinking she'd always be there. Wasn't that part of their vows? 'Til death do us part. But their parting had come long before death ever found Wallace, and with her exit, the crumbling of the life they'd built together. She left and Wallace threw himself into his work, but had it really been any different than when she'd been there? He remembered one of the last days of their marriage, when she'd stood in front of him, eyes cold, telling him he had to make a choice, that she wanted more than what he was offering.

He hadn't said a word.

It didn't matter. She heard all the things he didn't say. It wasn't her fault. None of it was, no matter what he'd tried to tell himself. It was why he hadn't contested the divorce, giving her everything she'd asked for. He'd thought it was because it was better to get it over with. He could see now it was because the guilt had been gnawing at him, though he hadn't given it a name at that point. He was too proud for that.

Or he had been, at least.

"No," he whispered. "I don't think I did."

Nelson nodded as if that was the answer he expected. "I see."

Wallace didn't want to think about it anymore. "Tell me something no one else knows."

Nelson grinned. "Fair." He rubbed his chin thoughtfully. "You can't tell anyone."

Wallace leaned forward, surprised at his own eagerness. "I won't."

Nelson glanced at the kitchen before looking down at Wallace. "There's a health inspector that comes here. Loathsome man. Chip on his shoulder. Thinks he's entitled to things he can't have. I haunt him while he's here."

"You what?"

"Little things. I knock his pen out of his hand or move his chair when he tries to sit down."

"You can do that?"

"I can do many things," Nelson said. "Man has it out for my Hugo. I make sure to reciprocate in kind."

Before Wallace could ask about it further, Apollo turned over, raising his head toward the kitchen. A moment later, Hugo appeared through the doors, Mei trailing after him.

He said, "What are you two talking about, and should I be concerned?"

"Most likely," Nelson said, winking at Wallace. "We're definitely up to no good."

Hugo smiled. "Wallace, could you come with me? I'd like to show you something."

Wallace looked to Nelson who nodded. "Go on. I have Mei and Apollo to keep me company."

Wallace sighed as he stood. "Another therapy session?"

Hugo shrugged. "If you want to think of it that way, sure. Or it could just be two people getting to know each other. Almost like friends, even."

Wallace grumbled under his breath as he followed Hugo down the hall.

They went outside again to the back deck overlooking the tea garden. Hugo turned on the strings of lights wrapped around the railings of the deck, white and twinkling.

Before Hugo closed the door to the house behind them, he reached in and switched off the deck light. The trees swayed in the darkness.

"Good talk with Grandad?" he asked, coming to stand next to Wallace near the steps.

"I guess."

"He can be a little . . . pushy," Hugo said. "Don't feel like you have to do whatever he says." He frowned. "Especially if it sounds like it'd be illegal."

"Not like that matters now, does it?"

"No," Hugo said. "I don't suppose it does. Still, humor me. For my own peace of mind." He reached up and smoothed out his pink bandana. "Your first full day here. How'd it go?"

"I stayed in the kitchen the whole time."

"Saw that." He leaned against the railing. "You don't have to."

"Is that supposed to make me feel better?"

"I don't know. Does it?"

"You know, for someone who said they aren't qualified to be a therapist, you really know how to act like one."

Hugo chuckled. "I've been doing this for a bit."

"Part of the gig," Wallace said.

Hugo seemed pleased that he remembered. Wallace wasn't sure why that felt important to him. He scratched at his chest, the hook tugging gently. "Exactly."

"What did you want to show me?"

"Look up."

Wallace did.

"What do you see?"

"The sky."

"What else?"

It was like it'd been the night before, walking down a dirt road with a strange woman at his side. The stars were bright. Once, when he'd been a kid, he'd gotten it in his head that he needed to count them all. Each night, he'd stared out the window of his bedroom, counting them one by one. He never made it very far before falling asleep, waking the next morning more determined to try again.

"Stars," Wallace whispered, even as he struggled to remember the last time he'd turned his face toward the sky before arriving at the tea shop. "All those stars." It wasn't like this in the city. The light pollution made sure of that, leaving only the barest hints of what hung in the sky at night. "There are so many of them." He felt very small.

"It's like that here," Hugo said. "Away from everything else. I can't imagine what it must be like where you're from. I don't know much else aside from this place."

Wallace looked at him. "Why? Don't you ever leave?"

"Can't really do that," Hugo said. "Never know when someone like you is going to come here. I always need to be ready."

"You're trapped here?" Wallace asked, sounding horrified. "Why the hell would you ever agree to that?"

"Not trapped," Hugo said. "That implies I don't—or didn't—have a choice. I did. I wasn't forced into being a ferryman. I chose to be. And it's not like I can't ever leave. I go into town all the time. I have my scooter, and sometimes, I go for a ride just to clear my head and breathe."

"Your scooter," Wallace repeated. "You ride that."

Hugo arched an eyebrow. "I do. Why?"

"Oh, I don't know," Wallace said, throwing up his hands. "Maybe because if you crash, you'll die?"

"Then it's a good thing I don't crash it." His lips quirked. "I'm careful, Wallace, but I appreciate your concern. Thank you for worrying about me." He sounded delighted, and Wallace refused to be charmed by it.

He failed miserably. "Someone has to," he muttered, and as soon as the words left his mouth, he wished desperately he could take them back. He plowed ahead, deflecting awkwardly. "This place is still a prison."

"It is? Why? I don't need much. I never have. I've got everything I want right here."

"But . . . that's . . ." Wallace didn't know what that was. Odd, surely. He'd never met someone so settled into their own skin. "Doesn't it get to you? All this death, all the time."

Hugo shook his head. "I don't think of it that way, though I get what you're trying to say. I think . . ." He paused as if choosing his words carefully. "Death isn't always something to be feared. It's not the be-all and end-all."

Wallace remembered what Mei had told him. "An ending. Leading to a new beginning."

"That's right," Hugo said. "You're learning. It can be beautiful, if you let it, though I can see why you wouldn't think so." He looked up at the stars. "The best way to describe it is the sense of relief most people feel when they're ready to go through the door. It may take them time to get to that point, but it's always the same." He hesitated. "I could tell you what it's like, what I've seen. The look on their faces the moment the door opens, the moment they hear the sounds coming from the other side. But I don't know that I can do it justice, because no matter what I say, it barely begins to scratch the surface. It changes you, Wallace, changes you in ways you don't expect. At least it did me. Call it faith, call it proof, whatever you like. But I know that I'm doing that right thing because I've seen the looks on their faces, filled with awe and wonder. I may not be able to hear what they hear, but I choose to believe it's everything they could've wanted."

"It doesn't bother you that you can't hear it?"

Hugo shook his head. "I'll find out one day. And until then, I'll do what I'm here for, preparing you to find out for yourself."

Wallace wished he could believe him. But the very thought of the door he had yet to lay eyes on terrified him. It made his skin crawl, and he deflected in the only way he knew how. "How did you become a ferryman?"

"Oof," Hugo said, though Wallace thought he wasn't fooled. "Just going for it, huh?"

"Might as well."

"Might as well," Hugo echoed. "It was by accident, if you can believe that."

He couldn't. At all. "You accidentally became the person who helps ghosts cross to . . . wherever."

"Well, when you say it like *that*, I can see how it could sound ridiculous."

"That's how you said it!"

Hugo looked at him. Wallace forced himself not to turn away. It was easier than he expected. "My parents died."

"I'm sorry," Wallace said, cognizant of the fact that apologies seemed to come easier now.

Hugo waved him away. "Thanks, but you don't need to apologize for it."

"It's what you're supposed to say."

"It is, isn't it? I wonder why. Did you mean it?"

"I . . . think so?"

Hugo nodded. "Good enough. Still lived at home. I grew up a few miles away from here. You probably passed by the house on your little adventure last night."

He wasn't sure if he should apologize again or not, so he kept quiet.

"It was fast," Hugo said, staring off into the darkness. He let his hands hang over the edge of the railing. "The roads were slick. Sleet and freezing rain had been falling all day, and Mom and Dad were going out on a date. They'd been thinking about staying in, but I told them to go ahead, so long as they were careful. They worked hard, and I thought they deserved a night out, you know? So I pushed them. Told them to go." He shook his head. "I didn't . . . it's weird. I didn't know it was the last time I'd see them as they were then. Dad squeezed my shoulder, and Mom kissed me on the cheek. I grumbled about it and told them I wasn't a kid anymore. They laughed at me and told me I was always going to be their little boy, even if I hadn't been little in a long time. They died. Car hit a patch of ice and slid off the road. It rolled. I was told it was over in an instant. But that stuck with me for a long time, because it was over for *me* in an instant, and yet it feels like it's still happening, sometimes."

"Shit," Wallace breathed.

"I fell asleep on the couch. I woke up because someone was standing above me. I opened my eyes, and . . . there they were. Just standing there, looking down at me, wearing their nice clothes. Dad hated his tie, said it felt like he was choking, but Mom made him wear it anyway, telling him he looked so handsome. I asked them what time it was. You know what they said?"

Wallace shook his head.

Hugo laughed wetly. "Nothing. They said nothing at all. They flickered in and out, and I thought I was dreaming. And then a Reaper appeared."

"Whoa."

"Yeah," Hugo said. "That was . . . something else. He took my parents by the hands, and I demanded to know who he was and what the hell he was doing in our house. I'll never forget the look of shock on his face. I wasn't supposed to be able to see him."

"How did you?"

"I don't know," Hugo admitted. "I'm not like Mei. I'd never seen ghosts before or anything like that. I never had any kind of touch or sight or whatever it is that makes people like Mei who they are. I was just . . . me. But here I was, trying to grab onto my parents, to pull them away from this stranger, but my hands kept going right through them. I reached for the unknown man, and for a moment, it worked. I felt him. It was like fireworks going off in my head, the explosions bright. They hurt. By the time my vision cleared, they were gone. I tried to tell myself I'd imagined it all, but then someone knocked on the door ten minutes later, and I knew it wasn't only in my head because the police were there, saying things I didn't want to hear. I told them it was a mistake, it had to be a mistake. I screamed at them to get the hell away from me. Grandad showed up shortly after, and I begged him to tell me the truth. He did."

"How old were you?"

"Twenty-five," Hugo said.

"Jesus."

"Yeah. It was . . . a lot. And then the Manager came to see me." His voice hardened slightly. "Three days after their funeral. One moment I was going through things in the house I thought could be donated to Goodwill, and the next he was standing in front of me. He . . . told me things. About life and death. How it's a cycle that never ends and never would. Grief, he said, is a catalyst. A transformation. And then he offered me a job."

"And you *took* it? You believed him?"

Hugo nodded. "The Manager is many things, most of which I can't even begin to describe. But he's not a liar. He speaks only in truths, even if we don't want to hear what he has to say. I didn't trust him right away. I don't know if I do even now. But he showed me things, things that should have been impossible. Death has a beauty to it. We don't see it because we don't want to. And that makes sense. Why would we want to focus on something that takes us away from everything we know? How do we even begin to understand that there's more than what we see?"

"I don't know the answer to that," Wallace admitted. "To any of it." That troubled him, because he felt like he *should* know, like the answer was on the tip of his tongue.

"Faith," Hugo said, and Wallace groaned. "Oh, stop it. I'm not talking about religion or God or whatever else you might be thinking. Faith isn't always . . . it's not just about those things. It's not something I can force upon you, even if you think that's what I'm doing."

"Aren't you?" Wallace asked, trying to keep his voice even. "You're trying to make me believe in something I don't want."

"Why is that, do you think?"

Wallace didn't know.

Hugo seemed to let it go. "The Manager said I was selfless, which is why I was under any consideration at all. He could see it in me. I laughed in his face. How could I be selfless when I would have given anything to have them back? I told him that if he put my parents in front of me along with a random person and said I had to choose who lived or died, I would pick my mom and dad without hesitation. That's not how a selfless person acts."

"Why not?"

Hugo looked surprised. "Because I would choose what made me happy."

"Doesn't mean you're not selfless. If we never wanted something just for ourselves, what would that make us? You were grieving. Of course that's what you would say."

"That's what the Manager said."

Wallace wasn't sure how he felt about that. In a way, *he'd* been a manager of sorts, and that comparison didn't sit well with him. "But you still said yes."

Hugo nodded slowly, picking at the string of lights on the railing.

"Not right away. He told me he'd give me time, but the offer wasn't always going to be on the table. And for a while after, I was going to say no, especially after he told me all it would entail. I couldn't . . . I wouldn't have a normal life. Not like everyone else. The job would come first, above all things. It was a commitment, one that if I agreed to, would be binding for as long as I drew breath."

Wallace Price had been accused of many things in his life, but selflessness was not one of them. He gave little thought to those around him, unless they stood in his way. And God help them if they did. But even so, he could feel the weight of Hugo's words, and it was heavy on his shoulders. Not necessarily because of what he'd said, but what it meant. They were alike in ways Wallace hadn't expected, choosing a job and putting it above all other things. But that was where the comparisons ended. Perhaps, when Wallace was young and bright-eyed, he'd started out with noble intentions, but those had fallen by the wayside quickly, hadn't they? Always about the bottom line and what it meant for the firm. For *Wallace*.

Maybe on a surface level, he and Hugo could be considered similar, but it didn't go much further than that. Hugo was better than he could ever be. Wallace didn't think Hugo would make the same choices he had. "What changed your mind?"

Hugo ran his hand over his hair. Such a small action, and a wonderfully human one at that, but it gave Wallace pause. Everything about Hugo did. He was struck by this man and the quiet power that emanated from him. Hugo was unexpected, and Wallace thought he was sinking once again. "Curiosity, maybe? A desire to understand that bordered on desperation. I told myself that if I did this, I might find answers to questions I didn't even know I had. I've been at this for five years now, and I *still* have questions. Not the same ones, but I don't know that I'll ever stop asking." He laughed, though it was strangled and soft. "I even convinced myself I might be able to see them again."

"You didn't, did you?"

Hugo looked out at the tea plants. "No. They . . . they were already gone. They didn't linger. There were days I was angry about that, but the more I did this job, the more I helped others in their time of need, the more I understood why. They lived a good life. They'd done right by themselves and me. There was nothing left for them to do here. Of course they'd cross."

"And now you're stuck with people like me," Wallace muttered.

The smile returned. "It's not so bad. The bikini was a nice touch."

Wallace groaned. "I hate everything."

"I don't believe that for a minute. You may think you do, but you don't. Not really."

"Well, I hate *that*."

Hugo made an aborted attempt to reach for him. His fingers fluttered above Wallace's hand on the railing before he pulled away, curling his hand into a fist. "We live and we breathe. We die, and we still feel like breathing. It's not always the big deaths either. There are little deaths, because that's what grief is. I died a little death, and the Manager showed me a way to cross beyond it. He didn't try to take it from me because he knew it was mine and mine alone. Whatever else he is, whether or not I agree with some of the choices he makes, I remember that. You think I'm a prisoner here. That I'm trapped, that *you're* trapped. And in a way, maybe we are. But I can't quite call it a prison when there's nowhere else I'd rather be."

"The pictures. The photographs. The posters hanging on the walls inside."

Hugo looked at him but didn't speak. He was waiting for Wallace to put it together, the little puzzle pieces scattered between them.

"You can't ever go to them," Wallace said slowly. "See them in person. They're a . . . reminder?" That didn't feel quite right. "A door?"

Hugo nodded. "They're photographs of places I can't even begin to imagine. There's a whole wide world out there, but I can only see it through these little glimpses. Do I wish I could see them in person? Of course I do. And yet I would make the same choice all over again if I had to. There are more important things than castles crumbling on cliffs over the ocean. It took me a long time to realize that. I won't say I'm happy with it, but I've made my peace because I know how crucial my work is. I still like to look at them, though. They remind me how small we really are in the face of everything."

Wallace rubbed at his chest, the hook aching. "I still don't get you."

"You still don't know me. But I promise I'm not all that complicated."

"I don't believe that for a moment."

Hugo watched him for a long moment, a slow smile forming. "Thank you, Wallace. I appreciate that."

Wallace flushed, hands tightening on the railing. "Don't you get lonely?"

Hugo blinked. "Why would I? I have my shop. I have my family. I have a job that I love because of what it brings to others. What more could I ask for?"

Wallace turned his face back toward the stars. They were really something else. He wondered why he'd never noticed them before. Not like this. "What about . . ." He coughed, clearing his throat. "A girlfriend. A wife, or, like . . ."

Hugo grinned at him. "I'm gay. Probably would be pretty hard to find me a girlfriend or wife."

Wallace was flustered. "A boyfriend, then. A partner." He glared down at his hands. "You know what I mean."

"I know. I'm just playing with you. Lighten up, Wallace. Not everything needs to be so serious." He sobered. "Maybe one day. I don't know. It'd be kind of hard to explain that my tea shop is actually just a front for dead people to have pseudo-intellectual conversations."

Wallace scoffed. "I'll have you know I'm *extremely* intellectual."

"Is that right? I never would have guessed."

"Asshole."

"Eh," Hugo said. "Sometimes. I try not to be. You just make it so easy. What about you?"

"What about me?"

Hugo shrugged, fingers twitching on the railing. "You were married."

Wallace sighed. "It was over a long time ago."

"Mei said she was there at the funeral?"

"I bet she did," Wallace mumbled. "Did she tell you what was said?"

Hugo's lips twitched. "Bits and pieces. Sounded like quite the show."

Wallace laid his head on the backs of his hands. "That's one way of putting it."

"Do you miss her?"

"No." He hesitated. "And even if I did, I wouldn't have the right. I messed up. I wasn't a good person. Not to her. She's better off without me. I think she's still screwing the gardener though."

"No shit?"

"No shit. But I don't blame her. He's pretty hot. I probably would have done the same if I thought he was interested."

"Wow," Hugo said. "I didn't see that coming. You contain multitudes, Wallace. I'm impressed."

Wallace sniffed daintily. "Yes, well, I do have eyes, so. He liked to work in the yard shirtless. He was probably messing around with half the women in the neighborhood. If I looked like that, I'd do the same."

Hugo looked him up and down, and Wallace fidgeted uncomfortably. "You're not so bad."

"Please, stop. You're far too kind. I can't stand it. How on earth are you still single with ammunition like that up your sleeve?"

Hugo squinted at him. "You think that's what I'd say?"

Abort. Abort. Abort. "Uh. I don't . . . know?"

"Multitudes," he said again as if that explained everything.

He glanced at Hugo, relieved he was ignoring Wallace's awkwardness. "Is that a good thing?"

"I think so."

Wallace picked at the peeling paint on the railing, barely realizing he was doing so. "I've never been very surprising to anyone before."

"There's a first time for everything."

And maybe it was because the stars were bright and stretched on forever across the sky. Or maybe it was because he'd never had a conversation like he'd just had with Hugo: honest, open. Real, all the bluster and noise of a manufactured life falling away. Or maybe, just maybe, it was because he was finding the truth within himself. Whatever the reason, he didn't try to stop himself when he said, "I wish I'd met someone like you before."

Hugo was quiet for a long moment. Then, "Before?"

He shrugged, refusing to meet Hugo's gaze. "Before I died. Things might have been different. We could have been friends." It felt like a great secret, something quiet and devastating.

"We can be friends now. There's nothing stopping us."

"Aside from the whole dead thing, sure."

He startled when Hugo stepped back from the railing, a determined look on his face. He watched as Hugo extended his hand toward him. He stared at it before looking up at Hugo. "What?"

Hugo wiggled his fingers. "I'm Hugo Freeman. It's nice to meet you. I think we should be friends."

"I can't—" He shook his head. "You know I can't shake your hand."

"I know. But hold out your hand anyway."

Wallace did.

And so, under the field of stars, Wallace stood before Hugo, their hands extended toward each other. Inches separated their palms, and though it still felt like an endless gulf between them, Wallace was sure, for a moment, he felt *something*. It wasn't quite the heat of Hugo's skin, though it felt close. He mirrored Hugo, raising his hand up and down, up and down in the approximation of a handshake. The cable between them flashed brightly.

For the first time since he'd stood above himself in his office, his breath forever gone, Wallace felt relief, wild and vast.

It was a start.

And it terrified the hell out of him.

CHAPTER 10

A few nights later, Wallace was determined. Irritated, but determined.

He stopped in front of a chair. Nelson had taken it off one of the tables, setting it in the center of the room. Around them, the house creaked and groaned as it settled. He could hear Mei snoring in her room. Hugo was probably doing the same somewhere above, a place Wallace hadn't dared go to yet for reasons he couldn't quite explain. He knew it had to do with the door, but he thought Hugo was part of it too.

The only people up were the dead, and Wallace wasn't a fan right now of two-thirds of them. Nelson was watching him calmly and Apollo had that goofy grin on his face as he lay next to Nelson's chair.

"Good," Nelson said. "Now, what did I tell you?"

He ground his teeth together. "It's a chair."

"What else?"

"I have to unexpect it."

"And?"

"And I can't force it."

"Exactly," Nelson said, as if that explained everything.

"That's not how any of this works."

"Really," Nelson said dryly. "Because you have such a good idea about how this works. What was I thinking."

Wallace grunted in frustration. He wasn't used to failing, especially not so spectacularly. When Nelson had told him he was going to start teaching Wallace the fine art of being a ghost, Wallace had assumed he'd take to it like he'd taken to everything else: with grand success and little care for whatever got in the way.

That had been the first hour.

And now here they were in the fifth, and the chair was just *sitting* there, mocking him.

"Maybe it's broken," Wallace said. "We should try another chair."

"Okay," Nelson said. "Then take another one off a table."

"Are you sure you don't want to cross?" Wallace asked. "Because I can go get Hugo right now and he can walk you to the door."

"You'd miss me too much."

"Keep telling yourself that." He took a deep breath, letting it out slow. "Unexpect. Unexpect. Unexpect."

He reached for the chair.

His hand went right through it.

And *oh*, did that piss him off. He growled at it, swinging for it again and again, his hand always passing through the wood as if it (or he) weren't there at all. With a yell, he kicked at it, which, of course, led to his foot going through the chair as well. The momentum carried his leg up and he teetered back before crashing onto the floor. He blinked up at the ceiling.

"That certainly went well," Nelson said. "Feel better?"

He started to say no but stopped himself. Because strangely, he *did* feel better.

He said, "This is so stupid."

"Right?" Nelson said. "It really is."

Wallace turned his head toward him. "How long did it take you to figure all of this out?"

Nelson shrugged. "I don't know that I've figured *all* of it out. But it did take me longer than a week, I'll give you that."

Wallace pushed himself up. "Then why do you think I'm going to be any different?"

"Because you have me, of course." Nelson smiled. "Get up."

Wallace pushed himself up off the floor.

Nelson nodded toward the chair. "Try again."

Wallace curled his hands into fists. If Nelson could do it, Wallace could too. Granted, Nelson wasn't exactly offering specifics on *how* to do it, but Wallace was determined.

He looked at the chair before closing his eyes. He let his thoughts drift, knowing the more he focused, the worse off he'd be. He tried to think about nothing at all, but there were little flickers of light behind his eyelids, like shooting stars, and a memory rose up around them. It was a trivial thing, something unimportant. He and Naomi had just started dating. He was nervous around her. She was out of his league and sharp as a tack. He didn't know what the hell she was doing with him, how they'd even gotten here in the first place. He hadn't had this before, too shy and awkward to ever instigate anything. There'd been furtive attempts at the end of high school and into college, women in his bed where he tried to pretend he knew what he was doing, and a man or two, though it was awkward fumblings in dark corners that carried a strange and exhilarating little thrill. It took him time to admit to himself that he was bisexual, something he'd felt relief over, at finally giving it a name. And when he'd told Naomi, a little nervous but firm, she hadn't cared either way, telling him that he was allowed to be whoever he wanted.

But that wouldn't happen for another six months. Now, it was their second—third?—date and they were in an expensive restaurant that he absolutely could not afford but thought she would enjoy. They'd gotten dressed up in fancy clothes (*fancy* being a relative term: his suit sleeves were too short, the pant legs rising up around his ankles, but she looked like a model, her dress blue, blue, blue) and a valet had taken his shitty car without so much as a raised eyebrow. He held the door open for her, and she'd *laughed* at him, a low, throaty chuckle. "Why thank you," she said. "You're too kind."

The maître d' eyed them both warily, his snooty little mustache wiggling as Wallace gave his name for the reservation. He led them to the table in the back of the restaurant, the smell of seafood thick and pungent, causing Wallace's stomach to twist. Before the maître d' could act, he hurried around the table, pulling the chair out for Naomi.

She laughed again, blushing and looking away before sitting down.

He thought how beautiful she looked.

Things would fall apart for them. They would hurl accusations like grenades, not caring they were both still in the blast radius. They did love each other, and they had good years, but it wasn't enough to keep it all from crumbling. For a long time, Wallace refused to accept any blame. *She* was the one who'd messed around with the gardener. *She* was the one who knew how important his job was. *She* was the one who'd pushed him to go all in with their own firm, even as his parents gave him nothing but dire warnings about how he'd be destitute and on the streets with nothing in a year.

Her fault, he told himself as he sat across from her in her lawyer's conference room, watching as he pulled the chair out for her. She thanked him. Her dress was blue. It wasn't the same dress, of course, but it could've been. It wasn't the same dress, and they weren't the same people they'd been on that second or third date when he spilled wine on his shirt and fed her bits of pricey crab cake with his fork.

And now, in a tea shop so far from everything he'd known, he felt a great wave of sadness for all that he'd had, and all that he'd lost. A chair. It was just a chair, and yet he couldn't even do that right. It was no surprise he'd failed Naomi.

"Would you look at that," he heard Nelson say quietly.

He opened his eyes.

He was holding the chair in his hands. He could feel the grain of the wood against his fingers. He was so surprised, he dropped it. It clattered against the floor but didn't fall over. He looked at Nelson with wide eyes. "I did it!"

Nelson grinned, flashing his remaining teeth. "See? Just needed a little patience. Try again."

He did.

Only this time, when he reached for the chair, there was a strange crackling the moment before he could grab onto it. The sconces on the walls flared briefly, and the chair rocketed across the room, smashing into the far wall. It fell on its side on the floor, one of the legs broken.

Wallace gaped after it. "I . . . didn't mean to do that?"

Even Nelson seemed shocked. "What the hell?"

Apollo started barking as the ceiling above them creaked. A moment later, Hugo and Mei came rushing down the stairs, both of them looking around wildly. Mei was in shorts and an old shirt, the collar stretched out over her shoulder, her hair a mess around her face.

Hugo was in a pair of sleep shorts and nothing else. There were miles of deep brown skin on display, and Wallace found something very interesting to stare at in the opposite direction that was not a thin chest and thick stomach.

"What happened?" Mei demanded. "Are we under attack? Is someone trying to break in? I am going to kick *so much ass*, you don't even know."

"Wallace threw a chair," Nelson said mildly.

Mei and Hugo stared at Wallace.

"Traitor," Wallace mumbled. Then, "I didn't *throw* it. I just . . . tossed it across the room with the power of positive thinking?" He frowned. "Maybe."

Mei went over to the chair, hunkering down beside it, poking the broken leg with her finger. "Huh," she said.

Hugo wasn't looking at the chair.

He was still staring at Wallace.

"What?" Wallace asked, trying to make himself smaller.

Hugo shook his head slowly. "Multitudes." As if that explained anything at all. He glanced at Nelson. "Maybe don't teach people to destroy my chairs."

"Bah," Nelson said, waving his hand. "A chair is a chair is a chair. He barely even *touched* it, Hugo. It took me weeks to even be able to feel it." He sounded oddly proud, and it was all Wallace could do to keep from puffing out his chest. "He's taking to this whole ghost thing pretty well, if you ask me."

"By murdering my furniture," Hugo said wryly. "Whatever you're planning, you get it out of your head right now."

"I have no idea what you're talking about," Nelson said. "I'm not planning anything at all."

Even Wallace didn't believe him. He didn't want to know what was going through Nelson's head to cause the expression of utter deviousness he wore.

Mei picked up the chair. The leg fell off onto the floor. "He's kind of got a point, Hugo. Have you ever seen someone do this only after a few days?"

Hugo shook his head, still looking at Wallace. "No. I don't suppose I have. Curious, isn't it?" Then, "How did you do it?"

"I . . . remembered something. From when I was younger. A memory."

He waited for Hugo to ask what memory it was. Instead, he said, "Was it a good one?"

It was. For all that came later, for all the mistakes he made, pulling out Naomi's chair was something he hadn't thought about in years, but apparently hadn't forgotten. "I think so."

Hugo smiled. "Try to keep my chairs in one piece, if you can."

"No promises," Nelson said. "I can't wait to see what else he can do. If we have to sacrifice a few chairs in the process, then so be it. Don't you dare think about stifling us, Hugo. I won't have it."

Hugo sighed. "Of course not."

They all fell into a schedule of sorts. Or, rather, they added Wallace to the one they already followed. Mei and Hugo were up before the sun, blinking blearily as they yawned and came down the stairs, ready to start another day at Charon's Crossing Tea and Treats. At first, Wallace wasn't sure how they did it, as the tea shop never had a day off, even on the weekend, and there were no other employees. Mei and Hugo ran everything, Mei mostly in charge of the kitchen during the day while Hugo ran the register and made the tea. They were a team, moving around each other like they were dancing, and he felt the hook tugging gently in his chest at the sight of it.

Those first days, Wallace stayed in the kitchen, listening to Mei's terrible music, watching Hugo through the portholes. Hugo greeted most everyone by name, asking after their friends and families and jobs while he punched the ancient keys of the register. He laughed with them, patiently nodding along with even the most long-winded of customers. Every now and then, he'd glance back at the kitchen doors, seeing Wallace looking out. He'd give a small smile before turning back to greet the next person in line.

It was on his eighth day in the tea shop that Wallace came to a decision. He'd spent a good portion of the morning working up the nerve, unsure of why it was taking him so long. The people in the tea shop wouldn't be able to see him. They'd never know he was even there.

Mei was telling him about how she'd tried to make tea but somehow had ended up almost burning down the kitchen, and therefore was never allowed to touch even the smallest of tea leaves again. "Hugo was horrified," she said, leaning over to look at a batch of cookies in the oven. "You would've thought I'd stabbed him in the back. I think these are burning. Or maybe they're supposed to look like that."

"Uh-huh," Wallace said, distracted. "I'm going out."

"Right? I mean, it wasn't *that* bad. Just smoke damage, but . . . wait. What?"

"I'm going out," he said again. And then he went through the doors and out into the tea shop, not waiting for a response.

Part of him still expected everyone to stop midsentence and turn slowly to stare at him. While he'd been able to move a chair (only breaking two more, though one did leave gouges in the ceiling when Wallace accidentally kicked it as hard as he could), he still hadn't figured out how to change his clothes. His flip-flops snapped against the floor, and he felt oddly vulnerable in his old shirt and sweats.

But no one paid him any mind. They continued on as if he weren't there at all.

He didn't know if he was relieved or disappointed.

Before he could make up his mind, he felt eyes on him and looked over at the counter. A tiny older woman prattled on about how there could be no nuts in her muffin, it couldn't even *touch* a nut of any kind or her throat would constrict and she'd die a terrible death, *Hugo, I know I've told you this before, but it's* serious.

"Of course," Hugo said, but he wasn't looking at her.

He watched Wallace, that quiet smile on his face.

"Don't make this into a big deal," Wallace muttered.

"I would never," Hugo said.

"Thank you," the old woman said. "My tongue gets swollen and my face balloons up, and I look like quite the fright. No nuts, Hugo! No nuts."

And after that, Wallace spent most of his days out in front of the tea shop.

Nelson was thrilled. "You can overhear some of the strangest things," he told Wallace as they walked between the tables. "People aren't very careful with their secrets, even when they're out in public. And it's not eavesdropping, not really."

"Yeah, I don't think that's true. At all."

Nelson shrugged. "Gotta get our kicks from somewhere. So long as we don't interfere, Hugo doesn't seem to mind."

"I mind a lot," Hugo muttered as he walked by them, carrying a tea tray to a couple sitting near the window.

"He says that, but he doesn't mean it," Nelson whispered. "Oh, look. Mrs. Benson is here with her girlfriends. They talk about butts all the time. Let's go listen in."

They *did* talk about butts. Including Hugo's. They giggled amongst themselves as they watched him, batting their eyelashes when he stopped by their table to ask if they needed anything else.

"Oh, the things I'd let him do to me," one of the women breathed as Hugo reached up to the board above the counter to write down a new special of the day: lemon balm tea. "Such lovely hands."

One of the other women said, "My mother would've called them piano hands."

"I'd certainly let him play my piano," Mrs. Benson murmured, twisting her gaudy wedding ring. "And by piano, I mean—"

"Oh, please," a third woman said. "He's one of those gays. You're lacking a few important pieces that would ever make you find out what his fingers could do."

"Watch this," Nelson whispered, elbowing Wallace in the stomach. Then, he raised his voice to a shout. "Hey, Hugo! *Hugo*. They're talking about your fingers in an inappropriate way again and it's making Wallace blush!"

The chalk in Hugo's hand crumbled as he jerked back from the board, clattering teacups on the counter.

Nelson cackled as his grandson glared at the both of them, ignoring the way others in the tea shop were staring at him curiously. "Sorry," he said. "Slipped a little."

"I'm not *blushing*," Wallace growled at Nelson.

"A bit," Nelson said. "I didn't even know you could still do that. Huh. Should I say something else to see how far that blush can go?"

Wallace should have stayed in the kitchen.

The woman came back. It wasn't every day, and sometimes it was in the morning, and other times it was late in the afternoon as the sun was beginning to sink in the sky.

It was always the same. She'd sit at the table by the window. Mei would come out front to work the register, and Hugo would carry a tea tray with a single cup and set it on the table. He'd sit across from her, hands folded on the table, and wait.

The woman—Nancy—barely acknowledged his presence, but Wallace could see the tightness around her eyes when Hugo pulled the chair out and sat down.

Some days, she seemed to be filled with rage, her eyes flashing, skin stretching over hollowed cheeks. Other days, her shoulders were slumped and she barely lifted her head. But she always looked exhausted, as if she too were a ghost and could no longer sleep. It caused a strange twist in Wallace's stomach, and he didn't know how Hugo could stand it.

He stayed away. Nelson did too.

Nelson watched as the woman stood, the chair scraping against the floor.

Nancy stopped when Hugo said, "I'll be here. Always. Whenever you're ready, I'll be here." It was the same thing he said every time she left. And every time, she stopped as if she was actually hearing him.

But she never spoke.

Most days, Hugo would sigh and collect the tea tray before carrying it back to the kitchen. He'd stay back there for a little while, Mei watching the doors with a worried look on her face. Eventually, he'd come back out, and it was as if it'd never happened at all.

But today was different.

Today, the door slammed shut, rattling in the frame.

Hugo stared out the window after her, watching as she walked down the road, shoulders hunched, pulling her coat tighter against the cool air.

He stood when she was out of sight, but he didn't pick up the tray. He went behind the counter, digging around in a drawer until he pulled out a set of keys. "I'll be back," he said to Mei.

She nodded. "Take your time. We'll hold down the fort. I'll let you know if something happens."

"Thanks, Mei."

Wallace was strangely alarmed when Hugo left the shop without so much as another word. He stood at the window and watched as Hugo went to the scooter. He lifted one leg up and over before settling down on the seat. The engine rumbled, and he pulled away, dust kicking up behind the tires.

Wallace wondered what it'd be like to ride with him, Hugo's back protecting him from the wind, hands gripping Hugo's waist. It was melancholic, this thought, though it was lost to a strange rising panic.

"He's leaving?" Wallace asked, voice high and scratchy. The cable stretched and stretched as Hugo disappeared around the corner. "I didn't think he could . . ." He swallowed thickly, barely resisting the urge to chase after Hugo. He expected the cable to snap. It didn't.

"He doesn't go far," Nelson said from his chair. "Never does. Just to clear his head. He'll be back, Wallace. He wouldn't leave."

"Because he can't," Wallace said dully.

"Because he doesn't want to," Nelson said. "There's a difference."

With nothing better to do, Wallace waited at the window. He ignored Mei when she turned the sign to CLOSED as the last customer left Charon's Crossing. He ignored Apollo who sniffed at his fingers. He ignored Nelson sitting in front of the fireplace.

It was dark by the time Hugo returned.

Wallace met him at the door.

"Hey," he said.

"Hi," Hugo said. "Sorry about that. I—"

Wallace shook his head. "You don't have to explain." Feeling strangely vulnerable, he looked down at his feet. "You're allowed to go wherever you want." He winced, because that wasn't exactly true, was it?

A beat of silence. Then Hugo said, "Come on. Let's go outside."

They didn't talk that night. Instead, they stood almost shoulder to shoulder. Every time Wallace opened his mouth to say something, *anything*, he stopped himself. It all felt . . . trivial. Unimportant. And so he said nothing at all, wondering why he felt the constant need to fill the quiet.

Instead, he watched Hugo out of the corner of his eye, hoping against hope that it was enough.

Before they went back inside for the night, Hugo said, "Thank you, Wallace. I needed that." He tapped his knuckles against the deck railing before heading inside.

Wallace stared after him, a lump in his throat.

CHAPTER 11

On the thirteenth day of Wallace Price's stay at Charon's Crossing, two things of note happened.

The first was unexpected.

The second was as well, though the chaos that followed could firmly be placed upon Mei and no one could convince Wallace otherwise, even if it was mostly his own fault.

Early morning. Alarm clocks would be going off soon, another day beginning at the tea shop. Hugo and Mei were asleep.

And Wallace wished he was anywhere but where he was.

"Would you stop *hitting* me?" he snarled, rubbing his arm where he'd been struck with the cane for what felt like the hundredth time.

"You're not doing it right," Nelson said. "You don't seem like a man who loves to fail, so why are you so good at it?"

Apollo woofed quietly as if in agreement, watching Wallace with a tilt to his head, ears perked.

"I'm going to make myself a cane and then hit *you* with it. See how you like it."

"Oh, I'm so scared," Nelson said. "Go ahead. Make a cane out of nothing. It'd certainly be better than standing here waiting for you to figure out how to change your clothes. At least *something* would happen that way." He sighed dramatically. "Such a waste. And here I was thinking you'd be different. I guess the chair was just a fluke."

Wallace bit back a sharp retort when the bottoms of his feet began to tingle. He looked down. The flip-flops were gone.

"Whoa," he whispered. "How did I . . . ?"

"You seem to react to anger more than anything else," Nelson said cheerfully. "Odd, that, but who am I to judge? I can hit you again if you'd think it'd help."

Wallace said, "No, don't. Just . . . hold on a minute." He frowned at his feet. He could feel the floor against his heels. There was a cookie crumb between his toes. He imagined his pair of Berluti Scritto's, the leather ones that cost more than many people made in a month.

They didn't appear.

Instead, he was suddenly wearing ballet slippers.

"Huh," Nelson said, also peering down at Wallace's feet. "That's certainly . . . different. Didn't know you were a dancer." He looked up, squinting at Wallace. "You've got the legs for it, I guess."

"What is it with you people and my *legs*?" Wallace snapped. Then, without waiting for an answer, "I don't know what happened."

"Right. Just like you don't know how the bikini happened. I believe you completely."

Wallace growled at him, but then the ballet slippers disappeared, replaced by a pair of old sneakers. And then slippers. And then flip-flops again. And then cowboy boots, complete with spurs. And then, much to his horror, brown sandals with blue socks.

He began to panic, hopping from one foot to the other as Apollo danced around him, yipping excitedly. "Oh my god, how do I make it stop? *Why isn't it stopping?*"

Nelson frowned at his feet just as the sandals and socks gave way to high heels better suited for an exotic dancer on a stage, making it rain. He shot up four inches, and then dropped back down as the heels were replaced by yellow rubber boots with ducks on the side. "Here," Nelson said. "Let me help."

He smacked Wallace's shins with his cane.

"*Ow,*" Wallace cried, bending over to rub his legs. "You didn't have to—"

"Stopped it, didn't I?"

He had. Wallace now wore . . . soccer cleats? He'd never played soccer in his life, and therefore had never worn cleats before.

Granted, he'd never worn stiletto heels or a bikini, but still. It was an odd choice, though Wallace wasn't sure *choice* was the right word.

"This is ridiculous," Wallace muttered as Apollo sniffed the cleats before sneezing obnoxiously.

"It is," Nelson agreed. "Who knew you were so eclectic. Perhaps these are simply manifestations of what your heart truly desires."

"I doubt that immensely." Wallace took a tentative step, the cleats unfamiliar. He waited for them to disappear, to change into something different. They didn't. He breathed a sigh of relief as he closed his eyes. "I think it's over."

"Um," Nelson said. "About that."

That didn't sound good. Wallace opened his eyes again.

The sweats were gone.

The Rolling Stones shirt was gone.

Oh, the cleats were still there, so he could be thankful for small favors, but he now wore a spandex jumpsuit that left absolutely nothing to the imagination. To make matters worse, it wasn't an ordinary spandex jumpsuit; no, because Wallace's afterlife was apparently an utter farce, the jumpsuit was imprinted with the outline of a skeleton on it, like a Halloween costume, though it was the end of March.

It was then that Wallace realized everything was terrible. He said as much to Nelson, sounding forlorn as he pulled at the spandex, watching it stretch. He shooed Apollo away when the dog tried to grab onto the material and rip it off.

"It could be worse," Nelson said, eyeing him up and down in a way that Wallace was sure was illegal in at least fifteen states. "Though, I will say congratulations on your business downstairs. Size doesn't matter of course, but it doesn't seem like you have to worry about that."

"Thank you," Wallace said distractedly as Apollo tried to squeeze through his legs, tongue lolling, a goofy expression of joy on his face. Then, "Wait, what?"

By the time Hugo and Mei came down, Wallace was in a state

of panic, seeing as how he was now wearing only brightly colored briefs and pleather thigh-high boots. Nelson was slowly losing his composure as Wallace stumbled around, making promises to whoever would listen that he'd never complain about sweats and flip-flops again. He stopped when he saw the new arrivals staring blearily at him.

"I can explain," Wallace said, covering himself as best he could. Apollo apparently decided that wouldn't do, biting Wallace's hand gently and tugging.

"It's too early for this," Mei muttered, but that didn't seem to stop her from getting an eyeful as she made her way to the kitchen.

"You've had a busy night," Hugo said mildly.

Wallace glared at him. "This isn't what it looks like."

Hugo shrugged as Apollo circled his legs. "That's fair, seeing as how I don't know what it's supposed to look like in the first place."

"Puts my Easter suit to shame," Nelson said, wiping his eyes.

Wallace blanched when Hugo stepped closer to him, fingers twitching at his sides. He waited for Hugo to mock him, but it never came.

"You'll get the hang of it," he said. "It's not easy, or so I'm told, but I think you'll figure it out." He frowned as he cocked his head. He started to reach for Wallace but stopped himself. "Depending on how much longer you're here, that is." He smiled tightly.

There it was. This thing that Wallace had been studiously avoiding. Aside from the first few days he'd been here, there'd been no further discussion of crossings or doors or what lay beyond the half-life Wallace was living in the tea shop. He'd been grateful, though wary, sure that Hugo was going to push. He hadn't, and Wallace had almost convinced himself that he'd forgotten. Of course Hugo hadn't. It was his job. This wasn't permanent. It never was, and Wallace was foolish to think otherwise.

He didn't know what to say. He was scared of what Hugo would do next.

Hugo said, "Better get to work," his voice strangely gruff. He turned toward the kitchen, Apollo prancing around his feet as he followed Hugo through the doors.

"Oh dear," Nelson said.

"What?" Wallace asked, staring after Hugo, the hook in his chest feeling heavier than it'd ever been before.

Nelson hesitated before shaking his head. "I . . . it's nothing. Don't worry about it."

"Because saying not to worry about something always makes me *not* worry."

Nelson sighed. "Focus. Unless you're good with what you're wearing, that is."

And so they began again as the sun rose, cool light stretching along the floor and wall.

By the time the second event of note occurred on Wallace's thirteenth day in the tea shop, he'd managed to dress himself in jeans and an oversized sweater, the sleeves too long and flopping over his hands. The boots were gone. In their place was a pair of loafers. He'd considered trying for one of his suits, but had dismissed the idea after thinking about it for a long moment. The right suit was made to show power. If worn correctly, it could cut an intimidating figure, making a very specific point that the wearer was important and knew what they were talking about, even when they didn't. But here, now, what purpose would it serve?

Nothing, Wallace thought. Hence the jeans and sweater.

The din of the shop was loud around them—it wasn't quite noon, though the lunch crowd was already forming—but Wallace was too impressed with himself to notice. He couldn't believe that such a little thing as a new outfit would bring him such peace. "There," he said, having waited ten minutes to make sure it wasn't a fluke. "That's better. Right?"

"Depends on who you're asking," Nelson muttered.

Wallace squinted at him. "What?"

"Some people might have enjoyed what you were wearing more than others."

Wallace didn't know what to do with that. "Oh, uh. Thank you? I'm flattered, but I don't think you and I are—"

Nelson snorted. "Yeah, that sounds about right. Don't always see what's right in front of you, do you, counselor?"

Wallace blinked. "What's right in front of me?"

Nelson leaned back in his chair, tilting his head toward the ceiling. "What a deep and meaningful question. Do you ask yourself that often?"

"No," Wallace said.

Nelson laughed. "Refreshing. Frustrating, but refreshing. How are your talks with Hugo going?"

The conversational whiplash threw Wallace off-balance, causing him to wonder if Nelson had picked up on one of his professional tricks. "They're . . . going." That might have been an understatement. The last few nights, they'd been speaking of nothing in particular. Last night, they'd argued for almost an hour over how cheating at Scrabble was acceptable in certain circumstances, especially when playing against a polyglot. Wallace couldn't be sure *how* their conversation had ended up there, but he was sure that Hugo was in the wrong. It was *always* acceptable to cheat at Scrabble against a polyglot.

"Are they helping?"

"I'm not sure," Wallace admitted. "I don't know what I'm supposed to be doing."

Nelson didn't seem surprised. "You'll know when the time is right."

"Cryptic bastard," Wallace muttered. "What do you think I'm—"

He never got the chance to finish.

Something tickled at the back of his mind.

He frowned, raising his head to look around.

Everything looked as it always did. People sat at the tables, their hands wrapped around steaming mugs of tea and coffee. They were laughing and talking, the sounds echoing flatly around the shop.

A small line had formed at the counter, and Hugo was putting pastries into a paper bag for a young man in a mechanic's uniform, the tips of his fingers stained with oil. Wallace could hear the radio through the kitchen doors. He caught a glimpse of Mei through the porthole windows, moving back and forth between the counters.

"What is it?" Nelson asked.

"I don't . . . know. Do you feel that?"

Nelson leaned forward. "Feel what?"

Wallace wasn't sure. "It's like . . ." He looked toward the front door. "Something's coming."

The front door opened.

Two men walked in. They wore black suits, their shoes polished. One was squat, as if he'd reached an invisible ceiling during his formative years and expanded outward rather than upward. His forehead had a sheen of sweat on it, his eyes beady and darting around the shop.

The other man couldn't have been more different. Though he was dressed similarly, he was as thin as a whisper and almost as tall as Wallace. His suit hung loosely on his frame. He appeared to be made of nothing but skin and bones. He carried an old briefcase in his hand, the sides worn and chipped.

The men moved to either side of the doorway, standing stock still.

The sounds of the tea shop at midday stopped as everyone turned to look at the new arrivals.

"Oh no," Nelson muttered. "Not again. Mei isn't going to like this."

Before Wallace could ask, a third person appeared in the doorway. She was a strange vision. She looked young, possibly around Hugo's age, or even younger. She was tiny, the top of her head barely reaching the squat man's shoulders. She moved with confidence, her eyes bright, her frizzy hair unnaturally red under an old-fashioned fedora with a crow's feather sticking up from the band. The rest of her outfit had probably been *en vogue* at the turn of the nineteenth century. She wore ankle boots with thick laces over black stockings. Her dress was calf-length, and looked heavy, the fabric black and red. It was cinched tightly at the waist and cut low on her chest, her bosom pale and generous. Her white gloves matched the pashmina shawl around her shoulders.

Everyone stared at her.

She ignored them. She raised one hand to the other and began to pluck at the glove one finger at a time. "Yes," she said, voice deeper than Wallace expected. She sounded as if she'd smoked at least two packs a day since she'd learned to walk. "Today feels . . . different."

"I agree," Squat Man said.

"Absolutely," Thin Man said.

She pulled off the glove from her left hand before holding the hand out in front of her, palm facing toward the ceiling. Her fingers wiggled. "Quite different. I believe we'll find what we seek today." She lowered her hand as she moved toward the counter, the floorboards creaking with every step she took.

The customers in the shop began to whisper as the men fell in step behind her. They passed Wallace and Nelson by without so much as a glance in their direction. Whoever this woman was, she wasn't the Manager that Wallace had been fearing. Unless she was ignoring him on purpose to gauge his reaction. Wallace kept his expression neutral, though his skin crawled.

Hugo, for his part, didn't look as perturbed as Wallace felt. If anything, he was resigned. The customers at the counter scattered as the woman approached. "Back so soon?" Hugo asked, voice even.

"Hugo," the woman said in greeting. "I expect you won't make things difficult for me, yes?"

Hugo shrugged. "You know you're always welcome, Ms. Tripplethorne. Charon's Crossing is open for all."

"Oh," she breathed. "Aren't you lovely, you silly flirt. Open for *all*, you say? What could you possibly mean by that?"

"You know what I mean."

She leaned forward. Wallace was reminded of a nature documentary he'd seen once about the mating habits of birds of paradise, their plumage on full display. She was obviously aware of her more . . . substantial features. "I do. And you know what *I* mean, sweet man. Don't think you have me fooled. The things I have seen across the world would be enough to strike fear into the very heart of you." She traced her finger on the back of Hugo's hand on the counter.

"I have no doubt," Hugo said. "So long as you don't bother my other customers, and stay out of—"

"Oh *hell* no," a voice growled. The doors behind the counter swung open, smacking against the wall and rattling the jars filled with tea as Mei stalked out of the kitchen, a small towel in her hands.

"—Mei's way, we'll be fine," Hugo finished.

"Mei," the woman said with no small amount of scorn.

"Desdemona," Mei snarled.

"Still back in the kitchen, I see. Good for you."

Hugo managed to hold Mei back before she launched herself over the counter.

The woman—Desdemona Tripplethorne, a mouthful if there ever was one—remained unaffected. She slapped her gloves against her hand as she looked upon Mei dismissively. "You should work on those anger issues, petal. They're unbecoming of a lady, even one such as yourself. Hugo, I'll take my tea at my usual table. Make it quick. The spirits are restless here today, and I won't miss my opportunity."

Mei wasn't having it. "You can take the tea and shove it up your—" But whatever threat she wanted to make was left to the imagination as Hugo pulled her back into the kitchen.

Desdemona turned and eyed everyone in the shop who was staring at her. Her lip curled in a close approximation of a sneer. "Continue on," she said. "These are matters far beyond your earthly understanding. Tut-tut."

Everyone turned away almost immediately, the whispers reaching a fever pitch.

Nelson grabbed Wallace by the hand, jerking him toward the kitchen. He looked back before they passed through the doors to see the woman and the two men heading toward a table near the far wall under the framed poster of the pyramids. She rubbed her finger along the tabletop before shaking her head.

"—and if you'll let me, I'll just put a *little* poison in her tea," Mei was saying to Hugo as they entered the kitchen. Apollo sat next to her, ear flopped over as he looked between the two of them. "Not enough to kill her, but still enough for it to be considered a felony for which I'll absolutely accept jail time. It's a win-win situation."

Hugo looked horrified. "You can't ruin tea like that. Every cup is special and putting poison in it would ruin the flavor."

"Not if it's tasteless," Mei countered. "I'm pretty sure I read that arsenic doesn't have a taste." She paused. "Not that I know where to get arsenic right this second. Dammit. I should've looked into that after last time."

"We don't murder people," Hugo said, and it didn't appear that this was the first time he'd said it to her.

"Maim, then."

"We don't do that either," Hugo said.

She crossed her arms and pouted. "Nothing's stopping us. You told me that we should always try to achieve our dreams."

"I didn't have murder in mind when I told you that," Hugo said dryly.

"That's because you think too small. Go big or go home." She glanced at Wallace. "Tell him. You're on my side, right? And you know the law better than any of us here. What does it say about killing someone who deserves it?"

"It's illegal," Wallace said.

"But not, like, *completely* illegal, right? Justifiable homicide is a thing. I think."

"I mean, there's always a plea of not guilty by reason of insanity, but that's difficult to pull off—"

Mei nodded furiously. "That's it. That'll be my defense. I'm so insane that I didn't know what I was doing when I put arsenic in her tea."

Wallace shrugged. "It's not like I can testify against you showing premeditation."

"Not helping," Hugo said.

Probably not, but it wasn't like he thought Mei would *actually* murder someone. Or so he hoped. "What's wrong with that woman? Who is she? What did she do besides have a terrible name?"

"She calls herself a medium," Mei spat. "A psychic. *And* she has a crush on Hugo."

Hugo sighed. "She does not."

"Right," Nelson said. "Because most people put their boobs up on the counter like she does. Perfectly natural."

"She's harmless," Hugo said, like he was trying to convince Wallace. "She comes in here every few months and tries to run a séance. But nothing ever happens and so she leaves. It's never for very long, and it doesn't hurt anyone."

"Are you *hearing* yourself?" Mei exclaimed.

Wallace was still stuck on the word *crush*. It made him bristle more than he expected. "I thought you were gay."

Hugo blinked. "I . . . am?"

"Then why does she flirt with you?"

"I . . . don't know?"

"Because she's awful," Mei said. "Literally the worst person in existence." She began to pace. "She gives people like me a bad name. She cons others out of money, telling them she'll help them communicate with their loved ones. It's messed up. All she does is give them false hope, telling them what they think they want to hear. She has no idea what I had to go through, and even if she *did*, I doubt it would stop her. She waltzes in here like she owns the place and makes a mockery of everything we do."

Hugo sighed. "We can't just kick her out, Mei."

"We *can*," Mei retorted. "It's very easy. Watch, I'll do it right now."

He stopped her before she could storm through the doors.

For a moment, Wallace thought it was all for show. That Mei was being overly dramatic, playing a part. But there was a twist to her mouth he'd never seen before, and a sheen to her eyes that hadn't been there a moment ago. She gnawed on her bottom lip as she blinked rapidly. He remembered what she'd told him about what it'd been like for her when she was younger, when no one would listen to her when she tried to tell them something was wrong.

"What does she do?" he asked.

"Ouija board," Nelson said. "She said she found it in an antique store, and that it once belonged to Satanists in the 1800s. There's a sticker on the bottom that says it was made by Hasbro in 2004."

"Because she's full of shit," Mei snapped.

"Pretty much," Nelson said. "She also records everything and puts it online. Mei looked it up once. She has a YouTube channel called Desdemona Tripplethorne's Sexy Seances." He made a face. "Not exactly quality content, if you ask me, but what do I know."

"But . . ." Wallace hesitated. Then, "If she tells people what they want to hear, what does it hurt?"

Mei's eyes flashed. "Because she's lying to them. Even if it makes them feel better, she's still lying. She doesn't know anything about what we do, or what comes after. Would you want to be lied to?"

No, he didn't think he would. But he could also see it from the other side, and if people wanted to give her money just to have reassurance, then wasn't it their business? "She charges for it?"

Mei nodded. Hugo wrapped an arm around her shoulder but she shrugged him off. "After what she did to Nancy, I really thought you'd see right through her. But here we are."

Hugo deflated. "I . . ." He scrubbed a hand over his face. "It was her choice, Mei."

"What did she do to Nancy?" Wallace asked.

Everyone stared at him, the silence deafening. Wallace wondered what fresh hell he'd stepped in now.

"She found Nancy," Mei finally said. "Or Nancy found her. I don't know which, but it doesn't matter. What matters is that Desdemona filled Nancy's head with all manner of crap about spirits and her ability to contact them. She gave Nancy false hope, and it was the cruelest thing she could have done. Nancy *believed* her when Desdemona said she could help. And then she came here looking more alive than she ever had since she first arrived. Nothing happened. Nancy was devastated, but Desdemona still collected her fee." By the time she finished, Mei's cheeks were splotchy, spittle on her lip.

Before Wallace could ask what had happened to Nancy for her to even talk to someone like Desdemona, Hugo said, "That's not . . . I'm not trying to—look, Mei. I get what you're saying. But it was Nancy's choice. She's reaching for anything she can to—"

It was then that Wallace Price came to a decision. He told himself it was because he couldn't stand to see the look on Mei's face, and that it certainly had nothing to do with the fact that Hugo was being flirted with.

It was time to take matters into his own hands.

He turned and walked through the doors, ignoring the others calling after him.

Desdemona Tripplethorne had taken a seat at a table. Squat Man and Thin Man stood next to her. The briefcase had been opened. There were candles lit on the table, the scent obnoxious and cloying, like someone had eaten a bushel of apples and then vomited them up and covered the remains in cinnamon. Most of the other customers had cleared out, though a few were still watching her warily.

The Ouija board had been set up on the table atop a black cloth that hadn't been there before. The theatricality of it all made Wallace grimace. A wooden planchette sat on the board, though Desdemona wasn't touching it. Next to the Ouija board lay a feather quill pen, resting on top of loose sheets of paper.

Desdemona sat in her chair ramrod straight, staring into a camera that had been set up next to the table on a tripod. A tiny red light blinked on the top. Without being told, Squat Man stepped forward, taking the shawl off her shoulders and folding it carefully. Thin Man pulled a vial of liquid from the briefcase along with a glass dropper. He dipped it into the vial and squeezed the top of the dropper, drawing up liquid. He held it over Desdemona's hands, two drops on each, before setting it aside. He rubbed the drops into the backs of her hands. It smelled of lavender.

"Yes," she breathed as Thin Man finished. "I feel it. There's someone here. A presence. Get the spirit box. Quickly." She smiled into the camera. "As my followers know, the Ouija board is my preferred choice of communication, but I'd like to try something new, if the spirits would allow for it." She trailed a finger along the feather quill. "Automatic writing. If the spirits are willing, I give full permission for them to take control of my hands and write whatever message they deem fit. Isn't this exciting?"

Squat Man reached into the briefcase and pulled out a device unlike anything Wallace had ever seen. It was the size and shape of a remote, though the comparison ended there. Out the top came stiff wires, each ending in a small bulb. Squat Man turned a switch on the side, and the device burst to life, lights flashing green. It squealed, a high-pitched mess filled with static. Squat Man looked down at it with wide eyes. He tapped it against his palm. The squeal died down, and the lights faded.

"Strange," he mumbled. "Never had it do that before."

"You're *ruining* the ambiance," Desdemona hissed out of the side of her mouth, never looking away from the camera. "Did you charge the damned thing?"

Squat Man wiped the sweat from his forehead. "I made sure of it. Battery's full." He swung it back and forth around him. Wallace stepped out of the way. It barely blipped when it came within inches of him.

"What are you doing?" a voice whispered beside him. "Whatever it is, count me in, especially if it causes trouble."

He looked over to see Nelson grinning obnoxiously. Wallace couldn't help but smile back. "I'm gonna mess with her."

"Ooh," Nelson said. "I approve."

Thin Man frowned. "Did you hear something?"

"Only the sound of your voice, which I *despise*," Desdemona said. She glared at the few remaining customers until they too got up and left. "Less talking, more focusing."

Thin Man snapped his mouth closed as Squat Man stood on a chair, raising the device toward the ceiling.

"Spirits!" Desdemona said shrilly. "I command that you speak with me! I know you're here." She placed her hands on the planchette. "This board will allow us to communicate with each other. Do you understand? There is nothing to fear. I only wish to speak with you. I'll not cause you harm. If you prefer the pen and paper, make your intentions known. Enter me. Allow me to be your voice."

Nothing happened.

Desdemona frowned. "Take your time."

Nothing.

"All the time you—would you stop *hovering*! You're ruining it!"

Thin Man stood upright quickly and stepped away.

"Weird," Squat Man muttered as he stopped near the fireplace. The device squealed again as he swung it over Nelson's chair. "It's as if something's here. Or was. Or might be. Or never was at all."

"Of course there was," Desdemona said. "If you had studied the file I'd given you, you would know that Hugo's grandfather lived here before he died. It's most likely his spirit I'm feeling today. Or perhaps this place once belonged to a serial killer, and his victims are reaching out from beyond the grave after being horribly mutilated and then murdered." She looked into the camera, wiggling her shoulders, chest rising and falling. Wallace didn't know why he hadn't noticed how violently red her lipstick was. "Just like when we were at the Herring House last year. Those poor, poor souls."

"Huh," Nelson said. "Maybe she can feel something after all."

"Get back in the kitchen," Hugo muttered as he walked by them, carrying a tray of tea. Wallace glanced back toward the kitchen to see Mei glaring daggers at them through the portholes.

"What was that?" Desdemona asked. "Did you say something, Hugo?" She looked into the camera again. "Followers of my channel will remember Hugo from our last visit. I know he's very popular with some of you." She giggled as Hugo set down the tray next to the Ouija board. Wallace wanted to gouge out her eyes. "A dear man, he is." She trailed a finger along Hugo's arm before he could pull away. "Would you like to stay and take part in what is surely to be the paranormal event of the decade? You could sit right by me. I wouldn't mind. We could even share a chair, if you'd like."

Hugo shook his head. "Not this time. Is there anything else I can get you, Ms. Tripplethorne?"

"Oh, there is," she said. "But children watch my videos, and I don't want to corrupt their precious minds."

"Oh my god," Wallace said. "How is she a *person*?"

Hugo coughed roughly. "That's . . . what it is." He stepped back. "If there's nothing else I can get for you, I'll get out of your way. In fact, if there was anyone else left in the room aside from you three, I'd tell them the same thing. Get out of the way."

Wallace snorted. "Oh, yeah. I'll do just that. Watch. Hugo. Are you watching? Look how much I'm getting out of the way."

Hugo glanced at him.

Wallace flipped him off.

Nelson cackled before doing the same.

Hugo wasn't pleased. He went back around the counter, took a rag out, and began to wipe it down while pointedly staring at Wallace and Nelson. When Desdemona and her lackies were distracted, he pointed two fingers at his eyes and then turned them toward Wallace. *Stop*, he mouthed.

"What was that?" Wallace said, raising his voice. "I can't hear you!"

Hugo sighed the weary sigh of the put-upon and furiously wiped the counter while mumbling under his breath. It probably didn't help that Mei was still at the window, but now had a large butcher's knife that she pretended to draw across her neck, eyes rolling back, tongue hanging out of her mouth.

As Squat Man continued his trek around the tea shop (agreeing rather quickly that he shouldn't step behind the counter when Hugo glared at him), Thin Man pulled out another pad of paper and a fountain pen from the briefcase. He stood next to Desdemona, ready to take notes of some kind. He wasn't aware of Apollo next to him, the dog lifting his leg, pissing on Thin Man's shoes. Wallace was momentarily distracted by the stream of urine that Thin Man didn't seem to be aware of, but then Desdemona put her hands back on the planchette and cleared her throat.

"Spirits!" she said again. "I am but your vessel. Speak through me and tell me the secrets of the dead. Be not afraid, for I am here only to help you." She wiggled her shoulders, fingers flexing on the planchette.

Wallace snorted. He rolled his neck side to side and cracked his knuckles. "Okay. Let's give her the ghostly experience she so desperately wants."

"Ooh," Desdemona breathed. "I can feel it." She sucked her bottom lip between her teeth. "It's warm and tingly. Like a caress against my skin. Ooh. *Ooh.*"

Wallace took a deep breath, shaking his hands before settling them on the opposite side of the planchette, ignoring the feather quill. At first, his fingers went through it, and he frowned. "Unexpect," he whispered. "Unexpect."

The planchette grew solid against his hands. He jerked in surprise, knocking the planchette slightly to the side.

Desdemona gasped, pulling her hands back quickly. "Did . . . did you see that?"

Thin Man nodded, eyes wide. "What happened?"

"I don't know." She leaned forward, face inches from the Ouija board. She then seemed to remember she was being recorded as she looked back up at the camera and said, "It begins. The spirits have chosen to speak." She put her hands back on the planchette. "O, dearly departed. Use me. Use me as hard as you can. Deliver unto me your message and I will reveal it to the world."

Wallace was not a fan of Desdemona Tripplethorne. He pushed against the planchette, trying to move it, but Desdemona had a firm grip on it. "It's moving," she muttered out of the corner of her mouth. "Get ready. This is going to get us four million views and a TV deal, I swear to god."

Thin Man nodded and scribbled on the pad of paper.

"What should we say?" Wallace asked Nelson.

Nelson's face scrunched up before smoothing out, a wicked

gleam in his eyes. "Something terrifying. Skip the yes or no on the board. That's boring. Pretend you're a demon, and you want to harvest her soul as well as her larynx."

"*No* harvesting souls," Hugo said loudly.

Desdemona, Thin Man, and Squat Man all turned to stare at him. "What was that?" Desdemona asked.

Hugo blanched. "I said . . . I'm thinking about offering burrito bowls?"

"Not in *my* tea shop you won't!" Mei shouted from the kitchen. She'd somehow found a second knife, and it was bigger than the first one. She looked quite the fright through the porthole. Wallace was impressed.

"She's right," Desdemona said to Hugo. "That wouldn't fit with your menu. Honestly, Hugo, know your consumer base." She turned back to the board, the tips of her fingers firmly pressed against the planchette. "Spirits! Fill me with your ghostly ectoplasm! Leave nothing to chance. Let me be your incredibly sensual voice. Tell me your secrets. *Oooh*."

"You got it, lady," Wallace said, and began to move the planchette. It took more concentration than he expected. Clothes were one thing; moving chairs was another. This was *small*, and yet it was more difficult than he thought it'd be. He grunted and if he was still capable of sweating, he was sure it'd be dripping down his forehead. Desdemona gasped as the planchette moved from side to side before it started spinning in slow circles.

"You actually have to pause on the individual letters," Nelson said.

"I'm *trying*," Wallace snapped. "It's harder than it looks." He furrowed his brow in concentration, tongue sticking out between his teeth. He moved slower, and it took only a few more moments before he got the hang of it.

"H," Desdemona whispered.

"H," Thin Man repeated, writing it down on the pad.

"I."

"I."

Wallace stopped.

Desdemona frowned. "That's . . . that's it?" She looked up at Thin Man. "What did it say?"

Thin Man paled as he turned the pad toward her, hands trembling.

Desdemona squinted at it before rearing back. "Hi. It says *hi*. Oh my god. It's real. It's really real." She coughed roughly. "I mean, of *course* it's real. I knew that. Obviously." She grinned at the camera, though more tightly than before. "The spirits are talking to us." She cleared her throat once more. "Hello, spirits. I have received your message. Who are you? What is it you want? Did you die horribly, perhaps by being bludgeoned to death with a hammer in a crime of passion, and have unfinished business that only I, Desdemona Tripplethorne of Desdemona Tripplethorne's Sexy Seances (trademark pending), can help you with? Who is your murderer? Is it someone in this room?"

"I'll straight up murder *you*!" Mei shouted from the kitchen.

"Yes," Desdomona said after Wallace moved the planchette over the same word on the board. "You *were* murdered. I knew it! Tell me, O great spirit. Tell me who murdered you. I will seek justice on your behalf and when I have my own TV deal in place, I promise I'll never forget you. Give me a *name*."

The planchette moved again.

"D," she whispered. "E. S. D. E. M. O. N—"

Thin Man let out a strangled noise. "That spells *demon*."

"Really scraping the bottom of the barrel with these two," Nelson said, eying Squat Man as he stood on a chair, holding his device toward the ceiling.

"A," Desdemona said as the planchette stopped moving. "That's not demon. It has too many letters. Did you get all of it?"

Thin Man nodded slowly.

"Well?" she demanded. "What does it say."

He showed her the pad of paper again.

In blocky letters, the page read: DESDEMONA.

She squinted at it, and then the Ouija board, and then back at the pad of paper as Thin Man turned and pointed the word toward the camera. "That's my name." The blood drained from her face as she pulled her hands away from the planchette. "Are you . . . are you saying that *I* murdered you?" She laughed uncomfortably. "That's impossible. I've never murdered anyone before."

Thin Man and Desdemona froze as the planchette began to move without her touching it. She rattled off the letters Wallace paused upon, and Thin Man wrote them down.

"You totally killed me," Desdemona read off the paper before blinking. "What? I did *not*. Who are you? Is this some kind of joke?" She bent over the underside of the table before sitting back up. "No magnets. Hugo. *Hugo*. Are you doing this? I don't like to be tricked."

"You're messing with forces you can't even begin to comprehend," Hugo said solemnly.

The planchette moved again.

"Ha, ha," Thin Man read aloud as he wrote the letters down. "You suck."

"What are you, ten?" Nelson asked, though he seemed to be fighting a smile. "You need to be scarier. Tell her you're Satan, and you're going to eat her liver."

"This is Satan," Thin Man said as the planchette moved. "I'm going to eat your diver."

"Liver," Nelson said. "*Liver*."

"I'm *trying*," Wallace said through gritted teeth. "It's slippery!"

"My diver?" Desdemona asked, sounding confused. "I've never been diving in my life."

The planchette moved again. "Sorry," Thin Man read as he wrote down the new message. "Stupid autocorrect. I meant liver."

Hugo put his face in his hands and groaned.

Desdemona stood abruptly, chair scraping against the floor. She looked around wildly. Thin Man was clutching the pad of paper against his chest, and Squat Man had joined them, holding the device out over the Ouija board. It squealed again, louder than it'd been before, the light bulbs across the top bright.

"We are meddling," Desdemona breathed, "in things we don't understand." She put the back of her hand against her forehead as her bosom heaved, and she looked into the camera. "You've seen it here first. Satan is here, and he wants to eat my liver. But I will *not* be intimidated." She dropped her hand. "Be you Satan or some other demon, you are not welcome here! This is a place of peace and overpriced confectionaries."

"Hey!" Hugo snapped.

Wallace moved the planchette faster. "You're the one who's not welcome here," he said under his breath, even as Thin Man said the same thing aloud. "Leave this place. Never return." He paused, considering. Then, "Also, be nicer to Mei or I'll eat your brain too."

"Look," Squat Man said, pointing a trembling finger.

Wallace turned his head to see Nelson standing near the sconces on the wall. He pressed his hands against them, and the light bulbs inside began to flicker. Wallace grinned when Nelson winked at him. The light bulbs rattled.

"Leave," Wallace said, moving the planchette faster. "Leave. Leave. Leave." When he finished, he pushed as hard as he could, knocking the planchette across the room. It landed in the fireplace and began to burn. The Ouija board flew off the table, clattering to the floor.

"I did *not* sign up for this shit," Squat Man said, backing away slowly. He yelped when he bumped into a chair, whirling around.

Nelson left the sconces and went to the camera. He studied it closely before nodding to himself. "This looks expensive." And then he knocked it over. It crashed to the ground, the lens cracking. "Oops."

Hugo sighed once again as Wallace said, "Yes, Nelson. *Yes*."

"We need to get out of here," Thin Man whispered feverishly. He started for the door, but Wallace kicked a chair toward him. It slid across the floor, banging into Thin Man's shins. He screamed and almost fell down, the pad of paper hitting the ground.

"I won't have this!" Desdemona exclaimed. "We won't be intimidated by the likes of you! I am Desdemona Tripplethorne. I have fifty thousand followers, and I *command* you to—"

But whatever Desdemona would have demanded was lost when Mei burst through the doors, both knives raised above her head, screaming, "I am Satan! I am Satan!"

The last Wallace saw of Desdemona, Thin Man, and Squat Man was their backs as they fled Charon's Crossing Tea and Treats. Thin Man and Squat Man tried to go through the door at the same time and became stuck until Desdemona crashed into them, knocking them onto the front porch. They cried out when she stepped on their backs and arms to get over them, her dress hiked up almost obscenely. She jumped off the steps and tore down the road without so much as a glance back at the shop, Thin Man and Squat Man managing to pick themselves up, chasing after her.

Silence fell in Charon's Crossing.

But it didn't last for long.

Nelson began to chuckle, softly at first, then louder and louder. Mei did the same, a hiccupping cough that turned into a wet snort before she cackled as she lowered her knives.

And then another sound filled the nooks and crannies of the tea shop, one never heard before. This sound caused Nelson and Mei to fall silent, Hugo to walk around the counter slowly.

Wallace was laughing. He was laughing as hard as he ever had, one arm wrapped around his stomach, his free hand slapping his knee. "Did you *see* that?" he cried. "Did you see the looks on their faces? Oh my god, that was *incredible*."

And still he laughed. Something loosened in his chest, something he hadn't even been aware had been knotted up and tangled. He felt lighter, somehow. Freer. His shoulders shook as he bent over, gasping for air he didn't need. Even as laughter dissolved into soft chuckles, that lightness didn't fade. If anything, it burned brighter, and the hook, that damnable thing that never ceased to be, finally didn't feel like a shackle, trapping him in place. He thought he had, perhaps for one of the first times in his life, done something good without expecting anything in return. How could he have never considered that before?

He wiped his eyes as he stood upright.

Nelson had a look of awe on his face. It matched his grandson's.

It was Mei who spoke first. "I'm going to hug the crap out of you."

That stunned him, especially when he remembered what Mei had told him about physical affection. "Only you could make that sound like a threat."

She set the knives on the closest table before tapping her fingers against her palm. There was a tiny pulse in the air around them, and then Mei was on him. He almost fell over as she wrapped her arms around his back, holding on tightly. He was stunned into inaction, but only for a moment. It was fragile, this, and Wallace couldn't remember the last time someone had hugged him. He pulled his arms up carefully, hands going to the small of Mei's back.

"Squeeze harder," she said into his neck. "I'm not going to break."

His eyes burned. He didn't know why. But he did as she asked. He squeezed as hard as he could.

When he opened his eyes, he found Hugo watching him, a strange expression on his face. They looked at each other for a long time.

CHAPTER 12

That night, Wallace followed the cable to find Hugo out back, leaning against the deck railing. It was cloudy, the stars hidden away. He paused in the doorway, unsure of his welcome. An odd sense of guilt washed through him, though he didn't allow it to grow any larger. It was worth it, seeing the smile on Mei's face.

Before he could turn back around and go inside, Hugo said, "Hello."

Wallace scratched the back of his neck. "Hello, Hugo."

"All right?"

"I think so. Do you . . . want to be left alone? I don't want to intrude or anything."

Hugo shook his head without turning around. "No, it's okay. I don't mind."

Wallace went to the railing, keeping a bit of distance between Hugo and himself. He worried Hugo was angry with him, though he didn't think Hugo should be upset over something so trivial as using a Ouija board to scare away a grifter. Still, it wasn't his place to tell Hugo what he could or could not feel, especially since this was his shop. His home.

Hugo said, "You're thinking about apologizing, aren't you?"

Wallace sighed. "That obvious, huh?"

"A little. Don't."

"Don't apologize?"

Hugo nodded, glancing at him before looking out at the tea garden. "You did the right thing."

"I told a woman I was Satan and was going to cannibalize her diver." He grimaced. "That's not something I ever thought I'd say out loud."

"First time for everything," Hugo said. "Can I ask you a question?"

"Okay."

"Why did you do it?"

Wallace frowned as he crossed his arms. "Mess with them like that?"

"Yes."

"Because I could."

"That's it?"

Well, no. But that he hadn't liked the way Desdemona had flirted with him wasn't something Wallace would *ever* admit. It made him sound ridiculous, even if there'd been a kernel of truth to it. Nothing could be done about it, and Wallace wasn't about to say something that made it sound like he had a crush of some sort. The very idea caused a wave of embarrassment to wash over him, and he felt his face grow warm. It was stupid, really. Nothing would come of it. He was dead. Hugo was not.

So he said the first thing he latched onto that didn't make him sound like he was about to swoon. "Mei." And with that one word, he knew it was the truth, much to his consternation.

"What about her?"

Wallace sighed. "I . . . She was upset. I didn't like the way Desdemona talked down to her. Like Mei was beneath her. No one should be made to feel that way." And because he was still Wallace, he added, "I mean, Mei did want to commit a felony, sure, but she's all right, I guess."

"That's quite a ringing endorsement."

"You know what I mean."

He was surprised when Hugo said, "I think I do. You saw something happening to someone you consider a friend and felt the need to intervene."

"I wouldn't call her a *friend*—"

"Wallace."

He groaned. "Fine. Whatever. We're friends." It wasn't as hard to say out loud as he thought it would be. He wondered if he'd always made things so difficult for himself. "Why did you let it happen?"

Hugo looked taken aback. "What do you mean?"

"This isn't the first time she's come here. Desdemona."

"No," Hugo said slowly. "It's not."

"And you know how Mei doesn't like her. Especially when she involved Nancy."

"Yeah."

"Then why didn't you put a stop to it?" He was careful not to put any censure in his voice. He wasn't *angry*, exactly—not at Hugo—but he didn't understand. He honestly expected more. He didn't know when that had started, but it was there all the same. "Mei's your friend too. Didn't you see how much it upset her?"

"Not as much as I should have," Hugo said. He stared off into the darkness of the woods around them.

"You know her history," Wallace said, unsure of why he was pushing this. All he knew was that it felt important. "What happened to her. Before."

"She told you."

"She did. I wouldn't wish that on anyone. I can't even imagine what it'd be like to have no one listen to you when you're . . ." He stopped himself, remembering how he'd screamed for someone to hear him after he collapsed in his office. How he'd tried to get someone, *anyone* to see him. He'd felt invisible. "It's not right."

"No," Hugo said. "I don't suppose it is." His jaw tightened. "And for what it's worth, I've apologized to Mei. I shouldn't have let it get as far as it did." He shook his head. "I think part of me wanted to see what you would do, even after I'd told you no."

"Why?"

"To see what you were capable of," Hugo said quietly. "You're not alive, Wallace. But you still exist. I don't think you realized that until today."

He could almost believe that, coming from Hugo. "Still shouldn't have done that to her. Or let Desdemona interfere with Nancy like she did."

"Yeah. I can see that now. I'm not perfect. I never claimed to be. I still make mistakes like everyone else, even though I try my best. Being a ferryman doesn't absolve me of being human. If anything, it only makes things harder. If I make a mistake, people can get hurt. All I can do is promise to do better and not let something like that happen again." He smiled ruefully. "Not that I think Desdemona will come back. At least not for a long time to come. You saw to that."

"Damn right," Wallace said, puffing out his chest. "Gave 'em the ol' what for."

"You really need to stop hanging out with Grandad."

"Eh. He's all right. Don't tell him I said that, though. He'd never let me hear the end of it." Wallace reached out to touch Hugo's hand until he remembered he couldn't. He pulled his arm away quickly. Hugo, for his part, didn't react. Wallace was thankful for that, even as he remembered the way it'd felt to have Mei hugging him as hard as she could. He didn't know when he'd become so desperate for contact.

He struggled with something to say, something to distract them both. "I made mistakes too. Before." He paused. "No, that's not quite right. I *still* make mistakes."

"Why?" Hugo asked.

Why, indeed. "To err is human, I guess. I wasn't like you, though. I didn't let it affect me. I should have, but I just . . . I don't know. I always blamed others and told myself to learn from *their* mistakes, and not necessarily my own."

"What do you think that means?"

It was a hard truth to face, and one he still wasn't sure he was ready for. "I don't know if I was a good person." He let the words float between them for a moment, bitter though they were.

"What makes a good person?" Hugo asked. "Actions? Motivations? Selflessness?"

"Maybe all of it," Wallace said. "Or maybe none of it. You said you don't know what's on the other side of that door, even though you see the looks on their faces when they cross. How do you know there's no Heaven or Hell? What if I walk through that door, and I'm judged for every wrong I've done and it outweighs all the rest? Would I deserve to be in the same place as someone who devoted their life to . . . whatever? Like, I don't know. A nun, or something."

"A nun," Hugo repeated, struggling against laughter. "You're comparing yourself to a nun."

"Shut up," Wallace grumbled. "You know what I mean."

"I do," he said, voice light and teasing. "Kinda would give almost anything to see you in a nun's habit, though."

Wallace sighed. "Pretty sure that's blasphemous."

Hugo snorted before sobering. He seemed to be mulling something over in his mind. Wallace waited, not wanting to push. Finally, Hugo said, "Can I tell you something?"

"Yeah. Of course. Anything."

"It's not always like this," Hugo said, voice hushed. "I could tell you I'm firm in my beliefs, but that wouldn't be entirely true. It's . . . like this place. The tea shop. It's sturdy, the foundation's set, but I don't think it'd take much to see it all come toppling down. A tremor. An earthquake. The walls would crumble, the floor would crack, and all that would be left is rubble and dust."

"You've had an earthquake," Wallace said.

"I have. Two, in fact."

He didn't want to know. He wanted to change the subject, to talk about anything else so Hugo wouldn't look as miserable as he did. But in the end, he said nothing at all. He didn't know which was more cowardly.

Hugo said, "Cameron was . . . troubled, when he came to me. I could see that the moment he walked through the door, trailing after my Reaper."

"Not Mei."

He shook his head. "No. This was before her." He scowled. "This Reaper wasn't . . . like her. We worked together, but we clashed more often than not. But I thought he knew what he was doing. He'd been a Reaper for far longer than I'd been a ferryman, and I told myself he knew more than I ever could, especially seeing as how I was new at all of this. I didn't want to cause trouble, and as long as I kept my head down, I figured we could make it work.

"He brought Cameron. He didn't want to be here. He refused to believe he was dead. He was angry, so angry that I could almost taste it. It's to be expected, of course. It's hard to accept a new reality when the only life you've known is gone forever. He didn't want to hear anything I had to say. He told me this place was nothing but a prison, that he was trapped here, and I was nothing but his captor."

There was the guilt Wallace had been trying to avoid. It clawed at his chest. "I didn't . . ."

"I know," Hugo said. "It's not . . . you're not like him. You never were. I knew all I had to do was give you time, and you'd see. Even if you didn't agree, even if you didn't like it, you'd understand. And I don't think you're quite there yet, but you will be."

"How?" Wallace asked. "How did you know that?"

"Peppermint tea," Hugo said. "It was so strong, stronger than almost any tea I've made for someone like you before. You weren't angry. You were scared and *acting* angry. There's a difference."

Wallace thought of his mother in the kitchen, candy canes in the oven. "What happened to Cameron?"

"He left," Hugo said. "And nothing I could do or say would stop him." His voice grew hard. "The Reaper told me to let him go. That he'd learn his lesson and come running back the moment he saw his skin starting to flake. And because I didn't know what else to do, I listened to the Reaper."

Wallace felt his own tremor, vibrating through his skin. "He didn't come back."

Hugo was stricken. Wallace could see it plainly on his face. It made him look impossibly young. "No. He didn't. I'd been warned, before, what could happen if someone like you left. What those people could become. But I didn't think it could happen so quickly. I wanted to give him space, to allow him to make the decision to come back on his own. The Reaper told me I was wasting my time. The only reason I went in the first place was the tie between us just . . . snapped. The Reaper was right, in his own way. By the time I found him, it was already too late." He hesitated. Then, "We call them Husks."

Wallace frowned. "Husks? What does that mean?"

Hugo bowed his head. "It's . . . apt. For what he is. An empty shell of who he used to be. His humanity is gone. Everything that made him who he is, every memory, every feeling, it's just . . . gone. And there's nothing I can do to bring him back. That was my first earthquake as a ferryman. I'd failed someone."

Wallace reached for him—to offer comfort?—but stopped when he remembered he couldn't touch Hugo. He curled his fingers as he dropped his hand. "But you didn't stop."

"No," Hugo said. "How could I? I told myself that I'd made a mistake, and even though it was a terrible one, I couldn't allow it to happen to anyone else. The Manager came. He told me that it was part of the job, and there was nothing I could do to help Cameron. He made his choice. The Manager said it was unfortunate, and that I needed to do everything in my power to make sure it didn't happen again. And I believed him. It wasn't until a couple of months later when the Reaper brought a little girl that I realized just how little I knew."

A little girl.

Wallace closed his eyes. Nancy was there in the dark, her eyes tired, the lines on her face pronounced.

"She was vibrant," Hugo said, and Wallace wished he would stop. "Her hair was a mess, but I think it was always that way. She was talking, talking, talking, asking question after question. 'Who are you? Where am I? What is this? When can I go home?'" His voice broke. "'Where's my mom?' The Reaper wouldn't answer her. He wasn't like Mei. Mei has this . . . innate goodness in her. She can be a little rough around the edges, but there's a reverence about her. She gets how important this work is. We don't want to cause further trauma. We have to offer kindness, because there is never a time in life or death when someone is more vulnerable."

"How did she die?" Wallace whispered.

"Ewing sarcoma. Tumors in the bones. She fought all the way until the end. They thought she was getting better. And maybe she was, at least for a little while. But it proved to be too much for her." Wallace opened his eyes in time to see Hugo wipe his face as he sniffled. "She was here for six days. Her tea tasted like gingerbread. She said it was because her mother made the most beautiful gingerbread houses and castles. Gumdrop doors and cookie towers. Moats made of blue icing. She was . . . wonderful. Never angry, only curious. Children aren't always as scared as adults are. Not of death."

"What was her name?"

"Lea."

"That's pretty."

"It is," Hugo agreed. "She laughed a lot. Grandad liked her. We all did."

And though he didn't want to know, he asked, "What happened to her?"

Hugo hung his head. "Children are different. Their connections to life are stronger. They love with their whole hearts because they don't know how else to be. Lea's body had been ravaged for years. Toward the end, she never saw the outside of her hospital room. She told me about a sparrow that would come to the window almost every morning. It would stay there, watching her. It always came back. She wondered if she would have wings where she was going. I told her that she would have anything she wanted. And she looked at me, Wallace. She looked at me and said, 'Not everything. Not yet.' And I knew what she meant."

"Her mother."

Hugo said, "Part of them lingers because they burn so brightly in such a short amount of time. While I slept, Lea thought of her mother. And it somehow manifested itself to Nancy. She was hundreds of miles away." His words took on a bitter twist. "I don't know quite how she found us. But she came here, to this place, demanding that we give her back her daughter." He looked stricken when he added, "She called the cops."

"Oh no."

Hugo sounded like he was choking. "They found nothing, of course. And when they learned what had happened to her daughter, they thought she was . . . well. That she'd just snapped. And who could blame her for that? None of them knew that Lea was *right there*, that she was shouting for her mother, that she was *screaming*. Lights shattered. Teacups broke. She said she wanted to go home. I tried to stop him. The Reaper. I tried to stop him when he grabbed her by the hand. I tried to stop him when he dragged her up the stairs. I tried to stop him as he forced her through the door. She didn't want to go. She was begging. 'Please don't make me disappear.'"

Wallace's skin turned to ice.

"The Reaper made her cross," Hugo said, his bitterness a palpable thing. "The door slammed shut before I could get to her. And when I tried to open it again, it wouldn't budge. It'd served its purpose, and there was no reason for it to open again. And oh, Wallace, I was so *angry*. The Reaper told me it was the right thing to do, that if we'd let it go on, then we ran the risk of only hurting both of them more. And more than that, it was what the Manager would want, what he told us we had to do. But I didn't believe him. How could I? We aren't supposed to force someone before they're ready. That's not our job. We're here to make sure they see that life isn't always about living. There are many parts to it, and it continues on, even after death. It's beautiful, even when it hurts. Lea would've gotten there, I think. She would have understood."

"What happened to him?" Wallace asked dully. "The Reaper."

Hugo's face hardened. "He screwed up. He'd never had the temperament I thought a Reaper needed, but what the hell did I know?" He shook his head. "He said that it was the only thing that could be done, and that in the end, I'd see that. But it only made me angrier. And then the Manager came."

Wallace could see the bigger picture, slowly forming in front of him. "What is he?"

"A guardian of the doors," Hugo said quietly. "A little god. One of the oldest beings in existence. Take your pick. Any will do. He says he's order in chaos. He's also a hard-ass who doesn't like it when things upset his order. He came to the tea shop. The Reaper tried to excuse what he'd done. 'Tell him, Hugo. Tell him that what I did was right, that it was *necessary*.'"

"Did you?" Wallace asked.

"No," Hugo said, voice as cold as Wallace had ever heard it. "I didn't. Because even though a Reaper is supposed to help a ferryman, it's not up to them to force a person into something they're not ready for. There is order, yes; the Manager thrives on it, but he also knows these things take time. One moment, the Reaper was standing next to me, begging to be heard, and all I could think about was how he sounded just like Lea. And then he was gone. Just . . . blinked out of existence. The Manager didn't even lift a finger. I was shocked. Horrified. And the *guilt* I felt then, Wallace. It was overwhelming. I'd done this. It was my fault."

"It wasn't," Wallace said, suddenly furious, though at what, he couldn't be sure. "You did everything you could. You didn't screw up, Hugo. He did."

"Did he get what he deserved?"

Wallace blanched. "I . . ."

"The Manager said he did. He said that it was for the best. That death is a process, and anything that undermines that process is only a detriment."

"Nancy doesn't know, does she?"

"No," Hugo whispered. "She doesn't. She was oblivious to it all. She stayed in a hotel for weeks, coming here every day, though she spoke less and less. I think part of her knew that it wasn't like it'd been before. Whatever she'd felt regarding Lea was gone because *Lea* was gone. There was a finality to it that she wasn't prepared for. She'd convinced herself that her daughter's death was a fluke. That somehow she was still here. She was right, in a way, until she wasn't. And that light in her eyes, that same light I'd seen in Lea's, began to sputter and die."

"She's still here," Wallace said, though he didn't know what that meant. The woman he'd seen appeared to be no different than he: a ghost.

"She is," Hugo said. "She left for a few months, and I thought that was the end of it, that she'd somehow begin to heal. The Manager brought Mei, and I told myself it was for the best. I was busy learning about my new Reaper, trying to make sure she wasn't like her predecessor. It took me a long time to trust her. Mei will tell you that I was a jerk at first, and that's probably true. It was hard for me to trust someone like her again."

"But you did."

Hugo shrugged. "She earned it. She's not like anyone else. She knows the importance of what we do, and she doesn't take it for granted. But above all else, she's kind. I don't know if I can adequately explain how significant that is. This life isn't an easy one. Day in and day out we're surrounded by death. You either learn to live with it, or let it destroy you. My first Reaper didn't get that. And people paid the price because of it, innocent people who didn't deserve what happened to them." He looked down at his hands, eyes dull in the dark. "Nancy came back. She rented an apartment in town, and most days, finds her way here. She doesn't speak. She sits at the same table. She's waiting, I think."

"For what?"

"Anything," Hugo said. "Anything to show her that those we love are never truly gone. She's lost, and all I can do is be there for her when she finds her voice again. I owe her that much. I'll never push her. I'll never force her into something she's not ready for. How could I? I already failed her once. I don't want that to happen again."

"It wasn't you. You didn't—"

"It *was*," Hugo snapped at him, and Wallace could barely keep from flinching. "I could have done more. I *should* have done more."

"How?" Wallace asked. "What more could you have possibly done?" Before Hugo could retort, Wallace continued. "You didn't force Lea through the door. You didn't cause her death. You were here when she needed you most, and now you're doing the same for her mother. What more can you give, Hugo?"

Hugo sagged against the railing. He opened his mouth, but no sound came out.

Without thinking, Wallace reached for him again, wanting to reassure him.

His hand went right through Hugo's shoulder.

He pulled away, face pinched. "I'm not really here," he whispered.

"You are, Wallace."

Three words, and Wallace wasn't sure he'd ever heard anything more profound. "Am I?"

"Yes."

"What does that mean?"

"I can't tell you that," Hugo said. "I wish I could. All I can do is show you the path before you, and help you make your own decisions."

"What if I make the wrong one?"

"Then we start again," Hugo said. "And hope for the best."

Wallace snorted. "There's that faith thing again."

Hugo laughed, looking surprised as he did so. "Yeah, I guess so. You're an odd man, Wallace Price."

A flash of memory. Of calling Mei strange. "That might be the nicest thing anyone has ever said to me."

"Is it? I'll keep that in mind." His smile faded. "It's going to be hard. When you leave."

Wallace swallowed thickly. "Why?"

"Because you're my friend," Hugo said, as if it were the easiest thing in the world. No one had ever said that to Wallace before, and he was devastated by it. Here, at the end, he'd found a friend. "You . . ."

He remembered what Nelson had told him. "Fit."

"Yeah," Hugo said. "You fit. I didn't expect that."

And because he could, he said, "You should have unexpected it."

Hugo laughed again, and they stood side by side, watching the tea plants sway back and forth.

The house was quiet.

Wallace sat on the floor.

He stared at the dying embers in the fireplace, Apollo's head in his lap. He rubbed the dog's ears absentmindedly, lost in thought.

He wasn't aware he was going to speak until he did. "I never got to grow old."

"No," Nelson said from his chair. "I don't suppose you did. And if you'd like, I can tell you that it's not so great, that all the aches and pains are terrible and that I wouldn't wish it on anyone, but that'd be a lie."

"I wouldn't like that."

"I didn't think you would." Nelson tapped Wallace's shoulder with his cane. "Do you wish you had?"

And wasn't that a conundrum? "Not as I was."

"How were you?"

"Not good," Wallace muttered. He looked down at his hands in his lap. "I was cruel and selfish. I didn't care about anything but myself. It's bullshit."

"What is?"

"This," Wallace said, tempering his frustration. "Seeing how I was, knowing that there's nothing I can do to change it."

"What would you do if you could?"

And wasn't *that* the crux of it? A question where any answer would serve only to show that he'd failed at almost every aspect of his life. And for what? In the end, what had it gotten him? Fancy suits and an impressive office? People who did whatever he told them the moment he said it? *Jump*, he'd say, and they'd do just that. Not because of any allegiance to him, but out of fear of reprisal, of what he'd do if they failed *him*.

They were afraid of him. And he'd used that fear against them because it was easier than turning it on himself, shining a light on all his dark places. Fear was a powerful motivator, and now, now, *now,* he knew fear. He was afraid of so many things, but particularly the unknown.

It was this thought that made Wallace push himself up off the floor, suddenly determined. His hands were shaking, skin prickling, but he didn't stop.

Nelson squinted up at him. "What are you doing?"

"I'm going to see the door."

Nelson's eyes bulged as he struggled to rise from his chair. "What? Wait, Wallace, no, you don't want to do that. Not until Hugo is there with you."

He shook his head. "I'm not going through. I just want to see it."

That didn't calm Nelson down. He grunted as he stood, using the cane to pull himself up. "That's not the point, boy. You need to be careful. Think, Wallace. Harder than you ever have in your life."

He looked toward the stairs. "I am."

He walked up the stairs, Nelson grumbling behind him. They paused on the second floor, the walls a pale yellow, the wooden floors silent underneath their feet, watching as Apollo walked down the hall toward a closed vibrant green door at the end. He walked through the door, tail wagging before it disappeared.

"Hugo's room," Nelson said.

Wallace knew that already, though he hadn't been inside. At the other end of the hall was Mei's room, the white door also closed, a sign hanging crooked on it that read: REMEMBER TO MAKE IT A GREAT DAY. The first day when he'd gone there and woken her up was the only time he'd been to the second floor.

He thought about going back downstairs, waiting for the alarm clocks to go off and another day to start.

He turned . . .

. . . and went up the stairs to the third floor.

The hook in his chest vibrated as he climbed each step. It felt almost hot, and if he focused hard enough, he thought he could hear whispers coming from the air around him.

He understood, then, that it wasn't from Hugo like he'd first thought. Not *just* from Hugo, at least. Oh, Wallace was sure Hugo was part of it, as were Mei and Nelson and Apollo and this strange house. But there was *more* to it, something much grander than he expected. The air around him filled with whispers, almost like a song he couldn't quite make out. It was calling for him, urging him upward. He blinked rapidly against the sting in his eyes, wondering if Lea had been able to hear any of this as she was pulled toward the door, fighting against the strong grip around her wrist.

He panted as he reached the landing on the third floor. To his right, an open loft, moonlight streaming in through the only window. A row of shelves lined the wall, filled with hundreds of books. Plants hung from the ceiling, their blooms gold and blue and yellow and pink.

To his left, a hallway with closed doors. Pictures hung on the walls: sunsets on white beaches, snow falling in thick clumps in an old forest, a church covered in moss with one stained glass window still intact.

"This is where I lived," Nelson said, hands gripping his cane tightly. "My room is down at the end of the hall."

"Do you miss it?"

"The room?"

"Life," Wallace said distractedly, the hook tugging him onward.

"Some days. But I've learned to adapt."

"Because you're still here."

"I am," Nelson said. "I am."

"Do you feel that?" he whispered. Weightless, like he was floating, the song, the whispers filling his ears.

Nelson looked troubled. "Yes, but it's not the same for me. Not anymore. Not like it once was."

And for the first time, Wallace thought Nelson was lying.

He continued up the stairs. The stairway was narrower, and he knew he was climbing toward the odd turret he'd first glimpsed upon his arrival with Mei. It'd been something out of a fairy tale, of kings and queens, a princess trapped in a tower. Of course this was where the door would be. He couldn't imagine it anywhere else.

He took each step slowly. "Did you try to stop him?"

"Who?"

Wallace didn't look back. "The Reaper. With Lea."

Nelson sighed. "He told you."

"Yes."

"I did," Nelson said, but it sounded faraway, like a great distance separated them. A dream, the edges hazy around a thin membrane. "I tried with all my might. But I wasn't strong enough. The Reaper, he . . . wouldn't listen. I did everything I could. Hugo did too."

The stairs curved. Wallace gripped the railing without thinking. The wood was smooth under his fingers. "Why do you think he did what he did?"

"I don't know. Maybe he thought it was the right thing to do."

"Was it?"

"No," Nelson said harshly. "He should never have laid a hand on that girl. He'd done his job by bringing her here. He should have left matters well enough alone. Wallace, are you sure about this? We could go back downstairs. Wake up Hugo. He wouldn't mind. He should be here for this."

Wallace wasn't sure of anything. Not anymore. "I need to see it."

And so he climbed.

Windows lined the walls, windows he hadn't seen on the outside of the house. He laughed when he saw sunlight streaming through them, even though he knew it was the middle of the night. He paused at one of the windows, looking out through it. There should've been a vast expanse of forest on the other side, perhaps even a glimpse of a town in the distance, but instead, the window looked out into a familiar kitchen. The faint sounds of Christmas music filtered in through the window pane, and a woman pulled homemade candy canes from the oven.

He continued on.

He didn't know how long it took to reach the top of the stairs. It felt like hours, though he suspected it was only a minute or two. He wondered if it was like this for everyone who'd come before him, and he almost wished Hugo were there, leading him by the hand. Such a funny little thought, he mused to himself. How it pleased him, the idea of holding Hugo's hand. He hadn't lied when he'd told Hugo he'd wished he'd known him before. He thought things could have been different, somehow.

He reached the fourth floor.

He was surrounded by windows, though the curtains had been drawn. A little chair sat next to a little table. On top of the table was a tea set: a pot and two cups. A vase had been placed next to the cups, filled with red flowers.

But no door.

He looked around. "I don't . . . Where is it?"

Nelson lifted one finger, pointing up. Wallace lifted his head. And there, above them, was a door in the ceiling.

It wasn't as he'd expected. In his fear, he'd built it up in his mind, a great metal thing with a heavy, foreboding lock. It'd be black and ominous, and he'd never work up the courage to walk through it.

It wasn't like that.

It was just a door. In the ceiling, yes, but it was still just a door. It was wooden, the frame around it painted white. The doorknob was a clear crystal with a green center in the shape of a tea leaf. The whispers that had followed him up the stairs were gone. The insistent tugging on the hook in his chest had subsided. A hush had fallen in the house around them as if it held its very breath.

He said, "It's not much, is it?"

"No," Nelson said. "It doesn't look like it, but appearances are deceiving."

"Why is it in the ceiling? That's a weird place for it. Has it always been there?" The house itself was strange, so he wouldn't be surprised if it'd been part of the original construction, though he didn't know what it could lead to aside from the roof.

"That's where the Manager put it when he chose Hugo as a ferryman," Nelson said. "Hugo opens the door, and we rise to whatever comes next."

"What would happen if I opened it?" Wallace asked, still staring at the door.

Nelson sounded alarmed. "Please. Let me get Hugo."

He tore his gaze away, looking back over his shoulder. Nelson was worried, his brow furrowed, but there was nothing Wallace could do about that now. He could barely move. "Can you feel it?"

He didn't need to explain. Nelson knew what he meant. "Not always, and not as strong as it was before. It fades over time. It's always there, at the back of my mind, but I've learned to ignore it."

Wallace wanted to touch the door. He wanted to wrap his fingers around the doorknob, to feel the tea leaf pressed against his palm. He could see it clear in his mind: he would turn the tea leaf until the latch clicked, and then . . .

What?

He didn't know, and not knowing was the scariest thing of all.

He stepped back, bumping into Nelson, who grabbed his arm. "Are you all right?"

"I don't know," Wallace said. He swallowed past the lump in his throat. "I think I'd like to go back downstairs now."

Nelson led him away.

The windows were dark as they descended the stairs. Outside, the forest was as it'd always been.

Before they reached the landing to the third floor, he looked out the last window to the long dirt road that led to the tea shop and strangely, a memory flitted through his head, one that didn't feel like his own. Of being outside, face turned toward the warm, warm sun.

The memory faded, the night returning, and he saw someone standing on the dirt road.

Cameron, looking directly at Wallace. He held out his arm, palm toward the sky, fingers opening and closing, opening and closing.

"What is it?" Nelson asked him.

"Nothing," Wallace said, turning away from the window. "Nothing at all."

CHAPTER 13

At the beginning of his twenty-second day at Charon's Crossing, a file appeared on the counter next to the cash register. The tea shop hadn't yet opened, and Mei and Hugo were in the kitchen, getting ready for the day to begin.

Nelson was sitting in his chair in front of the fireplace, Apollo at his feet.

Wallace moved around the shop, pulling the chairs down from the tables and tucking them underneath. It was getting easier for him, and it was the least he could do to help. He never thought he'd find joy in such menial work, but these were strange days.

He was lost in thought, pulling down the chairs, when the room seemed to shift slightly. The air grew thick and stagnant. The clock on the wall, ticking the seconds away, stuttered. He looked up to see the second hand move forward once, twice, three times before it moved *backward*. It twitched back and forth as the hairs on Wallace's arms stood on end.

"What the hell?" he muttered. "Nelson, did you see—"

He was cut off when the file folder burst into existence next to the cash register with a comical *pop*! Wisps of smoke drifted up around it as it settled onto the counter. It was thin, as if it only held a few pieces of paper inside.

"Oh boy," Nelson said. "Here we go again."

Before Wallace could figure out what *that* meant, Hugo and Mei came through the doors, Apollo trailing after them. Hugo frowned as he glanced up at the clock, the hands frozen.

"Dammit," Mei said. "Of course it comes when I'm making muffins." She grumbled as she headed for the stairs, untying her apron before pulling it up and over her head. "Don't let them burn," she called down. "I'll be very upset."

"Of course," Hugo said, looking down at the folder. He touched it with a single finger, tracing along the edges.

"What is that?" Wallace asked, going to the counter.

"We're going to have a new guest," Nelson said, rising from his chair. He hobbled over to Hugo and Wallace, cane tapping against the floor. "Doubling up. Haven't done that in a while."

"Another guest?" Wallace asked.

"Someone like us," Nelson replied. He stopped next to his grandson, peering down at the folder with barely disguised interest.

"Yes," Hugo said, touching the folder almost reverently. "Mei will retrieve them and bring them back here."

Wallace wasn't sure how he felt about that. He'd grown accustomed to having Hugo's undivided attention, and the thought of another ghost taking that away caused a strange twist in the hook in his chest. He told himself he was being foolish. Hugo had a job to do. There'd been many before Wallace, and there'd be even more after he was gone. It was temporary. All of this was temporary.

It stung more than he expected it to.

"What's that for?" he asked, rubbing his chest with a grimace. "The folder."

Hugo looked up at him. "All right?"

"I'm fine," Wallace said, dropping his hand.

Hugo watched him for a beat too long before nodding. "This tells me who's coming. It's not complete, of course. A life can't be broken down into bullet points and be comprehensive. Think of it as a sort of Cliff's Notes."

"Cliff's Notes," Wallace repeated. "You're telling me that whenever someone dies, you get Cliff's Notes about their lives."

"Uh-oh," Nelson said, looking between the two of them. Apollo whined, ears flattening against his skull.

"Yes," Hugo said. "That's what I'm telling you."

Wallace was incredulous. "And you didn't think to say anything about this before?"

"Why?" Hugo asked. "It's not like I can show you what's in here. It's not meant for—"

"I don't care about *that*," Wallace snapped, though it wasn't the whole truth. "You have one on me?"

Hugo shrugged. It was infuriating. "I did."

"What did it say? Where is it? I want to see it." And *that* wasn't quite the truth either. What if it was bad? What if across the top, written in bold letters (and in Comic Sans!) was a summation of Wallace Price's life that was less than flattering? **HE DIDN'T DO A WHOLE LOT, BUT HE HAD NICE SUITS!** or, worse, **NOT THAT GREAT, IF I'M BEING HONEST!**

"It's gone," Hugo said, looking back down at the folder on the counter. "Once I review it, it disappears again."

Wallace was incensed. "Oh, it does, does it? Just disappears back to wherever it came from."

"That's right."

"And you don't see the problem with that."

"No?" Hugo said. Or asked. Wallace wasn't sure.

Wallace threw up his hands in exasperation. "Who sends it? Where does it come from? Who writes it? Are they objective, or is it filled with nothing but opinionated drivel meant to defame? That's *libel*. There are *laws* against it. I demand you tell me what was said about me."

"Oof," Nelson said. "I'm too old and too dead for this." He shuffled away from the counter toward his chair. "Let me know when our new guest arrives. I'll put on my Sunday best."

Wallace glared after him. "You were wearing pajamas when I got here."

"Your observational skills are unparalleled. Good for you."

Wallace considered throwing a chair at him. In the end, he decided against it. He wouldn't want it going into a *file*.

"You're thinking too hard," Hugo said, chiding him gently. "There's no list of pros and cons, or of every action someone has taken, either good or bad. It's just . . . notes."

Wallace ground his teeth together. "What did my notes say?"

Hugo squinted at him. "Does it matter?"

"Yes."

"Why?"

"Because if someone has written something about me, I'd like to know."

Hugo grinned. "Did you look up reviews of your firm when you were alive?"

Every Tuesday morning at nine. "No," Wallace said. Then, "Unless that was written in my file. And if it was, I had a very good reason. I pissed off a lot of people, and everyone knows if you want to complain about something, you write it on the internet, even if you're a liar who doesn't know what he's talking about."

"Sounds like there's a story there."

Wallace scowled at him.

"Or not," Hugo said. He rubbed his chin thoughtfully. "You sure you want to know?"

Wallace balked. "Is it . . . bad? Like *really* bad? Lies! It's all lies! I was a mostly competent person." He cringed inwardly. Once, he might have fought tooth and nail to upsell himself, but now, he couldn't do it. It felt . . . well. Ridiculous was probably the best way to put it. Ridiculous and pointless.

Nelson snorted from his chair. "You shoot for those stars."

Wallace ignored him. "Never mind. I don't want to know. You just stand there acting smug like you always do."

"You wound me," Hugo said.

Wallace sniffed. "I highly doubt that. I don't even care. Look. Look at how much I don't care." And with that, Wallace turned on his heels, going back to the task at hand. He managed to take down two more chairs before he caved. Hugo was amused as he stalked back to the counter. "Shut up," Wallace muttered. "Just tell me."

"You lasted a whole minute," Hugo said. "Longer than I thought you would. I'm impressed."

"You're enjoying this far too much."

Hugo shrugged. "Gotta get my kicks from somewhere, right, Grandad?"

"Precisely," Nelson said as Wallace rolled his eyes.

Hugo glanced at Wallace. "But it's not like you're thinking. I wasn't lying when I said it's not meant to be a slight against you. Think of it more as a . . . an outline."

That certainly didn't make him feel better. "Written by whom? And don't say some esoteric bullshit like the universe or whatever."

"The Manager," Hugo said.

That stopped Wallace cold. "The Manager. The being you're all scared of who makes decisions on a cosmic level."

"I'm not *scared* of—"

"How does he know about me?" Wallace asked. "Was he *spying* on me?" He looked around wildly as he dropped his voice. "Is he listening to everything I'm saying right now?"

"Probably," Nelson said. "He's kind of a voyeur like that."

Hugo sighed. "Grandad."

"What? Man's gotta right to know that a higher being watched him poop or drop food on the floor and then pick it up and eat it." Nelson peered around his chair. "Did you pick your nose? He saw that too. Nothing wrong with it, I suppose. Humans are gross that way. It's in our nature."

"He didn't," Hugo said loudly. "That's not how it works."

"Fine," Wallace said. "Then I'll just see for myself." He was surprised when Hugo didn't try to stop him from picking up the folder. Surprised, that is, until he discovered that he *couldn't* pick it up. His hand passed right through the folder to the counter underneath. He jerked his hand back before trying again. And again. And again.

"Let me know when you're done," Hugo said. "Especially since I'm the only one who can pick it up and see what's inside."

"Of course you are," Wallace muttered. He sagged, hands flat against the counter.

Hugo reached for him again. It was happening more and more, as if he kept forgetting that he and Wallace couldn't actually touch each other. He paused, one hand above Wallace's. Wallace wondered what his skin would feel like. He thought it would be warm and soft. But he'd never find out. Instead, Hugo rested his hand between Wallace's, tapping his pointer finger. Wallace's own fingers twitched. Mere inches separated them. "It's okay," Hugo said. "I promise. Nothing bad. Your file said you were determined. Hard working. That you didn't take no for an answer."

A month ago, that would have pleased Wallace.

Now, he wasn't so sure.

"I'm more than that," he said dully.

"Glad to hear you say that," Hugo said. "I think so too." He picked up the file from the counter, flipping it open. Wallace attempted to lean in nonchalantly but ended up falling through the counter. Hugo eyed him above the top of the folder. Even his eyes were smiling.

"I dislike you immensely," Wallace said, feeling rather petulant as he stood upright.

"I don't believe that."

"You should."

"I'll keep that in mind."

"Jesus Christ," Nelson muttered. "Of all the obtuse . . ." Whatever else he had to say trailed off into mumbling under his breath.

Mei appeared down the stairs, dressed smartly in the same suit she'd worn to Wallace's funeral. She brushed her hair off her face. "I mean it about those muffins, man. If I come back and find they've burned, there'll be hell to pay. Who have we got now?" She plucked the file from Hugo and began to read, eyes darting back and forth. "Huh. Oh. *Oh.* Well. I see. Interesting." Her brow furrowed. "This . . . isn't going to be easy."

Wallace glared at Hugo. "You said you were the only one who could touch it."

"Did I?" Hugo asked. "My bad. Mei can too."

She grinned at Wallace. "Saw yours. Lots of good stuff in there. Question: Why did you think wearing parachute pants was cool in 2003?"

"You're all terrible people," Wallace announced grandly. "And I want nothing more to do with you." And with that, he went back to pulling down the chairs, refusing to even glance in their direction.

"Oh no," Mei said. "Please no. Anything but that." She shoved the file back into Hugo's hands. "All right. Number two, here we go."

"Make sure you don't show up three days late," Wallace said. "Heaven forbid you do your job correctly."

"Aw," Mei said. "You *do* care. I'm touched." She stood on her tiptoes and kissed Hugo's cheek. "Don't forget about—"

"The muffins. I know. I won't." He wrapped an arm around her shoulders, hugging her close. Wallace wasn't jealous. Not at all. "Be careful. This one isn't going to be like the others."

Wallace didn't like how worried he seemed to be.

"I will," Mei said, hugging him back. "I'll be back as soon as I can."

Wallace turned to tell her that the number of people who showed up at a funeral was *not* indicative of the value of a person, but Mei was already gone.

The clock on the wall resumed its normal pace, the seconds ticking by.

"I'll never understand how any of this works," Wallace said.

Hugo's only response was to laugh as he turned and walked through the kitchen doors.

The tea shop was busy all day. Since he was down Mei, Hugo never stopped moving, barely having time to acknowledge Wallace, much less answer more questions about what was in his file. It irritated him, though if pressed, he wouldn't be able to explain why.

It was Nelson who cut through the heart of the matter, much to Wallace's dismay. Wallace was lost in thought, sitting on the floor next to Nelson's chair. "He's not going to forget about you just because someone new is here."

Wallace resolutely didn't look at him. He stared into the fireplace, the flames snapping and popping. "I'm not worried about that at all."

"Right," Nelson said slowly. "Of course you're not. That'd just be preposterous."

"Exactly," Wallace said.

They sat in silence for at least ten more minutes. Then, "But *if* that's what you're worried about, don't. Hugo's smart. Focused. He knows how important this is. At least, I think he does."

Wallace looked up at him. Nelson was smiling, but at what, Wallace didn't know. "The new person coming here?"

"Sure," Nelson said. "That too."

"What are you talking about?"

Nelson waved his hand dismissively. "Just rambling, I suppose." He hesitated. "Did you love your wife?"

Wallace blinked. "What?"

"Your wife."

Wallace looked back at the fire. "I did. But it wasn't enough."

"Did you try your hardest?"

He wanted to say yes, that he'd done everything in his power to make sure Naomi knew she was the most important person in his entire world. "No. I didn't."

"Why do you think that was?" There was no censure in his voice, no judgment. Wallace was absurdly grateful for it.

"I don't know," Wallace said, picking at a string on his jeans. He hadn't worn anything close to a suit since he'd been able to change clothes. It made him feel better, like he'd shed an outer shell he hadn't been aware he'd been carrying. "Things got in the way."

"I loved my wife," Nelson said, and anything else Wallace had to say died on his tongue. "She was . . . vibrant. A spitfire. There wasn't anyone like her in all the world, and for some reason, she chose me. She loved me." He smiled, though Wallace thought it was more to himself than anything else. "She had this habit. Drove me up the wall. She'd come home from work, and the first thing she'd do was take off her shoes and leave them by the door. Her socks would follow, just laid out on the floor. A trail of clothes left there, waiting for me to pick them up. I asked her why she just didn't put them in the hamper like a normal person. You know what she said?"

"What?" Wallace asked.

"She said that life was more than dirty socks."

Wallace stared at him. "That . . . doesn't mean anything."

Nelson's smile widened. "Right? But it made perfect sense to her." His smile trembled. "I came home one day. I was late. I opened the door, and there were no shoes right inside. No socks on the floor. No trail of clothes. I thought for once she'd picked up after herself. I was . . . relieved? I was tired and didn't want to have to clean up her mess. I called for her. She didn't answer. I went through the house, room by room, but she wasn't there. Late, I told myself. It happens. And then the phone rang. That was the day I learned my wife had passed unexpectedly. And it's funny, really. Because even as they told me she was gone, that it had been quick and she hadn't suffered, all I could think about was how I'd give anything to have her shoes by the door. Her dirty socks on the floor. A trail of clothes leading toward the bedroom."

"I'm sorry," Wallace said quietly.

"You don't need to be," Nelson said. "We had a good life. She loved me, and I made sure she knew every day I loved her, even if I had to pick up after her. It's what you do."

"Don't you miss her?" Wallace asked without thinking. He winced. "Shit. That didn't come out like I meant it to. Of course you do."

"I do," Nelson agreed. "With every fiber of my being."

"But you're still here."

"I am," Nelson said. "And I know that when I'm ready to leave this place, she'll be waiting for me. But I made a promise that I'd watch over Hugo for as long as I was able. She'll understand. What's a few years in the face of forever?"

"What will it take?" Wallace asked. "For you to cross." He remembered what Nelson had told him when they'd stood below the door. "To rise."

"Ah," Nelson said. "That's the question, isn't it? What will it take?" He leaned forward, tapping his cane gently against Wallace's leg. "To know he's in good hands. That his life is filled with joy even in the face of death. It's not about what he *needs*, necessarily, because that might imply he's lacking something. It's about what he *wants*. There's a difference. I think we forget that, sometimes."

"What does he want?" Wallace asked.

Instead of answering, Nelson said, "He smiles more, now. Did you know that?"

"He does?" He thought Hugo was the type who always smiled.

"I wonder why that is," Nelson said. He sat back in his chair. "I can't wait to figure it out."

Wallace glanced at Hugo behind the counter, He must have felt Wallace watching him, because he looked over and grinned.

Wallace whispered, "It's easy to let yourself spiral and fall."

"It is," Nelson agreed. "But it's what you do to pull yourself out of it that matters most."

The second hand on the clock began to stutter a half hour after Charon's Crossing closed for the evening. Hugo placed a familiar sign in the window: CLOSED FOR A PRIVATE EVENT. He told Wallace it was just a precaution.

"We're not here," Hugo said. "Not really. When the clock begins to slow, the world moves on around us. If anyone were to come to the shop during a time such as this, they would see only a darkened house with the sign in the window."

Wallace followed him into the kitchen. His skin was itching, and the hook in his chest was uncomfortable. "Has anyone ever tried to get in?"

Hugo shook his head. "Not that I know of. It's . . . not quite magic, I don't think. More of an illusion than anything."

"For someone who's a ferryman, there's a lot you don't know."

Hugo chuckled. "Isn't it great? I'd hate to know everything. There'd be no mystery left. What would be the point?"

"But you'd know what to expect." He realized how it sounded the moment he said it. "Which is why we *un*expect."

"Exactly," Hugo said, as if that made any kind of sense. Wallace was learning it was easier just to go with it. It kept his sanity mostly intact. Hugo went to the pantry, frowning at the contents as he stood in front of it. Wallace looked over his shoulder. More jars lined the shelves, each with a different kind of tea inside. Unlike the ones behind the counter in the front of the shop, these weren't labeled. Most of them were in powder form.

"Matcha?" Hugo muttered to himself. "No. That's not right. Yaupon? No. That's not it either, though I think it's close."

"What are you doing?"

"Trying to find what tea will best fit our guest," Hugo said.

"You did this with me?"

He nodded as he pointed toward a dark powder toward the top of the shelf. "You were easy. Easier than almost anyone I'd ever had before."

"Wow," Wallace said. "First time anyone's said that about me. I don't know how I feel about that."

Hugo was startled into laughter. "That's not—oh, you know what I meant."

"You said it, not me."

"It's an art," Hugo said. "Or at least that's what I tell myself. Picking the perfect tea for a person. I don't always get it right, but I'm getting better at it." He reached for a jar, touching the glass before pulling his hand back. "That's not it either. What could—ah. Really? That's . . . an acquired taste." He took a jar from the shelf, filled with twisted, blackened leaves. "Not one of mine. I don't think I could grow it here. Had this imported."

"What is it?" Wallace asked, eyeing the jar. The leaves looked dead.

"Kuding cha," Hugo said, turning toward the opposite counter to prepare the tea. "It's a Chinese infusion. The literal translation is bitter nail tea. It's usually made from a type of wax tree and holly. The taste isn't for everyone. It's very bitter, though it's said to be medicinal. It's supposed to help clear the eyes and head. Resolves toxins."

"And this is what you're going to give him?" Wallace asked, watching as Hugo pulled a twisted leaf from the jar. The earthy scent was pungent, causing Wallace to sneeze.

"I think so," Hugo said. "It's unusual. I've never had someone take this tea before." He stared at the leaf before shaking his head. "Probably nothing. Watch."

Wallace stood next to him as Hugo poured hot water into the same set of teacups he'd used when Mei brought Wallace the first night. Steam billowed up as he set the teapot down. He held the leaf between two fingers as he lowered it gently into the water. Once it was submerged, the leaf unfurled like a blooming flower. The water began to darken to an odd shade of brown even as the leaf lightened in color to an off-green.

"What do you smell?" Hugo asked.

Wallace leaned forward and inhaled the steam. It clogged his nostrils, and he wiggled his nose as he pulled back. "Grass?"

Hugo nodded, obviously pleased. "Exactly. Underneath the bitterness, it has an herbal note with an aftertaste that's like lingering honey. You have to get through the bitter to find it, though."

Wallace sighed. "One of those things where you say one thing but mean something else."

Hugo smiled. "Or it's just tea. Doesn't need to mean something when it's already so complex. Try it. I think you might be surprised. It probably needs to steep longer, but it'll give you a good idea."

He thought back to the proverb hanging in the tea shop. Hugo must have been thinking the same thing as he handed Wallace the cup and said, "It's your second."

Honored guest.

Wallace swallowed thickly as he took the cup from Hugo. It wasn't lost on him that this was the closest they could ever get to touching. He felt Hugo's gaze on him as they both held the cup longer than was necessary. Eventually, Hugo dropped his hand.

The water was still clear, though the brown tinge had given way to a green closer to the color of the leaf. He brought it to his lips and sipped.

He gagged, the tea sliding down his throat and blooming hotly in his stomach. It was bitter, yes, and then the grass hit and it tasted like he'd eaten half a lawn. The honey afternote was there, but the sweetness was lost by the fact that Wallace hated everything about it. "Holy crap," he said, wiping his mouth as Hugo took the teacup back. "That's terrible. Who the hell would drink that willingly?"

He watched as Hugo brought the cup to his own lips. He grimaced as his throat worked. "Yeah," he said, pulling the cup away. "Just because I love tea doesn't mean I love every kind of tea." He smacked his lips. "Ah. There's the honey. Almost worth it."

"Have you ever been wrong picking out a tea?"

"For people who come in here alive? Yes."

"But not the dead."

"Not the dead," Hugo agreed.

"That's . . . remarkable. Bizarre, but remarkable."

"Was that another compliment, Wallace?"

"Uh, sure?" Wallace said, suddenly uncomfortable. He was standing closer to Hugo than he realized. He cleared his throat as he took a step back. "Man, that taste doesn't leave."

Hugo chuckled. "Sticks with you. I liked yours much better."

That shouldn't have made Wallace as happy as it did. "Was that a compliment, Hugo?"

"It was," Hugo said simply.

Wallace took those two words and held them close, the bitterness he felt no match against the sweet of the aftertaste.

Hugo pulled out more leaves from the jar, setting them on a small plate next to the teapot and cups. "There. How does it look?"

"Like you went outside and picked up the first thing you found on the ground."

"Perfect," Hugo said cheerfully. "That means we—"

At the front of the shop, the clock stuttered loudly and then stopped, the second hand twitching.

"They're here," Hugo said.

Wallace wasn't sure what he was supposed to do. "Should I just . . ." He waved his hand in explanation.

"You can come out with me if you'd like," Hugo said, picking up the tray. "Though, I ask that you let me handle him or any questions he may have. If he talks to you, you can respond, but do so evenly and calmly. We don't want him to be any more agitated than he already might be."

"You're worried," Wallace said. He didn't know how he'd missed the tightness around Hugo's eyes, the way his hands gripped the tray. "Why?"

Hugo hesitated. Then, "Death isn't always swift. I know you don't think so, but you were lucky. It's not like that for everyone. Sometimes, it's violent and shocking, and it follows you. Some are devastated, some are furious, and some . . . some let it become all they know. We get people like that more than you'd think, if you can believe that."

He could. He thought he knew what Hugo was implying, but he couldn't bring himself to ask. The world could be beautiful—and it showed on the walls of the tea shop with the pyramids and castles and waterfalls that seemed to drop from the greatest heights—but it was also brutal and dark.

Hugo looked toward the kitchen doors. "They're coming up the road. Do you trust me?"

"Yes," Wallace said immediately, and he had to fight the urge to block Hugo from leaving the kitchen. He didn't know what was coming, but he didn't like the sound of it.

"Good," Hugo said. "Watch. Listen. I'm counting on you, Wallace."

He walked through the doors, leaving Wallace to stare after him.

CHAPTER 14

Wallace paused in the doorway, frowning. The lights were on as normal, but they seemed . . . dimmer, as if the bulbs had been changed. Apollo whined, ears drooping as Nelson rubbed his head soothingly. "It's okay," Nelson said quietly. "It'll be all right."

Hugo had set the tea on one of the high-top tables, though it wasn't the same one he'd used for Wallace's arrival. Wallace went over to Nelson and Apollo, leaving Hugo to stand next to the table, hands clasped behind him.

He was different, now, even just standing there. It was subtle, and if Wallace hadn't been watching Hugo since he arrived, he might not have noticed it. But he had, and he catalogued all the little changes. It was in the set of Hugo's shoulders, the way his expression was carefully blank, though not disinterested. Wallace thought back to his own arrival, wondering if this was how Hugo had been then.

He tore his gaze away, looking around the room, trying to focus on something, anything, that would distract him. "What's wrong with the lights?" he asked Nelson. He glanced at the door. "Did you turn them down?"

Nelson shook his head. "This is going to be a rough one."

Wallace didn't like the sound of that. "Rough?"

"Most people don't want to be dead," Nelson muttered, running a finger along Apollo's snout. "But they learn how to accept it. Sometimes it comes with time, like you. But there are some who refuse to even consider it. 'These violent delights have violent ends, and in their triumph die, like fire and powder.'"

"Shakespeare," Wallace said, glancing at Hugo, who hadn't looked away from the door.

"Obviously," Nelson said. He reached up and grabbed Wallace's hand, squeezing it tightly. Wallace didn't try to pull away. He told himself the old man needed it. It was the least he could do.

The porch creaked as someone climbed the stairs. Wallace strained to hear voices, but no one was talking. He found that odd. With him, Mei had chattered the whole way down the road, even if it'd been because of Wallace's countless questions. The fact that no one spoke unsettled him.

Three taps on the door. The knocker. A beat of nothing, and then the door opened.

Mei entered first, a grim smile fixed on her face that didn't reach her eyes. She was paler than normal, her lips a thin slash with a hint of white teeth. She took in the room, starting with Hugo, then Nelson, Wallace, and Apollo. The dog tried to rise to go to her, but she shook her head, and he whined as he settled back on his haunches. Nelson squeezed Wallace's hand again.

If asked, Wallace wouldn't have been sure who he was expecting to walk in after her. The tea had given him a clue, but it was a small one, and he couldn't find a way to make it fit into the larger picture. The bitterness, harsh and biting, followed by grass like a field, and the finale of honey, so cloying it stuck in his throat.

Perhaps someone angry, more than he'd been. Someone shouting, filled with rage at the unfairness of it all. Wallace could certainly understand that. Hadn't he done the same? He thought it was part of the process, being firmly planted in denial and anger.

Whatever he thought, the man who entered Charon's Crossing this night was not what he expected. He was younger, for one, probably early twenties. He wore a loose black shirt over jeans with the knees torn out. His blond hair was long, messily swept back off his forehead as if he'd continuously been running his hands through it. His eyes were dark and glittering, his face a mask stretched tightly over bone. The man was unnerving as he took in the room before him, the light dim, gaze settling only briefly on Nelson and Apollo. He stared for a long moment at Wallace. His lips twitched like he was fighting back a terrible smile. His hand rubbed at his chest, and Wallace was startled when he realized he couldn't see the hook in his chest, the cable that should have stretched to Hugo. He didn't know why he hadn't considered it before. Did Nelson have one? Apollo? Mei?

Mei closed the door. The latch clicked again, and there was a finality to it that Wallace didn't like. She said, "This is Hugo. The ferryman, the one I told you about. He's here to help you." She gave the man a wide berth as she walked toward Hugo. Her expression never faltered, and she didn't look at Wallace and Nelson. She stopped next to Hugo. She didn't try to touch him.

The man stayed near the door.

Hugo said, "Hello."

The man twitched. "Hello. I've heard things about you." His voice was lighter than Wallace thought it would be, though it carried a palpable undercurrent of something darker, heavier.

"Have you?" Hugo asked lightly. "Nothing bad, I hope."

The man shook his head slowly. "Oh, no. It was good." He cocked his head. "All of it was good. Too good, if I'm being honest."

"Mei does talk me up," Hugo said. "Tried to get her to break that habit, but she doesn't listen."

"No, she doesn't," the man said, and *there* was the smile. The mask stretched tighter, cheek bones sharp. It chilled Wallace. "At all. Do you listen?"

"I try," Hugo said, hands still clasped behind his back. "I know it's difficult. Learning what you've learned. Knowing how things are never going to be the same. Coming here, to a place you've never been before with people you don't know. But I promise you that I'm here to help you as best I can."

"And if I don't want your help?"

Hugo shrugged. "You will. And I don't mean that flippantly. You're on a journey now, one unlike anything you've ever been on before. This is just a stop on that journey."

The man looked around again. "She said this was a tea shop."

"It is."

"Yours?"

"Yes."

He jerked his head toward Nelson and Wallace. "They are?"

"My grandfather, Nelson. My friend Wallace."

"Are they . . ." He closed his eyes briefly before opening them again. "Like you? Or like me?"

Wallace bit back a retort. They were nothing like him. There was a coldness emanating from him. It permeated the room, causing Wallace to shiver.

"Like you, in a way," Hugo said. "They have their own journey to make."

The man said, "Do you know my name?"

"Alan Flynn."

The skin under Alan's right eye twitched. "She said I'm dead."

"You are," Hugo said, moving for the first time. He brought his hands out from behind his back, settling them on the table in front of him. The teacups rattled on the tray as the table shifted slightly. "And I'm sorry about that."

Alan looked toward the ceiling. "Sorry," he said, sounding amused. "You're sorry. What are you sorry for? You didn't do this to me."

"No," Hugo said. "I didn't. But still, I am sorry. I know how it must seem for you. I won't pretend to understand all that you're going through—"

"Good," the man said sharply. "Because you have no idea."

Hugo nodded. "Would you like some tea?"

Alan grimaced. "Never been one for tea. It's bland." He rubbed at his chest again. "And boring."

"This isn't," Hugo said. "You can trust me on that."

Alan didn't seem convinced, but he took a careful step toward the table. The lights in the sconces flickered with a low electrical hum. "You're here to help me." He took another step. "That's what you said." Another step.

"I am," Hugo said. "It doesn't need to be today. It doesn't need to be tomorrow. But soon, when you're ready, I will answer every question I can. I don't know everything. I don't pretend to. I'm a guide, Alan."

"A guide?" Alan asked, voice taking on a sardonic note. "And just where are you supposed to guide me?"

"To what's next."

Alan reached the table. He tried to put his hands on it, but they went right through it. His mouth twisted down as he pulled his hands away. "Hell? Purgatory? This woman didn't feel like offering specifics." The scorn in his voice was crisp and biting.

"Not Hell," Hugo said as Mei narrowed her eyes. "Not Purgatory. Not somewhere in between."

"Then what is it?" Alan asked.

"Something you'll have to find out for yourself. I don't have those answers, Alan. I wish I did, but I don't. I wouldn't lie to you about that, or anything else. I promise you that, and that I'll do whatever I can to help you. But first, would you like a cup of tea?"

Alan looked down at the tray on the table. He reached out to touch the jar of leaves, but his fingers twitched and he dropped his arm again. "Those leaves. I've never seen tea like it before. I thought it came in bags with the little strings. My father, he . . ." He shook his head. "It doesn't matter."

"Tea comes in all shapes and forms," Hugo said. "There are many kinds, more than you could possibly imagine."

"And you think I'm going to drink your tea?"

"You don't have to," Hugo said. "It's an offering to welcome you to my tea shop. When people share tea, I've noticed it has the power to bring them closer together."

Alan snorted derisively. "I doubt that." He took in a deep breath, tilting his head from side to side. "I bled. Did you know that? I bled out in an alley. I could hear people walking by only a few feet away. I called for them. They ignored me." His gaze grew unfocused. The lights flickered again. "I asked for help. I *begged* for help. Have you ever been stabbed before?"

"No," Hugo said quietly.

"I have," Alan said. He raised his hand to his side. "Here." He moved his hand to his chest, fingers curling. "Here." To the side of his throat. "Here. I . . . I owed him money that I didn't have. I tried to explain that to him, but he . . . he flashed the knife, and I said I'd get it. I would. I was good for it. But I'd told him that before, time and time again, and . . ." His eyes narrowed. "I reached for my wallet to give him the few bucks I had on me. I knew it wouldn't be enough, but I had to try. He must have thought I was going for a weapon because he just . . . stabbed me. I didn't know what was happening. It didn't hurt at first. Isn't that strange? I could see the knife going into me, but it didn't hurt. Even with all the blood, it wasn't real. And then my legs gave out, and I fell in a pile of trash. There was a fast food wrapper on my face. It smelled awful."

"You didn't deserve that," Hugo said.

"Does anyone?" Then, without waiting for an answer: "He got away with seven dollars and a debit card he doesn't have the PIN for. I tried crawling, but my legs didn't work. My arms didn't work. And the people on the sidewalk just kept . . . walking. It's not fair."

"No," Hugo said. "It never is."

"Help me," Alan said. "Help me."

"I will. I promise I'll do what I can."

Alan nodded, almost relieved. "Good. We need to find him. I don't know where he lives, but if we just went back, I can find—"

"I told you," Mei said. "We can't go back." She looked perturbed. Wallace wondered what had happened to make her seem so spooked. "You can only move forward."

Alan didn't like that. He glared at Mei, teeth bared. "*You* said that, yes. But let's leave it up to your boss here, huh? You've already said enough. I don't like it when you talk. You don't tell me what I want to hear."

Hugo lifted the teapot and began to pour hot water into the cups on the tray. The steam billowed. He arched an eyebrow at Wallace and Nelson. Nelson shook his head. Hugo filled three cups before setting the pot back down. "What would you do?" he asked as he lifted tea leaves from the jar. He placed a single leaf in each of the cups. "If you could find him? If you knew where he was?"

Alan flinched, brow furrowing. His hands curled into fists. "I would hurt him like he hurt me."

"Why?"

"Because he deserves it for what he did to me."

"And that would make you feel better?"

"Yes."

"An eye for an eye."

"*Yes.*"

"This tea is called kuding cha," Hugo said. "It's unlike any tea I have here at my shop. I can't remember the last time I made it. It's not for everyone. It's said to have medicinal properties, and some people swear by it."

"I told you I don't want tea."

"I know," Hugo said. "And even if you did, I couldn't give it to you yet. It needs time to steep, you see. Good tea is patience. It's not about instant gratification, not like the bags with the little strings. Those can be fleeting, here and gone again before you know it. Tea like this makes you appreciate the effort you put into it. The more it steeps, the stronger the taste."

"The clock," Alan said. "It's not moving."

"No," Hugo said. "It's stopped to give us as much time as you need." He picked up a teacup and set it closer to Alan. "Give it another moment, then try it and tell me what you think."

A tear trickled down Alan's cheek. "You're not listening."

"I am," Hugo said. "More than you know. I'll never know what it was like for you in that alley. No one should ever have to feel alone like that."

"You're not *listening*." He turned toward the door.

"You can't leave," Mei said. She took a step toward him, but Hugo held her back. *Wait,* he mouthed to her. She sighed, shoulders sagging.

"I can," Alan said. "The door is right there."

"If you leave," Hugo said, "you'll begin to break apart, something that will only get worse the farther you go. Outside these walls is the living world, a world you don't belong to anymore. Alan, I'm so sorry for that. I know you may not believe me, but I am. I wouldn't lie to you, especially not about something as important as this. Leaving here will only make things worse. You will lose everything you are."

"I already *have*," Alan snapped.

"You haven't," Hugo said. "You're still here. You're still you. And I can help you. I can show you the way and help you cross."

Alan turned back around. "And if I don't want this crossing?"

"You will," Hugo said. "Eventually. But there's no rush. We have time."

"Time," Alan echoed. He looked down at the teacup. "Is it ready?"

"It is." Hugo sounded relieved, but Wallace was still wary.

"And I can touch the cup?"

"You can. Carefully, though. It'll be hot."

Alan nodded. His hand shook as he reached for the cup. Mei and Hugo did the same. Wallace thought back to how it'd been for him, the scent of peppermint in the air, the way his mind had been racing, trying to find a way out of this. He knew Alan would be the same.

Hugo and Mei waited until Alan took the first sip. He swallowed with a grimace.

Hugo drank from his own tea.

Mei did too, and if she didn't like the taste, she didn't show it on her face.

"I'm dead," Alan said, looking down into his cup. He swirled it around. Tea sloshed onto the table.

"Yes," Hugo said.

"I was murdered."

"Yes."

He set the teacup down on the tray. He flexed his hands. He took a deep breath, letting it out slow.

Then, Alan swept his arm across the tabletop, striking the teapot. It fell to the floor and shattered, liquid spilling. He took a step back, chest heaving. He raised his hands to the side of his head, clutching his skull before bending over and screaming. Wallace had never heard such a sound before. It burned as if the hot tea water had scalded his own skin. It went on and on, Alan's voice never breaking. The lights in the sconces flared brightly before they went out, casting the tea shop into darkness. Apollo growled, standing in front of Nelson and Wallace, hackles raised, tail ramrod straight.

Alan tried to overturn the tables, the chairs, anything he could get his hands on. He grew angrier when the chairs barely moved, the tables not at all. He kicked at them, but it was no use. He stalked around the room. Apollo snarled when he got too close to them. Wallace stood quickly, putting himself between Nelson and Alan, but Alan ignored them, eyes blazing as he tried to destroy as much as he could to no avail.

He tired himself out, eventually, hair hanging around his head as he bent over, hands on his knees, eyes bulging. "This isn't real," he muttered. "This isn't real. *This isn't real.*"

Hugo stepped forward. Wallace tried to stop him, but Nelson grabbed his arm, holding him back. "Don't," he whispered in Wallace's ear. "He knows what he's doing. Trust him."

Hugo stopped a couple of feet away from Alan, looking down at him with a sorrowful expression. He crouched down in front of Alan, who sagged to his knees, hands flat against the floor, rocking back and forth. "It's real," Hugo whispered. "I promise you. And you're right: it's not fair. It never really is. I don't blame you for thinking that. But if you let me, I'll do what I can to show you there is more to this world than you ever thought possible."

The man sat back up on his knees, tilting his head back toward the ceiling. He screamed again, the cords in his neck jutting out in sharp relief.

It never seemed to end.

Wallace tried to argue when Hugo asked them to leave, telling them that Alan needed space. He didn't like the idea of Hugo being left alone with him. He knew deep down that Hugo was more than capable, but the wild look in Alan's eyes was almost feral. Mei stopped him before he could tell Hugo in no uncertain terms that they *weren't* leaving. She jerked her head toward the back of the house.

"It's okay," Nelson said, though he too sounded worried. "Hugo can handle him."

Apollo refused to budge. No matter what Mei did or said, he wouldn't move. Hugo shook his head. "It's all right. He can stay. I'll let you know if I need you." He and Mei exchanged a look that Wallace couldn't parse. Alan growled at the floor, flecks of spittle on his lips.

The last thing Wallace saw was Hugo sitting cross-legged in front of Alan, hands on his knees.

He followed Nelson as he shuffled after Mei. They walked down the hall toward the back door. The air was colder than it'd been the last few nights, as if spring had momentarily lost its grasp. Wallace was dismayed when he realized he didn't know the date. He thought it was Wednesday, and it had to be April by now. Time was slipping here. He hadn't noticed, so wrapped up in living the life he found himself in. He'd been in Charon's Crossing for almost four weeks. Mei had said the longest anyone had stayed at the tea shop was two weeks. And yet no one had pushed him toward the door. No one had even mentioned it since the early days.

"You all right?" Nelson asked Mei as she paced back and forth on the deck. He reached out and took her by the wrist. "That had to be difficult."

She sighed. "It was. I knew it could be like that. The Manager showed me as much. He's not the first person I've dealt with who was murdered."

"But it's the first time you've been on your own," Nelson said quietly.

"I can handle it."

"I know you can. I never doubted that for a second. But it's okay not to be okay." She slumped against him, her head on his shoulder. "You did good. I'm proud of you."

"Thanks," she muttered. "I was half-convinced he was going to listen. At least at first."

"Where did you find him?" Wallace asked, looking out at the tea garden below. No one had thought to switch on the lights, and the moon was hidden behind clouds. The tea plants looked dead in the darkness.

"Near where he was murdered," she said. "He was . . . yelling. Trying to get someone's attention. He looked so relieved when he knew I'd heard him."

If Alan were anything like Wallace, it would have only been temporary. "Did you know?"

"Know what?"

He didn't look back at them. There was a thread he was pulling in his mind, one that he knew he should leave alone, but it was insistent. He worried at it as he chose his words carefully. "Was he already dead when the file came?"

There was a beat of silence. Then, "Yes, Wallace. Of course he was. It wouldn't have been sent to us otherwise."

He nodded tightly, hands gripping the deck railing. "And you . . . what? Take it on faith?"

"What are you talking about?" Nelson asked.

He wasn't sure. He tugged on the thread. "You get sent the files. *Our* files. But only after we die."

"Yes," Mei said.

"Why couldn't you get it sooner?" he asked into the night. "What's stopping the Manager or whoever from sending it *before* it happens?"

He knew they were staring at him. He could feel their gazes boring into his back, but he couldn't turn around. He was struggling, and he didn't want them to see it on his face.

"That's not how it works," Mei said slowly. "We can't . . . Wallace. There was nothing that could have been done to save y—him."

"Right," Wallace said bitterly. "Because it was his lot in life to die bleeding out in an alleyway."

"It's the way things are," Nelson said.

"That's messed up if you ask me."

"Death *is* messed up," Mei said. She moved toward him, the deck creaking with every step she took. "You won't hear me trying to argue otherwise, man. It's not . . . there's an order to things. A process we all have to go through. Death isn't something to be interfered with—"

Wallace scoffed. "Order. You're telling me that man is part of an order. That man who suffered and no one stopped to help him. *That's* what you believe in. That's your faith. That's your order."

"What would you have me do?" she demanded. She leaned on the railing next to him. "We can't stop death. No one can. It's not something to be conquered. Everyone dies, Wallace. You. Nelson. Alan. Me. Hugo. All of us. Nothing lasts forever."

"Bullshit," Wallace snapped, suddenly enraged. "The Manager could have stopped it if he wanted to. He could have told you what was going to happen to Alan. He could have warned you, and you could have—"

"Never," Mei said, sounding shocked. "We don't interfere with death. We *can't*."

"Why not?"

"Because it's *always there*. No matter what you do, no matter what kind of life you live, good or bad or somewhere in between, it's always going to be waiting for you. From the moment you're born, you're dying."

He sighed tiredly. "You have to know how bleak that sounds."

"I do," she said. "Because it's the truth. Would you rather have me lie to you?"

"No. I just . . . what's the point, then? To all of this? To any of it? If nothing we do matters, then why should we try at all?" He was spiraling, he knew. Rattled and spiraling. His skin was like ice, and it had nothing to do with the air around him. He clenched his jaw to keep his teeth from chattering.

"Because it's *your* life," Nelson said, coming to the other side of him. "It is what you make of it. No, it's not always fair. No, it's not always good. It burns and tears, and there are times when it crushes you beyond recognition. Some people fight against it. Others . . . can't, though I don't think they can be blamed for that. Giving up is easy. Picking yourself up isn't. But we have to believe if we do, we can take another step. We can—"

"Move on?" Wallace retorted. "Because you haven't. You're still here, so don't you try to spin the same bullshit. You can say all you want, but you're a hypocrite with the best of them."

"And that's the difference between you and me," Nelson said. "Because I never claimed not to be."

Wallace deflated. "Dammit," he mumbled. "I shouldn't have said that. I'm sorry. You didn't deserve it. Neither of you do. I . . ." He looked at Mei. "I'm proud of you. I've never said that before, and that's on me, but I am. I can't imagine doing what you do, the toll it must take on you. And dealing with people like him." He swallowed thickly. "Like *me* . . ." He shook his head. "I need a moment, okay?"

He left them behind, thoughts swirling in a massive storm.

He walked up and down the rows of the garden, letting his fingers pass gently over the tops of the plants, careful to avoid the delicate leaves. He stared beyond, into the forest. He wondered how far he could get before his skin began to flake. What would it feel like to give in? To let himself drift away? It should have scared him more than it did. From what he'd seen, it was empty and dark, a hollow husk of a life once lived.

And yet he still thought about it. Thought about finding a way to rip the hook from his chest, and rising, rising, rising up through the clouds into the stars. Or running, running until he could run no longer. It was fleeting, this, because if he did just that, he could become lost, turning into the one thing Hugo feared most. A Husk. What would that do to him, seeing Wallace dead-eyed and vacant? The guilt would consume him, and Wallace couldn't do that. Not now. Not ever.

Hugo was important. Not because he was a ferryman, but because he was Hugo.

Wallace started to turn back toward the deck, another apology on the tip of his tongue. He froze when he heard a sigh, a long, breathy sound like wind through dead leaves. The shadows around him grew thicker as if sentient, the stars fading until there was only black.

Movement, off to his right.

Wallace looked over, spine turning into a block of ice.

Cameron stood among the tea plants. Only a few feet away. Dressed as he'd been before. Dirty pants. Scuffed sneakers. Shirtless, his skin sickly and gray. Mouth open, tongue thick, teeth black.

Wallace didn't have time to react, didn't have time to make a sound. Cameron rushed forward, hands outstretched like claws. He grabbed Wallace's arm, and everything that made Wallace who he was whited out as fingers dug in, the skin leathery and cold.

Wallace whispered, "No, please, no," as Mei screamed for Hugo.

Cameron leaned forward, face inches from Wallace's, his eyes pools of inky black. He bared his teeth, a low growl crawling from his throat.

The dark colors of the world at night began to bleed around Wallace, melting like wax. He thought about pulling away, but it was a distant, almost negligible impulse. He was a tea plant, roots deep in the earth, leaves waiting to be plucked.

Great flashes of light crossed his vision, the brightest stars streaking across all the blackness. In each of these stars, a glimpse, an echo. He saw Cameron and then he *was* Cameron. It was discordant, harsh and rough. It was brilliant and numbing and terrible. It was—

Cameron laughed. A man sat across from him, and he was like the sun. On the hazy outskirts, a violinist moved by, the music from the strings sweet and warm. There was nowhere else Cameron wanted to be. He loved this man, loved him with every piece and part of him.

The man said, "What's that smile for?"

And Cameron said, "I just love you, is all."

Another star. The violin faded. He was young. Young*er.* He was hurting. Two people stood before him, a man and a woman, both severe. The woman said, "Such a disappointment you are," and the man said, "Why are you like this? Why are you so damn ungrateful? Don't you know what we've done for you? And this is how you choose to repay us?"

And *oh*, how crushing that was, how it *devastated* him. He was heartsore and nauseous, wanting to tell them he could be better, he could be who they wanted him to be, he didn't know how, he—

A third star. The man and woman were gone, but their disdain remained like an infection coursing through blood and bone.

The man like the sun rose again, except the light was fading. They were fighting. It didn't matter about what, just that their voices were raised, and they were clawing and scratching, each word like a punch to the gut. He didn't want this. He was sorry, so sorry, he didn't know what was wrong with him, he was trying, "I swear I'm trying, Zach, I can't—"

"I know," Zach said. He sighed as he deflated. "I'm trying to be strong here. I really am. You need to talk to me, okay? Let me in. Don't leave me guessing. We can't keep going on like this. It's killing us."

"Killing us," Cameron whispered as the stars rained down around them.

Wallace saw bits and pieces of a life that wasn't his. There were friends and laughter, dark days when Cameron could barely pull himself out of bed, a pervasive sense of acrimony as he stood next to his mother, watching his father take his last breaths from his hospital bed. He hated him and he loved him and he waited, waited, *waited* for his chest to stop rising, and when it did, his grief was tempered by savage relief.

Years. Wallace saw *years* flashing by where Cameron was alone, where he wasn't alone, where he was staring at himself in the mirror, wondering if it would ever get any easier as the dark circles under his eyes bloomed like bruises. He was a kid riding his bike in the heat of summer. He was fourteen and fumbling in the back seat of a car with a girl whose name he couldn't remember. He was seventeen when he kissed a boy for the first time, the scrape of the boy's stubble like lightning against his skin. He was four and six and nineteen and twenty-four and then Zach, Zach, Zach was there, the sunshine man, and *oh*, how his heart skipped a beat at the sight of him across the room. He didn't know what it was about him, what drew him so quickly, but the sounds of the party faded around him as he walked over to him, heart tripping. Cameron was awkward and tongue-tied, but he managed to get his name out when the sunshine man asked, and he *smiled*, oh god, he *smiled* and said, "Hi, Cameron, I'm Zach. Haven't seen you around before. How about that?"

It was good. It was so damn good.

In the end, they had three years. Three good, happy, terrifying years with ups and downs and blinking slowly in the morning light as they awoke side by side, their skin sleep-warm as they reached for each other. Three years of fights and passion and trips to the mountains in the snow and to the ocean where the water was cerulean and warm.

It was toward the end of the third year when Zach said, "I don't feel good." He tried to smile, but it split into a grimace. And then his eyes rolled back into his head, and he collapsed.

One moment, everything was fine.

The next, Zach was gone.

The destruction that followed was catastrophic. Everything they'd built was razed to its foundations, leaving Cameron screaming in the rubble. He howled and raged at the unfairness of it all, and nothing, *nothing* could pull him out of it. He faded, he faded until he was a shadow moving through the world by pure force of habit.

Wallace said, "Oh no, please no," but it was too late, it was already too late because this was in the past, this had already happened, it was already *done*.

Another star in the distance, but it wasn't Cameron's.

It belonged to Wallace.

What's the longest someone has been here?

Why? Thinking about setting down roots?

No. I'm just asking.

Ah. Right. Well, I know Hugo had someone who stayed for two weeks. That was . . . a hard case. Deaths by suicide usually are.

He said, "Cameron, I'm so sorry."

And Cameron said, "I'm still here. *I'm still here*."

The stars exploded, and he was pulled away, away, away.

Wallace jerked his head. He was in the tea garden, Mei's hand wrapped around his arm, and she was saying, "Wallace? *Wallace.* Look at me. You're okay. I've got you."

He struggled against her. "No, don't, you don't understand—" He looked over his shoulder to see Hugo standing in front of Cameron amongst the tea plants, near the one he'd been so proud of, the one that was ten years old. The Cameron he'd seen in the stars was gone, replaced by the horrible shell. His black teeth were bared, his eyes flat and animalistic.

"Cameron," Hugo said in a hushed whisper.

Cameron's fingers twitched at his sides. No sound came from his open mouth.

As Mei pulled Wallace up onto the deck, Apollo barking furiously, Nelson's eyes wide, Cameron turned and walked slowly toward the trees.

The last Wallace saw of him was his back as he disappeared into the woods.

Hugo turned toward the house. He looked devastated.

Wallace never wanted to see him like that again.

As the clouds slid away from the moon, they watched each other in this little corner of the world.

CHAPTER 15

Alan tried to leave.

He didn't make it very far before his skin began to flake.

He returned, expression stormy.

"What's happening to me?" he demanded. "What have you done?" He clawed at his chest. "I don't want this, whatever it is. It's a chain. Can't you see it's a chain?"

Hugo sighed. "I'll explain as best I can."

Wallace didn't think it would be good enough.

Charon's Crossing Tea and Treats opened as normal the next day, bright and early.

The people came as they always did. They smiled and laughed and drank their tea and ate their scones and muffins. They sat in their chairs, waking up slowly, ready to begin another day in this town in the mountains.

They couldn't see the angry man pacing through the tea shop, stopping to scream at each of them. A woman wiped her mouth daintily, unaware that Alan was shouting in her ear. A child had whipped cream on the tip of his nose, not knowing that Alan stood behind him, face twisted in fury.

"Maybe you should close the shop," Wallace muttered, staring out the porthole windows.

Mei had dark circles under her eyes. She and Hugo hadn't slept, kept awake by Alan causing a ruckus through the night. "He can't hurt anyone," she said quietly. "What would be the point?"

"I can move chairs. I can break light bulbs. And I wasn't half as angry as he is. You really want to take that chance?"

She sighed. "Hugo knows what he's doing. He won't let that happen."

Hugo stood behind the counter, a forced smile on his face. He greeted each customer as if they were a long-lost friend, but there was something off about it, though most didn't seem to notice. At best, the gaggle of elderly women told him that he needed to take better care of himself. "Get some rest," they scolded him. "You look exhausted."

"I will," Hugo said, glancing at Alan who tried to overturn a table with no success.

It wasn't until Alan started toward Nelson that Wallace went out into the tea shop for the first time that morning.

"Hey," he said. "Hey, Alan."

Alan whirled around, eyes blazing. "What? What the hell do you want?"

He didn't know. He'd only wanted to keep Alan away from Nelson. He didn't think Alan could hurt him, not really, but he didn't want to take that chance. Hugo started toward them, but Wallace shook his head, begging silently for Hugo to stay back. He couldn't stand the thought of Hugo putting himself in harm's way, not again.

Wallace turned back to Alan. "Knock it off."

That startled Alan, some of his rage fading slightly. "What?"

"Knock it off," Wallace repeated firmly. "I don't know what you think you're doing, but is it really helping your situation?"

"What the hell do you know?" Alan started to turn away.

"I'm like you," he said quickly, though it felt like a lie. "I'm dead, so I know what I'm talking about." He didn't believe that for a moment, but if *Alan* believed, then so be it.

Alan stopped and narrowed his eyes as he glanced back. "Then help me do something about it. I don't know what that was last night, but we can't be trapped here. I want to go home. I have a life. I have to—"

"You have two options. You can either stay right here, in this house. Or you can let Hugo take you upstairs and go through the door."

"Seems to me there's a third option. Figure out how to get out of here. Keep moving until I'm free of all of this."

Wallace hesitated. Then, "No one here wants to hurt you. They never have. That's not what this is about. It's a way station. A stop along the path we're all traveling on."

Alan shook his head. "You want to stay here? Fine. I don't give a shit what you do. If that old bastard over there wants to do the same? Good for him. I don't want this. I didn't *ask* for—"

"None of us did," Wallace snapped. "You think this is easy for any of us? You died. I can't even begin to imagine how it must have felt for you. But that doesn't mean you get to act like an asshole about it." Oh, the hypocrisy. Wallace cringed inwardly, remembering all he'd said and done to Hugo, to Mei, to Nelson, three people who were only trying to help him. He owed them everything, and he'd flung it back in their faces, all because he was afraid. Where did he get off scolding Alan when he'd acted the same way? He hated the comparison, but it was the truth, wasn't it? "You want to go? Then go. See how far you get. Maybe you'll get farther than I did, but it won't matter. You'll turn into nothing. You'll *be* nothing. Is that what you really want?" Alan started to speak, but Wallace overrode him. "I don't think it is. And deep down, I think you know that. For once in your life, use your damn head."

And with that, he spun on his heel and stalked away, leaving Alan behind.

"That went well," Nelson murmured when Wallace put his hand on the back of his chair.

Wallace sighed. "I don't know if I had the right to say any of that to him."

"What do you mean?"

"I just . . . he's me." The words were easier than he expected. "In a way I don't like to look at because it shows me for who I was. Hell, who I *am*. I don't know. It's all jumbled up in my head. How can I tell him he can't be an asshole about all of this when I acted exactly the same way?"

"You did," Nelson said evenly.

"I shouldn't have done that," Wallace whispered, ashamed. "I was scared, more than I'd ever been in my life, but that doesn't excuse the way I treated all of you." He shook his head. "Mei said something the first night she brought me here. That I needed to think about what I was saying. I didn't do that." Humbled, he looked at Nelson. "I'm sorry for how I treated you. I don't expect you to forgive me, but regardless, it's something I needed to say."

Nelson watched him for a long moment. Though Wallace wanted to look away, he didn't. Eventually, Nelson said, "Okay. I appreciate that. Mei's right. She usually is, but with this, she hit the nail on the head. And if there's hope for you, the same could be said about Alan."

"I don't know if it'll be enough," he admitted.

"Perhaps. But maybe it will be. Hugo will do the best he can. That's all anyone can ask for. I'm glad you're here, though. And I know I'm not the only one."

Wallace glanced at Hugo. He was handing a customer a mug filled with tea, that same fixed smile on his face.

But he seemed to only have eyes for Wallace.

The rest of the day was quieter than it'd begun. Alan stayed by the window, ignoring everyone else. His shoulders were stiff, and every now and then, he'd reach up and touch his stomach or his chest or his throat. Wallace wondered if there was a sort of phantom pain there. He hoped not. He couldn't imagine how that would feel.

When the last customer had left for the day, Hugo closed the door behind them, switching the sign in the window from OPEN to CLOSED. Mei was cleaning in the kitchen, her terrible music blasting loudly.

"Wallace," Hugo said. "Can I talk to you for a second?"

Wallace looked warily at Alan, still standing by the window.

"It's fine," Nelson said. "I can handle him if need be. I may look old, but I can kick ass and take names with the best of them."

Wallace believed him.

He followed Hugo down the hall toward the back door. He thought they were going out to the deck like they did most nights, but Hugo stopped near the end of the hall. He leaned against the wall, rubbing his hands over his face. His bandana—bright orange today—sat askew on his head. Wallace wished he could fix it for him. He suddenly found himself wishing for many impossible things.

Hugo spoke first. "It's going to be a little different for the next few days." He sounded apologetic.

"What do you mean?"

"Alan. I need to help him. Get him to try to talk, if I can." He sighed. "Which means we won't be able to talk like we normally do at night, unless we can do it after—"

"Oh, hey, no," Wallace said, even as a little flicker of jealousy flared within him. "I get it. He's . . . You have to do what you do. Don't worry about me. I know what's important here."

Hugo looked frustrated. "You are. Just as much as he is."

Wallace blinked. "Thank you?"

Hugo nodded furiously, looking down at the floor between them. "I don't want you thinking you're not. I . . . like it when we talk. It's one of my favorite parts of the day."

"Oh," Wallace said. His face felt warm. He cleared his throat. "I, uh. I like it when we talk too."

"You do?"

"Yeah."

"Good."

"Good," Wallace said. He didn't know what else to say.

Hugo gnawed on his bottom lip. "I act like I know what I'm doing. And I like to think I'm good at it, even when I'm out of my depth. It's . . . different. Each person is different. It's difficult, but death always will be. Sometimes we get people like you, and other times . . ."

"You get an Alan."

"Yeah," he said, sounding relieved. "And I have to work harder at it, but it's worth it if I can get through to them. I don't want anyone who comes here to turn around and do what Cameron did. To think that there's no hope. That they have nothing left."

"He's . . ." What? Wallace wasn't sure what he was trying to say. It felt too big. He pushed through it to the truth. "He took his own life."

Hugo blinked. "What? How did you know that?"

They hadn't had time to talk about what'd happened in the tea garden. All that he'd seen. All that he'd felt. All that Cameron had shown him. "I saw it when Cameron touched me. These stars, these pieces of him. Flashes. Memories. I felt his happiness and his sorrow and everything in between. And there was part of him that knew I could see it."

Hugo sagged against the wall as if his legs had given out. "Oh god. That's not . . . the Manager said . . ." He hung his head. "He . . . lied to me?"

"I don't know," Wallace said quickly. "I don't know why he said the things he did to you, but . . ." He struggled to find the right words. "But what if they're not as gone as you think? What if part of them still exists?"

"Then that would mean—I don't know what that would mean." Hugo lifted his head, eyes sad, mouth tugging down. "I tried so damn hard to get through to him, to make him see that he wasn't defined by his ending. That even though he saw no other choice, it was over now, and he couldn't be hurt again."

"He lost someone," Wallace whispered. The sunshine man.

"I know. And no matter what I said, I couldn't convince him that they'd find each other again." He looked toward the door that led to the garden.

"Has anyone ever come back from being a Husk?"

Hugo shook his head. "Not that I've heard. They're rare." His mouth took on a bitter twist. "At least that's what the Manager told me."

"Okay," Wallace said. "But even if that's the case, why aren't there hundreds of them? Thousands? He can't be the first. Why didn't I see any in the city after I died?"

"I don't know," Hugo said. "The Manager said that . . . it doesn't matter what he said, not now. Not if . . . *Wallace.* Do you know what this means?" He pushed himself off the wall.

"Uh. No?"

"I need to think about this. I can't . . . my head is too full right now. But thank you."

"For what?"

"Being who you are."

"It's not much," Wallace said, suddenly uncomfortable. "I wasn't that great to begin with, as you know."

Hugo looked like he was going to argue. Instead, he called for Mei.

The music briefly grew louder as she came through the doors, hurrying down the hall. "What? What is it? Are we under attack? Whose ass do I need to kick?"

And without looking away from Wallace, Hugo said, "I need you to do me a favor."

She glanced between them curiously. "Okay. What?"

"I need you to hug Wallace for me."

Wallace spluttered.

"Wow," Mei said. "I'm so glad I ran out here for this." She tapped her fingers against her palm. A little light burst before fading as quickly as it'd come. "Any specific reason?"

"Because I can't do it," Hugo said. "And I want to."

Mei hesitated, but only for a moment. And then Wallace stumbled against the wall as she latched onto him, arms around his waist, her head lying on his chest.

"Hug me back," she demanded. "It's weird if you don't. What the boss man wants, the boss man gets."

"This is already weird," Wallace muttered, but did as she asked. It felt good, having this. More than he expected it to. It wasn't like it'd been after Desdemona. It was . . . more.

"This is from Hugo," she told him, unnecessarily.

"I know," he whispered.

Alan looked like he was going to argue. He scowled, arms crossed defensively, ire clear. But he seemed to be listening.

"He'll get through to him," Nelson said, watching his grandson and their new guest.

Wallace wasn't so sure. He believed in Hugo, but he didn't know what Alan would do in response. He wasn't quite on board with the idea of them going off alone, even if it was only to the backyard. "What if he doesn't?"

"Then he doesn't," Nelson said. "And though it will be through no fault of his own, he'll carry the guilt with him just as he's done for Cameron and Lea. Remember what I told you? Empathetic to a fault. That's our Hugo."

"She didn't come in today."

Nelson knew who he meant. "She'll be back. Nancy might take a day or three, but she always comes back."

"Will she come around?"

"I don't know. I'd like to think she will, but there's . . ." He coughed into the back of his hand. "There's something about losing a child that destroys a person."

Wallace felt like an idiot. Of course Nelson would understand. Hugo had lost his parents, which also meant Nelson had lost a child. Guilt tugged at him that he'd never thought to ask. "Which one?"

"My son," Nelson said. "A good man. Stubborn, but good. Such a serious little boy, but he learned to smile in his own time. Hugo's mother saw to that. They were two peas in a pod. I remember the first time he'd told us about her. He had stars in his eyes. I knew then he was lost to her, though I hadn't even met her. I needn't have worried. She was a marvelous woman, so filled with hope and joy. But above all else, she was patient and kind. And they took the better parts of themselves and put them into Hugo. I see them in him, always."

"I wish I could have met them," Wallace said, watching as Alan trailed after Hugo down the long hallway toward the back deck, Apollo already barking from outside.

"They would've liked you," Nelson said. "Would've given you shit, of course, but you'd have been in on the joke with them." He smiled to himself. "I can't wait to see them again, to hold my son's face in my hands and tell him how proud I am of him. We think we have time for such things, but there's never enough for all we should have said." His glance was sly. "You'd do well to remember that."

"I have no idea what you're talking about."

Nelson chuckled. "I bet you don't." He sobered. "Is there anything you would say to someone left behind if you could?"

"No one would listen."

Nelson shook his head slowly. "I don't believe that for a moment."

Alan came back inside first. He looked bewildered. Spooked. The tea shop seemed heavier with his presence, and smaller, as if the walls had started closing in. Wallace didn't know if that was him projecting, or if it was coming from Alan himself. Alan, who Wallace almost felt sorry for as he turned over another chair and set it up on the table. This whole empathy thing wasn't all it was cracked up to be.

Mei paused, broom in her hand. "All right?" she asked, looking at Alan.

Alan ignored her. He stared at Wallace, jaw dropped. Wallace didn't like it. "What?"

"The chair," Alan said. "How are you doing that?"

Wallace blinked. "Oh, uh. Practice, I guess? It's not as hard as it looks, once you get the hang of it. It just takes time to learn how to focus—"

"You need to show me how to do it."

That certainly didn't sound like a good idea. Visions of chaos filled Wallace's head, customers screaming as chairs were flung around them by an unseen hand. "It took a long time, probably longer than you'll—"

"I can learn," Alan insisted. "How hard can it be?"

Mei set the broom against the counter, glancing at them before heading down the hall to the back deck.

"Well," Wallace said. "I . . . don't exactly know how to start."

"I do," Nelson said from his chair. "Taught him everything he knows."

Alan wasn't impressed. "You? Really. *You.*"

"Really," Nelson said dryly. "But you don't have to take my word for it. In fact, you don't have to take any word at all with that attitude."

"I don't need you," Alan said. "Wallace here can show me. Isn't that right, Wallace?"

Wallace shook his head. "Nope. Nelson is the expert. If you want to know anything, you go through him."

"He's too old to—"

Nelson disappeared from his chair.

Alan choked on his tongue.

And then he was knocked off his feet when Nelson appeared behind him, sweeping his legs out from underneath him with his cane. Alan landed roughly on his back, the lights in the sconces flaring briefly.

"Not too old to show you a trick or three, you insolent child," Nelson said coolly. "And if you know what's good for you, you'll bite your tongue before I show you what I can *really* do." He turned back toward his chair, but not before he winked at a gobsmacked Wallace.

"No, wait," Alan said, pushing himself up off the floor as the shop settled around them. "I . . ." He ground his teeth together. "I'll listen."

Nelson eyed him critically. "I'll believe it when I see it. Your first task is to sit there without talking. If I hear so much as a peep from you before I tell you to speak again, I won't teach you a damn thing."

"But—"

"Stop. *Talking.*"

Alan snapped his mouth closed, though he looked furious about it.

"Go check on them," Nelson said to Wallace as he sat back down. "I'll handle things in here."

Wallace believed it. He knew how much the cane hurt.

He glanced back only once as he hurried down the hallway.

Alan hadn't moved.

Maybe he would listen after all.

"—and you don't need to take that kind of abuse," Mei was saying hotly as Wallace walked through the door into the cool evening air. "I don't care *who* he thinks he is, no one gets to talk to you that way. Screw that guy. Screw him right in his stupid face."

Hugo smiled wryly. "Thanks, Mei. Pointed as always."

"Just because he's angry and scared doesn't give him the right to be a dick. Tell him, Wallace."

"Yeah," Wallace said. "I'm probably not the best person, seeing as how I used to be a dick."

Mei snorted. "Used to be. That's real cute." Then, "Did you leave Nelson alone with him?"

He held up his hands. "I don't think you need to worry about that. Nelson already put him in his place. I'm more worried about Alan than anything else."

Hugo groaned. "What did Grandad do?"

"Like . . . ghost karate?"

Mei laughed. "Oh, man, and I *missed* it? I need to go see if he'll do it again. You've got this, Wallace, right?" She didn't wait for an answer. She stood on her tiptoes, kissing Hugo on the cheek before heading back inside. Wallace heard her shouting for Nelson before she closed the door.

"Pain in the ass," Hugo muttered.

Wallace walked toward him. "Who? Nelson or Mei?"

"Yes," Hugo said before yawning, his jaw cracking audibly.

"You should go to bed," Wallace said. "Get some rest. I think he'll be quieter tonight." If they were lucky, Nelson would convince him to keep his mouth shut for at least a few hours.

"I will. Just . . . needed to clear my head for a moment."

"How did it go?"

Hugo started to shrug but stopped halfway. "It went."

"That good, huh?"

"He's angry. I get it. I really do. And as much as I want to, I can't take that away from him. It's his. The best I can do is to make sure he knows he doesn't have to hold onto it forever."

Wallace was dubious at best. "You think he'll listen to you?"

"I hope so." Hugo smiled tiredly. "It's too soon to tell. But if it starts getting out of hand . . ." A complicated expression crossed his face. "Well, let's just say it's best to avoid that if possible."

"The Manager."

"Yeah."

"You don't like him."

Hugo looked off into the dark. "He isn't the type of being *to* be liked. As long as the job gets done, nothing else matters. I'm not exactly ambivalent, but . . ."

"He scares you," Wallace said, suddenly sure.

"He's a cosmic being overseeing death," Hugo said dryly. "Of course he scares me. He scares everyone. That's kind of the point."

"You still listened to him when he offered you a job."

Hugo shook his head. "That has nothing to do with it. I took the job because I *wanted* to. How could I not? Helping people when they need it most, when they think all is lost? Of course I'd agree to it."

"Like Jesus," Wallace said solemnly. "Got that savior complex down pat."

Hugo burst out laughing. "Yeah, yeah. Point taken, Wallace." He sobered slightly. "And then there's the fact that he might be a liar given what he's said about the Husks, and that scares me even more. It makes me wonder what else he's kept from me."

"Make any headway with that?"

"Not yet. I'm still thinking. I'll get there. Just not yet."

They fell quiet, leaning against the railing.

"I think he'll listen," Hugo said finally. "Alan. I need to be careful with him. He's fragile right now. But I know I can get through to him. He just needs time to work through it. And once he's better and I can show him how to cross, we can go back to normal." He reached out for Wallace, only to stop himself and curl his fingers.

"Yeah," Wallace said. "Normal."

"That's not . . . I keep forgetting." His brow furrowed above a pinched expression as he breathed heavily through his nose. "That you're . . ."

"I know," Wallace said.

Hugo's face crumpled. "I'm losing focus. I keep thinking you're . . ." He shook his head. He started for the door, whistling for Apollo who barked from the tea garden.

And before he could walk through the open door, Wallace said, "Hugo."

He stopped but didn't turn around.

Wallace looked up at the stars.

Is there anything you would say to someone left behind if you could?

He said, "If things were different, if I were me, and you were you . . . do you think you'd ever see me as someone you could . . ."

He didn't think Hugo was going to answer. He'd walk through the door without a word, leaving Wallace alone and feeling foolish.

He didn't.

He said, "Yes." And then he went inside.

Wallace stared after him, burning like the sun.

CHAPTER 16

"Are you sure about this?" Wallace muttered, eyeing Alan warily. It was the third day with their new guest, and Wallace still wasn't sure what to make of him. Ever since Nelson had laid him out on his back, he'd . . . well, not *changed,* not exactly. He'd taken to watching their every movement, and though he didn't ask many questions, Wallace had the feeling he was taking it all in, not quite a cornered animal waiting to strike, but close. It certainly didn't help that he never looked away from Wallace when he started taking down the chairs each morning, getting the tea shop ready for yet another day. Every time Wallace grabbed hold of a different chair, he could feel Alan's gaze on him. It made his skin crawl.

"I can't imagine what it's like for him," Nelson said, voice low in case Alan was trying to listen in. "I know he's a little rough around the edges—"

"It's okay to be hyperbolic. Really. I swear. Don't hold back."

"—but murder victims have a harder time understanding that the life they knew is over." Nelson shook his head. "He died not because of his own choice, or because his body gave out on him, but because someone else took his life from him. It's a violation. We have to tread carefully, Hugo more than the rest of us."

Wallace was uneasy as he set down the last chair, hearing Mei singing in the kitchen at the top of her lungs. He glanced through the porthole windows and caught a glimpse of Hugo moving back and forth. They hadn't had the chance to talk more since their last night on the deck, though Wallace wasn't sure what more could be said. Hugo needed to put his focus on Alan, and Wallace was dead. Nothing was going to change that. It was ridiculous to think otherwise, or so that's what Wallace told himself. Declarations were meaningless in the face of life and death.

Wallace had never been a fan of the *what if.*

The problem with that was Wallace was also a liar, because it was getting harder to think of anything *but* the what if.

And it was dangerous, this. Because Wallace had been sitting in front of the fire the night before, barely listening as Nelson spoke with Alan, telling him that before he could even think of doing what he and Wallace could do, he needed to clear his head, he needed to *focus.* Wallace was far, far away. It was a sunny day. He found himself in a tiny little town. He was lost. He needed to stop and ask for directions. He found a curious little sign next to a dirt road advertising CHARON'S CROSSING TEA AND TREATS. He turned down the road. Sometimes he was in a car. Other times he was walking. Regardless, his destination never changed. He reached the house at the end of the dirt road, marveling at how such a thing could exist without collapsing. He walked in through the door.

And there, standing behind the counter, was a man with a bright bandana around his head, a quiet smile on his face.

What happened next varied, though the beating heart of it was the same. Sometimes, the man behind the counter would smile at him and say, "Hello. I've been waiting for you. My name is Hugo, what's yours?" Other times, Hugo would already know his name (how, it didn't matter; little dreams like these didn't need logic), and he'd say, "Wallace, I'm so happy you're here. You look like you could use some peppermint tea."

"Yes," Wallace would reply. "That sounds wonderful. Thank you."

And Hugo poured him a cup and then one for himself. They took it to the back deck, leaning against the railing. There were versions of this fantasy where they didn't speak at all. They sipped their tea and just . . . existed near each other.

There were other versions, though.

Hugo would say, "How long are you staying?"

And Wallace would reply, "I don't know. I haven't really thought about it. I don't even know how I got here. I was lost. Isn't that funny?"

"It is." Hugo glanced at him, smiling quietly. "Maybe it's fate. Maybe this is where you're supposed to be."

Wallace would never know what to say to this version of him, this Hugo who didn't have the weight of death on his shoulders, and a Wallace who had blood flowing through his veins. His face would grow warm, and he'd look down at his tea, muttering under his breath that he didn't really believe in fate.

Hugo laughed. "That's okay. I'll believe in it enough for the both of us. Drink your tea before it gets cold."

He startled when Nelson snapped his fingers inches from his face. "What?"

Nelson looked amused. "Where'd you go?"

"Nowhere," Wallace said, face hot.

"Oh boy," Nelson said. "Something on your mind you'd care to discuss?"

"I have no idea what you're talking about."

Nelson sighed. "I don't know what's worse. Whether you believe that or you don't and said it anyway."

"It doesn't matter."

Nelson smiled sadly. "No, I don't suppose it does."

The day went on as it always did, even if the tea shop felt a little more charged than normal. It wasn't as if Alan were threatening any of them. He wasn't. In fact, he barely spoke at all. He wandered around the tea shop as he had the day before, listening in on conversations, studying the customers. There were times he'd bend over in front of them, the tip of his nose inches from their own. No one knew anything was amiss, and rather than growing angrier, Alan looked delighted, and not in a way that seemed to be terrifying or menacing. It was an almost childlike glee, his smile appearing genuine for the first time since he'd arrived at the tea shop. Wallace could see the man he might have been before his decisions led him into that alley.

"It's like when I was a kid," Alan told Nelson. "You know when you think about wanting to be a superhero? Like lasers from your eyes, or the ability to fly. I always wanted the power to turn invisible."

"Why?" Nelson asked.

Alan shrugged. "Because if people can't see you, they don't know what you're doing and you can get away with anything."

And on the third day after Alan's arrival, Nancy came back to Charon's Crossing.

She walked through the door as she always did, mouth tight, the circles under her eyes like bruises. She went to her usual table and sat without speaking to anyone, though a few of the customers in the tea shop nodded at her.

Hugo went back into the kitchen, and before the doors had a chance to stop swinging, they opened again as Mei came out, standing at the register.

"Poor dear," Nelson murmured from his chair. "Still not sleeping. I don't know how much longer she can stand it. I wish there were more we could do for her."

"So long as it has nothing to do with Desdemona," Wallace said. "I can't believe she—"

"Who's that?"

They turned to look at Alan. He stood in the middle of the tea shop next to a table filled with people around his age. He'd been circling them since they'd arrived. He was stopped now, gaze trained on the table near the window and the woman who sat there.

He started to take a step toward her. Wallace moved even before he realized it. Alan blinked when Wallace appeared in front of him, a hand pressed against his chest. He looked down, frowning, and Wallace pulled his hand back. "What are you doing?"

"Leave her alone," Wallace said stiffly. "I don't care about what you do to anyone else here, but you stay away from her."

Alan's eyes narrowed. "Why?" He glanced over Wallace's shoulder before looking back at him. "It's not like she can see me. Who gives a shit?" He started to move around Wallace but stopped when Wallace gripped his wrist.

"She's off-limits."

Alan jerked his arm away. "You can feel it, can't you? She's like . . . a beacon. She's on fire. I can taste it. What's wrong with her?"

Wallace almost snapped that it didn't concern him. He course-corrected at the last moment, even though the idea of playing to Alan's humanity seemed so farcical it was ludicrous. "She's grieving. Lost her daughter to illness. It was . . . bad. The details don't matter. She comes here because she doesn't know where else to go. Hugo sits with her, and we leave them alone."

He was pleasantly surprised when Alan nodded slowly. "She's lost."

"Yes," Wallace said. "And whether or not she'll find her way isn't up to us. I don't give a crap who else you go near, but leave Nancy alone. Even if none of them can hear us, you don't want to run the risk of making things worse for her."

"Worse," Alan repeated. "You think *I'm* the one who could make things worse." He cocked his head. "Has Hugo told her about all of this? Is that why she comes here, because she knows Hugo helped her daughter cross?"

"No," Wallace said. "He hasn't. He's not allowed. It's part of being a ferryman."

"But he *did* help her girl cross," Alan said. "And somehow, part of her knows that, otherwise she wouldn't be here. What does that make Hugo if he's lying to her? And if part of her *does* know, that means she isn't like everyone else. Maybe she can see us. Maybe she can see *me*."

Wallace stepped in front of Alan again as he tried to move by. "She can't. And even if she could, you don't get to put her through that. I don't know what it's like to be you. I'll never understand what happened to you, or what it must have felt like. But you don't get to use her to try to make yourself feel better."

Alan opened his mouth to retort but stopped when Hugo walked through the kitchen doors. The din of the tea shop went on around them, but Hugo was staring at Wallace and Alan, a tea tray in his hands. Mei stood on her tiptoes and whispered something in his ear. He didn't react. She glanced at them, and if Wallace didn't know her, he'd have thought nothing of her blank expression. But he *did* know her, and she wasn't happy.

Hugo walked around the counter, fixing a smile on his face. He nodded at everyone who greeted him. As he passed Wallace and Alan, he spoke from the corner of his mouth. "Please stay away from her."

He continued on without stopping.

Nancy stared out the window as Hugo set the tea tray down on the table. She didn't react as he poured the tea into the cup. He set the cup in front of her before taking his seat opposite her, folding his hands on the table as he always did.

Alan watched them, waiting.

When nothing happened, he asked, "What's he doing?"

"Being there for her," Wallace said, wishing Alan would let it go. "Waiting for her to be ready to talk. Sometimes the best way to help someone is not to say anything at all."

"Bullshit," Alan muttered. He crossed his arms and glared at Hugo. "Did he screw up or something? He's got guilt written all over him. What'd he do?"

"If he wants to tell you, he will. Leave it alone."

And wonder of all wonders, Alan seemed to listen in his own way. He threw up his hands before stalking to the opposite side of the room toward a table where a small group of women sat.

Wallace sighed in relief as he looked back at Mei.

She nodded at him before rolling her eyes.

"Right," he said. "Kids these days."

She coughed into her hand, but he could see the curve of her smile.

And that should have been it. That should've been the end of it.

Nancy sitting there, not speaking. Hugo waiting, never pushing. The teacup in front of her, unacknowledged. After an hour (or maybe two), she'd stand, chair scraping against the floor, Hugo telling her he'd be there, always, whenever she was ready.

And then she'd leave. Perhaps she'd come back tomorrow and the next day and the next day, or perhaps she'd be missing for a day or two.

Nancy sat in her chair. Hugo sat across from her. After an hour, she stood.

Hugo said, "I'll be here. Always. Whenever you're ready, I'll be here."

She moved toward the door.

The end.

Except Alan shouted, "*Nancy!*"

The light bulbs in the sconces flared. Nancy stopped, her hand on the doorknob.

"*Nancy!*" Alan shouted again, stunning Wallace into immobility.

Nancy turned toward the sound of his voice as she frowned.

Alan jumped up and down in the center of the tea shop, waving his warms wildly, screaming her name over and over again. The tables on either side of him shifted as if someone had bumped into them, sloshing tea and knocking muffins over.

"What the hell?" a man asked, staring down at the table. "Did you feel that?"

"Yeah," his companion, a young woman with pink bubblegum lip gloss, said. "It shook, right? Almost like—"

The tables jumped again as Alan took a step toward Nancy.

Nancy, whose grip tightened on the doorknob until her knuckles turned white. "Who's there?" she asked, voice carrying, causing everyone to turn and look at her.

"Yeah," Alan panted. "Yes. I'm here. Oh my god, I'm *here*. Listen to me, you need to—"

Wallace didn't think.

One moment, he was a tea plant, unmoving. The next, he stood in front of Alan again, hand over his mouth, teeth scraping against his palm. "Stop it," he hissed.

Alan struggled against him, trying to shove him away. But Wallace was bigger than he was, and though he was rail thin, he held firm. Alan's eyes blazed in fury above Wallace's hand.

"Are you okay, sweetheart?" a woman asked Nancy, turning in her chair to look up at her.

Nancy didn't so much as glance at her. She continued to stare in Wallace and Alan's direction, but if she saw them, she didn't react. She opened her mouth as if to speak again, but shook her head before walking through the door, slamming it behind her.

Alan screamed into the hand covering his mouth before shoving Wallace as hard as he could. Wallace stumbled back, hitting a chair behind him. The man sitting in the chair looked around wildly as the legs scraped along the floor.

"She heard me," Alan snarled. "She *heard* me. She can—" He never finished. He hurried toward the door.

Hugo said, "If you walk out that door, you'll lose yourself. And I don't know how to bring you back."

Alan stopped, chest heaving.

Silence filled the nooks and crannies of Charon's Crossing. Everyone turned slowly to look at Hugo. Nelson groaned, face in his hands as Apollo growled at Alan.

"Right!" Mei said brightly. "Because if you haven't finished your cup of tea before you leave, you'll spend the rest of your day fretting over what you've lost. And we don't know how to bring it back, because reheated tea is the *worst*. Isn't that right, Hugo?"

Hugo didn't respond. He stared at Alan, unblinking.

"For the love of all that's holy, listen to him," Nelson said irritably. "I know you don't have a lick of common sense, but don't be an idiot. You've been told what will happen to you if you leave. You want that? Fine. Go. But don't expect any of us to come running to save you if you do."

Alan's shoulders were a rigid line. His throat worked as he swallowed, eyes wet and lost. "She could hear me," he whispered.

"Oh, look!" Mei said loudly. "I just realized today is National Free Tea and Scone Day. We need to celebrate. If anyone wants a free cup of tea or a scone, come up here and I'll hook you up."

Most everyone moved toward the counter, chairs scraping along the floor. After all, it was either continue to stare at the odd owner of Charon's Crossing, or get something for free. It seemed to be an easy choice.

Eventually, Alan stood down, though Wallace could still feel the anger and desperation emanating from him. He turned away and went to the far corner of the tea shop, leaning his forehead against the wall as he shook.

"Leave him be," Nelson said quietly. "I think he's learning what this all means. Give him time. He'll come around. I just know it."

Nelson was wrong.

The rest of the day went by in a blur.

Alan didn't move from the corner. He didn't speak. Wallace left him alone.

Mei stood behind the register, arms folded, watching, always watching. She smiled whenever someone came up to the counter to place their order, but it was forced, thin.

Nelson stayed in his chair, cane across his lap, eyes closed, head tilted back.

Hugo had disappeared into the kitchen, Apollo trailing after him, whining lowly. Wallace wanted to follow after them but found himself frozen in place, his thoughts racing.

She heard me. She heard *me.* That was what Alan had said.

And he'd been right. Wallace had seen it with his own eyes.

He didn't know what to do with that information, if anything at all.

Did it even matter?

He hated how much he focused on it, how *hopeful* it almost made him feel. Mei had told him Nancy was a bit like her, though nowhere near as strong. He didn't know if it had to do with the passing of her daughter—her grief manifesting itself into something extraordinary—or if she'd always been this way. Some dark part of him wondered if he could use that, somehow, use it to be seen and heard and—

He cut himself off, horrified.

No.

He wasn't . . . he could never do something like that. He wasn't like Alan. Not anymore.

Right?

He turned toward the kitchen.

Mei watched every step he took while ringing up a young couple, their faces flushed as the man smiled at his lady friend. "It's our second date," the man said, and he sounded so *awed* by it.

"Our third," the woman said, bumping his shoulder. "That time at the grocery store counted."

"Oh," the man said, and he smiled. "Our third, then."

Wallace walked through the double doors to an empty kitchen.

He frowned. Where had they gone? He hadn't heard the scooter start up, so he didn't think Hugo had left, and it wasn't as if Apollo could follow him even if he did. They had to be around here somewhere.

Wallace went to the door, looking out onto the back deck. The spring air still had a bite to it, though the tea plants and forest behind the shop were more vibrant than they'd ever been since Wallace arrived. What did this place look like in the throes of summer? Green, he expected, so green that he'd be able to taste it, something he hadn't known until this moment that he desperately wanted to see. The world outside Charon's Crossing marched ever on.

There, sitting against the railing, was Hugo.

Apollo sat at his feet, paws folded over each other. His ears were perked and twitching, head raised as he blinked slowly at Hugo.

Hugo, who looked slick with sweat, his breathing ragged.

Alarmed, Wallace hurried through the door.

Hugo didn't open his eyes as Wallace approached slowly, keeping his distance. He looked as if he was trying to get himself under control, breathing in through his nose and out his mouth. His bandana—purple today, with little yellow stars—sat crooked on his head.

Apollo turned his head, looking at Wallace. He whined again.

"It's all right," Wallace told him. "Everything is fine."

He kept his distance, stopping in the middle of the deck. He left the chairs alone, deciding to sit where he stood.

He waited.

It took a long time, but Wallace didn't push. He wouldn't. Not when Hugo was like this. It wouldn't help. So he sat there, head bowed, tapping his finger on the boards beneath him, a tiny sound to let Hugo know he was there. Tap. Tap. Tap. Quiet, soft, but a connection, a reminder. Tap, tap, tap. *You're not alone. I'm here. Breathe. Breathe.* He knew what this was. He'd seen it before.

Hugo sucked in ragged breaths, his chest heaving, face scrunched up, eyes unfocused, dazed. And Wallace didn't move, didn't try to talk to him. He kept on tapping on the deck, keeping the beat, like a metronome.

Wallace must have tapped his finger a hundred times before Hugo spoke. "I'm fine," he said, voice hoarse.

"Okay," Wallace said easily. "But it's all right if you're not, too." He hesitated. "Panic attacks are no joke."

Hugo opened his eyes, glassy and wet. He rubbed a hand over his face, groaning quietly. "That's an understatement. How did you know to . . ." He waved his hand at Wallace and the distance between them.

"Naomi had them when she was younger."

"Your wife?"

"Ex-wife," Wallace said automatically. "She . . . I didn't understand them, or what could trigger them. She explained it to me, but I don't know that I listened very well. They were few and far between, but when they hit, they were savage. I tried to help her, tried to tell her just to breathe through it, and she . . ." He shook his head. "She told me that it was as if a dozen hands were clawing at her, choking her. Squeezing her lungs. They were irrational, she said. Chaotic. Like her body was fighting her. And yet I still thought she could power through them if she really wanted to."

"If only that's how it worked."

"I know," Wallace said simply. Then, "Apollo helps."

Apollo thumped his tail at the sound of his name.

"He does," Hugo said. He looked exhausted. "Even though he flunked out of the service dog training, he still knows. It was worse for me, after . . . well. After everything. I didn't know how to stop them. I didn't know how to fight them. I couldn't even find the words to explain what they felt like. Chaotic is pretty close, I think. Anxiety is . . . a betrayal, my brain and body working against me." He smiled weakly. "Apollo's a good boy. He knows just what to do."

"I can go back inside," Wallace said. "If you want to be left alone. Some do, but Naomi liked having me near. Not touching her, but near so she knew she wasn't alone. I'd tap against the wall or the floor, just to let her know I was still there without speaking. It seemed to help her, so I took a chance it'd be the same with you."

"I appreciate that." Hugo closed his eyes again. "It's hard."

"What?"

Hugo shrugged. "This. Everything."

"That's . . ."

"Vague?"

"I was going to say all-encompassing."

Hugo snorted. "I suppose."

"I didn't know that it affected you this much," Wallace admitted.

"It's death, Wallace. Of course it does."

"No, I know. I didn't mean it like that." He paused, considering. "I guess I thought you were used to it."

Hugo opened his eyes again. They were clearer than they'd been before. "I don't know that I ever will be." He grunted as he shifted to a more comfortable position. "I don't want it to affect me as it does, but I can't always stop it. I know what I'm supposed to be doing, I know my job is important. But what I want and what my body does are sometimes two different things."

"You're human," Wallace whispered.

"I am," Hugo agreed. "And everything that comes with it. Just because I'm a ferryman doesn't mean all the other parts of me won't still be there, warts and all." Then, "What do you want?"

Wallace blinked. "To make sure you're—"

Hugo shook his head. "Not that. What do you want, Wallace? Out of your time here. Out of me. This place."

"I . . . don't know?" His own words confused him. There were many, many things he wanted, but each sounded more trivial than the last. And that was the rub, wasn't it? A life built upon inconsequential things made important simply because he desired them to be.

Hugo didn't look disappointed. If anything, Wallace's answer seemed to calm him further. "It's okay not to know. In a way, it makes things easier."

"How?"

Hugo settled his hands into his lap. Apollo lowered his snout to his paws, though he kept his gaze trained on Hugo, blinking slowly, tail curled around his haunches. "Because it's harder to convince someone of what they need versus what they want. We often ignore the truth because we don't like what it shows us."

"Alan."

"I'm trying," Hugo said. "I really am. But I don't know if I'm getting through to him. It's only been a few days, but he feels further away than he did when he first arrived." His mouth twisted down. "It's like Cameron all over again, only worse because there's no one trying to undermine my work."

Wallace startled. "They're not your fault."

"Aren't they? They came to me because I'm the one who's supposed to help them. But no matter what I say, no matter what I do, they can't listen. And I don't blame them for that. It's like a panic attack. I can try to explain it to you, but unless you've ever had one yourself, you'll never understand just how harsh they can be. And though I'm surrounded by death, I can never understand what it does to a person because I've never died."

"You're better than most," Wallace said.

Hugo squinted at him. "Another compliment, Wallace?"

"Yes," Wallace said, picking at the frayed ends of his jeans.

"Ah. Thank you."

"I could never be you."

"Of course not," Hugo said. "Because you're you, and that's who you're supposed to be."

"That's not what I meant. You do what you do, and I can't even begin to imagine the toll it takes. This gift you have . . . it's beyond me. I don't think I could ever be strong enough to be a ferryman."

"You underestimate yourself."

"Or I know my limits," Wallace countered. "What I'm capable of, even if I should've second-guessed some of the decisions I made." He paused. "Okay, maybe a lot of the decisions I made."

Hugo knocked his head back against the railing softly. "But isn't that life? We second-guess everything because it's in our nature. People with anxiety and depression just tend to do it more."

"Maybe that's Alan," Wallace said. "I won't pretend I get everything about him. I don't. But the world he knows is gone. Everything has changed. He'll see you for what you are, eventually. It just takes time."

"How do you know that?"

"Because I have faith in you," Wallace said, feeling brittle and exposed. "And all that you are. There's no one like you. I don't know if I would have made it this far without you. I don't even want to think what it would have been like with another ferryman. Or woman. Ferryperson?"

Hugo laughed, looking surprised as he did so. "You have faith in me."

Wallace nodded as he waved his hand awkwardly. "If this is a way station, if this is just one stop on a journey, you're the better part of it." He was silent for a moment. Then, "Hugo?"

"Yeah?"

"I wish for things too."

"Like what?"

Honesty was a weapon. It could be used to stab and tear and spill blood upon the earth. Wallace knew that; he had his fair share of blood on his hands because of it. But it was different, now. He was using it upon himself, and he was flayed open because of it, nerve endings exposed.

And perhaps that's why he said, "I wish I'd found you before. Not someone like you. But you."

Hugo inhaled sharply. For a moment, Wallace thought he'd crossed a line, but then Hugo said, "I wish that too."

"It's dumb, right?"

"No, I don't think it is."

"What do we do now?"

"I don't know," Hugo said. "Whatever we can, I guess."

"Make the most of the time we have left," Wallace whispered.

And Hugo said, "That's all anyone can ask of us."

The sun drifted slowly across the sky.

The last customer left for the day with a jaunty wave. Mei was back in the kitchen, Nelson in his chair. Apollo stayed close to Hugo, as if wanting to make sure he didn't relapse. Alan still stood in the corner, shoulders hunched up around his ears. They'd left him alone, but Wallace knew it couldn't last, especially when Nancy came back. They needed to make him understand that she was off-limits. Wallace wasn't looking forward to it.

Hugo flipped the sign in the window.

He was about to lock the door when he froze.

"Oh no," he breathed. "Not now."

"What is it?" Nelson asked. "Don't tell me we've got another guest coming. It's getting a little crowded as is." He glared at Alan.

"It's not that," Hugo said tightly.

In the distance, Wallace heard the rumble of a car engine coming down the road. He went to a window. Headlights were approaching. "Who is it?"

"The health inspector," Hugo said.

Nelson suddenly popped into existence next to Wallace, who yelped. Nelson ignored him, peering out the window. "*Again?* But he was just here a couple of months ago. I swear, that man has it out for you, Hugo. Quick! Turn off all the lights and lock the door. Maybe he'll go away."

Hugo sighed. "You know I can't do that. He'd just come back tomorrow and be in a worse mood." He glanced at Nelson. "Leave him alone this time."

"I have no idea what you're talking about."

"Grandad."

"Fine," Nelson said irritably. "I'll be on my best behavior." He lowered his voice so only Wallace could hear. "But mark my words, if he tries anything, I'm going to shove his pen up his ass."

Wallace grimaced. "You can do that?"

"Damn right I can. And he'd deserve it too. Prepare to meet the biggest waste of space you've ever met in your life."

"I know hundreds of attorneys."

Nelson rolled his eyes. "He's worse."

Wallace wasn't sure who he was expecting to climb out of the little car, but who he saw certainly wasn't it. The man was younger, around Hugo's age. He was coldly handsome, though his handlebar mustache made Wallace want to punch him in the face. He wore a smart suit—one Wallace might have worn when he was still alive, expensive, cut perfectly to his frame, the plaid tie completing the look—and a terrible sneer. Wallace watched as he reached back into his car, pulling out a clipboard. He took a fountain pen from the inner pocket of his suit jacket, pressing the tip against his tongue before he started scribbling notes.

"What's he writing?" Wallace asked.

"Who the hell knows," Nelson said. "Probably something bad. He's always looking for every little thing he can find to use against Hugo. He once tried to say that we had rats in the walls. Can you imagine? *Rats*. Odious man."

"And whose fault was that?" Hugo asked, stepping back from the door without locking it.

"Mine," Nelson said easily. "But I was trying to scare him, not make him think we had rodents." He raised his voice. "Mei! *Mei*. We've got company."

Mei burst through the door, a pot covered in dish soap in one hand and a butcher knife in the other. "Who? Are we under attack?"

"Yes," Nelson said.

"*No*," Hugo said loudly. "We're not. Health inspector."

Mei gasped. "Again? We *are* under attack. Lock the door! Maybe he'll think we're gone!" She waved the knife around until she glanced at Alan, who was eyeing her warily. She quickly hid it behind her. "I don't have a knife. You were seeing things."

"You're dripping water on the floor," Hugo told her. "Which he'll hold against us."

Mei growled as she spun around and hurried back into the kitchen. "Hold him off as much as you can. I'll make sure everything is good in here before he comes in."

"Shouldn't it be already?" Wallace asked.

"Of course it is," Nelson said as the health inspector pulled on a bit of peeling paint along the railing to the stairs. "But he won't see it that way. You should have seen the look on his face when he came here for the first time. I thought he was going to have a heart attack when he saw Apollo." He glanced at Wallace. "Is that still too soon or . . . ?"

Wallace glared at him. "You're not funny."

"I really am."

Wallace looked back out the window. "I don't see what's so bad. Surely he just wants to make sure the tea shop is clean, right? Why would he have it out for Hugo?" A terrible thought crossed his mind. "Jesus Christ, is it because he's Black? Of all the—"

"Oh, no," Nelson said. "Nothing as loathsome as that." He leaned forward, dropping his voice. "He asked Hugo out on a date once. Hugo said no. He wasn't happy about it and has been torturing us all ever since."

The skin under Wallace's right eye twitched. "What?"

Nelson patted his shoulder. "I knew you'd see it my way."

"Mei!" Wallace shouted. "Bring back the knife!"

Mei burst through the doors again, now carrying a knife in each hand.

"No knives!" Hugo barked.

She turned around and stalked back into the kitchen.

The door to Charon's Crossing Tea and Treats opened.

"Hmm," the health inspector said with a grimace as he looked around. "Not off to the best start, are we, Hugo?" He sounded as if he were affecting the most atrocious British accent the world had ever heard. Wallace despised him immediately, telling himself it had nothing to do with the fact that this man apparently wanted to climb Hugo like a tree. Even though this man couldn't see him, Wallace would remain the consummate professional.

"Harvey," Hugo said evenly.

"Harvey?" Wallace exclaimed. "His name is *Harvey*? That's ridiculous!"

Hugo coughed roughly.

Harvey stared at him.

Hugo held up his hand. "Sorry. Something in my throat."

"I can see that," Harvey said. "Probably all the dust that seems to coat this place. I do hope you've made a better attempt to keep things cleaner this time around." He sniffed daintily. "At least we don't have to worry about that mutt any longer. Pet dander around all that food? Bloody bollocks if you ask me."

Apollo barked angrily, spittle flying from his lips and landing on the floor.

"He's from Seattle," Nelson whispered. "Went to London once a few years ago and came back talking like that. No one knows why."

"Because he's ludicrous," Wallace said. "Obviously."

Hugo held himself together, insults about his dog notwithstanding. "I'm sure you'll find that everything is as it should be, just like it was when you were here in February. Speaking of, what brings you back so soon?"

Harvey scribbled furiously on his clipboard. "I'm a health inspector. I'm inspecting. And I'll be the judge of whether everything is as it should be. It's the point of surprise inspections. Doesn't allow you to cover up any . . . violations." He moved toward the display cases, unaware of the three ghosts (and one ghost dog) watching him with various shades of animosity. Wallace wasn't sure why Alan looked so aggravated, unless that was his default setting.

Harvey stopped in front of the display cases, bending over to peer into them. They were immaculate as always, the lights soft and warm on the remaining pastries left over from the day, few though they were. "Mei in the kitchen, I suppose? Tell her to cease all activities immediately. I'd hate to think she's covering up any crimes against humanity as she's wont to do."

Mei appeared in one of the portholes, a look of utter fury on her face. "Crimes? *Crimes?* Come in here and say that to my face, you—"

"She's doing what she normally does at the end of the day," Hugo said mildly. "As you well know."

"I'm sure she is," Harvey muttered. He stood upright, once again putting his pen to this clipboard. "I'm not the enemy here, Hugo. I'd never want to see this place shut down. I fear what it would do to Mei if she were forced onto the streets if I had to shut down your tea shop. She's rather . . . delicate."

Hugo stepped in front of the double doors in time to block Mei from bursting through them. He grunted when the doors struck his back, but otherwise didn't react.

Harvey arched an eyebrow.

Hugo shrugged. "She's exuberant today."

"Exuberant? I'll show *you* exuberant, you—"

Harvey sighed loudly. "Temper, temper. Though I may be a health inspector, I like to think the position allows me to comment on mental health as well. Hers appears to be in dire straits. I would suggest she get that seen to posthaste."

"How has he not been punched in the face?" Wallace demanded.

"Hugo said we can't," Nelson said.

"That's exactly right," Hugo said evenly.

"It is?" Harvey said, sounding taken aback. "Why thank you, Hugo. I do believe that's the first time you've ever agreed with me." He smiled, and Wallace felt his skin crawl. "It looks good on you." He sauntered up to the counter. "As would I."

"Oh my god," Wallace said loudly. "Does that actually work on anyone? Hugo, kick him in the nuts."

"I don't know if I can do that," Hugo said, never looking away from Harvey.

"Why not?" Harvey and Wallace asked at the same time.

"You know why," Hugo said.

Harvey sighed as Wallace threw up his hands in frustration. "I'll wear you down yet," Harvey said. "Just you wait and see. Now, back to the business at hand. I need to stick my thermometer in many things." He waggled his eyebrows.

"Wow," Wallace said. "That's sexual harassment. We're going to sue him. We're going to sue him for everything he's worth, just you wait and see. I'll draft up the papers just as soon as—oh. Right. I'm dead. Goddammit. Don't let him stick his thermometer in your baked goods!"

Hugo's eyebrows rose almost to his bandana.

Harvey pressed a finger against the counter, dragging it along the surface before pulling it away and inspecting the tip. "Spotless," he said. "That's good. Cleanliness is next to godliness, as I always say."

Wallace choked when Apollo stood next to Harvey, lifting his leg. A stream of urine sprayed onto Harvey's shoes. Apollo looked pleased with himself as he pranced away, Harvey none the wiser.

"Good boy," Nelson cooed. "Yes, you are. Yes, you *are*. You peed all over the bad man like a very good boy."

Harvey said, "Let's see what's in the kitchen, shall we? Perhaps you'd consider telling Mei to remove herself from the premises. Just because my restraining order against her was tossed out due to an utter lack of evidence doesn't mean she can still come within ten feet of me. Not after what happened last year."

"Dumped an entire bowl of icing on his head," Nelson told Wallace. "Said it was an accident. It wasn't."

Wallace was absurdly fond of Mei for reasons that had nothing to do with their current situation. He started to follow them toward the kitchen as Hugo pushed open the door but stopped when he heard a stuttering breath behind him. He turned to see Alan stepping out from his corner, his hands balled into fists, a strangely blank expression on his face.

"He looks like him," Alan said to no one, gaze boring into Harvey. "Looks just like him."

"Who?" Wallace asked.

But Alan ignored him.

The sconces on the wall flared with an electrical snarl.

Harvey glanced over his shoulder. "What was that? Rats chewing on your wiring, Hugo? You know that's . . . not . . ." He frowned, rubbing his chest. "Oh. Is it warm in here? It feels—"

Whatever else he meant to say was lost when the clipboard and pen slid from his hands, clattering on the floor. He took a stuttering step back, blood draining from his face.

Hugo's eyes widened. "Alan, *no*."

Too late. Before any of them could react, the light bulbs on the walls and ceiling shattered all at once, glass raining down around them. Harvey jerked as if he were a puppet on strings, head rocking back. His arms rose on either side of him, hands flexed, fingers trembling.

Alan ground his teeth together as he took another step forward.

Harvey rose a few inches off the floor, the tips of his shoes pointing down. Alan raised his hand toward him, palm toward the ceiling. He folded all but his pointer finger in, and as Wallace watched, moved it back and forth as if beckoning.

Harvey floated toward him even as Hugo shouted for Mei.

The whites of Harvey's eyes were bright in the dull light. He stopped, suspended, in front of Alan. "You look just like him," Alan whispered again. "The man. In the alley. It could almost be you."

Hugo was around the counter even as the kitchen doors flew open, Mei running through, tapping her fingers against her palm.

Alan said, "Stay back," and Wallace cried out as Hugo and Mei were flung away from him, each of them slamming into opposite walls, wooden picture frames cracking. Apollo lunged for Alan, teeth bared, and yelped when Alan waved his other hand. Apollo landed roughly on the ground near the fireplace, looking dazed as he raised his head.

Nelson vanished from his place next to Wallace, only to reappear behind Alan. He raised his cane above his head with a grunt. Wallace roared in fury when Alan jerked his arm back, elbowing Nelson in the gut, causing him to take a hard step back, cane falling to the floor.

Alan turned back toward Harvey, who still hung suspended in front of him. "Now *this* is what I expected being a ghost would be like," he said, almost conversationally. "It's not as hard as I thought it'd be. What I can do. It's anger. That's all it is. And I can use it because I'm *pissed off*."

Harvey choked, spittle dripping from his mouth and onto his chin.

"Don't do this," Hugo pleaded, struggling against whatever held him onto the wall. "Alan, you can't hurt him."

"Oh, I can," Alan said. "I can hurt him quite a bit."

"He's not your killer," Mei snapped. "He wasn't the one who hurt you. He would never—"

"It doesn't matter," Alan said. "It'll make me feel better. And isn't that what all this is about? Finding peace. This will bring me peace."

Wallace Price had never been what most would consider to be a brave man. Once, he'd seen someone being mugged on a subway platform and stepped away, telling himself he didn't want to get involved, that he was sure it'd all work out for the best. He'd barely felt a twinge of guilt. The mugger had gotten away with a purse, and Wallace knew whatever was inside could easily be replaced.

Bravery meant the possibility of death. And wasn't that funny? Because it took being dead for Wallace to finally be brave.

Hugo screamed his name as he rushed forward, but Wallace ignored him.

Wallace brought his shoulder down as he charged, steeling himself for the impact. It was still jarring when he collided with Alan's side. Wallace's teeth rattled in his gums as he nearly bit his tongue in two. Alan barely made a sound as he was knocked off his feet. Wallace lost his own footing, landing on top of Alan. He moved as quickly as he could, turning and straddling Alan's waist. Harvey collapsed to the floor and didn't move. Hugo and Mei also fell to the floor, Alan's hold over them having dissipated.

Alan's eyes glittered in the dark as he stared up at Wallace. "You shouldn't have done that."

Before Wallace could react (and really, he hadn't thought that far ahead; what was he going to do, choke the life out of a dead man?), the air shifted around him, and he was flung back. He gasped as the small of his back struck one of the display cases, the glass cracking underneath him.

Alan rose slowly to his feet, pointing a finger at Wallace. "You *really* shouldn't have—"

And then he stopped.

Wallace blinked.

He waited for Alan to finish his threat.

He didn't.

He seemed . . . frozen in place.

"Um," Wallace said. "What happened?"

No one answered him.

He turned his head to the left.

Mei had been in the process of pushing herself up off the ground, her hair hanging in her face.

She wasn't moving.

Wallace looked forward. Nelson had started to prop himself up with his cane, but only made it halfway before he too just . . . stopped.

Wallace turned his head to the right.

Apollo stood in front of Hugo, teeth bared in a silent snarl. Hugo himself was propping himself up against the wall, a look of anger mingled with despair on his face.

Wallace pushed himself off the display case, surprised when he did so without resistance.

"Guys?" he said, voice echoing flatly in the dark tea shop. "What's going on?"

No one answered him.

It was only then that he realized the second hand of the clock wasn't moving. It wasn't even *twitching*.

It'd stopped.

Everything had stopped.

"Oh no," Wallace whispered.

He didn't know what was happening. The only time the clock stopped was when a new ghost arrived at Charon's Crossing, but time hadn't stopped *inside* the tea shop.

"Hugo?" he whispered, taking a step toward him. "Are you—"

He raised his hand to shield his eyes as a bright blue light flashed from outside the tea shop. It filled the windows brilliantly, casting shadows that stretched long. The light pulsed again and again. He took a step toward the front of the shop, only to bring a hand to his chest.

The hook. The cable.

They felt dead.

They *were* dead.

"What is this?" he whispered.

He reached the closest window, looking out to the front of the tea shop, squinting against the bright light that lit up the forest, shadows dancing.

A vague shape stood out on the dirt road. As the light faded, the shape filled in, and Wallace saw it for what it was.

He remembered the brief glimpse he'd seen in the forest the night he'd tried to escape. The outline of a strange beast that he'd managed to convince himself was just a trick of the shadows.

Not a trick.

It was real.

And it was here.

There, standing in the road, was a stag.

CHAPTER 17

It was bigger than any stag Wallace had ever seen in pictures. Even from a distance, the creature looked as if it would tower over all of them. It held its head high, the many points of its antlers like a bony crown. As the stag stepped closer to the tea shop, Wallace could see flowers hanging from the antlers, their roots embedded into the velvet, blossoms in shades of ochre and fuchsia, cerulean and scarlet, canary and magenta. At the tips of its antlers were tiny white lights, as if the bones were filled with stars.

Wallace couldn't move, a sound falling from his mouth like he'd been punched in the gut.

The stag's nostrils flared, its eyes like black holes as it dug its hooves into the earth. Its hair was brown with white splotches along its back and considerable chest. Its tail swished back and forth. As the stag lowered its head, flower petals drifted down onto the ground.

Wallace said, "Oh. Oh. Oh."

The stag jerked its head back up as if it'd heard him. It bleated softly, a long, mournful cry that caused a lump to form in Wallace's throat.

He said, "Hugo. Hugo, are you seeing this?"

Hugo didn't answer.

The stag stopped a few feet from the stairs to the tea shop. The flowers growing from its antlers folded in on themselves as if shutting away against the night. The stag reared up on its hind legs. Its belly was completely white.

And then the stag was gone, a frame rate stutter, a glitch in reality. The stag was there, and then it wasn't.

In its place stood a child.

A boy.

He was young, perhaps nine or ten, with golden-brown skin, his eyes a strange shade of violet. Long, shaggy hair curled down around his ears, brown with streaks of white, unfurled flowers woven into the locks. He wore a T-shirt over jeans. It took Wallace a moment to make out the words on the shirt in the dark.

JUST A KID FROM TOPEKA

The boy's feet were bare. He flexed his fingers and toes, tilting his head from side to side before looking up at the window once more, directly at Wallace. The boy nodded, and Wallace felt his throat close.

The boy began to climb the stairs.

Wallace stumbled back from the window. He managed to keep upright, though it was close. He looked around wildly, for someone, anyone to see what he was seeing. Hugo and Mei were as they'd been. Apollo and Nelson too. Alan, the same.

He was alone.

The boy knocked on the door.

Once.

Twice.

Three times.

"Go away," Wallace croaked out. "Please, just go away."

"I can't do that, Wallace," the boy said, his voice light, the words almost like musical notes. He wasn't quite singing, but it wasn't normal speech either. There was a weight to him, a presence Wallace could feel even through the door, heavy and ethereal. "It's time we had a little chat."

"Who are you?" Wallace whispered.

"You know who I am," the boy said, voice muffled. "I'm not going to hurt you. I would never do that."

"I don't believe you."

"Understandable. You don't know me. Let's change that, shall we?"

The doorknob turned.

The door opened.

The boy stepped inside Charon's Crossing. The wooden floors

creaked under his feet. As he slowly closed the door behind him, the walls of the tea shop began to ripple like a breeze blowing across the surface of a pond. Wallace wondered what would happen if he tried to touch them, if he'd sink into the walls and drown.

The boy nodded at Wallace before looking around the room. He cocked his head at Alan, brow furrowing. "Angry, isn't he? It's odd, really. The universe is bigger than one can possibly imagine, a truth beyond comprehension, and yet all he knows is anger and hurt. Pain and suffering." He sighed, shaking his head. "I'll never understand, no matter how hard I try. It's illogical."

"What do you want?" Wallace asked. His back was pressed against the counter. He thought about running, but he didn't think he'd get very far. And he wasn't about to leave Hugo and Mei and Nelson and Apollo. Not while they couldn't defend themselves.

"I'm not going to hurt them," the boy said, and for a terrible moment, Wallace wondered if the child could read his mind. "I've never hurt anyone before."

"I don't believe you," Wallace said again.

"You don't?" The boy scrunched up his face. "Why?"

"Because of what you are."

"What am I, Wallace?"

And with the last of his strength, Wallace whispered, "You're the Manager."

The boy seemed pleased with his answer. "I am. Silly title, but it fits, I suppose. My real name is much more complicated, and I doubt your human tongue would be able to pronounce it. It'd turn your mouth to mush if you tried." He reached up and plucked a flower from his head, popping it into his mouth. His eyes fluttered shut as he sucked on the petals. "Ah. That's better. It's hard for me to take this form and keep it for long. The flowers help." He looked up at one of the potted plants hanging from the ceiling. "You've been watering these."

"It's my job," Wallace said faintly.

"Is it?" He poked a finger against the planter. Leaves grew. Vines lengthened. Soil trickled down onto the floor, little motes of dust and dirt catching the light from the dying fire in the fireplace. "Do you know what my job is?"

Wallace shook his head, tongue thick in his mouth.

"Everything," the boy said. "My job is everything."

"Are you God?" Wallace choked out.

The boy laughed. It sounded like he was singing. "No. Of course not. There is no God, at least not like you're thinking. He's a human construct, one capable of great peace and violent wrath. It's a dichotomy only found in the human mind, so of course he'd be made in your image. But I'm afraid he's nothing but a fairy tale in a book of fiction. The truth is infinitely more complicated than that. Tell me, Wallace. What are you doing here?"

He kept his distance, which Wallace was grateful for. "I live here."

"Do you?" the boy asked. "How do you figure?"

"I was brought here."

The boy nodded. "You were. Mei, she's good people. A little headstrong, but a Reaper has to be for all they deal with. There's no one like her in all the world. The same could be said for Hugo. And Nelson. Apollo. Even you and Alan, though not quite in the same way." He went to one of the tables and grabbed hold of a chair. He grunted as he pulled it down. It was bigger than he was, and Wallace thought it was going to crash down upon his head. It didn't, and he set it on the floor before climbing onto it and sitting down. His feet dangled as he kicked them back and forth. He folded his hands in his lap, twiddling his thumbs. "It's nice to finally meet you, Wallace. I know so much about you, but it's good to see you face to face."

A fresh wave of terror washed over him. "Why are you here?"

The boy shrugged. "Why are any of us here?"

Wallace narrowed his eyes. "Do you always answer a question with a question?"

The boy laughed again. "I like you. I always have, even when you were . . . you know. A bastard."

Wallace blinked. "Excuse me?"

"A bastard," the boy repeated. "It took you dying to find your humanity. It's hysterical if you think about it."

A flare of anger burned in Wallace's chest. "Oh, I'm so glad this is all such a riot to you."

"There's no need for that. I'm not being facetious. You're not as you once were. Why do you think that is?"

Wallace said, "I don't know."

"It's okay not to know." The boy tilted his head against the back of the chair, staring up at the ceiling. It too shimmered like the walls, as if liquid instead of solid. "In fact, an argument could be made it's better that way. Still . . . you're a curiosity. And that means you have my attention."

"Did you do this to them?" Wallace demanded. "If you're hurting them, I'll—"

"You'll what?" the boy asked.

Wallace said nothing.

The boy nodded. "I told you I wasn't going to hurt you or them. They're sleeping, in a way. When we're finished, they'll awaken and things will be as they always were and always will be. Do you like it here?"

"Yes."

The boy looked around, the movement strangely stiff as if the bones in his neck were fused together. "It doesn't seem like much from the outside, does it? A queer house made up of many different ideas. They should clash. They should crumble to the foundation. It shouldn't stand as it does, and yet you don't fear the ceiling collapsing onto your head." Then, "Why did you step in to protect them? The Wallace Price of the living world wouldn't have raised a finger unless it benefited himself."

"They're my friends," Wallace said, awash in unreality. The room around him felt hazy and muted, only the Manager crystal clear, a focal point, the center of everything.

"They are?" the boy asked. "You didn't have many of those." He frowned. "*Any* of those."

Wallace looked away. "I know."

"Then you died," the boy said. "And came here. To this place. To this . . . way station. A stop on a much larger journey. And you did just that, didn't you? You stopped."

"I don't want to go through the door," Wallace said, voice raising and cracking right down the middle. "You can't make me."

"I could," the boy said. "It would be easy. No effort on my part at all. Would you like me to show you?"

Fear, bright and glassy. It wrapped its hands around Wallace's ribs, fingers digging in.

"I won't," the boy said. "Because that's not what you need." He glanced at Hugo, expression softening. "He's a good ferryman, Hugo, though his heart often gets in the way. When I found him, he was angry and confused. Adrift. He didn't understand the way of things, and yet he had this light in him, fierce but in danger of flickering out. I taught him how to harness it. People like him, they're rare. There's beauty in the chaos, if you know where to look for it. But you would know about that, wouldn't you? You see it too."

Wallace swallowed thickly. "He's different."

"That's certainly one way to put it." The boy kicked his feet again as he settled back into the chair, hands on his stomach. "But yes, he is."

The anger returned, burning the fear away. "And you did this to him."

The boy arched an eyebrow. "Excuse me?"

Wallace's hands balled into fists. "I've heard about you."

"Oh boy," he said. "This should be good. Go ahead. Tell me what you've heard."

"You make the ferry . . . people."

"I do," the boy said, "though I don't want you thinking I pick them without rhyme or reason. Certain people . . . well. They shine brightly. Hugo happened to be one of them."

Wallace clenched his jaw. "You're supposed to be this . . . this *thing*—"

"Rude."

"—this grand thing that oversees life and death, delegating the responsibilities to others—"

"Well, yes. I'm the Manager. I manage."

"—and you put the weight of death on someone like Hugo. You make him see and do things that—"

"Whoa," the boy said, sitting up quickly. "Hold on a second. I don't make anyone do *anything*. Goodness gracious, Wallace, what have they been telling you about me?"

"You're callous," Wallace spat. "And cruel. How could you ever think putting something like that on a man who'd just lost his family was the right thing to do?"

"Hmm," the boy said. "I think we've got our wires crossed somewhere. That's not the case at all. It's a choice, Wallace. It all comes down to choice. I didn't *force* Hugo to do anything. I merely laid out the options before him and let him make up his own mind."

Wallace slammed his hands against the counter. "His parents had just *died*. He was suffering. He was *grieving*. And you opened a door to show him that there was something beyond what he knew. Of course he would take what you offered. You preyed upon him when he was at his weakest, knowing full well he wasn't in his right mind." Wallace was panting by the time he finished, palms stinging.

"Wow," the boy said. He squinted at Wallace. "You're protective of him."

Wallace blanched. "I . . ."

The boy nodded as if this were answer enough. "I didn't expect that. I don't know why. But with all I've seen, the most wonderful thing is that I can still be surprised by one such as you. You care about him very much."

"All of them," Wallace said. "I care about all of them."

"Because they're your friends."

"Yes."

"Then why don't you trust Hugo enough to make decisions for himself?"

"I do," Wallace said weakly.

"Do you? Because it sounds like you're second-guessing his

choices. I would hope you could tell the difference between being protective and doubting someone you call a friend."

Wallace said nothing. As much as he hated to admit it, the Manager had a point. Shouldn't he trust Hugo to know what was right for himself?

The boy nodded as if Wallace's silence was tacit agreement. He slid from the chair before turning around and lifting it up. He flipped it over and put it back on the table, wiping his hands on his jeans once he'd finished. He glanced at the health inspector and sighed. "People are so strange. Just when I think I have you all figured out, you go and make a mess of things." Absurdly, he sounded almost fond.

He turned back toward Wallace, clapping his hands. "Okay. Let's get a move on. Time is short. Well, not for me, but for the rest of you. Follow me, if you please."

"Where are we going?"

"To show you the truth," the boy said. He went to Alan, looking up at him and smiling sadly. He reached out and touched Alan's hip, shaking his head. "Oh. Yes. This one. I'm sorry for what you've been through. I'll do my best to make it better."

And then, before Wallace could do anything to stop him, he puckered his lips and blew a thin stream of air toward Alan, cheeks bulging. Wallace blinked as a hook materialized in Alan's chest, a cable growing and extending between him and Hugo. The Manager curled his fingers around the hook and yanked. It pulled free. The cable connecting Alan to Hugo dulled. The Manager dropped the hook, and as it hit the floor, it and the cable turned to dust. "There," he said. "That's better." He turned and headed farther into the house.

Wallace looked down at his own cable, still connecting him to Hugo. The cable flashed weakly, the hook shivering in his chest. He was about to touch it, to allow himself the reminder it was there, it was *real*, when Alan rose a few inches off the floor, floating though still frozen. The boy looked back at Wallace from the entry to the hallway. "Coming, Wallace?"

"If I say no?"

The boy shrugged. "Then you do. But I wish you wouldn't."

Wallace stumbled back when Alan began to rise toward the ceiling. "Where are you taking him?"

"Home," the boy said simply. He disappeared down the hallway. Wallace looked at Alan in time to see his feet disappear *through* the ceiling, concentric circles undulating outward.

He did the only thing he could.

He followed the Manager.

He knew where they were going, and though he'd never been more frightened in his life, he still climbed the stairs, each step harder than the last.

He passed by the second floor. The third. All the windows were black, as if all light had vanished from the world.

He stopped near the fourth floor landing, peering through the railing. The Manager stood below the door. Alan floated up through the floor, stopping next to him, suspended in air.

"I'm not going to force you through the door," the boy said mildly. "If that's what you're thinking."

"And Alan?" Wallace asked, climbing the last few stairs.

"Alan's a different case. I'll do what I must for him."

"Why?"

The boy laughed. "So many questions. Why, why, why. You're funny, Wallace. It's because he's becoming dangerous. Obviously."

"You're going to make him go through the door."

The boy looked back at him over his shoulder. "Yes."

"How is that *fair*?"

The boy looked confused. "Death? How is it not? You're born, yes. You live and breathe and dance and ache, but you die. Everyone dies. Every*thing* dies. Death is cleansing. The pain of a mortal life is gone."

"Tell that to Alan," Wallace growled. "He's hurting. He's filled with anger—"

The boy turned, frowning. "Because he's still stuck here. He doesn't see the way things should be. Not everyone can adapt as well as you." He gnawed on his bottom lip. "Or Nelson or Apollo. I like them too. They wouldn't be here if I didn't."

"And Lea?" Wallace snapped. "What about her? Where were you when she needed you? When Hugo needed you?" A thought struck him, terrible and harsh. "Or did what happened to Cameron keep you away?"

The boy's shoulders slumped. "I never claimed to be perfect, Wallace. Perfection is a flaw in itself. Lea was . . . it shouldn't have happened the way it did. The Reaper was out of line, and he paid for it dearly." He shook his head. "I manage, Wallace. But even I can't manage everyone all the time. Free will is paramount, though it can get a bit messy at times. I don't interfere unless there's no other way."

"And so they're supposed to suffer because of what you can't do?"

The boy sighed. "I can see where you're coming from. Thanks for the feedback, Wallace. I'll take it into consideration going forward."

"Feedback?" Wallace said, outraged. "That's what you're calling it?"

"It's either that or you're telling me what I can and cannot do. I'm giving you the benefit of the doubt, because I choose to believe you can't possibly be *that* stupid." He turned his face up toward the door. It vibrated in its frame, the leaves and flowers carved into the wood bursting to life. The crystal leaf in the doorknob glittered.

"I like you," the boy said again without looking at him. He raised his hand toward the door, curling his fingers. "Which is why I'm going to tell you how things will go." He twisted his hand sharply.

The doorknob on the ceiling above them turned.

The latch clicked, the crystal leaf flashing brightly.

The door opened slowly, swinging down toward them.

Hugo had told him what he'd seen when the door opened, how it made him feel. And still, Wallace wasn't prepared for what happened next. Light spilled out so bright that he had to look away. He thought he heard birds singing on the other side, but the whispers from the door were too loud for him to be sure. He lifted his head in time to see the Manager push gently on the bottom of Alan's feet. Before Wallace could open his mouth, Alan rose swiftly, passing through the doorway. The light pulsed before it faded. The door slammed shut. It took only seconds.

"He'll find peace," the boy said. "With time, he'll find himself again." He turned and sank to the floor, legs crossed in front of him. He looked up at Wallace still standing near the stairs.

"What did you do?" Wallace whispered.

"Helped him along his journey," the boy said. "I find that sometimes people need a little push in the right direction."

"What happened to free will?"

The boy grinned. It chilled Wallace to the bone. "You're smarter than I gave you credit for. Fun! Think of it as . . . hmm. Ah. Think of it as a gentle nudge in the right direction. Can't have him turning into a Husk. I don't like to think what that would do to Hugo. Not again. He took it so hard the first time. It's why I've allowed Nelson and Apollo to stay as long as they have, to keep him from abandoning his calling."

"So we only have free will until . . . what? It interferes with your order?"

The Manager chuckled. "Precisely! Good for you, Wallace. Order is absolutely paramount. Without it, we'd be stumbling in the dark. Which brings me to you. You've been here a long time, much longer than any other aside from Nelson and Apollo. And for what? Do you even know? What is your purpose?"

Wallace felt like he was on fire. "I . . ."

"Yes," the Manager said. "I thought as much. Let me help you answer that. Your being here makes you a distraction in ways Nelson and Apollo aren't. A distracted ferryman is one who'll make mistakes. Hugo has a job to do, one that is far more important than his *feelings*." He grimaced. "Terrible things, those. I've watched and waited, allowing this farce of a happy little home to play out, but it's time to move things along to ensure Hugo does what he was hired to do." He grinned. "Which is why I'm going to tell you what'll happen next."

Wallace didn't like the sound of that. "What?"

The boy cocked his head as he studied Wallace. "How to put this in ways you can understand. How . . . to . . . put—Ah!" He clapped his hands. "You're a lawyer." His lips quirked. "Well, you *were*. I'm like you, in a way. Death, my dear man, is the law, and I'm the judge. There are rules and regulations. Sure, the bureaucracy of it all can be a little tiresome, and the monotony is killer, but we need the rule of law so we know how to be, how to act." The smile slid from his face. "And yet, it's always *why*. Why, why, why. I hate that question above all others." And then his voice changed, becoming a frightened woman's. "Why do I have to go?" His voice changed again, becoming a man's, old and frail. "Why can't I have more time?" Again, this time a child. "Why can't I stay?"

"Stop," Wallace said hoarsely. "Please stop."

When the Manager spoke again, his voice returned to normal. "I've heard it all." He frowned. "I *hate* it. But never more so than I do right now, because I find *myself* asking why. Why is Wallace Price still here? Why doesn't he move on?" He shook his head as if disappointed. "That leads to *me* asking myself why I should care at all. You want to know what I realized?"

"No," Wallace whispered.

"I realized that you're an aberration. A flaw in the system that's worked so well. And what does one do with flaws as someone in charge, Wallace? To keep the things running as they should?"

Fire them. Remove them from the equation. Replace the part so the machine can run smoothly. Distantly, Wallace thought of Patricia Ryan, sitting across from him in his office.

"Exactly," the Manager said as if Wallace had spoken aloud. He tapped his fingers against his knee. The bottoms of his feet were dirty. "Which is why I've made an executive decision." He grinned, the violet of his eyes moving like liquid. "One week. I'll give you one more week to put your affairs in order. This isn't meant to be forever, Wallace. A way station such as this exists to allow you to regroup, to accept the inevitable. You've changed in the weeks since your arrival. So different from the man I saw fleeing in the dead of night."

"But—"

The boy held up his hand. "I'm not finished. Please don't interrupt me again. I don't like being interrupted." When he saw Wallace snap his mouth closed, he continued. "You've been given more than enough time to process your life spent on this Earth. You were not a kind man, Wallace, or even a just one. You were selfish and mean. Not quite as cruel as you claim I am, but it was close. I don't recognize that man in you. Not anymore. Death has opened your eyes. I can see the good in you now, and what you're willing to do for those you care about. Because you do care about them, don't you?"

"Yes," Wallace said gruffly.

"I figured. And really, I can see why. They're certainly . . . unique."

"I know they are. There's no one like them."

The boy laughed again. "I'm glad we can at least agree on that." He sobered. "One week, dear Wallace. I'll give you one more week. In seven days, I shall return. I'll bring you to this door. I will see you through it because that's the way it's supposed to be."

"And if I refuse?"

The boy shrugged. "Then you do. I hope you won't, but I can't promise that this will go on for much longer. You aren't meant to be here. Not like this. Perhaps in another life, you could have found your way to this place, and made the most of it."

"I don't want to go," Wallace said. "I'm not ready."

"I know that," the boy said, for the first time sounding irritated. "Which is why I'm giving you a week rather than making you go now." His face darkened. "Don't mistake my offer for anything but what it is. There is no loophole, no last-minute bit of evidence you can fling upon the courtroom in a display of your legal prowess. I can make you do things, Wallace. I don't want to, but I can."

Dazed, Wallace said, "I . . . maybe it'd be different. I've changed. You've said as much. I—"

"No," the boy said, shaking his head. "It's not the same. You aren't Nelson, the grandfather who guided Hugo after the loss of his parents. You aren't Apollo, who helped Hugo to breathe when his lungs collapsed in his chest. You are an outsider, an anomaly. The options I've laid out for you—going through the door or running the risk of losing all you've gained—are your *only* options. You're a disruption, Wallace, and though I've allowed certain . . . concessions in the spirit of magnanimity, don't make the mistake of thinking I'll look the other way for you. This was always temporary."

"And what about Cameron?" Wallace demanded. "And all the others like him?"

The boy looked surprised. "The Husks? Why do you care?"

I'm still here. I'm still here.

"He's not gone," Wallace said. "He's still there. Part of him still exists. Help him, and I'll do whatever you want."

The boy shook his head slowly. "I'm not here to bargain with you, Wallace. I thought you were beyond that stage already. You're into the fabled land of acceptance, or at least you were. Don't backtrack on me now."

"It's not *for* me," Wallace snapped. "It's for him."

"Ah," the boy said. "Is it? What would you have me do? Cure him? He knew the risks when he chose to leave the grounds." He stood, wiping his hands off on the front of his jeans. "I'm glad we've had this talk. It's been a pleasure meeting you, and believe me, that's not something I say often." He grimaced. "Humans are untidy. I'd rather keep my distance if possible. It's easier when they agree with me, as you have."

"I didn't agree to anything!" Wallace cried.

The boy pouted. "Aw. Well, I'm sure you'll come around to it. One week, Wallace. What will you do with the time you have left? I can't wait to find out. Tell the others, or don't. It doesn't concern me either way. And don't worry about the health inspector. He won't remember a thing." The boy tipped Wallace a jaunty salute. "See you soon."

And then he vanished.

Wallace's knees felt weak, loose, and he grabbed onto the railing to hold himself up as he heard yelling come from the bottom floor below him. He closed his eyes when Hugo began to shout his name frantically. "Here," he whispered. "I'm still here."

CHAPTER 18

Hugo said, "Alan. Wallace, where's Alan?"

Wallace looked at the door in the ceiling. "He's crossed."

Hugo was bewildered. "What? On his own? How?"

Wallace shook his head. "I don't know. But he's gone. He found his way through, and he's gone."

Hugo stared at him. "I don't . . . are you all right?"

Wallace smiled, but the weight of it was heavy. "Of course."

Back downstairs, Harvey said, "I do believe I lost myself for a little while. Excuse me, won't you? I need to go home. I've got a terrible headache." He was pale as he walked toward the door. "Keep this place up to code, Hugo. You won't like what'll happen if you don't."

He walked through the door, closing it quietly behind him.

"What the hell?" Mei muttered. "What happened?"

"I don't know," Nelson said, hands rubbing his forehead. "I feel like I've just woken up. Isn't that strange?"

Hugo didn't say a word. His gaze never left Wallace.

And Wallace looked away.

Seven days.

What will you do with the time you have left?

Wallace pondered this as the sun rose on the first day.

He didn't know.

He'd never felt more lost in his life.

Grief, Wallace knew, had the power to consume, to eat away until there was nothing left but hollowed-out bones. Oh, the shape of the person remained as it was, even if the cheeks turned sallow, and dark circles formed under the eyes. Hollowed out and left raw, they were still recognizably human. It came in stages, some smaller than others, but undeniable.

These were the stages of Wallace Price:

On the first of his remaining days, he was in denial.

The shop opened as it always did, bright and early. The scones and muffins were placed in the display case, the scent of them warm and thick. Tea was brewed and steeped, poured into cups and sipped slowly. People laughed. People smiled. They hugged one another as if they hadn't seen each other in years, patting backs and gripping shoulders.

He watched them all through the portholes in the kitchen, burdened with the knowledge that they could leave this place whenever they wished. The bitterness he felt was surprising, tugging at the back of his mind. He kept it in place, not allowing it to roar forward no matter how much he wanted it to.

"It's not real," he muttered to himself. "None of it is real."

"What was that?"

He glanced over his shoulder. Mei stood next to the sink, a look of concern on her face. He shook his head. "Nothing."

She didn't believe him. "What's wrong?"

He laughed wildly. "Nothing at all. I'm dead. What could possibly be wrong?"

She hesitated. "Did something happen? With Alan, or . . . ?"

"I told you already. He went through the door. I don't know how. I don't know why. I don't even know how he got there. But he's gone."

"So you said. I just . . ." She shook her head. "You know you can talk to us, right? Whatever you need."

He left her in the kitchen, heading out the back door.

He walked amongst the tea plants, fingers trailing along the leaves.

The first night was anger.

Oh, but was he angry.

He snapped at Nelson. At Apollo. They were hovering. Nelson held up his hands as Apollo put his tail between his legs. "What's gotten into you?" Nelson asked.

"None of your business," Wallace snarled. "Leave me alone for one damn second."

Nelson was hurt, shoulders stiff as he pulled Apollo away. "You should see a doctor."

Wallace blinked. "What? Why?"

"To get that stick up your ass removed."

Before he could retort, Hugo was in front of him, brow furrowed. "Outside."

Wallace glared at him. "I don't want to go outside."

"Now." He turned and headed down the hallway, not looking back to see if Wallace would follow.

He thought about staying right where he was.

In the end, he didn't.

Hugo stood on the deck, face turned toward the sky.

"What do you want?" Wallace grumbled, staying near the door.

"Scream," Hugo said. "I want you to scream."

That startled Wallace. "What?"

Hugo didn't look at him. "Yell. Scream. Rage. As loud as you can. Get it all out. It'll help. Trust me. The longer it sits in you, the more you're poisoned. It's best to get it out while you can."

"I'm not going to scream—"

Hugo sucked in a deep breath and yelled. It was deep, the sound of it rolling through the forest around them. It was as if all the trees were screaming. His voice cracked near the end, and when his voice died, his chest heaved. He wiped spittle from his lips with the back of his hand. "Your turn."

"That was stupid."

"Do you trust me?"

Wallace sagged. "You know I do."

"Then do it. I don't know what's happened to cause this regression, but I don't like it."

"And you think screaming into nothing will make me feel better."

Hugo shrugged. "What could it hurt?"

Wallace sighed before joining Hugo at the railing. He felt Hugo's gaze on him as he looked up toward the stars. He'd never felt smaller than he did at that moment. It hurt more than he cared to admit.

"Do it," Hugo said quietly. "Let me hear you."

He wondered when the threshold had been crossed that he couldn't refuse Hugo anything.

So he screamed as loud as he could.

He put everything into it he had. His parents, telling him he was an embarrassment. His mother, taking her last breaths, his father next to him, though he felt like a stranger. When he died two years later, Wallace didn't shed a tear. He told himself he'd cried over them long enough.

And Naomi. He'd loved her. He really had. It hadn't been enough, and she didn't deserve what he'd turned into. He thought about the last good days they had, when he could almost convince himself that they'd make it work. It'd been foolish to think that way. The death knell had already sounded, they'd just ignored it for as long as they'd been able to in hopes that it wasn't the end. They went to the coast, just the two of them, a couple of days away from everything. They held hands on the drive there, and it was almost like it'd used to be. They laughed. They sang along with the radio. He had rented a convertible, and the wind whipped through their hair, the sun shining down. They didn't talk about work or children or money or past arguments. Deep down, he had known this was it, the last chance.

It hadn't been enough.

They had made it a single day before they were fighting again. Wounds he long thought scarred over reopened and bled again.

The car ride back was silent, her arms folded defensively. He ignored the tear that trickled down her cheek from underneath her sunglasses.

A week later, she served him with divorce papers. He didn't fight it. It was easier this way. She'd be better off. It was what they both wanted.

He'd drowned, unaware that he'd slipped beneath the surface.

And so here, now, he screamed as loud as he could. Tears prickled his eyes, and he was almost able to convince himself they came from the exertion. Spit flew from his mouth. His throat hurt.

When he could scream no longer, he put his face in his hands, shoulders shaking.

Hugo said, "It's life, Wallace. Even when you're dead, it's still life. You exist. You're real. You're strong and brave, and I'm so happy to know you. Now, tell me what happened with Alan. All of it. Leave nothing out."

Wallace told him everything.

The third stage of grief was bargaining, and it also came on the first night.

But it wasn't Wallace who bargained.

It was Hugo.

He bargained by shouting, demanding the Manager show himself to explain what the hell he'd meant. Mei stood speechless. She hadn't said a word since Hugo had told her and Nelson the truth. Nelson's mouth was still hanging open, hands curled tightly around his cane.

"I'm calling you," Hugo snapped as he paced the main room of the tea shop, glaring up at the ceiling. "I need to talk to you. I know you're there. You're always there. You owe me this. I never ask for anything, but I'm asking you to be here now. I'll listen. I swear I'll listen."

Apollo trailed after him, back and forth, back and forth, ears alert as he listened to his owner grow angrier.

Wallace tried to stop Hugo, tried to tell him that it was fine, that it was okay, that he'd always known it would come to this. "This isn't forever," he said. "You know that. You told me that. It's a stop, Hugo. One stop on a journey."

But Hugo didn't listen.

"Manager!" he cried. "Show yourself!"

The Manager didn't come.

As the clock moved toward midnight, Mei convinced Hugo he needed to sleep. He argued bitterly, but in the end, he agreed. "We'll figure it out tomorrow," he told Wallace. "I'll think of something. I don't know what, but I'll figure it out. You aren't going anywhere if you don't want to."

Wallace nodded. "Go to bed. The day starts early."

Hugo shook his head. Muttering under his breath, he climbed the stairs, Apollo following him.

Mei waited until the door slammed shut above them before she turned to Wallace. "He'll do what he can," she said quietly.

"I know," Wallace said. "But I don't know if he should."

She narrowed her eyes. "What?"

He sighed as he looked away. "He has a job to do. Nothing is more important than that. He can't throw it away because of me."

"He's not throwing anything away," she said sharply. "He's fighting to give you the time you deserve, to make your own choice about when you're ready. Don't you see that?"

"Does it matter?"

"What the hell is *that* supposed to mean?"

"I'm dead," he said. "There's no going back from that. A river only moves in one direction."

"But—"

"It is what it is. You've all taught me that. I didn't listen at first, but I learned. And it made me better because of it. Isn't that the point?"

She sniffled. "Oh, Wallace. It's more than that now."

"Maybe," he said. "Maybe if things were different, we'd . . ." He couldn't finish. "There's still time left. The best thing I can do is to make the most of it."

Soon after, she went to bed.

The clocked ticked, ticked, ticked the seconds and minutes and hours away.

Nelson said, "I'm glad you're here."

Wallace jerked his head up. "What?"

Nelson smiled sadly. "When you first arrived, I thought you were just another visitor. You'd stay for a little while, and then you'd see the light." He chuckled. "Forgive the expression. Clichéd, I know. Hugo would do what he does, and you'd move on without muss or fuss, even though you were adamant you wouldn't. You'd be like all the others who'd come before you."

"I am."

"Perhaps," Nelson allowed. "But that doesn't discount what you've done in your time here. The work you've put in to making yourself a better person." He shuffled toward Wallace, setting the cane against the table Wallace was leaning on. Wallace didn't flinch when Nelson reached up and cupped his face. His hands were warm. "Be proud of what you've accomplished, Wallace. You've earned that right."

"I'm scared," Wallace whispered. "I don't mean to be, but I am."

"I know you are," Nelson said. "I am too. But as long as we're together, we can help each other until the end. Our strength will be your strength. We won't carry you because you don't need us to. But we'll be by your side." Then, "Can I ask you something?"

Wallace nodded as Nelson dropped his hands.

"If things were different, and you were still . . . here. I don't know how. Say you took a trip on your own, and you ended up in our little town. You found your way to this tea shop, and Hugo was as he was, and you were as you were. What would you do?"

Wallace laughed wetly. "I'd probably make a mess of things."

"Of course you would. But that's the beauty of it, don't you think? Life is messy and terrible and wonderful, all at the same time. What would you do if Hugo was before you and there was nothing stopping you? Life or death or anything else. What would you do?"

Wallace closed his eyes. "Everything."

Depression hit on the second morning, brief though it was. Wallace allowed himself the sadness that stirred within him, remembering how Hugo had told him grief wasn't only for the living. He stood on the back deck, watching the sunrise. He could hear Hugo and Mei moving around in the kitchen. Hugo had wanted to close the shop for the day, but Wallace told him to go on as he always did. He had Mei on his side, and Hugo finally relented, though he wasn't happy about it.

The sunlight filtered through the trees, melting the thin layer of frost on the ground. He gripped the railing as the light stretched toward him. It touched his hands first. And then his wrists, and arms, and finally his face. It warmed him. It calmed him. He hoped wherever he was going that there'd still be the sun and the moon and the stars. He'd spent a majority of his life with his head turned down. It seemed only fair that eternity would allow him to raise his face toward the sky.

The sadness receded, though it didn't leave entirely. It still bubbled underneath the surface, but he floated on top of it now. This was a different kind of grief, he knew, but it was still his all the same.

He accepted that.

What will you do with the time you have left?

And that's when he knew.

"Are you out of your damn *mind*?" Mei snapped at him. She stood in the kitchen, glaring at him as if Wallace were the stupidest person she'd ever laid eyes on. Hugo manned the register out front, the shop busy.

He shrugged. "Probably? But I think it's the right thing to do."

She threw up her hands. "Nothing involving Desdemona Tripplethorne is the right thing to do. She's a terrible person, and when she finally bites the big one, I'm going to—"

"Help her like you've helped everyone else if she gets assigned to you?"

Mei deflated. "Of course I will. But man, I won't like it. And you can't make me."

"I wouldn't dream of it. I know you don't care for her, Mei. And you have very good reason not to. But you said Nancy trusts her, for whatever reason. If it came from you or Hugo, she might not listen. At least with Desdemona, we'd have a chance. And if what I have in mind works, she won't be here very long." He shook his head. "I won't do this, though, without your okay."

"Why?"

She was really going to make him say it, wasn't she? "Because you matter."

She startled, a slow smile blooming on her face. "I matter?"

He groaned. "Shut up."

She looked away, though he could tell she was pleased. "Hugo's not going to be happy about this."

"I know. But the point of all of this is to help as many people as you can, right? And Nancy needs help, Mei. She's stuck, and it's killing her. Maybe it won't work, and it won't make anything better. But what if it does? Don't we owe it to her to try?"

Mei wiped her eyes. "I think I liked you better when you were an asshole."

He laughed. "I like you too, Mei."

He wrapped his arms around her when she lunged at him, holding her close.

"No," Hugo said.

"But—"

"No."

"Told you," Mei muttered as she pushed her way through the double doors. "I'll watch the register."

"She needs this, Hugo," Wallace said as the doors swung shut. "Something, anything to show her that all is not lost, even though it can seem that way."

"She's fragile," Hugo said. "Breakable. If it went wrong, I don't want to think what that would do to her."

"We owe it to her to try," Wallace said. He held up his hand as Hugo started to retort. "Not just you, Hugo. All of us. What happened to her and Lea isn't your fault. I know you think it is, and I know you think you should have done more, but what the other Reaper did is on him, not you. Still, it's heavy. Grief. You know that better than anyone. It'll crush you if you let it. And she's being crushed. If I were where she is now, I'd hope someone would do the same for me. Wouldn't you?"

"She might not even agree," Hugo muttered, refusing to look at Wallace. He was frowning, brow knitted, shoulders hunched. "Nothing happened the first time."

"I know," Wallace said. "But it's going to be different this time around. You knew Lea, at least for a little while. You spoke with her. You cared for her."

Wallace thought Hugo would still refuse. Instead, he said, "What are we going to do?"

On the third evening, Hugo switched the sign in the window to CLOSED FOR A PRIVATE EVENT.

"Are you sure about this?" Nelson whispered, watching his grandson move around the tea shop, preparing for their guests.

"As much as I can be," Wallace whispered back.

"A delicate matter requires delicate hands."

"You don't think we can do it?"

"That's not what I meant. You're blunt and sharp, but you've learned a bit of grace, Wallace. Kindness and grace."

"Because of you," Wallace said. "You and Mei and Hugo."

Nelson grinned at him. "You think so?"

He did. "I wish—"

But whatever Wallace wished stayed within him as lights filled the windows.

"They're here," Mei said as Hugo went back into the kitchen. "You're serious about this?"

"As a heart attack," Wallace said, Nelson chuckling beside him.

He heard car doors opening and closing, and Desdemona speaking loudly, though he couldn't make out the words. He knew who she was speaking to. If they'd done what Hugo had asked, they'd driven separately. It was now or never.

Squat Man opened the door. Desdemona entered first, head held high, dressed as ridiculously as she'd been before. Her towering hat was black and covered with lace, her frizzy red hair tied back into a thick braid that hung over one shoulder. Her dress was black-and-white striped, the hem just below her knees. Her legs were sheathed in red stockings, and her boots looked as if they'd been recently shined.

"Yes," she breathed as she all but sashayed into the tea shop, removing her gloves. "I can feel it. It's like it was the last time. The spirits are active." She turned her head slowly, taking in the room. Her gaze slid over Nelson and Wallace without stopping. "I believe we're going to get somewhere. Mei, how lovely to see you're still . . . alive."

Mei glared at her. "Grave robbing is illegal."

Desdemona blinked. "I beg your pardon?"

"Whatever grave you desecrated to get that dress will—"

Nancy appeared in the doorway. Squat Man and Thin Man crowded behind her, looking as if they'd rather be anywhere else. Nancy gripped the strap of her purse tightly, her expression pinched, her breaths light and quick. She looked exhausted, but determined in ways Wallace hadn't seen before. She stepped into the tea shop slowly, biting her lip as if nervous.

Hugo came through the doors, a tray of tea in his hands.

"Hugo," Desdemona said, looking him up and down. "I was surprised to receive your invitation, especially after you returned my Ouija board to me without so much as a note attached to the post. It's about time you started appreciating my work. There is more to this world than we can see. It's heartening to know you're beginning to understand that."

"Desdemona," Hugo said in greeting, setting the tray down on a table. "I'll take your word on that." He turned to Nancy. "Thank you for coming. I know it's a little later than when you're normally here, but I only want to help."

Nancy glanced at the tray of tea before looking back at Hugo. "So you say." Her voice was rough and gravelly, as if she wasn't used to speaking. Wallace ached at the sound of it. "Desdemona said you invited us here."

"I did," Hugo said. "I can't promise anything will come of it. And even if it doesn't, I want you to know that you're always welcome. Whatever you need."

She nodded tightly but didn't respond.

Squat Man and Thin Man began to set up. Thin Man pulled out a camera, a newer model as the last one had been broken. He positioned it on the tripod, pointing it toward where Desdemona would be sitting. Squat Man had the same device he'd had before, switching it on. It squealed almost immediately, the lights flashing brightly. He frowned down at it, banging it against his hand before shaking his head. "I don't even know why I use this stupid thing," he muttered before waving it around the room.

Thin Man pulled the Ouija board from his bag, setting it on the table along with a new planchette. The last one had burned in the fireplace, becoming nothing but ash and smoke thanks to Wallace. Next to the Ouija board, he set down the feather quill and loose sheets of paper.

Desdemona pulled out a chair for Nancy. "Sit here, dear. That way, you'll still be in frame but won't be blocking me."

"Oh boy," Nelson muttered as Mei scoffed.

Nancy did as asked, clutching her purse in her lap. She didn't look at any of them, quietly refusing the offer of tea from Hugo as Desdemona took a seat next to her.

Desdemona smiled at her. "I know we didn't quite make contact the last time you and I were here. But that doesn't mean it won't happen now. When we came a couple of weeks ago, the spirits were . . . active. I don't think any of them were Lea, but you weren't with us then. It'll help having you here to focus. I have a feeling today will bring the answers you seek." She reached over and touched Nancy's elbow. "If you need a break, or want to stop entirely, say the word."

Nancy nodded. She looked down at the Ouija board. "You think we'll get something this time?"

"I hope so," Desdemona said. "Either through the board or automatic writing. But if we don't, we'll try again. You remember what to do, right? Direct your questions toward me, keeping them to yes or no answers if you can. I'll ask whatever you want, and if all goes well, the spirit energy will run through me. Be patient, especially if another spirit is trying to speak first."

"Okay," Nancy whispered as she sniffled.

Desdemona glanced at Thin Man. "Is everything ready?"

"As it'll ever be," Thin Man mumbled as he pressed a button on the camera. It beeped, and a red light began to blink. He pulled out a pad of paper and a pen from his bag. He looked around nervously, as if remembering the last time they'd been here, and the chaos that'd ensued.

"And as we discussed," Desdemona said to Nancy, "we're not streaming live per your request. We'll post the video later, but only after you've seen the edited version and agreed to it. Anything you don't want shown, we'll keep to ourselves."

Nancy gripped her purse tighter.

"Do you have any questions before we begin? If you do, that's okay. You can ask me anything you want. I won't start until you're ready."

She shook her head.

Desdemona wiggled her shoulders, breathing in through her nose and out through her mouth. She cracked her knuckles before settling her hands on the planchette in the middle of the Ouija board. "Spirits! I command that you speak with me! I know you're there. This will allow us to communicate with each other. Do you understand? There is nothing to fear. We aren't here to harm you. If you would prefer the pen, give me a sign."

The planchette didn't move. Neither did the pen.

"It's okay," Desdemona said to Nancy. "It takes a little time." She raised her voice again. "I am here with Nancy Donovan. She believes the spirit of her daughter, Lea Donovan, resides in this place, for reasons I'm still not quite clear on, but no matter. If Lea Donovan is here, we need to hear from her. If there are any other spirits, we ask that you step aside and allow Lea her moment to say what she must."

"Are you sure about this?" Nelson asked quietly.

"Yes," Wallace said. "We wait."

For the next hour, Desdemona tried all manner of questions, some sweet and coaxing, others more forceful and demanding. Nothing changed. The planchette remained still.

Desdemona grew frustrated, Thin Man covering up a yawn with the back of his hand as Squat Man carried the spirit box around the room, the machine silent.

Eventually, Desdemona sat back in her chair with a sigh. "I'm sorry," she muttered, glaring down at the Ouija board. "I really thought something would happen." She forced a smile. "It doesn't always work. They can be a fickle thing, spirits. They only do what they want when they want."

Nancy nodded, though Wallace could see how hurt she was by it. He ached at the pain radiating from her, silently begging her to hold on just a little bit longer.

Nancy didn't move as Thin Man and Squat Man packed away the Ouija board and the camera. Desdemona spoke quietly to Nancy, holding her hands, telling her that she couldn't give up, that they'd try again as soon as they could. "Give it time," she said quietly. "We'll figure it out."

Nancy nodded, expression slack and blank.

She rose from her chair as the others headed for the door, holding her purse against her chest like a shield. Thin Man and Squat Man left without looking back. Desdemona paused at the doorway, glancing at Hugo. "You know there's something here."

Hugo didn't respond.

"Come, dear," Desdemona said to Nancy. "You can follow us back into town, so we know you're safe."

Mei cocked her head as if confused, glancing back and forth between Desdemona and Nancy.

Hugo cleared his throat. "I'd like to have a word with Nancy in private, if she'll allow it."

Desdemona narrowed her eyes. "Anything you want to say to her, you can say with me present."

"If that's what she wants," Hugo said. "If not, but she wants to share what I tell her, then that's okay too."

"Nancy?" Desdemona asked.

Nancy studied Hugo before nodding. "It's . . . it's fine. Go. I won't be long."

Desdemona hesitated, looking as if she was going to argue. Instead, she sighed. "All right. If you're sure."

"I am," Nancy said.

Desdemona squeezed her shoulder and left the tea shop.

Silence fell, all of them waiting until the sound of a car started up, the engine rumbling. It faded, the clock ticking, ticking.

"Well?" Nancy asked, voice trembling. "What do you want?"

Hugo took in a deep breath, letting it out slow. "Your daughter isn't here."

Nancy recoiled as if slapped. Angry tears filled her eyes. "What?"

"She's not here," Hugo said gently. "She's gone to a better place. A place where nothing can hurt her again."

"How dare you," Nancy whispered. "What the hell is wrong with you?" She took a step back toward the door. "I thought you'd . . ." She shook her head furiously. "I'm not going to stand here and let you be so cruel. I can't." Her chest hitched. "I won't." With one last glare, she turned toward the door.

She gripped the doorknob and Wallace knew it was now or never. Alan—frightened, doomed Alan—had shown him the way. Nancy burned like fire, her grief a never-ending fuel. Whatever she was—like Mei or something else—she'd heard him when Alan had screamed her name.

Which is why Wallace shouted, "*Nancy!*"

She froze, back stiff, shoulders hunched near her ears.

"*Nancy!*"

She turned slowly, tears spilling onto her cheeks. "Did you . . . did you hear that?"

"I did," Hugo said. He held up his hands as if calming a spooked animal. "And I promise there is nothing to be afraid of."

She barked out a laugh, wet and harsh. "You don't get to tell me what I—"

She gasped when Wallace grabbed a chair, lifting it up off the ground. The blood drained from her face, hand going to her throat. Wallace didn't bring the chair to her, not wanting to frighten her more than she already was.

Instead, he carried the chair behind the counter toward the blackboard. "Careful, Wallace," Nelson warned. "Don't give her more than she's ready for."

"I know," Wallace said through gritted teeth, nudging Apollo out of the way as he jumped around him, trying to figure out why Wallace was carrying a chair. He seemed to want to help, biting down on one of the chair legs before getting distracted by his tail.

Wallace set the chair on the floor before glancing back. Nancy hadn't moved, jaw dropped at the sight of a chair floating through the air. He grunted as he climbed up on the chair. "Sorry about this," he muttered before wiping his hand across the blackboard. The words—specials, prices, all around the quote about tea and family—smeared in white.

"Oh my god," Nancy whispered. "What is this? What's happening?"

Wallace lifted a piece of chalk from the base of the blackboard. He wrote one word.

SPARROW.

Nancy let out a strangled sob before rushing forward. "Lea? Oh my god, *Lea*?"

Underneath SPARROW, Wallace wrote: NO. NOT YOUR DAUGHTER. NOT HERE. I WISH SHE WERE. SHE HAS MOVED ON TO A BETTER PLACE.

"Is this a joke?" Nancy demanded, voice thick, eyes wet. "How the hell did you know about the sparrow? It . . . outside her hospital room. It always . . . who are you?"

Wallace wiped away the words before writing again, chalk scraping against the blackboard.

I DIED. HUGO IS TAKING CARE OF ME.

"Why are you even talking to me, then?" Nancy asked, wiping her face angrily. "You're not who I want."

I KNOW. BUT I HOPE IN HEARING FROM ME, YOU'LL UNDERSTAND THERE IS SOMETHING MORE BEYOND WHAT YOU KNOW.

"How am I supposed to believe you?" Nancy cried. "Stop. Stop playing with me. It hurts. Can't you see that? It hurts so much." Her voice broke.

THE GIVING TREE.

Nancy flinched. "What?"

"Hugo," Wallace whispered. "I . . . can't. It's too much. It's up to you now." He dropped the chalk to the floor. It shattered. He almost fell off the chair, but Nelson was there, grabbing onto his legs, keeping him from collapsing. He sat down roughly, his strength draining.

"No," Nancy whispered, taking a stuttering step forward. "No, no, come back. Come *back*!"

"Nancy," the ferryman said.

Nancy turned, bone white.

"It was her favorite book," Hugo said quietly, and Wallace sat upright, Nelson gripping his hand tightly. Apollo sat next to them, tail swishing back and forth. Mei looked pale, her hand at her throat. "She loved the voices you did when you read it to her. Even though she learned to read on her own, she always wanted you to read it to her. There was something about your voice, something warm and beautiful that she always wanted to hear."

"You can't know that," she said hoarsely. "It was just her and me. Our thing." She sounded as if she were choking.

"She told me," Hugo said. "She was so happy when she did. She spoke of picking apples in the fall, and the way you laughed when she ate more than she picked."

Nancy covered her mouth with her hand.

Hugo took a step toward her, slow and deliberate. "She was sad, too, because she missed you." His voice cracked, but he pushed through it. "Her body was tired. She fought as hard as she could, but it was too much for her. She was brave because of you. *For* you. You taught her joy and love and fire. You went to the zoo because she wanted to see polar bears. You took her to the museum because she wanted to touch dinosaur bones. You danced in your living room. The music was loud, and you danced. Once, she knocked over a vase. You told her it was just a little thing, and there was no need to be upset when it could be replaced."

Nancy began to sob. It crawled from her chest, the monster of grief, trying to drag her down into the depths.

"Fight," Wallace whispered. "Oh, please, fight it."

"She loved you," Hugo continued, "and she loves you still. No matter what comes next, that will never change. One day, you'll see her again. One day, you'll look upon her face. There will be no more pain. There will be no more sorrow. You'll know peace because you'll be together. But that day is not today."

"Why?" Nancy said, and it was such a desperate thing that Wallace bowed his head. "Why can't I have her? Why does it have to hurt so much? Why can't I breathe?"

Hugo stopped in front of her. He hesitated before touching the back of her hand briefly. Nancy didn't try to pull away. "She isn't gone. Not really. Just . . . moved on."

"Who are you?" she whispered.

"Someone who cares," Hugo replied. "I . . . lied to you. Before.

When you first came here. And for that, I'm sorrier than you could know. I didn't mean to hurt you. I didn't mean to make you feel worse. I help people. Like her. I help them cross. And we . . ." He swallowed thickly. "And I—*we* did that. We showed her the path forward. Lives don't end. They move on." He paused. "Do you remember the last thing you said to her?"

Nancy deflated, curling in on herself. "Yes."

"You said go. Go wherever you need to go. To the center of the earth. To the stars. To the—"

"To the moon to see if it's made of cheese," she whispered.

Hugo smiled. "The sickness is gone."

Nancy glanced at the blackboard, the smear of words, before turning back to Hugo. "Did you do this?"

He shook his head. "It wasn't me. But it was someone very important to me. And you can believe every single word written."

She watched him for a long time. "I'll be here. Whenever you're ready, I'll be here. That's what you keep telling me."

He nodded.

"Why?" she asked as she trembled. "Why do you care so much?"

"Because I don't know how else to be."

For a moment, Wallace thought it'd be too much for her. That they'd pushed too hard. He was surprised when she squared her shoulders. She looked at Mei, who waved at her with a small smile. Then, to Hugo, "I'd like a cup of tea, if that's all right."

"Okay," Hugo said. "I've always thought tea was a good place to start. And whenever you're ready, if you're ready, you'll know where to find me." He nodded toward the table where the tea tray sat. "Milk or sugar?"

"No. Just as it is."

Wallace looked on as Hugo poured the tea into two cups, one for her, and one for him. He handed Nancy a cup before taking his own. He watched her as she brought the teacup toward her face, inhaling deeply. Her hands started to shake, though no tea spilled. "Is that . . ."

"Gingerbread," Hugo said. "Her favorite."

Another tear slipped down Nancy's cheek. She drank deeply, throat working as she swallowed. She took another sip before setting the cup down back on the tray. She took a step away from Hugo. "I'd like to leave now. I've seen enough for one day."

Mei rushed forward, taking Nancy by the elbow and guiding her toward the door. Nancy stopped before Mei could open it for her. She looked back at Hugo, the color slowly returning to her face. "What are you?"

"I'm Hugo," he said. "I run a tea shop."

"Is that all?"

"No," he said.

Nancy looked as if she were going to speak again, but shook her head as Mei opened the door for her. She hurried down the porch, glancing back only once. A moment later, lights from her car illuminated the tea shop as it backed slowly, turning around before she drove away.

Mei closed the door, turning and leaning against it. She wiped her eyes as she sniffled.

Hugo rushed to Wallace. "Are you okay?" he demanded. He reached out for Wallace and looked stricken when his hands passed right through him. Wallace felt the same. "You—"

Wallace smiled weakly. "I'm fine. It's . . . I'm okay. Really. It took more out of me than I expected. You did it, though. I knew you could. Do you think it helped?"

Hugo gaped at him. "Do I think it *helped*?"

"That's . . . what I asked, yes."

Hugo shook his head. "Wallace, we gave her hope. She . . . maybe she has a chance now." Wallace was stunned to see Hugo's own eyes were wet. "Mei. I need you to—"

"No," Wallace said before Mei could move. "This wasn't about me. This is your moment, Hugo. You did this." He looked at Mei. "Can you do me a favor?"

"Yes," she said. "Yes."

"I need you to hug Hugo for me. Because I can't, and I want to more than anything."

Hugo's eyes widened comically as Mei launched herself at him, legs wrapping around his waist, her arms around his neck. It took Hugo a second, but he lifted his arms and held her close, her face in his neck, his in her hair. Apollo yipped excitedly, dancing around them, tongue hanging from his mouth. "We did it, boss," Mei whispered. "Oh my god, we did it."

Wallace watched with fierce pride as Nelson moved toward them, and though he couldn't touch them, he did the next best thing. He stood with his grandson and Mei.

Wallace smiled and closed his eyes.

CHAPTER 19

Acceptance.

It was easier than Wallace had expected.

Whatever he'd felt before he'd met the Manager, whatever he'd resigned himself to, it hadn't been like this.

His head was clear.

He didn't think it was peace he was feeling, at least not yet. He was still scared. Of course he was. The unknown always brought fear. His life, what there was of it, had been strictly regimented. He woke up. He took a shower. He dressed. He drank two cups of terrible coffee. He went to work. He met with the partners. He met with clients. He went to court. He'd never been one for theatrics. Just the facts, ma'am. He felt comfortable in front of a judge. In front of opposition. Most times he won. Sometimes he didn't. There were highs and lows, setbacks and victories. The day would be long gone by the time he went home. He'd eat a frozen dinner in front of the television. If he was feeling particularly indulgent, he'd have a glass of wine. Then he'd go into his home office and work until midnight. When he finished, he'd take another shower before going to bed.

Day after day after day.

It was the life he knew. The life he was comfortable with, the one he'd made for himself. Even after Naomi had left and it felt like everything was crumbling, he held it all together by sheer force of will. It was *her* loss, he'd told himself. It was *her* fault.

He'd accepted it.

"You're a white man," his assistant told him at the office Christmas party, her cheeks flushed from one too many Manhattans. "You'll fail up. You always do."

He'd startled her when he'd laughed loudly. He'd been a little drunk himself. She'd probably never seen him laugh before.

If only she could see him now.

Here, in Charon's Crossing, with three days left until the Manager returned, Wallace ran through the backyard as night gave way to the rising sun, Apollo chasing after him in a sort of game of tag, barking brightly. Wallace worried for a moment about disturbing the tea plants, but he and Apollo were dead. The plants wouldn't be bothered if he didn't want them to be.

"Got you," he said, pressing his fingers between Apollo's ears before taking off again.

He laughed when Apollo jumped on him, paws hitting his back, knocking him off his feet. He landed roughly on the ground and managed to roll over in time to get his face spectacularly licked. "Ugh!" he cried. "Your breath is awful."

Apollo didn't seem to mind.

Wallace allowed it to go on for a few moments longer before pushing the dog off. Apollo crouched down on his front paws, ears twitching, ready to play again.

"Did you ever have a dog?" Nelson asked him from his perch on the back deck.

Wallace shook his head as he pushed himself off the ground. "Too busy. Seemed a little mean to get one, only to be gone for most of the day. Especially in the city."

"When you were younger?"

"My father was allergic. We had a cat, but it was an asshole."

"Cats usually are. He's a good boy. I worried, when we knew his time had come. We didn't know what happened to dogs when they passed. They take a piece of our souls with them when they leave. I thought . . . I didn't know what it'd do to Hugo." He nodded toward the tea plants. "Toward the end, Apollo could barely walk. Hugo had to make a hard choice. Let him stay as he was, and be in pain, or give him the ultimate gift. It was an easier decision for him than I expected it to be. The vet came here, and they laid a blanket out in the garden. It was quick. Hugo said his goodbyes. Apollo smiled in that way that dogs do, like he knew what was happening. He took a breath and then another and then another. And then . . . he didn't. His eyes closed. The vet said it was done. But he couldn't see what we could."

"He was still here," Wallace said as Apollo pressed his head against his knee, trying to get him to run again.

"He was," Nelson agreed. "Full of pep and vigor as if all the ailments and trappings of life had just faded away. Hugo tried to take him up to the door, but Apollo refused. Stubborn, he is."

"Sounds like someone I know."

Nelson laughed. "I suppose, though the same could be said about you." His smile faded. "Or at least it used to be. Wallace, you don't have to—"

"I know," Wallace said. "But what choice do I have?"

Nelson was quiet for a long moment, and Wallace almost convinced himself the conversation was over. It wasn't. Nelson smiled sadly and said, "It's never enough, is it? Time. We always think we have so much of it, but when it really counts, we don't have enough at all."

Wallace shrugged as Apollo pranced around the tea plants. "Then we make the most of it."

Nelson didn't reply.

He spent the day in the kitchen with Mei. He'd recovered enough from the séance with Nancy that he was able to pull trays of pastries from the oven and to lift the kettles from the stove. If anyone had looked through the portholes, they'd have seen kitchenware floating through the air with the greatest of ease.

"Why don't you just heat the water in the microwave?" he asked, pouring the water into a ceramic teapot.

"Oh my god," Mei said. "Don't ever let Hugo hear you say that. No, you know what? I changed my mind. Tell him, but make sure I'm there when you do. I want to see the expression on his face."

"Wouldn't be too happy, huh?"

"Understatement. Tea is serious business, Wallace. You don't heat water for tea in the freaking microwave. Have a little class, man." She picked up the tray Wallace had been working on and backed through the doors. "But still, tell him. I want to record his reaction." The doors swung shut behind her.

He went to the portholes, looking out into the tea shop. It was as busy as usual. The lunch crowd had arrived, and most of the tables were filled. Mei moved expertly around the people before setting the tray on a table. He glanced at the far corner. Nancy's table was empty. He wasn't surprised. He thought she'd be back, but it probably wouldn't be until he was gone. He didn't know if what they'd done had been enough. He wasn't foolish enough to think he'd alleviated her pain, but he hoped she'd at least have the foundation to start to build again if she wanted.

Hugo stood behind the register, smiling, though it was distant. He'd been quiet that morning, as if lost in thought. Wallace didn't want to push. He let Hugo be.

The front door of the tea shop opened, and a young couple walked in, their hair windswept, eyes bright. They'd been here before, the man saying it was their second date, when it was actually their third. He held the door open for his lady friend, and she laughed when he bowed slightly. Even above the din, Wallace could hear him. "After you, my queen."

"You're so weird," she said fondly.

"Only the best for you."

She grabbed his hand, pulling him to the counter. He kissed her on the cheek as she ordered for the both of them.

And Wallace knew the next thing he needed to do with the time he had left.

"You don't have to do this," Hugo said after the tea shop had closed for the night. Wallace had asked Mei and Nelson to give them some privacy. They'd agreed, though Nelson waggled his eyebrows suggestively as Mei pulled him into the kitchen, Apollo trailing after them.

"Maybe. But I think I do. If you can't, I can ask Mei to—"

Hugo shook his head. "No. I'll do it. What do you want me to say?"

Wallace told him. It was short and simple. He didn't think it was enough. He didn't know what else to add.

If he still had a beating heart, he thought it'd be in his throat as Hugo set the phone to speaker after he'd dialed the number Wallace had given him. He didn't know if anyone would answer. It'd be a strange number appearing on her screen, and she'd probably end up ignoring it as most people did.

She didn't.

"Hello?"

Hugo said, "Can I speak with Naomi Byrne?"

"Speaking. Who's calling, please?" The last word was quieter, and Wallace knew she had pulled the phone away to look at the number, frowning as she did so. He could see her clear as day in the corners of his mind.

"Ms. Byrne, my name is Hugo. You don't know me, but I know your husband."

A long pause. "Ex-husband," she said finally. "If you mean Wallace."

"I do."

"Well, I'm sorry to be the one to have to tell you this, but Wallace died a couple of months ago."

"I know," Hugo said.

"You . . . do? You spoke of him in the present tense, and I just assumed—it doesn't matter. What can I do for you, Hugo? I'm afraid I don't have long. I have a dinner meeting to get to."

"I won't take much of your time," Hugo said, looking up at Wallace who nodded.

"Were you a client of his? If there's a legal issue, you need to call the firm. I'm sure they would be happy to assist—"

"No," Hugo said. "I wasn't a client of his. I guess you could say he is—"

"*Was*," Wallace hissed. "*Was*."

Hugo rolled his eyes. "He *was* a client of mine, in his own way."

A longer pause. "Are you his therapist? I don't recognize the area code. Where are you calling from?" Then, "And *why* are you calling?"

"No," Hugo said. "I'm not a therapist. I own a tea shop."

Naomi laughed. "A tea shop. And you say *Wallace* was a client of yours. Wallace Price."

"Yes."

"I don't think I ever saw him drink a cup of tea in his life. Forgive me for sounding dubious, but he wasn't exactly the tea type."

"I know," Hugo said as Wallace groaned. "But I think you'd be surprised to hear that he learned to enjoy it regardless."

"Did he? That's . . . odd. Why would he—it doesn't matter. What do you *want*, Hugo?"

"He was a client of mine. But he was also my friend. I'm sorry for your loss. I know it must have been difficult."

"Thank you," Naomi said stiffly, and Wallace *knew* she was wracking her brain, trying to figure out what angle Hugo was working. "If you knew him, I'm sure you're aware we divorced."

"I know," Hugo said.

She was growing irritated. "Is there a point to this conversation? Or was that it? Look, I appreciate you calling, but I—"

"He loved you. Quite a bit. And I know it got rough, and you went your separate ways for good reason, but he never regretted a single moment he spent with you. He wanted you to know that. He hoped you found happiness again. That you would have a full life, and that he was so sorry for what happened."

Naomi didn't speak. Wallace would have thought she disconnected, but he could still hear her breathing.

"Say it," he whispered. "Please."

Hugo said, "He told me about your wedding day. He said there had never been anyone more beautiful than you were at that moment. He was happy. And even though things changed, he never forgot the way you smiled at him in that little church." He laughed quietly. "He said he panicked right before the ceremony. You had to talk to him through a door to try to get him to calm down."

Silence. Then, "He . . . he said he couldn't get his tie to work. That we might as well call the whole thing off."

"But you didn't."

Naomi sniffled. "No. We didn't, because it was just something so Wallace that I . . . Christ. You had to call and ruin my makeup, didn't you?"

Hugo chuckled. "I don't mean to."

"No, I don't expect you do. Why are you calling me now with this?"

"Because he thought you deserved to hear it. I know you hadn't spoken in a long while before he passed, but the man I know—knew, was different than the man you remember. He learned kindness."

"That doesn't sound like Wallace at all."

"I know," Hugo said. "But people can change when faced with eternity."

"What's that supposed to mean?"

"It is what it is."

She sounded uncertain when she said, "You knew him."

"Yes."

"Really knew him."

"Yes."

"And he told you what happened with us."

"He did."

"So you just decided to call me out of the blue, out of the goodness of your heart."

"Yes."

"Look. Hugo, was it? I don't know what you're gunning for here, but I don't—"

"Nothing. I want nothing. All I wanted to do was tell you that you mattered to him. Even when all was said and done, you mattered."

She didn't respond.

"That's it," Hugo said. "That's all I needed to say. I apologize for interrupting your evening. Thank you for—"

"You cared for him."

Hugo startled. He glanced at Wallace before looking away. "I do."

"Friends," she said, almost amused. "*Just* friends?"

"Hang up!" Wallace said frantically. "Oh my god, hang up the *phone*!" He tried to swipe at it, but Hugo was quicker, plucking it off the counter and holding it out of reach.

"Just friends," Hugo said, hurrying around the counter to keep Wallace from the phone. Wallace snarled at him, prepared to do what he had to in order to make this fresh hell end as quickly as possible.

"Are you sure? Because—and I can't believe I know this—you sound like the kind of guy he'd go for. He didn't think I noticed, but he would swoon whenever—"

"I don't *swoon*!" Wallace bellowed.

"Really?" Hugo said into the phone. "Swoon, you say?"

"Yes. It was embarrassing. There was this one friend of mine—kind of talked like you, the same cadence—who Wallace would fawn over. He would deny it, of course, but I wouldn't be surprised if that was the case with you."

"I have the worst ideas," Wallace muttered. "Everything is terrible."

"Good to know," Hugo said to Naomi. "But no, we were just friends."

"Doesn't matter now though, does it?" Naomi asked. "Because he's gone."

Wallace stopped, hands pressed flat against the counter. He bowed his head and squeezed his eyes shut.

"I don't know that he truly is," Hugo said finally. "I think a part of him remains."

"Pretty thoughts, and nothing more. Did . . ." She huffed out a breath. "Did you love him? God, I can't believe I'm having this conversation. I don't know you. I don't even *care* if you and he were—"

"We weren't," Hugo said simply.

"That doesn't answer my question."

"I know," he said, and Wallace felt hot and cold, all at the same time. "I don't know how to answer that question."

"Yes or no. It's not hard. But you not saying no is all the answer I need." She sniffled again. "You weren't at the funeral."

"I didn't know."

"It was . . . quick. For him. I'm told he didn't suffer. There and gone as if he never were at all."

"But he was," Hugo said, and he never looked away from Wallace. "He was."

She laughed, though it sounded like a sob. "He was, wasn't he? For better or worse, he was. Hugo, I don't know who you are. I don't know how you knew Wallace, and I don't believe for a minute it was because of tea. I'm . . . sorry. For your loss. Thank you, but please don't call me again. I'm ready to move on. I *have* moved on. I don't know what else to say."

"You don't need to say anything else," Hugo said. "I appreciate your time."

The phone beeped as she disconnected the call.

Silence filled the tea shop.

Wallace broke. "You can't . . . *Hugo*."

"I know," Hugo said, sounding strangely vulnerable. Wallace looked up to see him fiddling with his bandana, green with white dogs imprinted on it. "But it's mine. It's for me. And you can't take that away."

"I'm not *trying* to," Wallace snapped. "It's—you're . . ." His chest hitched. The hook felt molten hot. "You're making it harder. Please don't do this to me. I can't stand it. I just can't."

"Why?" Hugo asked. "What's so bad about it?"

"Because I'm *dead*!" Wallace shouted.

He left Hugo standing in the main room of the tea shop, the shadows stretching further.

CHAPTER 20

The next day was hard.

Wallace brooded, pacing back and forth like a caged animal. The others gave him a wide berth as he muttered, "Two days. Two more days."

He shuddered. He shook. He *quaked.*

And there was nothing he could do to stop it.

He looked out the front window.

There, parked in front of the tea shop as it always was, sat Hugo's scooter. Pea green with whitewall tires. A side mirror with a little trinket hanging from it, a cartoon ghost with a little word bubble that read BOO! The seat was small, but there were metal handlebars on the back.

He remembered the way the sun had felt on him as he'd stood on the back deck. Again. Again. He needed to feel it again. Such a small thing, but the more he thought about it, the more he couldn't shake it. The sun. He wanted to feel the sun. It was calling to him, the hook in his chest vibrating, the cable brighter now than it'd been before. Whispers caressed his ears, but it wasn't like the voices from the door. Those were soothing and calm. This felt urgent.

He went to Mei in the kitchen. She eyed him warily as if she expected him to bite her head off. He felt guilty. "Can you watch the shop this afternoon?"

She nodded slowly. "I guess. Why?"

"I need to get out of here."

She looked alarmed. "What? Wallace, you know what'll happen if you try to—"

"I know. But I won't go far. I know how long I lasted the first time. I can handle it."

She wasn't convinced. "You can't take that risk. Not when you're so close to . . ." She didn't need to finish. They both knew what she meant.

He laughed wildly. "If not now, when? Oh, and I'm taking Hugo with me."

Mei blinked. "Taking him with you *where*?"

He grinned. He felt crazed, and it burned within him. "I don't know. Isn't it wonderful?"

Hugo listened as Wallace explained. He didn't answer right away, and Wallace thought he was going to refuse. Finally, he said, "Are you sure?"

Wallace nodded. "You'll know, won't you? How long we can go. How far."

"It's dangerous."

"I need this," Wallace said plainly. "And I want it to be with you."

It was the wrong thing to say. Hugo's expression shuttered. "Changed your mind? Last night, you seemed pretty certain you didn't want to hear how I feel."

"I'm scared," Wallace admitted. "And I don't know how not to be. But if this is it, if this is what I have left, then I want to do this. With you."

Hugo sighed. "It's really what you want?"

"Yes."

"I need to ask Mei if she'll—"

"Already done," Mei said, peeking her head through the kitchen doors. Wallace snorted when he saw Nelson peering under her arms. Of course they'd been listening. "I got it, boss. Give the man what he wants. It'll do you both some good. Fresh air and blah, blah, blah. We'll hold down the fort."

"We don't even know if he can ride it," Hugo said.

Wallace puffed out his chest. "I can do anything."

He couldn't do anything.

"What the hell?" he growled as he fell through the scooter to the ground for the fifth time.

"People are staring," Hugo muttered out the side of his mouth.

"Oh, I'm so *sorry*." Wallace pushed himself up off the ground. "And it's not like they can see me. For all they know, you're talking to your scooter like a weirdo."

Hugo crossed his arms and glared at his feet.

Wallace frowned at the scooter. It should be easy. It was just like the chairs. "Unexpect it," he mumbled to himself. "Unexpect it. Unexpect it."

He lifted his leg once more, throwing it over the back of the scooter. He knew he looked ridiculous as he lowered himself slowly, but he was beyond caring. He was going to do this if it was the last thing he did.

He crowed in triumph when he felt the back seat of the scooter pressed against his rear and thighs. "Hell yeah! I'm the best ghost *ever*!"

He looked over at Hugo, who fought a smile. "You're going to fall off and—"

"Kill myself? I have a feeling I don't need to worry about that. Get on. Come on, come on, come *on*." He patted the seat in front of him.

It was awkward, more so than Wallace thought it would be. The scooter was small and Hugo and Wallace were not. Swallowing thickly, Wallace studiously avoided looking at Hugo's rear as he threw his leg over one side and settled on the seat. The scooter creaked as Hugo propped it up, raising the kickstand with the heel of his shoe. They were close, so close that Wallace's legs disappeared into Hugo. The cable stretched between them tightly. It was oddly intimate, and Wallace wondered what it would be like to wrap his arms around Hugo's waist, holding on as tightly as he could.

Instead, he reached back and gripped the metal bars at his sides, settling his feet on the footrests.

Hugo turned his head. "We're not going far."

"I know."

"And you'll tell me when it starts getting bad."

"I will."

"I mean it, Wallace."

"I promise," he said, and he'd never meant it more. The whispers he'd heard in the house were louder now, and he could no longer ignore them. He didn't know what they were calling him toward, but it wasn't the door. They were calling him *away* from the tea shop.

Hugo turned the key. The scooter's engine whined, the seat vibrating underneath Wallace pleasantly. His laugh turned into a yelp when they started rolling forward slowly, picking up speed as dust kicked up behind them.

Wallace felt the pull the moment they hit the road. He gritted his teeth against it. He hadn't known what it'd been before. He did now. He looked down at his arms, expecting to see his skin beginning to flake off. Not yet, but soon.

Wallace thought Hugo would turn toward town, perhaps driving down the main drag and back to the shop.

He didn't.

He went the opposite direction, leaving everything behind. The forest grew thicker on either side of the road, the trees swaying in a cool breeze, limbs clacking together like bones. The sun sank lower in front of them, the sky pink and orange and shades of blue that Wallace couldn't believe existed, deep, dark, like the farthest depths of the ocean.

No one followed them; no cars on the road passed them by. It was as if they were the only two people in the entire world on a lonely stretch of road that led to nowhere and everywhere all at once.

"Faster," he said in Hugo's ear. "Please go faster."

Hugo did, the engine of the scooter whining pathetically. It wasn't built for speed but it didn't matter. It was enough. The wind whipped through their hair as they leaned into every curve, the road a blur beneath them, flashes of white and yellow lines shooting across Wallace's vision.

It was only a few minutes later that Wallace's skin began to rise and flake away, trailing behind them. Hugo saw it out of the corner of his eye, but before he could speak, Wallace said, "I'm all right. I swear. Go. Go. Go."

Hugo went.

Wallace wondered what would happen if they never stopped. Perhaps if they went far enough, Wallace would drift away into nothing, leaving all the pieces of him behind. Not a Husk. Not a ghost. Just motes of dust along a stretch of mountain road, ashes spread as if he'd mattered.

And maybe he had. Not to the world at large, not to very many people in the grand scheme of things, but here, in this place? With Hugo and Mei and Apollo and Nelson? Yes, he thought maybe he mattered after all, a lesson in the unexpected. Wasn't that the point? Wasn't that the great answer to the mystery of life? To make the most of what you have while you have it, the good and the bad, the beautiful and the ugly.

In death, Wallace had never felt more alive.

He squeezed his thighs against the sides of the scooter, holding himself in place. He raised his arms out like wings, pieces of his arms flaking off behind them. He tilted his head back toward the sun and closed his eyes. There, there, there it was, the warmth, the light covering him completely. Never wanting it to end, he shouted his wild joy toward the sky.

Hugo seemed to have a destination in mind. He turned down a road that Wallace would have missed had he been on his own. It wound its way through the forest on an incline. The pull of his shedding skin was negligible. A dark curl flickered at the back of his mind, but he had it under control. The whispers were fading.

On the side of the road ahead was a little pullout, nothing more than a gravel patch. Hugo steered the scooter toward it. Wallace gasped when he saw what lay on the other side of the guardrail.

The pullout was set on a cliff. The drop-off was steep, though the tops of the trees below rose in front of them. The sun set in the west, and as the scooter came to a stop, Wallace jumped off, rushing toward the guardrail. In his haste, he almost ran *through* it, but managed to skid to a stop just before.

"That would've been bad," he said, looking down, the thrill of vertigo washing dizzily over him.

He heard Hugo turn the scooter off and prop it up on the kickstand before climbing off himself. "We can't stay long. It's getting worse."

It was. The flakes were larger. The curl in his mind was stronger. His jaw ached. His hands were shaking. "Just a few minutes," he whispered. Hugo joined him at the guardrail. "Why here? What's this place to you?"

"My father used to bring me up here," Hugo said, face awash with dying sunlight. "When I was a kid. This was where we'd talk about all the important things." He smiled ruefully. "This is where I got the sex talk. This is where I got grounded because I was failing algebra. This is where I told him I was queer. He told me if he'd known, the sex talk would have gone a hell of a lot different."

"Good man?"

"Good man," Hugo agreed. "The best, really. He made mistakes, but he always owned up to them. He would have liked you." He paused. "Well, how you are *now*. He wasn't fond of lawyers."

"No one is. We're masochists that way."

As the sun set, they stood side by side, Hugo's shadow stretching behind them.

"When I'm gone," Wallace said, "please don't forget me. I don't have many people who'll remember me, at least not in a good way. I want you to be one of them." His fingernails began to break apart.

Hugo's throat worked as he swallowed. "How could I ever forget you?"

Wallace thought it would be very easy. "You promise?"

"I promise."

The sunset was brilliant. He wished he'd taken more time to turn his face toward the sky. "Do you think we'll see each other again?"

"I hope so."

It was the best answer he could ask for. "But not for a long time.

You've got work to do." He blinked away the burn in his eyes. "And it will—"

But he never got to finish. The curl deepened. It tugged. It pulled. It *yanked.* The cable flashed. "Oh," Wallace grunted as he stumbled.

"We have to go back," Hugo said, sounding worried. "Now."

"Yeah," Wallace whispered as the sun dipped below the horizon.

He felt as if he were floating on the ride back. Hugo pushed the scooter as fast as it could go, but Wallace wasn't worried. He wasn't scared, not like he'd been before. There was a sense of calm about him, something akin to relief.

"Hold on!" Hugo shouted at him, but he sounded so very far away. The whispers had returned, growing louder, more insistent.

His head cleared when they hit the road that led to the tea shop. By then, his hands were gone, his arms were gone, and he thought he'd lost his nose. He groaned as they reformed, the bits and pieces snapping back into place like a complex puzzle. He gasped when Hugo jerked the scooter to the right. He thought they were going to crash, and for a wild moment, he wondered why he hadn't insisted Hugo wear a helmet. But the thought was gone when he saw what had caused Hugo to lose control out of the corner of his eye.

Cameron.

Standing in the middle of the road.

I'm still here.

Rocks and dust kicked up around the tires as they skidded. A tree loomed in front of them, a great old thing with cracked bark leaking sap like tears. Wallace reached *through* Hugo, wrapping his hands around the handlebars, squeezing the brakes as hard as he could. They squealed and the scooter wobbled. The back tire lifted off the road momentarily before slamming back down as the scooter stopped, the front tire inches from the tree.

"Holy crap," Hugo muttered. He looked down as Wallace pulled his hands back. "If you hadn't—"

Wallace was off the scooter before Hugo could finish. He turned toward the road.

Cameron's face was turned toward the stars, mouth open, black teeth bared. His arms were limp at his sides, fingers dangling. He lowered his head as if he could feel Wallace watching him, eyes flat and cold.

The hook in Wallace's chest vibrated as hard as he'd ever felt it. It was almost like it was alive. The whispers were now a storm, spinning around him, the words lost, but Wallace knew then what they meant, why he'd felt the drive to leave the tea shop in the first place.

It was Cameron calling to him.

Behind him, Hugo lowered the kickstand on the scooter before switching it off, but Wallace wasn't to be distracted. Not now. He said, "Cameron. You're still in there, aren't you? Oh my god, I hear you."

Cameron blinked slowly.

Wallace remembered how he'd felt in the tea garden, Cameron's hands wrapped around him. The happiness. The fury. The bright moments of the sunshine man, of *Zach, Zach, Zach.* The thunderous grief that overtook him when all was lost. He'd been told later it'd only lasted seconds, their strange union, but he'd felt a lifetime of peaks and valleys. He *was* Cameron, he'd seen all that Cameron had seen, had suffered alongside him through the extraordinary unfairness of life. He hadn't understood the nuances then; it'd all been too much, too fast. He didn't think he could understand it now, not completely, but the bits and pieces were clearer than they'd been before.

Even as Hugo screamed for him to stop, Wallace reached out and took Cameron's hand in his. "Show me," he whispered.

And so Cameron did.

Memories rose like ghosts, and Zach said, "I don't feel good."

He tried to smile.

He failed.

His eyes rolled up in his head.

Alive, then dead.

But it hadn't been that quick, had it? No, there'd been more, so much more that Wallace hadn't been able to parse through the first time. Now, he caught glimpses of it, flashes like staccato film, reels of tape that jerked from frame to frame. He *was* Cameron, but not.

His name was Wallace Price. He'd lived. He'd died. And yet, he'd persisted, on and on and on, but that was insignificant, that was minor, that was *gone,* because Cameron took over, showing him all that lay hidden beneath the surface.

"Zach," Wallace whispered as Cameron said, "Zach? *Zach?*" moving forward, but he (they?) couldn't catch Zach before he collapsed, head bouncing on the floor with a terrible *thunk.*

Wallace was no longer in control, caught up in the bleeding memories that surrounded him like an endless universe, Cameron on the phone, screaming at the 911 operator that he didn't *know* what was wrong, he didn't *know* what to do, help us, oh please god, help us.

"Help us," Wallace whispered. "Please."

Another jump, harsh and grating, and Cameron threw open the front door, paramedics pushing by him, lights flashing from an ambulance and a fire truck in front of the house.

Cameron demanded to know what was wrong as they loaded Zach onto a gurney, the paramedics talking quickly about pupils dilating and blood pressure dropping. Zach's eyes were closed, body limp, and Wallace felt Cameron's horror as if it were his own, his mind blaring *WHAT IS HAPPENING WHAT IS HAPPENING* over and over again.

He was in the back of the ambulance as they opened Zach's shirt, asking Cameron if he knew of any history of illness, if he took drugs, if he'd overdosed, you need to tell us everything so we know how to help him.

He could barely think. "No," he said, sounding incredulous. "He's never taken a drug in his life. He doesn't even like taking aspirin. He's not sick. He's never been *sick.*"

He stood in the hospital, numb as if his entire body had been submerged in ice, surrounded by friends and Zach's family when the doctor came out and broke their entire world apart. Bleeding in the brain, the doctor said. A rupture. A fissure. Aneurysmal subarachnoid hemorrhage.

Brain damage.

Brain damage.

Brain damage.

Cameron said, "But you can help him, right? You can fix him, right? *You can make him better, right?*" He screamed and screamed, hands on his shoulders, hands on his arms, holding him, keeping him from lunging at the doctor, who backed away slowly.

They took Zach into surgery immediately.

He died on the operating table.

Cameron wore his finest suit to the funeral.

He made sure Zach had the same.

A choir sang a hymn of light and wonder, of God and His divine plan, and Wallace screamed in his head, but not as himself. As Cameron, shrieking silently for this all to be a dream, that it couldn't be real. *Wake up!* Cameron bellowed in his head. *Please, wake up!*

The priest spoke of pain and grief, that we can never understand why someone so full of life could be taken so soon, but that God never gave us more than what he thought we could handle.

Everyone cried.

Cameron didn't.

Oh, he tried. He tried to force the tears, tried to force himself to feel *anything* but the numbing, encroaching cold.

The casket was open.

He couldn't look at the body that lay inside.

"Are you sure?" a friend asked him. "Don't you want to go say goodbye before . . ." Her words cut off in a wet choke.

Cameron stood next to a hole in the ground as the same priest droned on and on about God and His plans and the mysterious, unknowing world. He watched as Zach was lowered into that hole, and still he felt nothing but cold. It was all he knew, and no matter what Wallace did, no matter how hard he tried, he couldn't chase the cold away.

People stayed the night with him. For weeks on end, he wasn't alone.

They said, "Cameron, you need to eat."

They said, "Cameron, you need to shower."

They said, "Cameron, let's go outside, huh? Get you some fresh air."

And finally, they said, "You sure you're going to be all right by yourself?"

"I'll be fine," he told them. "I'll be fine."

He wasn't.

He lasted four months.

Four months of haunting their home, moving from room to room, calling out for Zach, saying, "We were going to do so many things. *You promised me!*"

And still the tears didn't come.

He was cold all the time.

There were days when he didn't get out of bed, days when he didn't have the strength to do anything but roll over, pulling the comforter over his head, chasing the scents of Zach, who smelled like woodsmoke and earth and trees, so many trees.

Toward the end, his friends came back. "We're worried about you," they said. "We need to make sure you're going to be okay."

"I'll be fine," he told them. "I'll be fine."

On the last day, he woke up.

On the last day, he ate a bowl of cereal. He washed the bowl and spoon in the sink before putting them away.

On the last day, he wandered around the house, but he didn't speak.

On the last day, he gave up.

It didn't hurt, really.

The end.

He was only numb.

And then he was gone.

Except he *wasn't,* was he?

No.

Because he stood above himself, watching his lifeblood spill from him, and he said, "Oh. This is Hell."

And he was still alone.

Until a man came. He called himself a Reaper. He smiled, though it didn't reach his eyes. There was a curl to his lips that wasn't kind.

"I'll take you away," the Reaper said. "It'll all make sense, I promise. Even though you gave your life away like it was nothing, I'll take care of you."

He stood in front of a tea shop at dusk, looking at a sign in the window.

CLOSED FOR A PRIVATE EVENT

Hugo waited for him inside. He offered Cameron tea.

Cameron refused.

"I'm sorry," Hugo told him. "For all that you've lost."

The Reaper snorted. "He did it on his own."

And it was like poison in Cameron's ears.

There was a door, he knew, but he didn't trust it. The Reaper had told him that it could lead to just about anywhere. He didn't know. Hugo didn't know. No one did. "It could be just endless darkness," the Reaper mused late at night while Hugo slept. "It could be just nothing at all."

Cameron fled the tea shop.

His skin flaked away.

The cable snapped and disappeared.

The hook in his chest dissolved.

He made it to the town before he fell to his knees in the middle of the road.

His last lucid thought was of Zach, and how he smiled like the sun, and Wallace knew his desire to feel the same hadn't only come from himself. It was the last, forceful gasp of the man whose mind he now shared, the sun the last thing he'd held onto before the end of his humanity.

And here, now, Wallace said, "It isn't fair. None of it is."

"Help me," Cameron said.

Wallace looked down as his chest burned as if on fire.

A curve of metal stuck out from his sternum. The end was attached to the thick, glowing cable that stretched toward Hugo. A connection, a tether, a lifeline between the living and the dead, keeping them from floating away into nothing.

Wallace reached for the hook, hesitating briefly. "I see it now. It's not always about the things you've done, or the mistakes you've made. It's about the people, and what we're willing to do for one another. The sacrifices we make. They taught me that. Here, in this place."

"Please," Cameron whispered. "I don't want to be lost anymore."

"Unexpect it," Wallace said.

He gripped the hook, the metal hot against his palms and fingers, but it didn't burn. He pulled as hard as he could, the pain immense, causing him to grit his teeth together. Tears flooded his eyes, and he cried out as the hook came free. The heaviness loosened its grip, a wave of relief washing over him that felt like the sun and the stars.

He raised the hook above his head.

And slammed it into Cameron's chest.

His eyes flashed open when his head rocked to the side from a vicious slap. "*Ow!* What the hell?"

He blinked as Mei glared down at him. They were in the tea shop, Wallace looking up from the floor. "You *bastard,*" Mei snapped at him. "What the hell did you think you were doing?"

He rubbed the side of his face, cheek still stinging as he sat up. "What are you . . ." His eyes bulged. "Oh shit."

"Yeah, you dick. *Oh shit* is right. Do you have any idea what you've—"

"Did it work?" he asked desperately. "Did it work?"

She sighed, shoulders slumping. "Look for yourself." She reached down, grabbing his arm and pulling him up from the floor. He yelped in surprise when he *shot* up, feet leaving the ground as if he weighed nothing. With wide eyes, he looked down. He gasped when he saw himself floating a few inches above the floor. He waved his arms *up*, trying to push himself *down*. It didn't work. Mei glared at him as he tried again. "Yeah, that's your own fault. You're lucky we still had Apollo's leash or you'd be gone by now." She pointed at his ankle. Wrapped around him was a dog leash. He followed the leash until he saw Nelson holding the other end.

"What's wrong with me?" he whispered.

Nelson leaned forward, kissing the back of his hand, lips dry and chapped. "You foolish man. You foolish, wonderful man. You're floating because there's nothing left holding you in place. But don't worry. I've got you. I won't let you float away. Unexpect it, Wallace, and trust that we have you."

Apollo nosed Wallace's ankle, licking frantically at the leash as if to make sure Wallace was still there. "I am," Wallace whispered, his voice soft and dreamy. "I'm still here."

He raised his head, and everything else fell away. Mei. Apollo. Nelson. The leash, the tea shop, the fact that he couldn't feel the ground. All of it.

Because a man stood next to Hugo in front of the fireplace, head bowed. He was handsome, though his cheeks were sunken, his eyes red-rimmed as if he'd been crying recently. His light-colored hair hung down around his face. He wore a pair of jeans and a thick sweater, the sleeves hanging over the backs of his hands.

"Cameron?" Wallace asked, voice cracking.

Cameron lifted his head. His smile trembled. "Hello, Wallace." He stepped away from Hugo, looking uncertain. A tear trickled down his cheek. "You . . . you found me."

Wallace nodded dumbly.

And then he was being hugged within an inch of his life, Cameron's face pressed against his stomach as Wallace rose into the air as far as the leash allowed. It was different than it'd been before. Gone were the flashes of the life once lived. Cameron wasn't cold like he'd been. His skin was fever-hot, and his shoulders shook as he held on as tightly as he could. Wallace was helpless to do anything but put his hands in Cameron's hair, holding on gently.

"Thank you," Cameron whispered against his stomach. "Oh my god, thank you. Thank you. Thank you."

"Yeah," Wallace said roughly. "Yes. Of course."

CHAPTER 21

The next day, Charon's Crossing Tea and Treats didn't open as it normally did. The windows were shuttered, lights off, a blind pulled down on the window to the front door. Those who came for their daily tea and pastries were disappointed to find the door locked, a sign in the window.

DEAR VALUED FRIENDS:
CHARON'S CROSSING WILL BE CLOSED FOR THE NEXT TWO DAYS DUE TO SOME MINOR RENOVATIONS.
WE LOOK FORWARD TO SERVING YOU AGAIN WHEN WE REOPEN!
HUGO & MEI

Wallace floated a few feet above the back deck, watching Apollo run through the tea plants, chasing a cadre of squirrels that didn't know he was there. He laughed quietly when the dog tripped over his own feet, tumbling to the ground before picking himself up and tearing through the tea plants again. Wallace barely felt the leash tugging at his ankle, tied to the deck railing to keep him from floating away.

He looked down at the man standing next to him, Wallace's knees at the same level as the man's shoulders.

"I don't really remember," Cameron said, and Wallace wasn't surprised. "What it was like being . . . a Husk. There are flashes, but I can barely make them out, much less remember them."

"It's probably for the best." Wallace didn't know what it'd do to a person to remember their time as a Husk. Nothing good.

"Two years," Cameron whispered. "Hugo said it was over two years."

"You can't blame him. He didn't know. He was told there was nothing that could be done when someone—"

"I don't blame him," Cameron said. Wallace believed him. "I made my own choice. He warned me what would happen if I left, but I couldn't listen."

"It didn't help that the Reaper tried to force your hand," Wallace said bitterly.

Cameron sighed. "Yeah, but that's not Hugo's fault. All he wants to do is help, and I wasn't willing to let him. I was so angry at everything. I thought I'd found a way to make it stop. Everything I was feeling. It was a slap to the face when I realized it wasn't over. It goes on and on. Do you know what that's like?"

"I do." Then, "Maybe not to the extent you mean, but I get it."

Cameron glanced up at him. "You do, don't you?"

"I think so. It's a lot for anyone to realize that we go on, even when our hearts stop beating. That the pain of life still can follow us even through death. I don't blame you for what happened. I don't think anyone could. And you shouldn't blame yourself. Learn from it. Grow from it, but don't allow it to consume you again. Easier said than done, I know."

"But look at you," Cameron said. "You're . . ."

Wallace laughed against the lump in his throat. "I know. But I don't want you worrying about that. I think . . . I think you helped to teach me what I was supposed to learn."

"Which was what?" Cameron asked.

Wallace looked toward the sky, tilting back until he was almost horizontal with the ground. Clouds passed by, fluffy white things with no real destination in mind. He raised his hands, backlit by the warm sun. "That we have to let go, no matter how scary it can be."

"I've wasted so much time. Zach must be angry with me."

"You'll find out soon enough. Do you love him?"

"Yes." It was said with such a tangible fierceness that Wallace could taste it in the back of his throat, the remnants of a fire that smoldered and sparked.

"And he loves you?"

Cameron laughed wetly. "Impossibly. I wasn't the best person to be around, but he took the worst parts of me and dragged them out into the light." He hung his head. "I'm scared, Wallace. What if it's too late? What if I took too long?"

Wallace turned over in midair, looking down at Cameron. He didn't cast a shadow. Neither of them did, but it didn't matter. They were here. They were real. "What're a couple of years in the face of eternity?"

Cameron sniffled. "You think so?"

"Yeah," Wallace said. "I do."

Time seemed to move in fits and starts for the rest of the day. Hugo spent most of it with Cameron. For a brief moment, Wallace was intensely jealous, but he let it go. Cameron needed Hugo more. Wallace had made his choice.

"What's it like?" Mei asked him. They were in the kitchen, Mei moving back and forth between one of the ovens and the stove. Just because the shop was closed, she'd told him, didn't mean the work stopped too.

"What?" The leash was tied around the bottom of the refrigerator, cinched tightly so that his feet brushed the ground.

She hesitated. "Hugo said you . . ." She motioned at her chest.

He shrugged. "It is what it is."

"Wallace."

"Untethered," he said finally.

She took her hand in his, tugging gently so his feet bumped the floor. "I've got you."

He smiled at her. "I know you do."

"I won't let you float away. You're not a balloon."

He laughed until he could barely breathe.

He didn't know what they were planning.

He should have known it was something. They weren't the types to let things lie as they were.

He wandered the bottom floor of the tea shop, Apollo happily tugging on the leash to hold him in place, Wallace doing his best to ignore the little whispers at the back of his head. They weren't like what he'd heard with Cameron. These whispers were more forceful, coming from the door, and though he couldn't make the words out, they had a cadence to them that felt like speech, frightening and enthralling him in equal measure. He was haunting the tea shop, a little boat in a vast ocean. His feet never touched the floor.

Nelson watched him from his chair in front of the fireplace. When Apollo tugged Wallace by him, Nelson said, "You feel it, don't you?"

"What?" Wallace asked, voice wistful and off-kilter.

"The door. It calls to you."

"Yes," Wallace whispered. He spun lazily in the air.

"This hook. The cable. You had one."

Wallace blinked slowly, coming back to himself. At least a little bit. "You do too. Of course you do. I never thought to ask. What is it?"

"I don't know," Nelson admitted. "Not really. It's always been there. I think it's a manifestation of a connection, tying us to Hugo, reminding us that we're not alone."

"It's gone now," Wallace whispered, staring down at the crackling fire. He closed his eyes. Hugo was there, smiling in the dark.

"Perhaps," Nelson said. "But what it represented isn't. That can never be taken away from you. Remember what I told you about need versus want? We don't need you because that implies you had to fix something in us. We were never broken. We *want* you, Wallace. Every piece. Every part. Because we're family. Can you see the difference?"

Wallace laughed quietly. "But I haven't had my third cup of tea."

Nelson tapped his cane on the floor. "No. I don't suppose you have. Let's change that, shall we?"

Wallace opened his eyes. "What?"

Nelson nodded toward the kitchen.

Hugo and Mei appeared through the double doors. Hugo carried a tray filled with familiar cups and a clay teapot. Cameron trailed after them, eyes bright.

Hugo set the tray down on a table. He motioned for them to join them at the table. He said, "Cameron, I have something for you."

Cameron blinked. "For me? I thought this was for . . ." He glanced at Wallace.

Wallace shook his head. "No. This is for you. Your first."

Nelson rose from his chair, tugging the leash from Apollo's mouth. The dog thought they were playing and tried to pull it back. Wallace jerked from side to side, smiling so wide he thought his face would split in half. Apollo eventually let go, barking at Wallace's feet as Nelson pulled him toward the table.

"Has it steeped long enough?" Wallace asked as the scent of . . . oranges? Yes, the scent of oranges filled the tea shop.

"It has," Hugo said. His hands shook as he lifted the teapot. Mei put her hand on the back of his to steady him. He poured the tea into each cup. Once he'd finished, he poured more tea into a little bowl with the same markings as the teacups. He set the pot down before lifting the bowl and placing it on the floor in front of Apollo. The dog sat in front of it, head cocked as he waited. "It's ready."

Cameron hesitated before leaning over the teapot, inhaling deeply. "Oh. That's . . ." He looked up at Hugo with wide eyes. "I know that smell. We . . . had this orange tree. In our back yard. It was . . . Zach liked to lie underneath it and look up at the sunlight through the branches." He closed his eyes as his throat worked. "It smells like home."

"Hugo knows what he's doing," Wallace said. "He's good like that." He looked at all of them. "How does it go again?"

They knew what he meant. "The first time you share tea, you are a stranger," Mei said.

"The second time you share tea," Nelson said, "you are an honored guest."

Hugo nodded. "And the third time you share tea, you become family. It's a Balti quote. I took those words to heart because there's something special about the sharing of tea. Grandad taught me that. He said that when you take tea with someone, it's intimate and quiet. Profound. The different flavors mingle, the scent of it strong. It's small, but when we drink, we drink together." He handed each of them a cup. First Cameron. Then Mei. Then Nelson. Wallace was last. The tea sloshed as he took the cup from Hugo, their fingers close but not touching, never touching. He was careful as he spun in air, pointing his feet toward the ground as Nelson tied off the leash against a table leg. "Please, drink with me."

He waited for Cameron to go first. Cameron lifted the cup to his lips, inhaling again, eyes fluttering shut. His lips curved into a quiet smile before he drank. Mei went next, followed by Nelson, then Hugo. Apollo did too, lapping at the bowl.

Wallace raised the cup to his lips, breathing in the orange mingling with spice. He could almost picture it, lying on the ground in the grass, looking up at a tree heavy with fruit, the leaves swaying softly in a cool breeze, sunlight trickling through the branches. He drank deeply, the tea sliding down his throat, warming him from the inside out.

Once the tea was finished, Wallace felt like he had only a moment before.

Except . . .

Except that wasn't quite true, was it?

Because he'd had his third cup of tea. His gaze drifted to the Balti proverb hanging above the counter.

Stranger. Guest. Family.

He belonged to them now just as much as they belonged to him.

He set the teacup back on the table before he could drop it. It clattered against the table, but the remains of the tea didn't spill. Cameron did the same. He stared down at the teacup, a look of wonder on his face. "I can . . ." He turned his gaze up toward the ceiling. "Can you hear that? It's . . . it sounds like a song. It's the loveliest thing I've ever heard."

"Yes," Nelson said quietly as Apollo barked.

"Me too," Wallace said.

Mei shook her head.

Hugo looked stricken, but Wallace hadn't expected him to hear what they could. It wasn't meant for him, at least not yet.

"It's calling me," Cameron whispered.

Wallace smiled.

They stood around the table, Wallace floating amidst them, drinking the tea until there was nothing left but the dregs.

Hugo found him on the back deck, floating horizontal to the ground, hands folded behind his head as he gazed up at the night sky. Mei had tied the leash to a deck railing after he'd asked, telling him he wasn't allowed to untie it for any reason. The stars were as bright as they always were. They stretched on forever. He wondered if there were stars where he was going. He hoped so. Perhaps he and Hugo could look up at the same sky at the same time.

Hugo sat next to him, wrapping his arms around his legs, knees against his chest.

"Another session, Doctor?" Wallace asked as he grabbed the leash, pulling himself closer to Hugo. His rear bumped the deck. He reached behind him to grab the edge of the deck, holding himself in place.

Hugo snorted before shaking his head. "I don't know if there's anything left to tell you."

"Where's Cameron?"

"With Grandad and Mei." He cleared his throat. "He's, uh. Tomorrow."

"What about tomorrow?" A big question, but never more than now.

"He's going to cross."

Wallace turned his head toward Hugo. "Already?"

Hugo nodded. "He knows what he wants."

"And he wants this."

"Yeah. I told him there was no rush, but he wouldn't hear of it. Thinks he's wasted too much time. He wants to go home."

"Home," Wallace whispered.

"Home," Hugo agreed, throat bobbing. "It'll be first thing." He stared at Wallace for a long moment. Then, "We can help them. If . . . if it worked for Cameron, maybe it can work for others." He looked out at the tea plants. "The Manager won't like it, though."

Wallace chuckled. "No, I don't expect he will. But regardless of what else he is, he's a bureaucrat. And even worse than that, he's a *bored* bureaucrat. He needs what I did."

"What's that?"

"A shock to the system."

"A shock to the system," Hugo repeated, mulling over the words. "I . . ." He shook his head. "Will you come with me? I want to show you something."

"What is it?"

"You'll see. Come on."

Wallace pushed himself off the deck, floating upward. He bounced when the leash grew taut. He swayed back and forth, blinking slowly. He wondered what would happen if he untied the leash, if he would continue to rise and rise and rise until he took his place amongst the stars. It was a terribly wonderful thought.

Instead, Hugo pulled him into the house, careful so that Wallace didn't bump his head on the doorframe.

The clock ticked the seconds by.

Mei and Cameron sat on the floor in front of the fireplace, Apollo on his back, legs in the air. Nelson was in his chair. They didn't speak as Hugo climbed the stairs, Wallace trailing after him, feet never touching the floor.

He thought Hugo would take him to the door and speak more of what it could mean, what might lay on the other side. He was surprised when Hugo went to one of the closed doors on the second floor.

The door that led to his room, the only one Wallace hadn't been into.

Hugo paused, his hand on the doorknob. He looked back at Wallace. "You ready?"

"For what?"

"Me."

Wallace laughed. "Absolutely."

Hugo opened the door and stepped to the side. He motioned for Wallace to go through.

Gripping the frame, he pulled himself into the room, ducking his head.

It was smaller than he thought it'd be. He knew the master bedroom was on the third floor, and that it'd belonged to Nelson and his wife before they'd passed.

This room was neat and tidy. Harvey, the health inspector, would undoubtedly be pleased. There wasn't a single speck of dust, not a bit of clutter or a thing out of place.

Much like the first floor, the walls were covered with posters and pictures of faraway places. A never-ending forest of ancient trees. An ancient statue on the banks of a green river. Bright ribbons hanging over a colorful marketplace filled with people in flowing robes. Homes with thatched roofs. The sun rising over a field of wheat. An island in the middle of a sea, a strange home set on its cliffs.

But they weren't all out-of-reach dreams.

A man and a woman who looked like Hugo smiled from a framed picture hanging in the center. Below it was another photograph, this one of a mangy dog looking grumpy as Hugo gave it a bath. Next to this one was Hugo and Nelson standing in front of the tea shop, arms folded across their chests, both of them grinning widely. Underneath this one was a picture of Mei in the kitchen, flour dotting her face, eyes sparkling, a spatula pointed at the camera.

And on and on they went, at least a dozen more, telling a story of a life lived with strength and love.

"This is wonderful," Wallace said, studying a photograph of a young Hugo on the shoulders of a man who looked to be his father. The man had a thick, bushy mustache and a devious spark in his eyes.

"They help me remember," Hugo said quietly, closing the door behind him. "All that I have. All that I've had."

"You'll see them again."

"You think so?"

He nodded. "Maybe I can find them first. I can . . . I don't know. Tell them about you. All that you've done. They'll be so proud of you."

Hugo said, "This isn't easy for me."

Wallace turned around in air. Hugo frowned, his forehead lined. He reached up and slid the bandana off his head. "What isn't easy?"

"This," Hugo said, motioning between the two of them. "You and me. I spend my life talking, talking, talking. People like you come to me, and I tell them about the world they're leaving behind, and what lies ahead. How there's nothing to fear and that they will find peace again even when they're at their lowest."

"But?"

Hugo shook his head. "I don't know what to do with you. I don't know how to say what I want to say."

"You don't have to do anything with—"

"Don't," Hugo said hoarsely. "Don't say that. You know that's not true." He dropped the bandana to the floor. "I want to do *everything* with you." Then, in a whisper, as if saying it any louder would break them completely, Hugo said, "I don't want you to go."

Six little words. Six words no one had ever said to Wallace Price before. They were fragile, and he took them in, holding them close.

Hugo lifted his apron above his head, letting it fall next to the bandana. He toed off his shoes. His socks were white, a hole near one of his toes.

Wallace said, "I . . ."

"I know," Hugo said. "Stay with me. Just for tonight."

Wallace was devastated. If they were anyone else, this could be the start of something. A beginning rather than an end. But they weren't anyone else. They were Wallace and Hugo, dead and alive. A great chasm stretched between them.

Hugo switched off the light, casting the room in semidarkness. He went to the bed. It was simple. Wood frame. Large mattress. Blue sheets and comforter. The pillows looked soft. The bed creaked when Hugo sat on it, hands dangling between his legs. "Please," Hugo said quietly.

"Just for tonight," Wallace said.

He looked down at his own feet, hovering above the wood floors. He scrunched up his face, and his shoes disappeared. He didn't worry about the rest. He wouldn't sleep.

Hugo looked up as Wallace floated toward him. He had a strange expression on his face, and Wallace wondered why Hugo had chosen him, what he'd done in life to deserve this moment.

Hugo nodded, sliding back on the bed, stretching out against the far side. He grabbed the dangling leash, tying it off to the headboard.

Wallace reached down and pressed his hands against the bed, wishing he could lie down next to Hugo. His fingers curled in the soft comforter. He pulled himself down until his face pressed against the blanket, breathing in deeply. It smelled like Hugo, cardamom and cinnamon and honey. He sighed, moving until he floated above Hugo, who rested his head on the pillow, eyes glittering in the dark as he watched Wallace.

They didn't speak at first. Wallace had so many things he wanted to say, but he didn't know how to start.

Hugo did. He always did. "Hello."

Wallace said, "Hello, Hugo."

Hugo raised his hand toward Wallace, fingers outstretched. Wallace did the same, their hands inches apart. They couldn't touch. Wallace was dead, after all. But it was good. It was still good. Wallace imagined he could feel the heat from Hugo's skin.

Hugo said, "I think I know why you were brought to me."

"Why?" Wallace asked.

Voices low, soft. Secret.

Hugo lowered his hand back to the bed, and the grief Wallace felt over it was enormous. "You make me question things. Why it has to be this way. My place in this world. You make me want things I can't have."

"Hugo." He cracked right down the middle.

"I wish things were different," Hugo whispered. "I wish you were alive and found your way here. It could be a day like any other. Maybe the sun is shining. Maybe it's raining. I'm behind the counter. The door opens. I look up. You walk in. You're frowning, because you don't know what the hell you're doing in a tea shop in the middle of nowhere."

Wallace snorted. "That sounds about right."

"Maybe you're passing through," Hugo continued. "You're lost, and you need help finding your way. Or maybe you're here to stay. You come up to the counter. I say hello, and welcome you to Charon's Crossing."

"I tell you I've never had tea before. You look outraged."

Hugo grinned ruefully. "Maybe not outraged."

"Yeah, yeah. Keep telling yourself that. You would be so irritated. But you'd also be patient."

"I'd ask you what flavors you like."

"Peppermint. I like peppermint."

"Then I have just the tea for you. Trust me, it's good. What brings you here?"

"I don't know," Wallace said, caught in a fantasy where everything was beautiful and nothing hurt. He'd been here before in secret. But now it was out in the open, and he never wanted it to end. "I saw the sign near the road and took a chance."

"Did you?"

"Yeah."

"Thank you for taking a chance."

Wallace struggled against closing his eyes. He didn't want to lose this moment. He forced himself to memorize every inch of Hugo's face, the curl of his lips, the stubble he'd missed on his jaw when shaving earlier. "You'd make the tea. Put it into a little pot and set it on a tray. I'd be sitting at the table near the window."

"I'd bring the tray out to you," Hugo said. "There'd be a second cup, because I want you to ask me to sit down with you."

"I do."

"You do," Hugo agreed. "Sit a spell, you say. Have a cup of tea with me."

"Will you?"

"Yes. I sit in the chair opposite you. Everything else fades away until it's only you and me."

"I'm Wallace."

"I'm Hugo. It's nice to meet you, Wallace."

"You pour the tea."

"I hand you the cup."

"I wait for you to pour your own."

"We drink at the same time," Hugo said. "And I see the moment the flavor hits your tongue, the way your eyes widen. You didn't expect it to taste like it does."

"It reminds me of when I was younger. When things made sense."

"It's good, right?"

Wallace nodded, eyes burning. "It's very good. Hugo, I—"

Hugo said, "And maybe we just sit there, wasting away the afternoon. We talk. You tell me about the city, the people who hurry everywhere they go. I tell you about the way the trees look in the winter, snow piling on the branches until they hang low to the ground. You tell me about all the things you've seen, all the places you've visited. I listen, because I want to see them too."

"You can."

"I can?"

"Yes," Wallace said. "I can show you."

"Will you?"

"Maybe I decide to stay," Wallace said, and he'd never meant it more. "In this town. In this place."

"You'd come in every day, trying different kinds of tea."

"I don't like a lot of them."

Hugo laughed. "No, because you're very particular. But I find the ones you do like, and make sure I always have them on hand."

"The first cup I'm a stranger."

"The second you're an honored guest."

And Wallace said, "And then I have one more. And then another. And then another. What does that make me?"

"Family," Hugo said. "It makes you family."

"Hugo?"

"Yeah?"

"Don't forget me. Please don't forget me."

"How can I?" Hugo said.

"Even when I'm gone?"

"Even when you're gone. Don't think about it now. We still have time."

They did.

They didn't.

Hugo's eyes grew heavy. He fought it, eyes blinking slowly, but he'd already lost. "I think it'd be nice," he said, words slurring slightly. "If you came here. If you stayed. We'd drink tea and talk and one day, I'd tell you that I loved you. That I couldn't imagine my life without you. You made me want more than I ever thought I could have. Such a funny little dream."

His eyes closed and didn't reopen. He breathed in and out, lips parting.

After a time, Wallace said, "And I would tell you that you made me happier than I'd ever been. You and Mei and Nelson and Apollo. That if I could, I'd stay with you forever. That I love you too. Of course I do. How could I not? Look at you. Just look at you. Such a funny little dream."

For the rest of the night, he floated above Hugo, watching, waiting.

CHAPTER 22

The next morning—the seventh, the final, the last—Cameron said, "Will you go with me to the door?"

Wallace blinked in surprise as he looked down at Cameron. "You want me there?"

He nodded.

"I'm not . . . I can't go—not yet. I'm not going through yet."

"I know," Cameron said. "But I think it'll help, having you there."

"Why?" Wallace asked helplessly.

"Because you saved me. And I'm scared. I don't know how I'm going to climb the stairs. What if my legs don't work? What if I can't do it?"

Wallace thought of all he'd learned since walking through the doors of Charon's Crossing for the first time. What Hugo had taught him. And Mei. And Nelson and Apollo. He said, "Every step forward is a step closer to home."

"Then why is it so hard?"

"Because that's life," Wallace said.

Cameron gnawed on his bottom lip. "He'll be there."

Zach. "He will."

"He'll yell at me."

"Will he?"

"Yes," Cameron said. "That's how I'll know he still loves me." His eyes were wet. "I hope he yells as loud as he can."

"Until you think your eardrums will burst," Wallace said, patting him on the top of the head. "And then he'll never let you go."

"I'd like that." He looked away. "I'll find you. When you come. I want him to meet you. He needs to know you and what you've done for me."

Wallace couldn't. Everything was hazy. The colors were melting around him. His strings had been cut, and he was floating away, away, away.

"Then yes," Wallace said. "I'll be there when you go."

Cameron hugged Mei.

He hugged Nelson.

He patted Apollo on the head.

He said, "Will it hurt?"

"No," Hugo said. "It won't."

He looked to Wallace, holding out his hand. "Will you?"

Wallace didn't hesitate. He took Cameron's hand in his own. Cameron clutched him tightly as if to keep Wallace from floating away.

Mei, Nelson, and Apollo stayed on the bottom floor.

"I expect you to come right back, Wallace," Nelson called out. "I'm not done with you yet."

"I know," Wallace said, squeezing Cameron's hand to get him to stop. He looked back at them. "We won't be long."

Nelson didn't look like he believed him, but Wallace couldn't do anything about that now.

Hugo led the way up the stairs to the second floor.

"Can you hear that?" Cameron asked. "It's singing."

To the third floor.

"Oh," Cameron said, tears streaming down his cheeks. "It's so *loud.*" He looked out the windows as they passed them by, and he laughed and laughed. Wallace didn't know what he saw, but it wasn't meant for him.

To the fourth floor.

They stopped at the landing.

The flowers carved into the wood of the door bloomed on the ceiling above them.

The leaves grew.

"When you're ready, remove the hook and let it go. I'll open the door. Just tell me when," Hugo said.

Cameron nodded and looked up at Wallace floating above them. He squeezed Wallace's hand before pulling him down to eye level. "I know," he whispered. "When you brought me back, when you put your hook into my chest, I felt it. They're yours, Wallace. And you're theirs. Make sure they know that. You don't know when you'll get the chance again."

"I will," Wallace whispered back.

Cameron kissed his cheek before letting Wallace go. Hugo grabbed the leash, eyes soft and sad.

Cameron breathed in and out once, twice, three times. He said, "Hugo?"

"I'm here."

"I found my way back. It took a little while, but I did. Thank you for believing in me. I think I'm ready now." And with that, he grasped the hook Wallace couldn't see. Cameron grimaced as he pulled it from his chest. He gasped in relief as he opened his hand.

"It's gone," Hugo said quietly. "It's time."

"I feel it," Cameron said, looking up toward the door. "I'm rising. Hugo, please. Open the door."

Hugo did. He reached up, fingers grazing against the doorknob. He gripped it and twisted it once.

It was as it'd been with Alan. Light spilled down, so bright Wallace had to look away. The whispers gave way to birds singing. Wallace heard Cameron gasp as his feet left the floor. He raised his hand to shield his eyes, trying to make out Cameron in all the blinding light.

"Oh my god," Cameron breathed as he rose in the air toward the open doorway. "Oh, Wallace. It's . . . the sun. *It's the sun.*" Then, the moment before he rose through the doorway, a great and powerful joy filled his voice as he said, "Hello, my love. Hello, hello, hello."

The last Wallace saw of him were the bottoms of his shoes.

The door slammed shut behind him.

The light faded.

The flowers curled in on themselves.

The leaves shrank as the door settled in its frame.

Cameron was gone.

They stood under the door for what felt like hours, the leash in Hugo's hand as Wallace floated. It was almost time. Not yet, but close.

They drank tea as if it were any other day, the morning turning into afternoon as they pretended nothing was changing.

They laughed. They told stories. Nelson and Mei reminded Wallace of how he'd looked in a bikini. Nelson said if only he was a couple of decades younger, he might consider going after Wallace himself, much to Hugo's dismay. Wallace made Nelson show him the rabbit costume. It was quite startling. The basket of brightly colored eggs only made it worse, especially when his ears flopped all over the place, his nose wiggling. Nelson didn't need to open the eggs for Wallace to know they were filled with cauliflower.

Wallace had to grip the underside of the table to keep from rising farther. He tried to be inconspicuous about it, but they knew. They all knew. He'd forgone the leash, not wanting any distractions for what came next.

As the sun moved across the sky, Wallace reflected back on the life he'd had before this place. It wasn't much. He'd made mistakes. He hadn't been kind. And yes, there were moments of outright cruelty. He could have done more. He should have *been* more. But he thought he'd made a difference, in the end, with help from the others. He remembered how Nancy had looked before she'd left the tea shop the last time. The way Naomi had sounded on the phone. The relief on Cameron's face when the Husk he'd become melted away, life returning to the dead.

Wallace had done more in death than he ever had in life, but he hadn't done it alone.

And maybe that was the point. He still had regrets. He thought he always would. Nothing could be done about that now. He'd found within himself the man he had thought he'd become before the heaviness of life had descended upon him. He was free. The shackles of a mortal life had fallen away. There was nothing holding him here. Not anymore.

It hurt, but it was a good hurt.

Hugo tried to keep up appearances, but the closer it came to dusk, the more agitated he became. He fell silent. He frowned. He crossed his arms defensively.

Wallace said, "Hugo?" as Mei and Nelson quieted. Wallace gripped the table.

Hugo shook his head.

"Not now," Wallace said. "I want you to be strong for me."

He had a stubborn set to his jaw. "What about what I want?"

Nelson sighed. "I know this is hard on you. I don't think that—"

Hugo laughed hoarsely as his hands curled into fists. "I know. I just . . . I don't know what to do."

Mei laid her head on his shoulder. "What you have to," she whispered. "And we'll be there with you. The both of you. Each step of the way." She peered up at Wallace. "You turned into a pretty good dude, Wallace Price."

"Not as good as you, Meiying . . . what the hell is your surname?"

She chuckled. "Freeman. Changed it last year. Best name I've ever had."

"Damn right," Nelson said.

He had so much more to say to all of them. But before he could, Apollo growled, going to the window that looked out to the front of the tea shop. The hands of the clock began to stutter as time slowed down.

"No," he whispered as a blue light began to fill Charon's Crossing. "Not yet. Please, not yet—"

Apollo howled, a long and mournful sound as the light faded. The clock froze completely, the hands unmoving.

A light tapping on the door: *thump, thump, thump.*

Hugo rose slowly from his chair, footsteps heavy as he walked toward the door. He hung his head, his hand on the doorknob.

He opened it.

The Manager stood on the porch. He wore a shirt that read IF YOU THINK I'M CUTE, YOU SHOULD SEE MY AUNT. Flowers hung from his hair, opening and closing, opening and closing.

"Hugo," the boy said in greeting. "How nice to see you again. You're doing well, I see. Or as well as can be expected."

Hugo took a step back but didn't respond.

The Manager walked into the tea shop, the floor creaking under his bare feet, the walls and ceiling beginning to ripple as they had before. He looked at each of them in turn, gaze lingering on Mei before turning to Nelson and Apollo, who growled at him but kept his distance.

"Good dog," the boy said.

Apollo barked savagely in response.

"Well, mostly a good dog. Mei, you've taken to this Reaper business like a fish to water. I knew assigning you to Hugo was the right thing to do. I'm impressed."

"Frankly, I don't give two shits what you—"

"Ah," the boy said. "No need for that. I am your boss, after all. I'd hate to think you'd need a mark on your permanent record." He sniffed. "Nelson. Still here, I see. How . . . expected."

"Damn right I am," Nelson growled. He pointed his cane at the Manager. "And don't think you're going to be making anyone do anything they don't want to do. I won't have it."

The boy stared at him for a long moment. "Interesting. I actually believed that threat, as inconsequential as it was. Please remember there is little you could do to me that would stop what must happen. I am the universe. You're a speck of dust. I like you, Nelson. Please don't make me regret that."

Nelson eyed him warily, but didn't reply.

The Manager approached the table. Wallace sat stock-still as Hugo closed the door. The lock clicked.

The boy stopped at the table across from Wallace, inspecting the teapot and cups. He traced a finger along the spout of the pot. He caught a drop of liquid from the tip before pressing it against his tongue. "Peppermint," he said, sounding amused. "Candy canes. Isn't that right, Wallace? Your mother made them in the kitchen in winter. How strange it is that a memory so comforting comes from someone you grew to despise."

"I don't despise her," Wallace said stiffly.

The boy arched an eyebrow. "Is that so? Why not? She was, at best, distant. Both of your parents were. Tell me, Wallace, what will you do when you see them again? What will you say?"

He hadn't thought about it. He didn't know what that made him.

The boy nodded. "I see. Well, I suppose that's better left to you than me. Have a seat, Hugo, so that we may begin."

Hugo walked back to the table, pulling the chair out before sitting back down, expression blank and cold. Wallace hated to see it on him.

The boy clapped his hands. "That's better. Hold on just a second." He went to the table near them, pulling the chair out and dragging it along the floor back to their table. He pushed it between Mei and Nelson before he climbed onto it, sitting on his knees. He rested his elbows on the table, his chin in his hands. "There. Now we're all the same. I'd like a cup of tea. I always did like your tea, Hugo. Would you pour it for me?"

And Hugo said, "No. I won't."

The boy blinked slowly, his eyelashes black soot against golden skin. "What was that?" he asked, voice pitched high and sweet, like candy-coated razors.

"You're not getting tea," Hugo said.

"Oh." The boy cocked his head. "Why not?"

"Because you're going to listen to me, and I don't want you distracted."

"Ooh," the boy breathed. "Is that right? This should be interesting. You've got my attention. Go ahead. I'm listening." He cast a sly glance at Wallace before looking back at Hugo. "But I'd hurry if I were you. Appears our Wallace here is having a hard time staying seated. I wouldn't want him to float away while you're . . . how do you all put it? Giving me the ol' what for."

Hugo folded his hands on the table in front of him, the pads of his thumbs pressed together. "You lied to me."

"Did I? About what, exactly?"

"Cameron."

"Ah," the Manager said. "The Husk."

"Yes."

"He went through the door."

"Because we helped him."

"Did you?" He tapped his fingers against his cheeks. "Fascinating."

Wallace felt like screaming, but he kept his mouth closed. He couldn't let his emotions get the best of him, not when this counted more than anything. And he trusted Hugo with every fiber of his being. Hugo knew what he was doing.

Hugo's voice was even when he said, "You let him be as he was. You told me there was nothing we could do."

"Did I say that?" the Manager chuckled. "I suppose I did. Glad to know you were listening."

"You could've stepped in at any time to help him."

"Why would I have done that?" the Manager asked, sounding baffled. "He made his choice. As I told Wallace, free will is paramount. It's vital for—"

"Until you decide that it's not," Hugo said flatly. "This isn't a game. You don't get to pick and choose when you intervene."

"Don't I?" the boy asked. He glanced around at the others as if to say *Can you believe this guy?* His gaze lingered on Wallace for a moment before he looked back at Hugo. "But, for the sake of argument, why don't you tell me what I, an endless being of dust and stars, should've done."

Hugo leaned forward, face stony. "He was suffering. Lost. My former Reaper knew that. He fed off it. And still you did nothing. Even after Cameron turned into a Husk, you didn't lift a finger. It wasn't until Lea that you decided to do something about it. It should never have taken that long."

The boy scoffed. "Perhaps, but it all worked out in the end. Lea's mother is on the road to healing. Cameron found himself again and continued his journey to the great and wild beyond. I don't see the problem here. Everyone is happy." He grinned. "You should feel proud of yourself. Kudos all around. Hooray!" He clapped his hands.

"Could you have helped him?" Mei asked.

The Manager turned his head slowly toward her.

She didn't look away.

"Well," the Manager said, dragging the word out for several syllables. "I mean, sure, if we're getting down to brass tacks. I can pretty much do anything I want to." He narrowed his eyes. Wallace felt a chill run down his spine as the boy's voice became clipped. "I could have stopped your parents from dying, Hugo. I could've kept Wallace's heart beating its jazzy little jam. I could've grabbed Cameron by the scruff of his neck the day he decided to flee and forced him through the door."

"But you didn't," Hugo said.

"I didn't," the boy agreed. "Because there is an order to things. A plan, one that goes far above your pay grade. You would do well to remember that. I'm not sure I like your tone." He pouted, his bottom lip sticking out. "It's not very nice."

"What is that plan?" Wallace asked.

The boy looked to him again. "Pardon me?"

"The plan," Wallace said. "What is it?"

"Something far beyond your capability to comprehend. It's—"

"Right," Wallace said. "What's on the other side of the door?"

It was subtle, there and gone in a flash, but Wallace saw the bewildered expression before it disappeared. "Why, everything, of course."

"Specifics. Tell me one thing besides what we already know."

His bottom lip stuck out farther. "Oh, Wallace. There's nothing for you to fear. I've told you that. You will find—"

"Yeah, see, I don't think you know," Wallace said. He leaned forward as Mei sucked in a breath, as Nelson tapped his cane on the floor. "I think you want to. You try to emulate us. You try to make us think you understand, but how could you? You don't have our humanity. You don't know what it's like to have a beating heart, to feel it crack. You don't know what it means to be happy, what it means to grieve. Maybe some part of you is jealous of all the things we are that you can never be, and though you may not believe me, I wish that for you more than you know. Because *I* know there's something on the other side of that door. I've felt it. I've heard the whispers. I've heard the songs it sings. I've seen the light that spills from it. Can you even begin to imagine what that's like?"

"Careful, Wallace," the Manager said, pout melting away into steel. "Remember who you're talking to."

"He knows," Hugo said quietly. "We all do."

The Manager frowned as he glanced at Hugo. "Do you? I should hope so."

"What are the Husks?" Wallace paused, thinking as hard as he ever had. "A manifestation of a fear-based life?" That seemed like the right direction, but he couldn't quite get the picture to come into focus. "They . . . what? Are more susceptible to . . ."

"Fear-based life," the Manager repeated slowly. "That's . . . huh." He squinted at Wallace. "Figured that out on your own, did you? Good for you. Yes, Wallace. Those who lived in fear and despair are more . . . how did you put it? *Susceptible.* All they know is dread, and it follows them across. Though it doesn't affect them all the same way, people like Cameron sometimes can't accept their new reality. They run from it and . . . well. You know what happens next."

"How many of them are there?" Hugo asked.

The Manager reared back. "What?"

Hugo stared at the Manager, barely blinking. "People like Cameron. People who've been brought to the ferrypeople all over the world and lost their way. How many of them are there?"

"I don't see what that has to do with—"

"It's the entire *point!*" Wallace exclaimed. "It's not about any one person. It's about all of us, and what we do for one another. The door doesn't discriminate. It's there for everyone who is brave enough to look up at it. Some people lose their way, but that's not their fault. They're scared. My god, of course they are. How could they not be? Everyone loses their way at some point, and it's not just because of their mistakes or the decisions they make. It's because they're horribly, wonderfully *human*. And the one thing I've learned about being human is that we can't do this alone. When we're lost, we need help to try to find our way again. We have a chance here to do something important, something never done before."

"We," the Manager said. "Don't you mean *they*? Because, in case you forgot, you're dead."

"I know," Wallace said. "I know."

The boy frowned. "I told you once, Wallace. I don't make deals. I don't bargain. I thought we were past that." He sighed heavily. "I'm so disappointed in you. I was very clear on the matter. And you talk about the Husks as if you know anything about them."

"I've seen them," Wallace said. "Up close. Cameron. I saw what he was, regardless of what he'd turned into."

"One," the Manager said. "You've seen *one* of them."

"It's enough," Hugo said. "More than, even. Because if the rest of the Husks are anything like Cameron, then they deserve a chance, the same as we do." He leaned forward, gaze never leaving the Manager. "I can do this. You know I can." He looked around at the others at the table. "*We* can do this."

The Manager was silent for a long moment. Wallace had to stop himself from fidgeting. He barely kept from shouting in relief when the Manager said, "You have my attention. Don't waste it."

Closing arguments, but it didn't come from Wallace. It couldn't. He looked to the one person who knew life and death better than anyone else in the tea shop. Hugo squared his shoulders, taking a deep breath and letting it out slow. "The Husks. Bring them here. Let us help them. They don't deserve to stay as they are. They should be able to find their way home like everyone else." He glanced at Wallace, who still held onto the table as tightly as he could. It was getting harder to do. His rear lifted from the chair a few inches, his knees pressed to the underside of the table, his feet off the floor.

And if he listened hard enough, if he really tried, he could hear the whispers from the door once more. It was almost over.

The Manager stared at him. "Why would I agree to this?"

"Because you know we can do it," Mei said. "Or, at the very least, we can try."

"And because it's the right thing to do," Wallace said, and he'd never believed anything more. How simple. How terrifyingly profound. "The only reason the Husks chose as they did was out of fear of the unknown."

The Manager nodded slowly. "Say I entertain this. Say, for a moment, that I consider your offer. What will you give me in return?"

And Wallace said, "I'll let go."

Hugo was alarmed. "Wallace, no, don't—"

"How strange you are," the Manager said. "You've changed. What caused it? Do you even know?"

Wallace laughed, wild and bright. "You, I think. Or at least you're part of it, even if nothing you do makes any sense. But that's par for the course with existing, because life is senseless, and on the off chance we find something that *does* make sense, we hold onto it as tightly as we can. I found myself because of you. But you pale in comparison to Mei. To Nelson. Apollo." He swallowed thickly. "And Hugo."

Hugo stood abruptly, chair tipping over and falling to the floor. "No," he said harshly. "I won't let you do this. I won't—"

"It's not about me," Wallace told him. "Or us. You've given me more than I could ever ask for. Hugo, can't you see? I am who I am because you showed me the way. You refused to give up on me. Which is how I know you'll help all those who come after me and need you as much as I did."

"Fine," the Manager said suddenly, and all the air was sucked from the room. "You have a deal. I'll bring the Husks here, one by one. If he heals them, then so be it. If he doesn't, they stay as they are. It'll be a lot of work either way, and I don't know how successful it'll be."

Wallace's grip on the table grew slack as his jaw dropped. "You mean it?"

"Yes," the Manager said. "My word is my bond."

"Why?" Wallace asked. The Manager had agreed quicker than Wallace expected. There had to be more.

The Manager shrugged. "Curiosity. I want to see what happens. With order comes routine. Routine can lead to boredom, especially when it goes on forever. This is . . . different." His eyes narrowed as he looked at Hugo and Mei. "Don't mistake my acquiescence for a sign of complacency."

"You swear?" Wallace insisted.

"Yes," the Manager said, rolling his eyes. "I swear. I've heard the closing argument, counselor. The jury has come back with a verdict in your favor. We've reached a deal. It's time, Wallace. It's time to let go."

Wallace said, "I . . ."

He looked at Mei. A tear trickled down her cheek.

He looked at Nelson. His eyes were closed as he frowned deeply.

He looked at Apollo. The dog whined and bowed his head.

He looked at Hugo. Wallace remembered the first day he'd come to the tea shop, and how scared he'd been of Hugo. If only he'd known then what he knew now.

What will you do with the time you have left?

He knew. Here, at the end, he knew. "I love you. All of you. You've made my death worth it. Thank you for helping me live."

And then Wallace Price let go of the table.

Unmoored, untethered, he rose.

The tops of his knees hit the table, causing it to jump. The teapot and cups rattled on the table. How freeing it was, letting go. Finally, at last. He wasn't scared. Not anymore.

He closed his eyes as he floated toward the ceiling.

The pull of the door was as strong as it'd ever been. It was singing to him, whispering his name.

He opened his eyes when he stopped rising.

He looked down.

Nelson had a hold of his ankle, fingers digging in, a look of determination on his face which changed into surprise when he too started to lift from the floor.

But then Apollo leapt forward, jaws closing around the end of Nelson's cane, holding him in place. He whined when his front paws rose from the floor, the top of Wallace's head near the ceiling.

Mei grabbed onto Apollo's hindquarters, his tail hitting her in the face. "No," she snapped. "It's not time. You can't do this. *You can't do this.*"

Then she started to rise, feet kicking as they left the floor.

Hugo tried to grab her, but his hands went through her again and again.

Wallace smiled down at them. "It's okay. I promise. Let me go."

"Never in your life," Nelson grunted, grip tightening around Wallace's ankle. Nelson's hand slipped to Wallace's shoe. His eyes widened. "No."

"Goodbye," Wallace whispered.

The shoe came off. Nelson and Apollo and Mei fell to the floor in a heap.

Wallace turned his face up. The whispers grew louder.

He rose through the ceiling of the first floor to the second. He heard the others shouting below him as they ran for the stairs. Nelson appeared out of thin air, reaching for him, but Wallace was too high. Mei and Hugo made it to the second floor in time to see him rise through the ceiling.

"Wallace!" Hugo cried.

The third floor. He wished he'd spent more time in Hugo's room. He wondered what sort of life they could have made for themselves had he found his way to this little place before his heart had given out. He thought it would have been wonderful. But it was better to have had it for as long as he did than to never have had it at all. What a tremendous thought that was.

But then it was a tremendous death, wasn't it? Because of what he'd found after life.

The whispers of the door called for him, singing his name over and over, and in his chest, a light, like the sun. It burned within him. He was horizontal to the floor below him, arms spread like they'd been when he'd ridden behind Hugo on the scooter. He hit the ceiling of the third floor, and it gave way as he rose through it to the fourth floor.

He wasn't surprised to see the Manager already waiting for him below the door, head cocked. For a moment, Wallace thought he'd continue up and up and up. Maybe the door wouldn't open, and he'd rise through the roof of the house into the night sky and the never-ending stars. It wouldn't be such a bad way to go.

But he didn't.

He stopped, suspended in air. Nelson appeared near the landing, but he didn't speak.

For the first time, the Manager looked unsure. Just a little boy with flowers in his hair.

Wallace smiled. "I'm not afraid. Not of you. Not of the door. Not about anything that came before or will come next."

Nelson put his face in his hands.

"Not afraid," the Manager repeated. "I can see that. You let go of the table as if . . ." He stared at Wallace for a long moment before looking up at the door as the whispers grew louder, more unintelligible. "I wonder. What would it be like if . . ."

The whispers turned into a maelstrom. The Manager shook his head stubbornly, a child being told no. "No, I don't think that's quite true. What if—You know what? I'm getting pretty tired of your—"

The maelstrom became a hurricane, furious and loud.

"I've done whatever you've asked. Always." He glared up at the door. "And where has it gotten us? If this is for everyone, then it needs to *be* for everyone. Don't you want to see what could happen? I think they could end up surprising us all. They've proven themselves as it is. And they'll need all the help they can get. What could it hurt?"

The door rattled in its frame, the leaf in the doorknob unfurling.

"Yes," the Manager said. "I know. But this . . . this is a choice.

My choice. And it will be on me, whatever happens. You have my word. I will be responsible for whatever happens next."

The hurricane blew itself out, silence falling on the fourth floor of the tea shop.

"Huh," the Manager said. "I can't believe that worked. I wonder what else I can do?" He looked up at Wallace before jerking his head. Wallace fell to the floor, landing roughly on his feet, but managing to stay upright. For the first time since he'd given Cameron his hook, he felt grounded, like he had weight.

Mei reached the landing, panting as she bent over, hands on her knees. Apollo's nails slid along the floor as he jumped the last few steps, tumbling end over end before landing on his back. He blinked up at Wallace, tongue lolling out of his mouth as he grinned, tail wagging.

Hugo came last. He stopped, mouth agape.

"There's been a change of plans," the Manager said, sounding oddly amused. "*I've* made a change in plans." He laughed loudly, shaking his head. "This is going to be *fun*." The air around them thickened before exploding in a comical *pop*! The Manager held a file folder, frowning down at it as he flipped it open, mouth moving as he read silently, riffling through the pages. Wallace tried to see what he was reading, but the Manager closed the folder before he could get close enough. "Interesting. Your résumé is very thorough. Too thorough, if you ask me, but since no one did, that's apparently neither here nor there."

Wallace felt his eyes bulge. "My what?"

The Manager threw the folder up into the air. It hung suspended briefly before it winked out of existence. "Job interviews," he said. "All this damn paperwork, but death is a business, so I suppose it's a necessity. Who would have thought this would turn into an office job?" He shuddered. "No matter. Congratulations, Wallace. You're hired." He grinned sharply. "On a temporary basis, of course, one whose terms will be negotiated should this move on to a more permanent position."

"For *what*?"

The Manager reached up and plucked a flower from his hair, the vine snapping. The petals were yellow and pink and orange. He held it out to Wallace, palm toward the ceiling. The leaf on the crystal doorknob above them fluttered as if caught in a breeze. The flower floated above his hand as it bloomed brilliantly. "Having the Husks brought here will be a bigger job than you think. The others will need the help. As per your résumé, you certainly seem qualified, and though I would have preferred someone a little less . . . you, a résumé such as this doesn't lie. Open your mouth, Wallace."

"What?" Wallace asked, rearing back. "Why?"

The Manager grumbled under his breath before saying, "Do it before I change my mind. If you knew what I was risking here, you'd *open your damn mouth.*"

Wallace opened his mouth.

The Manager puffed his cheeks, blowing a stream of air against the flower above his palm. It grew bigger as it floated toward Wallace. The petals brushed against his lips. They tickled his nose. They folded into his mouth, pressing down on his tongue. They tasted sweet, like honey in tea. He gasped and coughed as the flower filled his mouth. He bit down, trying to hold it back to no avail. The flower slid down his throat.

He fell to the floor on his hands and knees, head bowed as he gagged.

He felt it the moment the flower hit his chest and bloomed.

It pulsed once.

Twice.

Three times.

Again and again and again.

Someone crouched next to him. "Wallace?" Hugo asked, sounding worried. "What did you do to him?"

"Um, Hugo?" Mei said, voice trembling.

"What I wanted to," the Manager said. "It's time for a change. They don't like it, but they're old and stuck in their ways. I can handle them."

"*Hugo.*"

"*What*, Mei?"

She whispered, "You're touching him."

Wallace lifted his head.

Hugo was next to him on his knees, hand on Wallace's back, rubbing up and down. It stilled when Mei spoke, the heavy weight of it like a brand.

Hugo choked out, "Are you . . . ?"

"Alive?" the Manager asked. "Yes. He is. A gift for you, Hugo, and one not to be taken lightly." He sniffed. "It can just as easily be taken away. And I'll be the first one here for it in case the need arises. Don't disappoint me, Wallace. I'm taking a chance on you. I would prefer not to regret that. I'm pretty sure the repercussions would be endless."

"My heart," Wallace croaked as the pulse in his chest thundered against his ribcage. "I can feel my—"

Hugo kissed him. His hands cupped Wallace's face, and he kissed him as if it were the last thing he would ever do. Wallace gasped into his mouth, his lips warm and soft. Hugo's fingers dug into his cheeks, a pressure unlike anything Wallace had ever felt before.

He did the only thing he could as stars burst in his eyes.

He kissed Hugo back. He breathed him in, chasing the remnants of peppermint on Hugo's tongue. Wallace kissed him for all he was worth, giving everything he could. He was crying, or Hugo was crying, or they were *both* crying, but it didn't matter. He kissed Hugo Freeman with all his might.

Hugo pulled away, but only just, pressing their foreheads together. "Hello."

"Hello, Hugo."

Hugo tried to smile, but it collapsed. "Is this real?"

"I think so."

And Hugo kissed him again, sweet and shining, and Wallace felt it down to the tips of his toes.

He kissed Wallace on the lips and the cheeks and on his eyelids when Wallace could no longer bear to look at him so closely. He kissed away the tears, saying, "You're real. You're real. *You're real.*"

Eventually, they broke apart.

Eventually, Hugo stood, knees popping.

He held a hand out toward Wallace.

Wallace didn't hesitate.

Hugo's grip was strong as he pulled Wallace up. He stared down at their joined hands in wonder before tugging Wallace close. He lowered his head to Wallace's chest, ear pressed against the left side of his ribcage. "I can hear it," he whispered. "Your heart."

And then he stood upright and hugged Wallace tightly. Wallace's breath was knocked from his chest as Hugo squeezed him as hard as he could. He was lifted off his feet as Hugo laughed, spinning them both around.

"Hugo!" Wallace shouted, dizzy as the room spun around them. "You're going to make me sick if you don't put me down!"

Hugo did. He tried to step back, but Wallace didn't let him get far. He interlocked his fingers with Hugo's, palm to palm. He barely had time to react before Mei jumped on him, legs wrapped around his waist, her hair in his nose. He laughed when she began to beat her fists against his chest, demanding that he never do anything so stupid again, and how could you be so dumb, Wallace, how could you possibly think you could ever say goodbye?

He kissed her hair. Her forehead. She squealed when he tickled her side, jumping back off him.

And then Nelson and Apollo came running.

Except they passed right through him.

Nelson almost fell to the floor. Apollo did, smashing into the wall behind them. The windows rattled in the turret. He got up, shaking his head, looking confused.

"He's alive," the Manager said dryly. "You can't touch him. At least not yet. Mei will have to show you how."

They looked at the Manager. "What do you mean?" Wallace asked, still dazed. "How can I—"

Mei said, "A Reaper."

The Manager nodded. "The job will be bigger than you can handle. If you're going to see to the Husks, then you'll need another

Reaper to assist you. Wallace already understands how it works. Everyone knows it's cheaper to keep the employees you have rather than hiring someone new. Wallace, hold out your hand."

Wallace looked at Hugo, who nodded. He held out his hand.

"Mei," the Manager said. "You know what to do."

"Damn right," Mei said. "Wallace, watch me, okay?" She lifted her own hand, fingers flexing. She brought up her other hand and tapped a familiar pattern into her palm. A light pulsed briefly in her hand.

Wallace let go of Hugo, though he was loath to do so. He tapped the same pattern onto his own hand.

At first nothing happened.

He frowned. "Maybe I did it wr—"

The room shuddered and shook. His skin vibrated. Gooseflesh prickled along the back of his neck. His hands trembled. The air around him expanded as if it lay on the surface of a soap bubble. The bubble popped.

Wallace looked up.

The colors of the fourth floor were sharper. He could see the grains in the walls, the finite cracks in the floor. He reached for Hugo, and his hand went right through him. He panicked until the Manager said, "You can change back, like Mei. Repeat the pattern, and you'll be amongst the living once more. It's part of being a Reaper. This will allow you to interact with those who've passed." He made a face. "With the Husks, unfortunate creatures that they are."

Apollo approached him slowly, nostrils flaring. He craned his neck until his snout pressed against Wallace's hand. His tail started wagging furiously as he licked Wallace's fingers.

"Yes," Wallace said with a grimace. "I'm happy to feel you too."

And then Nelson was on him, hugging him almost as hard as his grandson had. "I knew it," Nelson whispered. "I knew we'd find a way."

Wallace hugged him back. "Did you?"

Nelson scoffed as he pulled away. "Of course I did. I never doubted it, even for a second."

"Switch back," the Manager said.

Wallace repeated the same pattern on his palm. The room stuttered around him again, the sharpness fading as quickly as it'd arrived. Needing reassurance that it'd worked, he reached for Hugo once more, taking his hand. He lifted Hugo's hand to his lips, kissing the back of it. Hugo stared at him in wonder. "It's real," Wallace whispered to him.

"I don't understand," Hugo admitted. "How?"

They turned to the Manager once more. The boy sighed as he crossed his arms. "Yes, yes. You're alive again. How wonderful for you." He looked grim. "This isn't something to be taken lightly, Wallace. In all of history, there has only been one person who was brought back to life in such a way."

Wallace gaped at him. "Holy shit. I'm like Jesus?"

The Manager scowled. "What? Of course not. His name was Pablo. He lived in Spain in the fifteenth century. He was . . . well. It's not important who he was. All that matters is you know this is a gift, and one that can be taken away just as easily." He shook his head. "You cannot go back to the life you lived, Wallace. For all intents and purposes, that life is still dead. The people who knew you, the people who . . . put up with you, to them, you're dead and buried with nothing left but a stone marker to show you existed at all. You can't return. It would create disorder, and I won't have it. You've been given a second chance. You won't be given another. I'd suggest getting that heart looked at as quickly as possible. Better to be safe than sorry. Do you understand?"

No. He really didn't. "What if someone sees me who used to know me?" He thought the chance miniscule, but the last weeks had shown him how strange the world really was.

"We'll deal with it then," the Manager said. "I mean it, Wallace. Your place is—"

"Here," Wallace said, squeezing Hugo's hand because he could. "My place is here."

"Exactly. You have much work ahead of you. It's up to you to prove to me that my faith in you isn't misplaced. No pressure." The Manager yawned widely, jaw cracking. "I think that's enough excitement for one day. I'll be back shortly to outline what's next. Mei will act as your trainer. Listen to her. She's good at what she does. Maybe even the best I've seen."

Mei blushed even as she continued to glare at the Manager.

"I'm leaving now," the Manager said. "I'll be keeping tabs on all of you. Consider it an evaluation of those in our employ. Reorient yourself with the living world." He glanced at Hugo before looking back at Wallace. "Do what it is humans do when they're enamored with each other. Get it out of your system. I don't want to come back and catch you two *in flagrante delicto*." He made an obscene gesture with his hands, something Wallace never wanted to see a child do, even if said child seemed to be as old as the universe.

Hugo sputtered.

"Oh my god," Wallace mumbled, knowing his cheeks were red.

"Yes," the Manager said. "I know. It's terribly vexing. I don't know how you put up with it. Love seems positively dreadful." He turned toward the stairs, antlers beginning to grow from his head, flowers blooming from the velvet. He paused, looking back over his shoulder. He grinned, winked, and descended the stairs. By the time he reached the bottom, they could hear the sound of hooves on the floor of the tea shop. A blue light flashed through the window that pointed toward the front of the house.

And then it—*he*—was gone.

They stood silently, listening as the clocks in the tea shop began ticking once more.

Nelson spoke first. "What a strange day this has been. Mei, I think I could use a cup of tea. Would you join me?"

"Yep," she said, already heading for the stairs. "I'm thinking something fancy to celebrate."

"Great minds think alike," Nelson replied. He hobbled toward the stairs, Apollo and Mei trailing after him. Like the Manager, he stopped before descending. When he looked back at Wallace and

Hugo, his eyes were wet, and he was smiling. "My dear boy," he said. "My lovely Hugo. It's your time now. Make the most of it."

And with that, he walked down the stairs, telling Mei and Apollo he was thinking along the lines of the Da Hong Pao tea, something that made Mei gasp in delight. The last they saw of them was the tip of Apollo's tail as it flicked back and forth.

"Christ," Wallace said, scrubbing a hand over his face. "I can't believe how tired I am. I feel like I could sleep for a—"

"I love you too," Hugo said.

Wallace sucked in a breath as he closed his eyes. "What?"

He felt Hugo standing before him. His hand caressed the side of his face. He leaned into it. How he'd lasted all these weeks without his touch, Wallace would never know. "I love you too," Hugo said again, and it came with a hushed reverence akin to prayer.

Wallace opened his eyes. Hugo filled the world until he was all Wallace could see. "You do?"

Hugo nodded.

Wallace sniffed. "Damn right you do. You're very lucky to have—"

Hugo kissed him once more.

"I think," Wallace said against Hugo's lips, "that we should forgo the tea, at least for now."

"What did you have in mind?" Hugo asked, nose brushing against Wallace's own.

Wallace shrugged. "Perhaps you could give me a tour of your bedroom."

"You've seen it before."

"Yes," Wallace said. "But that was when I was wearing clothes. I expect it'll be different if we got rid of—" He yelped when the world tilted as Hugo lifted him up, throwing him over his shoulder. He was stronger than he looked. "Oh my god. Hugo, put me down!" He beat his hands against Hugo's back, laughing as he did so.

"Never," Hugo said. "Never, ever, ever."

Wallace raised his head and looked up at the door as Hugo headed for the stairs. For a brief moment, he saw the flowers and leaves growing along the wood. "Thank you," he whispered.

But the door was just that: a door.

It didn't respond.

It would, one day. It waited for all of them.

The tour of Hugo's bedroom went smashingly. It really was better without clothing.

EPILOGUE

On an evening in the middle of summer, Nelson Freeman said, "I think it's time."

Wallace looked up. He was washing the counter after another day manning the register of Charon's Crossing Tea and Treats. Hugo and Mei were in the kitchen, getting their prep done for the following morning. It was good work, hard work. He was tired more than he wasn't, but he went to bed every night with a sense of accomplishment.

It certainly didn't hurt that he and Hugo worked as well together as they did. After the Manager had left, and once the fiery shine of living had faded slightly, Wallace worried that it was too much too soon. It was one thing having a ghost living in your home. It was something else entirely to have them made flesh and blood and sharing a bed. He'd thought about moving somewhere in town to give them some space or, at the very least, to another room in the house.

Nancy had decided to move back to where she'd come from, and her apartment had become available. She'd come to say goodbye, hugging Hugo before she left. She looked . . . brighter, somehow. She wasn't healed, and probably wouldn't be for a long time, if ever, but life was slowly returning to her. She told Hugo, "I'm starting again. I don't know if I'll ever come back. But I won't forget what happened here."

And with that, she left.

Hugo had shot down the idea of Wallace taking her apartment over with a grumpy expression, arms folded. "You can stay here."

"You don't think it's too soon?"

He shook his head. "We've got the hard part out of the way, Wallace. I want you here." He frowned, looking unsure. "Unless you want to leave."

"No, no," Wallace said hastily. "I rather like where I'm at."

Hugo grinned at him. "Do you? And what exactly do you like about it?"

Wallace blushed, mumbling under his breath how cocky Hugo had become.

And that was the last time he'd mentioned it.

Shortly after his resurrection (a word he tried not to think too much about), he had Hugo call his former law firm. At first, no one would listen, but Hugo was persistent, Wallace feeding him the right words to say. Wallace had made an awful mistake, and Patricia Ryan should be rehired immediately, her daughter's scholarship restored. It took nearly a week for Hugo to get one of the partners on the phone—Worthington—and when Hugo told him why he was calling, Worthington said, "Wallace wanted this? Wallace Price? Are you sure? He was the one who fired her. And if you knew Wallace, you know he never admitted to mistakes."

"He did this time," Hugo said. "Before he died, he sent me a handwritten letter. I didn't receive it until a few days ago."

"Post office," Worthington said. "Always running behind." Silence. Then, "You're not having me on, right? This isn't some joke from beyond the grave that Wallace wanted you to pull?" He snorted. "Never mind, that can't be it. Wallace didn't know how to joke."

Wallace muttered under his breath about the ridiculousness of lawyers.

"I can send you the letter," Hugo said. "You can verify his handwriting. He's very clear about wanting Mrs. Ryan to have her job back."

Sweat trickled down the back of Wallace's neck as he waited, staring down at the phone on the counter.

Worthington sighed. "I never thought she deserved what happened to her. She was good. More than, even. I've actually been thinking about calling her and . . ." He paused. "Tell you what: send me what you have, and I'll take a look at it and go from there. If she wants to come back to work with us, then we'd be glad to have her."

"Thank you," Hugo said as Wallace cheered silently. "I appreciate that. I know Wallace would—"

"How did you know Wallace?" Worthington asked.

Wallace froze.

Hugo did not. He looked at Wallace as he said, "I loved him. I love him still."

"Oh," Worthington said. "That's—I'm sorry for your loss. I didn't know he . . . had someone."

"He does," Hugo said simply.

Worthington disconnected, and Wallace hugged Hugo as hard as he could. "Thank you," he whispered into Hugo's shoulder. "Thank you."

It wasn't easy. Of course it wasn't. Wallace was learning how to live again, an adjustment that proved harder than he expected. He still made mistakes. But he wasn't like he'd been before his heart had stopped.

They argued, sometimes, but it was always small, and they didn't leave things unsaid. They were making it work. Wallace was sure they always would.

And it wasn't as if they were in each other's back pockets all the time. They all had jobs to do. Mei took on her role as Wallace's trainer with gusto. She was quick to point out when he messed up, but never held it against him. She worked him hard but only because she knew what he was capable of. "One day," she told him, "you'll be doing this on your own. You gotta believe in yourself, man. I know I do."

It was more than he expected. He never thought about death until he died. And now that he'd returned, he sometimes struggled with the bigger picture, the point of it all. But he had Mei and Nelson and Apollo to fall back on when things got confusing. And Hugo, of course. Always Hugo.

The Manager had returned a week after bringing Wallace back

to life. And with him came their second Husk, a woman with black teeth and a vacant stare. Wallace frowned at the sight of her, but he wasn't afraid.

"Do what you will," the Manager said, offering no further assistance. He sat in a chair, munching on a plate of leftover scones.

"You're not going to help?" Wallace asked.

The Manager shook his head. "Why should I? A successful manager knows how to delegate. You figure it out."

They did, eventually, because of Mei. As the Manager looked on, she stood in front of the Husk. She took her hand. Mei grimaced, and if it was anything like it'd been with Cameron, Wallace knew she was seeing flashes of the woman's life, all the choices she'd made that had led to her becoming as she was. By the time she let the woman go, she was crying. Hugo reached for her, but Mei shook her head. "It's all right," she said weakly. "It's just . . . a lot. All at once." She wiped her eyes. "I know how to help her. It's like it was with Wallace and Cameron. Hugo, it's up to you."

Hugo stepped forward, and though Wallace couldn't see it, he knew Hugo grabbed the hook in his own chest, pulling it out with a grunt. The air in the tea shop grew hot as he pressed the hook into the Husk. She gagged as her skin filled with the colors of life. She bent over, clutching her sides as the black of her teeth turned to white.

"Wh-aaat," the woman said. "Wha-aaaat is . . . this? What. Is happening?"

"You're safe," Hugo said. He glanced at Wallace who arched an eyebrow, a pointed look at Hugo's chest. Hugo nodded, and Wallace breathed a sigh of relief. Another hook had appeared in Hugo's chest, connecting him to the woman. It'd worked. "I've got you. Can you tell me your name?"

"Adriana," she whispered.

The Manager muttered through a mouthful of scone.

Since that day, they'd helped a dozen more Husks. Sometimes it was Mei. Other times, it was Wallace. There were days when they'd leave to find the Husks themselves, and others when the Husks would appear on the road leading to the tea shop, surrounded by hoofprints in the dirt. Some were harder than others. One had been a Husk for close to two hundred years and didn't speak English. They'd managed to help him by the skin of their teeth, but Wallace knew that it would only get easier from there. They'd do what they could for all who came to them.

The people of the town were curious about this new addition to Charon's Crossing. It didn't take long for rumors to spread about Wallace and his relationship with Hugo. People came in to gawk at him. The older women cooed, the younger women seemed disappointed that Hugo was off the market (as did a few of the men, much to Wallace's complicated glee), and it wasn't long before the newness of it all faded and Wallace became yet another fixture of the town. They waved at him when they saw him on the sidewalk or in the grocery store. He always waved back.

Wallace Price became Wallace Reid. At least, that's what his new ID and Social Security card said. Mei told him not to ask too many questions when she'd handed them to him after returning from a three-day trip to visit her mother, which she said had gone better than she expected. "Mom knows people," she said, lips quirking. "She picked out the last name for you. Showed her a couple of pictures of you, and she told me to tell you the surname is because you're thin as a reed, and that you need to eat more."

"I'll write her a thank-you note," Wallace said, distracted as he brushed a finger over his new name.

"Good. She's expecting you to."

Desdemona Tripplethorne returned to the tea shop, telling them she wanted to see the new employee at Charon's Crossing for herself. Squat Man and Thin Man crowded behind her, staring at Wallace. Desdemona studied him as he fidgeted. Finally, her brow furrowed, and she said, "Have . . . have we met? I swear I know you from somewhere."

"No," Wallace said. "How could we have? I've never been here before."

"I suppose you're right," she said slowly. She shook her head. "My name is Desdemona Tripplethorne, I'm sure you've heard of me. I'm a clairvoyant—"

Mei coughed. It sounded strangely like *bullshit*.

Desdemona ignored her. "—and I come here from time to time to speak to the spirits that haunt this place. I know how it sounds. But there is more to the world than you could possibly know."

"Is there?" Wallace asked. "How do you know?"

She tapped the side of her head. "I have a gift."

She left an hour later, disappointed when the planchette on her Ouija board and the feather quill hadn't moved even a millimeter. She would be back, she announced grandly before leaving the tea shop in a swirl of self-entitlement, Thin Man and Squat Man hurrying after her.

It went on, life did, ever forward. Good days, the not-so-good days, the days when he wondered how he could stand being surrounded by death for much longer. It hit Hugo too; though few and far between, he still had panic attacks, days when his breath would catch in his chest, lungs constricting. Wallace never tried to force him through the attacks, just sat on the back deck with him, tap, tap, tapping, Apollo alert at Hugo's feet. When Hugo recovered, breaths slow and deep, Wallace whispered, "All right?"

"I will be," Hugo said, taking Wallace's hand in his own.

It wasn't always Husks. Spirits still came to them, spirits who needed someone like Hugo as their ferryman. Often, they were angry and destructive, bitter and cold. Some of them stayed for weeks, ranting and raving about how they didn't want to be dead, that they didn't want to be trapped here, they were going to *leave*, and nothing was going to stop them, pulling at the cables extending from their chests to Hugo's, threatening to remove the hook that kept them grounded.

They didn't.

They always stayed.

They listened.

They learned.

They understood, after a time. Some just took longer than others.

But that was okay.

Each of them found their way to the door, and to what came after.

After all, Charon's Crossing was nothing but a way station.

At least for the dead.

It was the living who found their roots growing deep in the earth. Tea plants, Hugo had once told Wallace, required patience. You had to put in the time and have patience.

Which is why, on a summer evening, when Nelson said, "I think it's time," Wallace knew what he meant.

But any reply he had dried up in his throat when he saw who stood before him.

Gone was the elderly man leaning on a cane.

In his place stood a much younger man, back straight, hands clasped behind him as he looked out the window, cane gone as if it'd never been there at all. Wallace recognized him immediately. He'd seen this very man in many of the photographs hanging on the walls of the tea shop and in Hugo's room, mostly in black and white or grainy color.

"Nelson?" he whispered.

Nelson turned his head and smiled. His wrinkles were gone, replaced by the smooth skin of someone far younger. His eyes were twinkling. He was bigger, stronger. His hair sat in a black Afro on his head, much like his grandson's. Decades had melted away until before Wallace stood a man who looked as young as Hugo. What had Nelson said?

It's simple, really. I like being old.

"You stayed as you were because it's how Hugo knew you when you were alive," Wallace said hoarsely.

"Yes," Nelson said. "I did. And I'd do it all over again if I had to, but I think it's time for what I want. And Wallace, I want this."

Wallace wiped his tears away. "You're sure."

He looked back out the window. "I am."

Mei made them tea as the rest gathered in the darkened tea shop, moonlight bathing the forest around them. Hugo sat in a chair, bandana in his lap (black with little yellow ducks), looking around the tea shop with a quiet smile on his face.

Mei brought the tea tray out, setting it on the table. The scent of chai filled the room, thick and heady. Hugo poured tea for each of them, the cups filled to the brim. He handed them each a cup, setting a bowl down on the floor for Apollo, who began to lap at the liquid frantically. Wallace couldn't bring himself to drink from his own cup, worried his hands would shake too much.

"This is nice," Hugo said as Mei sat next to him. He had yet to comment on his grandfather's appearance. He'd looked momentarily stunned when he'd seen Nelson as he was now, but had quickly covered it up. Wallace knew he was waiting for Nelson to bring it up. "We should do this more often. Just us, at the end of the day." He looked at each of them in turn, smile fading when his gaze found Wallace, who failed miserably in his attempt to school his expression. "What is it? What's wrong?"

Wallace cleared his throat and said, "Nothing. It's nothing. I—"

"Hugo," Nelson said, a thin line of chai on his upper lip. "My dear Hugo."

Hugo looked at him.

And just like that, he knew.

Empathetic almost to a fault.

Hugo set his cup down on the table.

He closed his eyes.

He said, "Grandad?" in a small voice.

"It's time," Nelson said. "I've lived a long life. A good life. I've loved. I've been loved in return. I made something out of nothing. This place. This tiny tea shop. My wife, my heart. My children. And you, Hugo. Even when it became just the two of us, I held on as tightly as I could. I worried that I wouldn't be enough, that you wanted more than I could give you."

"I didn't," Hugo croaked. "I didn't want anything else."

"Perhaps not," Nelson agreed gently. "But you've found it all the same. You've found it in Mei and Wallace, but even before them, you were already on your way. You've built this life, this wonderful life with your own hands. You took the tools I gave you and made them your own. What more could a man ask for?"

"It hurts," Hugo said as he lifted his head. He pressed a hand against his chest above his heart.

Mei sobbed into her hands, little hiccupping breaths.

"I know," Nelson said. "But I can leave now, secure in the knowledge that you stand on your own two feet. And when the days come that you don't think you'll be able to, you'll have others to ensure you will. That's the point, Hugo. That's the point of all of this."

"Grief," Hugo choked out. "It's grief." Apollo tried to nose at his hand, ever the service dog he'd been in life. He settled on the floor next to Hugo's feet, nose inches from Hugo's toes.

"It is," Nelson agreed. "We'll see each other again. But not for a long, long time. You have a life to live, and it'll be filled with such color and joy that it'll take your breath away. I just wish . . ." He shook his head.

"What?" Hugo asked.

"I wish I could hug you," Nelson said. "One last time."

"Mei."

"On it, boss," Mei said. She moved quickly, tapping her finger against her palm. The air stuttered, and then she was hugging Nelson with all her might. Nelson laughed brightly, face toward the ceiling, tears streaming down his face.

"Yes," he said. "This is fine. This is fine, indeed."

When Mei pulled away, Nelson smiled.

"When?" Hugo asked.

"I think at sunrise."

Those who came to Charon's Crossing Tea and Treats the next morning were surprised to find the front door locked once more, a sign in the window with an apology, saying that the tea shop would be closed that morning for a special event. It was okay. They would come back.

Inside, Hugo rose unsteadily to his feet. They'd spent the night together in front of the fireplace, Nelson in his chair, the fire crackling. Wallace and Mei and Apollo had listened as the two men told stories of their youth, tales of their family who'd gone on before them.

But a river only moves in one direction, no matter how much we wish it weren't so.

The night sky began to lighten.

Nelson's eyes were closed. He whispered, "I can hear it. The door. The whispers. The song it's singing. It knows I'm ready."

Hugo gripped Wallace's hand tightly. "Grandad?"

"Yes?"

"Thank you."

"For?"

"Everything."

Nelson chuckled. "That's quite a lot to be thankful for."

"I mean it."

"I know you do." He opened his eyes. "I'm a little frightened, Hugo. I know I shouldn't be, but I am all the same. Isn't that funny?"

Hugo shook his head slowly. He squared his shoulders and became the ferryman he was. "There's nothing for you to fear. You'll no longer know pain. You'll no longer know suffering. There will be peace for you. All you have to do is rise through the door."

"Will you help me?" Nelson asked.

And Hugo said, "Yes. I'll help you. Always."

Nelson rose from his chair slowly. He was unsteady on his feet, swaying side to side. "Oh," he whispered. "It's louder now."

Hugo stood. He looked down at Mei and Wallace and Apollo. "Will you come with us?"

Mei hung her head. "Are you sure?"

"Yes," Hugo said. "I'm sure. Grandad?"

"I'd like that very much," Nelson said.

And so they did.

They followed Nelson and Hugo up the stairs to the second floor.

To the third.

To the fourth.

They gathered below the door. Wallace knew what Nelson was hearing, though he could no longer hear it himself.

Nelson turned to face them. "Mei. Look at me."

She did.

"You have a gift," Nelson told her. "One that cannot be denied. But it's the immensity of your heart that makes you who you are. Never forget where you come from, but don't allow it to define you. You have made your place here, and I doubt there will ever be a better Reaper than you."

"Thank you," she whispered.

"Wallace," Nelson said. "You were an asshole."

Wallace choked.

"And yet, you've managed to move beyond it to become the man who stands before me. An honorary Freeman. Perhaps one day you'll become an actual Freeman, like Mei. I can think of no better man to share a name with."

Wallace nodded dumbly.

"Apollo," Nelson said. "You—"

"Should go with him," Hugo said quietly.

Apollo cocked his head up at Hugo.

Hugo crouched before him. Apollo tried to lick his face, but his tongue went through Hugo's cheek. "Hey, boy," Hugo said. "I need you to listen to me, okay? I have a job for you. Sit."

Apollo sat promptly, cocking his head as he watched Hugo.

Hugo said, "You're my best friend. You did more for me than almost anyone else. When I was lost and couldn't breathe, you grounded me. You reminded me that it was okay to hurt so long as I didn't let it consume me. You did your part, and now I need to do the same for you. I want you to do me a favor. Keep an eye on Grandad for me. Make sure he doesn't get into too much trouble, okay? At least until I can join you."

Apollo's ears flattened against his skull as his head drooped. He whined softly, trying to butt his head against Hugo's knee to no avail.

"I know," Hugo whispered. "But I swear we'll run together again one day. I won't forget it or you. Go, Apollo. Go with Grandad."

Apollo stood. He looked between Hugo and Nelson as if unsure. For a moment, Wallace thought he'd ignore Hugo's order and stay right where he was.

He didn't.

He barked at Hugo, a low woof before he turned toward Nelson. Apollo circled Nelson, sniffing at his legs before pressing his snout against Nelson's hand. Nelson smiled down at him. "You ready, Apollo? I think we're going on an adventure. I wonder what we'll see?"

Apollo licked his fingers.

Hugo rose from his crouch. He moved until he stood in front of his grandfather. Wallace thought he'd hesitate, if only for a moment. He didn't. He raised his hand toward Nelson's chest, and the moment his fingers closed around the hook only he and Nelson could see, Nelson said, "Hugo?"

Hugo looked at him.

Nelson said, "I'll be seeing you, okay?"

Hugo grinned brilliantly. "Damn right you will." And then he pulled the hook free. He turned and did the same to Apollo, the dog yipping once.

Hugo stood upright, taking a deep breath as he raised his hand above his head toward the doorknob. His fingers covered the leaf, and with a twist of his wrist, the door opened.

White light spilled out, the song of life and death like a symphony.

"Oh," Nelson said, voice hushed in reverence. "I never . . . I never thought . . . All this light. All these colors. I think . . . yes. Yes, I hear you. I see you, oh my god, I *see* you." He laughed wildly as his feet left the floor, Apollo looking comically surprised as his did the same. "Hugo!" Nelson cried. "Hugo, it's real. All of it is real. It's life. It's *life*."

Blinking against the blinding light, Wallace saw the outline of Nelson and Apollo as they rose through the air. Apollo looked around, tongue hanging out. It almost looked as if he were grinning.

And then they both crossed through the doorway.

Before the door closed, Wallace heard Nelson's voice one last time as Apollo barked happily.

He said, *"I'm home."*

The door slammed shut.

The light faded.

Nelson and Apollo were gone.

Silence settled like a blanket over the fourth floor of the tea shop.

"What do you think he saw?" Mei finally asked as she wiped her eyes.

Hugo stared up at the door. Though his face was wet, he smiled. "I don't know. And isn't that the point? We don't know until it's our time. Can you give me a moment? I want . . . I'll be down shortly."

Wallace touched the back of his hand before following Mei down the stairs. He thought he heard Hugo speaking quietly, almost like a prayer.

That night, Wallace found Hugo on the back deck. Mei was in the kitchen, her terrible music blaring loudly, causing the bones of the house to shake. He shook his head as he closed the back door behind him.

Hugo glanced back at him. "Hello."

"Hello, Hugo," Wallace said. "You all right?" He winced as he joined Hugo at the railing. "Stupid question."

"No," Hugo said as he lay his head on Wallace's shoulder. "I don't think it is. And honestly? I don't know if I'm all right. It's strange. Did you hear his voice at the end?"

"I did," Wallace said.

"He sounded . . ."

"Free."

Wallace felt Hugo nod against him. He wrapped an arm around Hugo's waist. "I can't even begin to imagine the relief he must have felt. I . . ." He hesitated. Then, "Are you angry with him?"

"No," Hugo said. "How could I be? He's watched over me for long enough, and helped to teach me how to be a good person. And besides, he knew I was in good hands."

"Are you?"

Hugo laughed. "I think so. You are pretty good with your—"

Wallace groaned. "I'm trying to have a moment here."

Hugo turned his head so he could kiss the underside of Wallace's jaw with a loud smack. Wallace grinned against his hair. "I am," Hugo whispered. "In good hands. The best, really. And he's right: this isn't goodbye. We'll see each other again. All of us. But before then, we still have work to do. And we'll do it together."

"We will," Wallace agreed. "I think—"

The back door opened.

Light spilled out.

They turned.

Mei stood in the doorway. "Stop being all gross and lovey and blech. A new file appeared."

Hugo stepped away from the railing. "Tell me."

Mei began to recite the contents of the file from memory. Hugo didn't interject, listening as Mei rattled off facts about their new guest.

Wallace glanced back at the tea plants.

Their leaves fluttered in the warm breeze. They were strong, firmly rooted in the soil. Hugo had seen to that.

"Wallace," Hugo called from the doorway. "You coming?"

"Yeah," Wallace said, turning away from the garden. "Let's do this. Who's our new guest going to be?"

When he reached the door, Wallace took Hugo's outstretched hand without hesitation. The door closed behind them. A moment later, the light on the back deck switched off, the tea garden bathed only in moonlight.

If they'd looked back one last time, they would've seen movement in the forest. At the tree line, there, in the dark, a great stag lowered its head toward the earth in veneration, flowers dangling from its antlers. Before long, it moved back amongst the trees, petals trailing in its wake.

ACKNOWLEDGMENTS

Under the Whispering Door is a deeply personal story to me; therefore, it was very hard to write. It took a lot out of me to finish, as it forced me to explore my own grief over losing someone I loved very much, more than I ever had before—outside of therapy, at least. There is a catharsis to grief, though we don't usually see that in the midst of it. I won't say writing this book helped heal me, because that would be a lie. Instead, I'll say that it left me feeling a bit more hopeful than I had before, bittersweetly so. If you live long enough to learn to love someone, you'll know grief at one point or another. That's just how the world works.

Some amazing people helped bring this book to you, so I'd like to thank them now.

First is Deidre Knight, my agent, who fiercely champions my books and believes in them, perhaps more than anyone else. She is the best agent an author could ask for. Thanks to Deidre and the team at The Knight Agency, including Elaine Spencer, who handles all the foreign rights to my books. She's the reason *The House in the Cerulean Sea* and *Under the Whispering Door* are being translated into so many different languages.

Ali Fisher, my editor, gave me the absolute best writing advice I've ever gotten. While we were in the middle of edits for this book, she told me one word that changed how I looked at Wallace's story: *decentralize*. That won't mean much to you, but believe me when I say that it was like the sun bursting through the clouds for the first time in weeks, and it allowed me to put the focus where it should've been in the first place. This story is as good as it is because of her. Thanks, Ali.

Also on the editing side is assistant editor Kristin Temple. Kristin had key input on the character of the Manager (as I tend to try to break my own in-world rules), and that strange boy who is not really a boy is who he is because of her. Thanks, Kristin.

Next, the sensitivity readers. Not to diminish the work anyone else did on this book, but the sensitivity readers were, perhaps, some of the most important. Of the five central characters—Wallace, Hugo, Nelson, Mei, and Apollo—three are characters of color. The sensitivity readers sifted through various iterations with a fine-toothed comb and provided extremely beneficial notes. I'd like to thank the sensitivity readers at Tessera Editorial, as well as moukies, who made the character of Hugo that much better.

Saraciea Fennell and Anneliese Merz are my publicists and cheerleaders, and all around some of the best people an author could ask for on their team. I don't know how they do what they do, but we're all the better for them and the tireless work they do.

The higher up are Tor Publisher Devi Pillai, President of TDA Fritz Foy, VP and Director of Marketing Eileen Lawrence, Executive of Publicity Sarah Reidy, VP of Marketing and Publicity Lucille Rettino, and Chairman/Founder of TDA Tom Doherty. They believe in the power of queer storytelling, and I'm grateful they are letting me make the fantasy genre that much gayer.

Becky Yeager is the marketing lead, meaning it's her job to get the word out about my books. One of the big reasons they've been read as widely as they have is her work. Thanks, Becky.

Rachel Taylor, the digital marketing coordinator, runs the Tor social-media accounts and makes sure everyone sees my dumb tweets about my books. Thanks, Rachel.

On the production side of things, you have production editor Melanie Sanders, production manager Steven Bucsok, interior designer Heather Saunders, and jacket designer Katie Klimowicz. They make everything look as good as it does. In addition, I'd like to thank Michelle Foytek, senior manager of publishing operations, who coordinates with production to get all the exclusive materials into the right editions.

And the jacket, man. The *jacket*. Go stare at it for just a moment. See how freaking rad that is? That's because of Red Nose Studios.

Chris has the uncanny ability to somehow dig around in my brain and make my imagination come to life in the form of the amazing jacket art he's made for me. I am in constant awe of the work he does. Thanks, Chris.

I'd also like to thank the Macmillan sales team for all their support and hard work in getting this book—and all my others—out to bookstores everywhere. They are the best cheerleaders an author could ask for.

Thanks to Lynn and Mia, my beta readers. They get to read the stories before anyone else, and so far, they haven't run screaming yet, so I count that as a win.

Thank you to Barnes & Noble for selecting *Under the Whispering Door* as an exclusive edition (if you haven't seen the little something extra in the B&N edition, you should definitely check that out). Also, to the indie booksellers and librarians all over the world who've championed my books to readers, thank you. I am forever in your debt and will do whatever you ask of me, even if that means helping you hide a body.

Last, to you, the reader. Because of you, I get to do this whole writing thing as my job. Thank you for letting me do what I love most. I can't wait for you to see what comes next.

TJ Klune
April 11, 2021